WIRED

Douglas E. Richards

This book is a work of fiction. The characters, incidents, and dialogues are products of the author's imagination and are not to be construed as real. Any resemblance to actual events or persons, living or dead, is entirely coincidental.

eBook Published by Paragon Press, 2011

ParagonPressSF@gmail.com

E-mail the author at doug@san.rr.com, Friend him on Facebook at Douglas E. Richards Author, or visit his website at www.douglaserichards.com

ISBN: 978-0-9826184-9-3

First Edition

ABOUT THE AUTHOR

Douglas E. Richards is the *New York Times* and *USA Today* bestselling author of *WIRED*, its sequel, *AMPED,* and *THE CURE*. He has also written six middle grade/young adult novels widely acclaimed for their appeal to boys, girls, and adults alike. In recognition of his work, he was selected to be a "special guest" at San Diego Comic-Con International, along with such icons as Stan Lee, Ray Bradbury, and Rick Riordan. Douglas has a master's degree in molecular biology (aka "genetic engineering"), was a biotechnology executive for many years, and has authored a wide variety of popular science pieces for *National Geographic*, the *BBC*, the *Australian Broadcasting Corporation, Earth and Sky*, *Today's Parent*, and many others. Douglas currently lives in San Diego, California, with his wife, two children, and two dogs.

Also By Douglas E. Richards

***AMPED* (The WIRED Sequel)**

THE CURE

Middle Grade/YA
(Enjoyed by kids and adults alike, ages 9 to 99)

The Prometheus Project: Trapped (Book 1)

The Prometheus Project: Captured (Book 2)

The Prometheus Project: Stranded (Book 3)

The Devil's Sword

Ethan Pritcher, Body Switcher

Out of This World

WIRED

Douglas E. Richards

Paragon Press

"What is good? All that heightens the feeling of power in man, the will to power, power itself. What is bad? All that is born of weakness. What is happiness? The feeling that power is growing, that resistance is overcome."

—Friedrich Nietzsche, Philosopher (1844-1900)

PROLOGUE

Bill Callan extended his silenced Ruger .45 and crept soundlessly toward the woman calling herself Angela Joyce. She was seated at an old wooden desk with her back to him, busily manipulating an expensive laptop computer. She was undeniably cute, reflected Callan, not for the first time. But he liked his women on the sleazy side, and her look was too wholesome for his taste—even though her appearance was probably the *only* thing wholesome about her. And she was too smart for his liking as well. Far too smart.

Her driver's license pegged her at twenty-seven, but she looked younger, as if she had just finished college. Except for her eyes. There was a maturity there, a street savvy, far beyond her actual age or appearance that suggested this soft-looking girl had seen her share of hard times.

Why did she need to hire two mercenaries to protect her? Not bodyguards, but mercenaries. And how was she able to afford them without any visible means of support? She had fed them a story about having been the girlfriend of a mobster who wasn't prepared to let her go, but Callan hadn't bought it for a second. So he had made a study of her. And sure enough, his investigation had hit pay dirt. Pay dirt far richer than he could ever have imagined.

The girl was so engrossed in the computer she was completely oblivious to Callan's approach. He cleared his throat and she spun around, startled. "Oh," she said in relief, noticing it was him, but her relief was short-lived as she saw the gun pointed at her, ominously fitted with a silencer. "What's going on, Bill?" she said anxiously. And while she kept her face passive, Callan had an unmistakable sense that her agile mind was racing; evaluating these new circumstances and weighing possibilities.

"You need to come with me," said Callan evenly. And then, raising his eyebrows he added, "*Kira.*"

Her eyes widened for just an instant before she caught herself. "What the hell is going on?" she demanded. "Why are you pointing that at me? And why did you call me Kira?"

"Because that's your real name," he said simply. "Kira Miller."

She shook her head in annoyance. "If this is your idea of a joke, Bill, it isn't funny."

Callan ignored her. "Catch," he said, tossing her a set of car keys. She snatched them from the air with athletic ease, her gaze never wavering from his.

"I took the liberty of removing the pepper spray from your key ring," he told her. "Let's go. You're driving."

"Where's Jason?" she asked.

"He's in the garage," replied Callan with a sly smile. "Waiting for us."

"I'm not going *anywhere* until you tell me what this is about!" she snapped.

Callan closed the gap between them in the blink of an eye and shoved the long barrel of the silencer roughly against the side of her head. He reached out with his other hand and grabbed her chin, forcing her face mere inches from his. Callan was a muscular six-foot-three and his meaty paws were enormous.

"For a smart chick, you're just not getting it," he hissed. "Things have changed. I don't work for you anymore. I'm the one giving the orders now! You'll do as I say or I'll break you in half." He gave her chin and lower face a quick, powerful squeeze, so strong that several of her teeth cut into the inside of her mouth, drawing blood. "Have I made myself clear!" he whispered through clenched teeth, finally releasing her chin.

She rubbed her chin and glared at him with such a feral intensity he expected holes to appear in the back of his head.

"Admit your real name is Kira Miller or I'll break your left arm," he growled fiercely.

She continued to glare at him as she considered his threat. "*Okay*," she said finally. "So I'm Kira Miller. So what? I'm paying you and Jason a small fortune to protect me, and you're putting that in serious jeopardy."

Callan laughed. "You think?" he said sarcastically. He shook his head. "Thanks for your concern, but I won't be needing your small fortune anymore. I'm trading it for a *large* one." He grabbed her arm and shoved her in the direction of the garage. "Let's go," he barked. "I'm *not* going to ask again."

As she walked toward the garage she detoured a few yards to snatch a jean jacket draped over the back of a chair, and quickly slipped it on. Callan shook his head in disbelief. It was still almost sixty degrees outside. In *November*. Positively balmy. Callan had lived in Chicago much of his life, but he knew that after only a few years of being spoiled in the paradise climate of San Diego the pathetic residents became hypersensitive to cold.

As they reached the door that led to the garage, she turned completely around to face him, looking as though she wanted to ask a question, her right hand now buried in the coat's right pocket. Callan reacted instinctively, twisting away from her before his conscious mind knew why, just as a small caliber bullet tore through her pocket and dug a shallow, five-inch-long groove across his stomach. If he had not turned when he did, the bullet would have bored a hole straight through his gut.

Callan threw his massive body into Kira Miller and slammed her into the door before she could get off another shot. While she was still dazed, he wrestled her arm from her pocket and easily ripped the Glock subcompact she had hidden there from her fingers.

He could feel the wetness of his blood as it slid from his wound and soaked into his now-torn shirt, but he knew the injury was superficial and not in need of immediate attention. He spun his former client around roughly and began to frisk her, something he should have done from the start. He had assumed she was content to leave security to her two hired mercenaries, but it was clear she had taken additional precautions of her own. He found a small canister of pepper spray attached to her lower leg, but no other weapons.

He considered roughing her up a bit as punishment for her attack, but decided against it. If he injured her, she would be more difficult to manage, and it was his carelessness that had allowed the attempt anyway. Besides, he had made certain she was all out of surprises.

Callan opened the door to the garage and shoved her through, hitting the light switch as he did so. The girl almost tripped over the body of Jason Bobkoski lying face down on the gray concrete floor, a hole drilled through his heart from behind by a silenced weapon at point blank range. Streams of bright-red blood branched out from the body like so many fingers and disappeared under Kira's white Lexus sedan.

Kira glared at Callan with contempt, but said nothing. Most women would have shrieked in horror had they been surprised by a bloody corpse, but apparently not this one. After her bold attack just moments before, he shouldn't have been surprised. His instincts had been dead on: this bright, attractive girl was far more than she seemed.

They were on the road minutes later. Kira was at the wheel and Callan sat in the passenger seat with his gun trained on her. The sun had set a few hours earlier, but despite the darkness the roads were still fairly active. A crescent moon hung in the still night sky, and the typical Southern California assortment of tropical flowers and palms made steady appearances outside the windshield, a living testament to a growing season and a summer that never seemed to end.

"Where are we going?" asked Kira finally, breaking a long silence.

"You'll know when we get there," said Callan.

"How did you learn my true identity?"

"This isn't twenty questions."

"Look, I paid you well and you're obviously selling me out in return. The least you could do is answer a few questions. What's the big deal?"

Callan considered for several seconds and then shrugged. "Okay," he said. "Why not. I never bought your bullshit story from the start. Your driver's license and credit cards are flawless, but I dug a little and became certain you were using a false identity. This intrigued me. Not many people have fake documents and superficial histories as good as yours." He paused. "Then I got lucky. I found a crumpled United Airlines luggage tag inside the outer pocket of your suitcase, with the name Kira Miller scribbled on it in pencil." He pointed ahead to the next intersection. "Turn left here," he said.

Kira did as instructed. "So how did you go from finding a luggage tag to abducting me at gunpoint?"

"I made some public inquiries into Kira Miller's background," he explained, "and let it be known I had stumbled onto information that might lead me to you. It was a fishing expedition. I baited my hook with your name and waited for an interested party to bite. I had no idea I'd be catching *Moby fucking Dick*," he said in amazement, shaking his head as if still unable to believe his good fortune. "The government contacted me almost immediately. They told me you were a fugitive and warned me you were highly dangerous." Callan glanced down at his bloody shirt and decided he should have taken their warning more seriously. "They wouldn't tell me anything more, but they offered me a massive finder's fee if I could bring you to ground." The corners of his mouth turned up into a broad, self-satisfied smile. "After a little negotiation, we settled on two million dollars."

Kira shook her head in disgust. "You're an *idiot,* Bill. Did you consider they were lying about being with the government?"

He smiled. "Of course. But I don't really give a shit who they are and why they're after you. So long as I get paid."

"What if they're lying about the money also?" pressed Kira.

"After I convinced them I could find you, they wired half a million into my numbered account as a gesture of good faith. A half million bucks buys a lot of credibility."

"So this is just about money?" she said in contempt. "Betraying a client. Killing Jason in cold blood. With absolutely no idea of what's really going on or what's at stake."

"What the fuck did you expect!" he snapped. "That's the very definition of the word *mercenary* for Christ's sake: someone who's just in it for the money."

"I thought you guys had some sort of code."

Callan laughed. "Not for two million dollars we don't." He shook his head irritably. "And spare me your preaching. You're not innocent. Innocent people don't have flawlessly forged identities. And innocent people who feel threatened hire bodyguards. *Guilty* people hire mercenaries."

"Keep telling yourself that if it makes you feel better," said Kira bitterly. "But you're wrong. You're in way over your head, Bill. You're playing with fire. The people who contacted you *aren't* from the government. And you're *never* going to see the rest of that money. In fact, no matter what else happens, you're a dead man walking right now, Bill. You're on borrowed time, and you're too clueless to know it."

She said it with such chilling conviction that she gave Callan pause. But this was her intention, he realized. She was bluffing. Trying to get him to second-guess himself.

"So you're taking me to them now?" said Kira.

He nodded. "That's right. At a location I specified," he said.

"They insisted I had to be delivered alive and well or the deal was off, didn't they? They told you that if you screwed up and I ended up dead, your own funeral wouldn't be far behind. Didn't they, Bill?"

"So what?" he said dismissively, trying not to show how much she was beginning to unnerve him.

"Any idea why they were so adamant?" she pressed. She shot him a look of disgust, as if unable to believe the depth of his stupidity. "Of course you don't," she continued, not waiting for an answer. "Because you have absolutely no clue as to what you've gotten yourself into. If you want any hope of living through the night, you'll let me go now and disappear."

Callan's eyes narrowed. She was probably bluffing, but could he afford to take that chance? Maybe he *was* in over his head. As eager as he was to get his hands on the rest of the money, with stakes this high, perhaps it did pay to interrogate her properly and gain a clear picture of what he had gotten himself into. He could always reschedule the handoff. They wouldn't be happy, but they'd go along with a short delay. He'd bet they'd do almost *anything* to get her.

"Turn the car around," he said finally. "We're going back to your house. Since you're so eager to tell me what's really going on, I'm going to give you that chance."

She raised her eyebrows. "What's the matter, Bill?" she taunted. "I thought you didn't give a shit who I was or why they're really after me."

"Turn around!" he barked angrily.

They drove for several minutes, maintaining a tense silence. They were in the far left lane, slowing for a red light that shined like a beacon against the night sky, a hundred yards distant, when Kira pressed the button near her waist, retracting her seatbelt.

"Put it back on," ordered Callan.

"You bruised my shoulder and the belt is aggravating it," she said.

"I said, put it back on!"

"Okay, okay," she said as they neared to within fifteen yards of the intersection, reaching for her belt.

But she never touched it.

She threw the door open instead, and without a moment's hesitation launched herself from the car onto the grassy median that paralleled the road. She tried for a gymnastics roll, but hit hard on her right shoulder and half rolled, half skidded into the trunk of a small palm tree planted in the median.

Callan was stunned by her audacity. He could have shot her as she dived from the car but he couldn't risk killing her; something she must have counted on. He frantically released his own belt and hurled himself toward the driver's seat to take control of the runaway car, when he realized with a sinking feeling that he was too late. Kira's rudderless Lexus shot through the red light, and Callan heard the wail of a horn and the screeching of tires coming from his right. The driver of the oncoming car, a small Honda, managed to reduce his speed considerably, but couldn't stop from slamming into the passenger door of the Lexus, creating a violent and unmistakable explosion of sound that could only arise from the collision of two steel-and-glass missiles, each weighing thousands of pounds.

The collision occurred just as Callan was reaching the driver's side to take control of the car, and it threw him violently against the side of the steering wheel, fracturing one of his ribs. While the air bags had inflated instantly, Callan had been unbelted, and in such an awkward position they had been unable to prevent injury.

He shook off the severe pain, put the car in park, and stumbled out of the door as the air bags began deflating automatically. He spotted the girl running out of sight through a brightly lighted gas station on the opposite corner, noting with satisfaction that her daredevil stunt had not left her unscathed. A jagged hole had been torn in her pants and grass-stain and blood now decorated her exposed thigh.

Callan went after her as fast as he could given the pain in his ribcage, ignoring the startled shout of, "Hey, where are you going?" from the owner of the Honda.

He made it to the gas station and scanned the area in all directions, searching frantically for his multimillion dollar ticket to retirement. He entered the station's large food mart and stormed into the women's room, yanking open the stall, but it was empty. He raced back outside, his eyes darting in all directions.

And he spotted her.

The bitch had circled back to her car.

Smart. Despite a massive cave-in on the passenger side, the car was probably still drivable, and he had left the keys in the ignition. The driver of the Honda was yelling something at her, but she ignored him, gunning the engine and taking off in the direction the car was pointed. Bits of glass from the door's shattered window rained onto the pavement as she hastily drove off.

Callan scanned the gas station. A Mercedes with a powerful engine was just pulling up to a pump. *Perfect.* The driver was a plump man with a short beard, and when he exited the car to fill the tank, Callan emerged from behind the car with a gun pointed at his gut. "The keys!" he demanded. "Now!"

The man was stunned but managed to hold out his hand helplessly.

Callan snatched the keys and seconds later was tearing onto the street after Kira. She had a considerable head start, but her severely damaged car was easy to identify from a distance, even at night, and the car he was now in had more than enough horsepower to catch her.

As he cut the distance between them, she shot onto the onramp to highway 52, heading east. The Lexus was like a wounded animal and he caught up to her struggling vehicle only minutes after she had entered the highway. She was in the far left lane. He brought his car parallel to hers, one lane over, close enough that they could see each other's dark silhouette by the glow of their dashboard lights, and gestured her over menacingly with his gun.

She ignored him.

Callan wasn't sure what to do next. Shooting a tire or trying to force her off the road could cause her to lose control of the car, and he couldn't have that. He needed to deliver her alive and well, and he could tell from her determined face, unconcerned by his presence beside her, that she knew full well the advantage this gave her.

As they approached the eastbound bridge that crossed Tecolade Canyon, the girl slammed on her brakes and skidded noisily, her squealing tires leaving a trail of rubber behind her. As her speed plummeted below thirty, she veered sharply to the left, leaving the highway and entering a twenty-yard wide strip of grass that separated the eastbound and westbound lanes of the 52. The car bouncing jarringly, its shocks no match for the unpaved terrain. She came to a stop just ten yards short of a concrete barrier that had been erected in the median to prevent cars from inadvertently plummeting into the canyon, and then calmly completed her turn. With her car now pointing to the west, she picked up speed and carefully entered the westbound lanes of the 52.

Callan slammed on his brakes to follow, but was too late. Her timing had been perfect. As she had no doubt planned, in the few seconds it had taken him to react, he had continued onto the eastbound bridge over Tecolade Canyon. The westbound bridge was only twenty yards away, but instead of a grassy median separating them, there was now nothing but air, leaving him no way to mimic her maneuver short of flying.

He screeched to a halt in the middle of an active lane and several cars behind him were just able to swerve in time to avoid hitting him. Additional cars shot past him, leaning on their horns angrily. He briefly considered backing up against the oncoming traffic, but realized it would be suicide.

Furious, he picked up speed and continued to cross the long bridge, stopping the Mercedes on the shoulder when he had done so. He exited the car and surveyed the westbound lanes. As he expected, the girl's battered Lexus was nowhere in sight.

He slammed both hands against the top of the car in rage. "*Shit!*" he thundered angrily.

As he stood there, fuming, he could just make out three helicopters in the distance, their powerful searchlights probing the darkness in an ever-widening pattern whose epicenter was over the exact part of town at which the hand-off was supposed to have taken place. They were looking for Kira Miller. Somehow he was sure of it.

But he was beginning to doubt they would catch her.

Who in the hell was she? he thought in frustration.

And what could she possibly have done to warrant this kind of attention?

PART ONE
Pursuit

1

Ten Months Later

David Desh stopped at the gatehouse and lowered the window of his green Chevrolet Suburban as a uniformed guard approached him. "David Desh to see Colonel Jim Connelly," he said, handing the guard his driver's license.

The guard consulted his clipboard for several long seconds, examined the license, and then handed it back. "Go right in, sir, he's expecting you. Welcome to Fort Bragg. Do you need directions?"

Desh smiled wistfully and shook his head. "Thanks, but I've been here before." He rolled past the guard station, halfway expecting to be saluted as he passed.

The leaves of several of the trees peppered throughout the sprawling North Carolina base had transformed into a pageant of striking colors in the cool autumn air. It was the most picturesque season to return to Fort Bragg, home of a number of military units, among them USASOC; the US Army Special Operations Command. It was also home to the unit in which Desh had served; Special Forces Operational Detachment Delta, tasked with counterterrorist operations outside the United States.

As Desh passed many familiar buildings and landmarks, including a three-story climbing wall, eighty-foot rappel tower, and Olympic-sized training pool, he fought to suppress a number of conflicting emotions that welled up inside him. This was his first time back to Bragg since he had left the military and his return was bittersweet.

He arrived at his destination and parked. A few minutes later he entered Jim Connelly's office, shook hands firmly with the uniformed man behind the desk, and took a seat facing the colonel, lowering his briefcase to the floor beside him as he did so. Desh had been in this office many times before, but never as a civilian. Books on military history and strategy were organized in perfect precision on a bookshelf. The colonel was an accomplished fencer, and a large, framed photograph of two fencers locked in battle, shot in vibrant clarity by a professional photographer, was centered behind his desk.

The colonel had angular features, light-brown hair of military length, and a matching, neatly trimmed mustache. At forty-eight, he was seventeen years Desh's senior, but despite their different ages each man had an aura of fitness, competence, and easy self-assurance that was typical of those who had undergone the rigorous training demanded of the Special Forces.

"Thanks for coming, Captain," said Connelly. He raised his eyebrows. "I guess I should be calling you David nowadays."

Desh sighed. "Disappointed?"

"What, that you left the service?"

Desh nodded.

"After what happened in Iran, who could possibly blame you?"

Desh had been found nine months earlier in a bloody heap just on the Iraq side of the Iraq/Iran border, the only surviving member of his team after an operation in Iran had gone terribly wrong. He had lost three men who had each been like a brother to him. Desh found himself revisiting the horrific mission often, cursing himself for not being smarter, or faster, or more careful. He blamed himself for the deaths of his men and was consumed by guilt for being alive when they were not. The psychiatrist the military had provided insisted this was a natural reaction, but this knowledge brought him little comfort.

"I'm not sure you answered the question," persisted Desh.

"Okay then," said Connelly. "As a Special Forces colonel, I am disappointed. You're as good as it gets, David. Bright, decisive, innovative. I hate to lose a man like you." He opened his mouth to continue but thought better of it.

"Go on," prompted Desh.

Connelly stared at his visitor for a long while and then sighed. "As a friend, on the other hand," he said earnestly, "while I'm sorry the decision was brought on by tragedy, I think you did the right thing. And I'm happy for you." He paused. "As good as you are," he continued, choosing his words with great care, "you didn't belong in the service. Not because you're irreverent and don't suffer fools gladly—which is true—but because you think too deeply. And you've never gotten numb to the necessity of taking lives. You may be unmatched as a warrior, but nothing will ever change the fact that you have the soul of a scholar." Connelly shook his head. "The military was sapping your natural optimism and sense of humor. Even before Iran."

Desh's eyes narrowed as he considered Connelly's words. He had always had a knack for seeing the humor in anything and everything. But the more he thought about it, the more he realized the colonel was right; this key facet of his personality had been steadily eroding for years.

After leaving the service he had joined Fleming Executive Protection, the largest bodyguarding service in Washington outside of the Secret Service. But while the protection business was thriving and the pay was good, Desh knew his heart wasn't into this type of work anymore. He was in the process of deciding what would come next in his life, and while he wasn't sure what this might be, he knew it wouldn't involve guns or adrenaline or life and death challenges.

In the final analysis, the colonel was right. Just because you were good at something didn't mean it was a match with your personality or psyche.

"Thanks Colonel," said Desh earnestly. "I appreciate your honesty." He waited a few seconds and then added,

"But how are things with you?" signaling he no longer wanted to be the subject of conversation.

Connelly shrugged. "Nothing much has changed since you left. We're still winning the war on terror hundreds of times each day." He frowned and added, "The only problem, of course, is that we have to win every round and they only have to win once. Which means I don't have the luxury of ever making a mistake." There was a long pause. "But I didn't ask you here to burden you with all of my troubles," he finished.

Desh raised his eyebrows. "Only one of them, right?"

Connelly laughed. "True enough," he said.

There was an awkward silence in the room for several seconds. Finally the colonel lowered his eyes and let out a regretful sigh. "David, as good as it is to see you," he began, "I wish it were under different circumstances. But you know I wouldn't have asked you here if this wasn't of the utmost importance."

"I know that, Colonel," said Desh. He forced a smile. "That's what worries me."

The colonel opened his desk drawer, withdrew a brown accordion folder, and slid it across the desk to Desh, who dutifully picked it up. At Connelly's request he pulled out a separate file from within the folder, which contained a series of eight-by-ten photographs, and examined the one on top. It was of a woman who looked to be about twenty-five, wearing well-worn jeans and a simple V-neck sweater. Cute. Desh's physical taste exactly. Fresh-faced. Girl next door. He glanced at Connelly and raised his eyebrows questioningly.

"Kira Miller," began Connelly. "Twenty-eight years old. Five foot seven. Weight: One hundred and twenty-two pounds."

Desh glanced back at the photo. The girl's blue eyes sparkled almost playfully and she wore an unselfconscious, relaxed smile that conveyed a down-to-earth, friendly personality—although Desh knew better than to judge someone's personality based on a single photograph.

"Born in Cincinnati Ohio, attended Middlebrook High School," continued Connelly mechanically. "Parents deceased. One older brother, Alan; also deceased. Valedictorian of Middlebrook High at age sixteen. Graduated from the University of Chicago, summa cum laude, with a BS in molecular biology—at nineteen. Obtained a Ph.D. from Stanford in molecular neurobiology at twenty-three."

"When do most people get their doctorates?"

"Twenty-seven or Twenty-eight," replied Connelly.

Desh nodded. "Cute *and* geeky-brilliant. Just my type."

"I forgot to mention, star of her high school track team as well."

"Maybe not so geeky at that," allowed Desh. He turned to the photo once again and found himself hoping that this Kira Miller turned out to be the damsel in distress in Connelly's unfolding story rather than the villain.

Desh was almost six feet tall, with green eyes and short brown hair. And while he had never thought of himself as particularly handsome, the open, friendly nature of his face seemed to appeal to women far out of proportion to his looks. But while the most beautiful of women were often attracted to him, a woman's intelligence, confidence, and sense of humor had come to matter to him far more than her appearance. He couldn't stand to be around an empty-headed woman, no matter how beautiful, or one who didn't have a down-to-earth personality. He wondered what Kira Miller might be like.

A part of him realized that this primitive, lizard brained interest in a girl who was nothing but a picture and a profile was foolish—but perhaps it was also a sign of returning health. He had felt numb inside since Iran, during which time he had lost all interest in starting any type of relationship. On the other hand, perhaps nothing had really changed. Perhaps he allowed himself a glimmer of interest in this woman because she was just an inaccessible two-dimensional profile, and one sure to have some unusual baggage at that, rather than a relatively safe, flesh-and-blood women whose picture *wasn't* inside a top-secret military folder.

Despite this, Desh found himself hoping that this newfound spark, tiny and foolish though it was, would not be extinguished immediately. It was time to find out. "She sounds too good to be true," he said pointedly.

The corners of Connelly's mouth turned up in a slight, humorless smile. "Well, you know what they say about things that sound too good to be true."

Desh frowned. "They usually are," he finished.

Connelly nodded.

Desh had his answer. Too bad, he thought.

Not the damsel after all.

2

Jim Connelly reached into a small white refrigerator that was tucked away against the wall of his office, pulled out two chilled plastic bottles of spring water, and handed one to Desh. Desh nodded his thanks, unscrewed the cap, and took an appreciative sip, while Connelly slid a wooden coaster across to him.

The colonel took a drink from his own bottle. "From what we understand, Kira Miller is even more of a genius than her record would suggest," he said. "Especially when it comes to gene therapy. In this field, scientists who have worked with her think she might just be the most brilliant, intuitive scientist alive today."

"Gene therapy?"

"It's just like the name suggests," explained Connelly. "It's a therapy to cure disease, or even birth defects, by correcting faulty genes. Or by inserting totally new ones," he added.

"That's possible?"

"For quite a while now. I wasn't aware of it either. I guess those involved in this field haven't done a good job of spreading the word."

"Or you and I have had our heads in the sand."

The colonel chuckled. "I wouldn't rule that out either," he said, amused.

"How is it done?"

"The most popular way is to use viruses, which insert genes into host cells naturally. These viral genes commandeer our cellular machinery to make endless copies of themselves. Some types, like herpes viruses and retroviruses, actually insert their genes right into human chromosomes."

Desh's face showed a hint of disgust. Even though it occurred at the submicroscopic level, the thought of a virus inserting its genetic material into a human chromosome was disturbing. "Retroviruses," said Desh. "You mean HIV?"

"The AIDS virus is in the retrovirus family, yes. But regardless of the virus type, the idea of gene therapy is to use modified versions of these viruses as delivery vehicles, forcing them to insert human genes into our cells rather than their own. If you cut out all the nasty parts of a retrovirus and add back in a human gene—say, insulin—the virus will insert perfect, working copies of insulin genes into your chromosomes. Presto—no more diabetes. Simple as that."

"So the AIDS virus could actually be used to save lives?"

"Properly hollowed out and genetically engineered, yes. Ironic, isn't it?"

"Very," said Desh. He was intrigued. Rather than treating the symptoms of a disease, gene therapy offered an outright cure: virus-aided microsurgery on the genes themselves. "It sounds ideal," offered Desh.

"In many ways it is," responded Connelly thoughtfully. "Unfortunately, the field hasn't progressed as quickly as scientists had hoped. It might sound simple on paper, but I'm told it's treacherously complicated."

"It doesn't even sound simple on paper," noted Desh wryly.

The corners of Connelly's mouth turned up into a slight smile. "Apparently she had quite a knack for it," he said. He lifted the water bottle to his lips and gestured at the photographs lying on the desk in front of Desh.

Desh flipped the picture of Kira Miller on its back and revealed the second photo in the stack. It was a two-story yellow brick building, not particularly attractive, with a large placard over the door that read, *NeuroCure Pharmaceuticals.*

"She joined NeuroCure, a publicly traded biotech company in San Diego, right out of Stanford," continued Connelly. "She was well liked, and by all accounts performed as brilliantly there as expected."

He gestured again and Desh dutifully flipped to the next photo, a small, nondescript building in the middle of an industrial strip. The building had an address affixed to it but no name.

"NeuroCure's animal research facility," explained the colonel. "The building that Kira Miller worked out of, and for which she was responsible. Notice there's no way to tell it's at all associated with NeuroCure, or that there are animals inside. Biotechs don't like to advertise these facilities. Not with all the PETA types running around."

Connelly stroked his mustache absently with the tips of two fingers, something he had had a tendency to do ever since Desh had known him. "Kira was a model employee her first two years at NeuroCure, performing with the level of brilliance expected of her. During this time she was promoted twice, which is fairly unprecedented." He raised his eyebrows. "Then again, so is graduating Stanford with a Ph.D. at twenty-three." Connelly leaned forward in his chair. "Which brings us to about a year ago," he said meaningfully, a hint of weariness in his voice.

"Let me guess," said Desh dryly. "That's when all hell starts to break loose."

"You could say that."

"Interesting," noted Desh. "Up until now, at least, you've painted Kira Miller as a model citizen. It must have been *some* year."

"You have no idea," said Connelly ominously.

3

The colonel motioned for Desh to flip to the next photograph in his thin stack. It showed a short, slightly pudgy man with a hard look, holding a cigarette loosely.

"Larry Lusetti," said Connelly. "Private Investigator; ex-cop. One morning about eleven months ago he's found dead in Kira Miller's condo in La Jolla, his skull bashed in with a heavy marble bookend and his body severely lacerated. After he was bludgeoned, he fell through a picture window in the front of the condo, which explains the lacerations." He paused. "Kira must have managed to pull him back inside and close the shutters, but a neighbor heard the glass shattering and went to investigate. When no one answered the neighbor's knock—and then Kira sped out of her garage and raced right past him—he called the police.

"Kira Miller couldn't be located, but later that morning police found that the victim's apartment had been broken into and turned upside down. Turns out Lusetti had installed a motion-activated nanny-cam inside a hanging plant in the apartment. Because of the nature of his work he tended to be a bit paranoid."

You're not paranoid if they really are out to get you, thought Desh dryly, but he didn't interrupt.

"Lusetti's secretary alerted the authorities to the existence of the camera, which recorded some nice footage of Kira Miller ransacking the place and leaving with a large file folder and Lusetti's laptop. They were able to enhance the footage enough to make out the label on the file she took. Turns out it was a file Lusetti had on *her*."

"Interesting. Do we know why she was under investigation?"

Connelly shook his head. "No. Lusetti's secretary knew nothing about it. And Kira Miller's file was the only one he kept at home. There were no other records ever located that made any mention of her at all—other than the ones she took, of course."

Connelly gestured at the photographs and Desh flipped to the next one.

"Alan Miller," said Connelly. "Kira's older brother."

Desh studied the photo. Blue eyes. Handsome. He could see the family resemblance.

"Around midnight that same day, brother Alan turned up dead in Cincinnati. His house was found burned to the ground with his charred remains inside."

"Arson?"

"No question about it. A rental car was found abandoned near the house with traces of acetone inside, the fire accelerant used in the arson. The DNA from a strand of hair found on the driver's seat of the car matched Kira Miller's DNA from hair samples police had taken from her condo."

"And she had rented the car?"

"Yes. Using an alias. The name and license she used to rent it turned out to be untraceable. But the rental car agent identified her picture from ten that were shown to him. Later, police found a cab driver who recognized her picture. The Cabbie said he had picked her up a few miles from the brother's house, about an hour after the fire, and had taken her to the airport." Connelly frowned. "This is where the trail ends. We presume she took a flight, but if she did she used fake identification."

Desh pulled Kira Miller's eight-by-ten from the photo pile and examined her once again. She had such a friendly and appealing look. But this was just a carefully constructed mask. Being burned alive was one of the more horrible ways to die. Killing anyone in cold calculation in such a sadistic fashion—especially a family member—pointed to a psychopathic or sociopathic personality. And these soulless monsters were hard to spot. In fact, Desh knew, they were often quite intelligent and charismatic, and highly skilled at hiding their true nature.

Connelly nodded toward the last photo Desh held in his hand. It was of a tall man, probably in his early fifties, with wavy, seemingly uncombed salt-and-pepper hair, dressed in business casual slacks and shirt. He had a long, thin face and a wild, faraway look in his eye that reminded Desh of a stereotypical professor.

"Tom Morgan. He was NeuroCure's Chief Scientific Officer and Kira's boss when she joined. He was killed in an auto accident almost exactly three years after Kira Miller's hire. In light of future events, we now think there's a good chance it wasn't an accident."

Desh frowned and was silent for several long seconds, digesting what he had been told so far. "You said her parents were deceased. How did they die?"

"I figured you'd jump to this question," said Connelly approvingly. "You really do have a singular talent for connecting dots."

"Thanks, Colonel," said Desh. "But these particular dots aren't exactly difficult to connect."

"You'd be surprised. Anyway, to answer your question, her parents both died in the same auto accident. While she was in high school. As with Morgan, the police didn't suspect foul play at the time and didn't do much of an investigation. But in light of everything else, it's not hard to imagine that their daughter was behind it."

Desh knew signs of sociopathy were usually present from a very young age if anyone was looking in the right direction. If Kira Miller could torch her brother in cold blood, she wouldn't likely be squeamish about killing her parents either. A thorough examination of mysterious deaths and disappearances with her as epicenter was almost certain to be revealing. Perhaps brother Alan had been helping this private investigator, Larry Lusetti. This was as good a conjecture as any for why she killed him so soon after recovering the file Lusetti had on her. Alan Miller could probably have pulled any number of skeletons from his little sister's closet—perhaps literally.

"Any other unexplained accidents in her wake?" said Desh.

Connelly nodded grimly. "An uncle drowned while swimming alone when she was twelve. And he was known to be a very strong swimmer. There were two other incidents involving teachers at Kira's high school the next year. One turned up dead in her apartment, her face so badly eaten away by sulfuric acid it was unrecognizable. The other went missing and was never found. Neither case was ever solved."

So the breathtaking, fresh-faced girl smiling in the photo was a psychopath, and was at the very least a double murderer. The tale Connelly had spun was truly grisly. But Desh knew the worst was yet to come. There was only one reason any of this would warrant the colonel's attention. "So what's the terrorism connection?"

Connelly sighed heavily, as if he had hoped he could somehow avoid this discussion. He rubbed his mustache once again and said, "As the Lusetti investigation and hunt for Kira Miller continued, the police found evidence that she had been in communication with several known terrorist organizations, including Al-Qaeda and Islamic Jihad."

"Nice groups," said Desh dryly.

"The case was turned over to Homeland Security. There's a detailed report in the accordion file, but they quickly found that she had millions of dollars deposited in banks throughout the world, well hidden, including several numbered Swiss accounts. They're certain they haven't found it all. The methods she used to obscure the trail between herself and her money were quite sophisticated. They also found several false identities, and are convinced she has more."

"Working with Jihadists is an interesting choice for a Western woman, even for a sociopath. These groups aren't exactly known for being progressive when it comes to a woman's place in society."

"It's a puzzle alright. She's not Muslim and there's no evidence she ever supported this ideology. She could be in it just for money, but somehow I think there's something we're missing."

"Do you think she's attracted to the danger of working with terrorists?"

Connelly shrugged. "It's impossible to say. Normal motives don't necessarily apply to psychopathic personalities. Jeffrey Dahmer murdered and cannibalized seventeen people, three of whose skulls were found in his refrigerator."

"That's *perfectly* rational behavior," said Desh sarcastically. "He just didn't want them to spoil."

A smile flashed across Connelly's face, but only for a moment. "You'll read in the report that they found a flotation tank in her condo," he continued. "Top of the line. That's a pretty unusual device to have taking up space in your living room."

"Flotation tank?"

"They used to be called sensory deprivation chambers. Basically a giant coffin filled with water and Epsom salt. Seal yourself up in one and you bob around like a cork, weightless, in total silence and total darkness. You receive virtually no sensory input while inside." Connelly grimaced. "One can only imagine what she was doing with it. Performing bizarre rituals? Locking people in for days at a time as a means of torture?" he shuddered. "This girl is our worst nightmare: brilliant and totally unpredictable. No conscience; no remorse."

The room fell silent. Both men were alone with their thoughts. Desh knew that any problem Connelly had that he couldn't solve with his vast resources and was important enough for him to summon Desh had to be very, very ugly. He wasn't sure he really wanted to know what it was. Maybe he should just leave now. What did it matter, anyway? Stop one villain and another would always spring up to take his place. But he couldn't bring himself to walk away, at least not until his curiosity was satisfied.

Desh took a deep breath and locked his eyes on Connelly. "So let's cut to the chase, Colonel. What are we really talking about here, biological warfare?"

Connelly frowned. "That's right. And she's the best around—maybe ever." Connelly's demeanor, already fairly grim due to the nature of the events he had been reporting, took a sharp turn for the worse.

"With her skills and experience engineering viruses," said Desh, "I'm sure she could make them more deadly and contagious. But to what end? You can't contain them. They could easily boomerang back on the terrorists. I know these groups aren't very selective in who they kill, but their leaders, at least, aren't in any hurry to meet the seventy-two virgins awaiting them in heaven."

"My bioweapons experts tell me someone with her skill can get around the containment issue by designing in molecular triggers. The DNA not only has to be inserted, it has to be read and turned into gene products," explained Connelly. "There are promoter regions on the DNA that control under what circumstances this happens. Triggers. Someone as talented as Kira Miller can engineer these to her specifications. Like a Trojan Horse virus that infects your computer. It lies dormant until whatever predetermined time the asshole who invented it has specified. Then it emerges and demolishes your files."

Connelly took a deep breath and then continued. "We think she's engineering the common cold virus to insert specific Ebola virus genes into human chromosomes like a retrovirus does," he said gravely. "As with any cold, it would spread quickly. But now, in addition to a runny nose, those infected would get a bonus: the genes responsible for the massive hemorrhagic fever associated with Ebola. This is almost always fatal. Victims suffer from fever, vomiting, diarrhea, and uncontrollable bleeding, both internally and externally—from the corners of their eyes, their nose—everywhere."

Desh's stomach tightened. Ebola was the deadliest virus known. He shouldn't have been surprised that something as promising as gene therapy and molecular biology could be bastardized to kill rather than cure. Humanity seemed to have a singular ability to find destructive uses for any constructive technology. Invent the computer, and you could be certain someone would invent computer viruses and other ways to attack it. Invent the Internet, an unimaginable treasure trove of information, and you could bet it would be used as a recruiting tool for hate mongers and instantly turned into a venue for child pornographers, sexual predators, and scam artists. Humanity never failed to find a way to become its own worst enemy.

"I still don't see how the terrorists can be certain of avoiding the Ebola genes themselves," said Desh.

"They can't be. But there's more to the story. This is where the molecular trigger comes in. Remember, the genes don't only have to be inserted, they have to be activated."

"So what activates them?"

"We believe she's trying to engineer them to be triggered by a chemical. One specific to a certain food. Ingest this chemical and the inserted Ebola genetic material begins to be expressed by victims' cells. And once the genes have been triggered, there's no stopping them. People's own cells are transformed into ticking time bombs. A few days to a few weeks later, boom!—you're dead." Connelly raised his eyebrows. "Any guesses as to what food sets it off?"

Desh looked blank.

"Pork."

Desh's eyes widened. Of course it would be pork. What else? Only those at the pinnacle of the Jihadist pyramid would know of the plot, but since ingestion of pork was forbidden in the Muslim religion, their followers would be safe. And Desh knew how these people thought. In their eyes, any Muslim around the world who ignored this prohibition and *did* eat pork deserved to die anyway.

"Our organic chemists tell me there are several complex molecules that are swine-specific. We believe the Ebola genes are set to be triggered by one of them. But even though the genes are triggered, the viral parts aren't present, so it isn't infectious like the natural Ebola. That's what keeps the terrorists safe. As long as they don't eat pork, they have nothing to worry about."

Desh's lip curled up in disgust. It was a masterful plan from the terrorist's perspective. And as utterly horrific as their strategy was, it was not without its boldness or creativity. Ironically, in addition to devout Muslims, religious Jews would also be spared. This would be the only fly in the ointment of an otherwise ideal plan from the terrorists' perspective. The fact that their most hated enemy would remain untouched would sit like open sores in their stomachs.

"Can she really pull it off?" he asked

"This is as difficult a genetic engineering project as there is, but if anyone in the world can do it, Kira Miller can. She's that good."

"And the expected casualties?"

"Depends on how efficiently her designed virus can insert the genes, and how efficiently the pork-specific organic chemicals can trigger them. Worst case, hundreds of millions around the world. Best case, given the high quality of medicine in the West, maybe a few hundred thousand."

The color drained from Desh's face. This attack had the potential to be more costly in human lives than a nuclear bomb set off in a population center. And the very nature of the attack would unleash a raging wildfire of irrationality and panic that could have an incalculable effect on civilization. "And this would be only the beginning," he whispered to Connelly.

"That's right," said Connelly. "People would fear they had other Trojan Horses buried in their genetic material, primed to go off with one wrong bite. No one would know what foods to trust. Rumors would race around the world. Fear would be at a fever pitch. Economies would collapse. The most ordered societies would degenerate into chaos and devastation almost overnight."

Desh knew this plan could set civilization back hundreds of years—which is exactly what the Jihadists wanted. No wonder Kira Miller was so wealthy. If she could convince Al-Qaeda she could execute on this plan, she could name her price. Death and devastation on a vast scale wouldn't trouble a soulless psychopath like her in the least.

"At some point, we may be forced to issue a warning not to eat pork," said Connelly. "But this wouldn't buy us all that much. The warning itself would incite some of the panic we're trying to avoid. Many wouldn't get the message and still others would ignore it, believing it to be a government conspiracy. And we believe the Jihadists have a contingency version ready to go, with a different trigger. So sounding the alarm would just push them into plan B. The terrorist leaders would still know which foods to avoid, although since they'd only risk sharing this secret with a select few, they'd lose far more of their followers under this scenario."

Desh shook his head in disgust. If it came to that, the need to sacrifice scores of their followers for the cause would not give them the slightest pause.

Desh placed the photographs back inside the folder and reinserted it into the accordion file. Before arriving at Fort Bragg he had already felt dead inside. Being on the grounds, a reminder of a past he so desperately wanted to forget, had made things worse. And now this. He felt ill. He needed to conclude this meeting and get some air. "So tell me," he said pointedly. "Why am *I* here?"

Connelly sighed deeply. "Kira Miller has been off the grid since her brother's murder—for about a year now. She's vanished. Like magic. We have reason to believe she was in San Diego last November, but she could be anywhere now. Only Bin Laden and a few others have been the subject of bigger manhunts, and we've basically gotten nowhere. There are those who think she must be dead, but we can't make that assumption, obviously."

"I ask again," said Desh. "Why am I here? Plan B? Send in a solitary man when entire armies fail?"

"Believe me, we didn't wait until now to try the Lone Ranger approach. We've been sending in individual agents for several months. The best and brightest. They've gotten nowhere."

"So what am I, then," remarked Desh. "Plan E? What do you expect I can do that your first choices couldn't?"

"First of all, you *would* have been my first choice had you remained in the military. You know that, David. You know my opinion of your abilities. I didn't think I could get authorization to recruit a civilian, so I never recommended you."

Desh looked confused. "Then how am I here?"

"Someone up the food chain realized your value and asked me to recruit you. I was thrilled that they did. Not only are you unequaled as a soldier, you found more top-level terrorists on the lam than anyone when you were in the service. No one is as creative and tenacious on the hunt as you are. Kira Miller has a knack for gene therapy. *You* have a knack for finding those who are off the grid."

Connelly leaned forward and fixed an unblinking stare on Desh. "And you're someone I trust absolutely, someone outside the system. This woman has massive amounts of money and is quite persuasive. I wouldn't put it past her to have found a way to monitor us, or to compromise some of our people."

"So you think you have a mole?"

"Honestly . . . no. But with the stakes this high, why take chances?"

Desh nodded. He couldn't argue the point.

"We failed as an organization. The individuals who have tried have also failed. There could be many other good explanations for this, but now it's time to try something different." He rubbed his mustache absently. "You have a singular talent for this and you don't report through military channels. Let's keep it that way. Use your own resources, not ours. In the file you'll find the reports of your predecessors: all the information they gathered on Kira Miller."

"I assume it will also detail their attempts to locate her?"

"Actually, no," said Connelly. "We don't want you to be polluted with what came before. You'll be starting with a clean slate. And don't communicate with me. I don't want to know what you're doing. You'll find a contact number to use when you find her. The person at the other end will handle the rest. Follow his instructions from there on in."

"*When* I find her?"

"You'll find her," said Connelly with absolute conviction. "I'm certain of it."

"That's two questionable assumptions you're making," said Desh. "The first one is that I'll agree to take the job in the first place."

Connelly said nothing. The silence hung in the room like a thick fog.

Desh was torn. There was a significant part of him that just wanted to walk away. Connelly would find a way to solve his problem—or he wouldn't. But the world would keep revolving, with or without Desh on the case. There were other talented men outside the system. Let someone else be the hero. He had tried the hero business and had failed.

On the other hand, what if he really did have some special quality that would turn the tide? If he walked away and the attack succeeded, how could he live with himself? He beat himself up every day for surviving the operation in Iran when his men had not. Guilt and loss were eating away at his soul already, but would pale in comparison to the question that would torment his every waking moment—what if he really had been the only one able to find, and stop, Kira Miller?

And even though he had wanted to clear his head and put distance between himself and anyone he had known from his past life, his relationship with Connelly had been very close, and almost certainly would be again someday. There were few men he admired as much as he did Jim Connelly.

Desh stared long and hard at the colonel. "Okay," he said wearily, a look of resignation on his face. "I'll help you." He shook his head bitterly, and it was clear he was annoyed with himself for being unable to refuse. "I'll give it my best," he added with a sigh. "That's all I can do."

"Thanks, David," said Connelly in relief. "That's all anyone can do."

The colonel paused and now looked somewhat uneasy. "Now that you're on board, I need to insist that you don't go after her yourself, under any circumstances. Your job is to find her. Period. The job of the person at the end of the telephone number I gave you is to reel her in." He paused. "Before you leave, I have to be sure you're crystal clear about this."

Desh stared at Connelly in disbelief. "I'm clear on it, all right, Colonel. What I'm not clear on is why. What if I found her and was in the perfect position for capture? I need to be able to strike when the iron's hot. By the time I call someone in and they arrive, she could slip through the noose. She's too elusive and too important to allow that to happen." He shook his head in disbelief. "It's an idiotic strategy," he snapped.

The colonel sighed. "I couldn't agree more," he said. "But those are my orders. I made all the points you just made as emphatically as I could, but I didn't win the day. So this is what we're left with."

"Okay then," said Desh in annoyance. "I'm just a civilian now. If someone up the chain of command just had a frontal lobotomy, there's nothing *I* can do about it."

"On the bright side," continued Connelly, pressing ahead, "I *was* able to win one important argument with my superiors." He smiled slyly. "I convinced them it wouldn't be easy to entice you back. They've authorized me to pay you two hundred thousand dollars upon initiation of the assignment as a draw against expenses. It's all set to be wired into your account. You'll have access to it within the hour." He leaned forward intently. "There's another *million* upon success."

Desh's eyes widened. A payment of this magnitude would dramatically change the course of his life. It would allow him to leave the violent world he had known behind and immediately start down whichever new path he finally chose for himself. "Thanks, Colonel," he said. "That's a hell of a lot of money." Desh paused. "But you do know I agreed to help because of you, and because of the nature of the threat, and not for the money."

A twinkle came to Connelly's eye. "I know that," he said. "Notice that I only brought up the money *after* you had agreed." The colonel smiled. "Considering the bounty for Bin Laden went as high as twenty-five million dollars, and considering the devastating consequences of failure, you're the biggest bargain the government has ever had."

Desh smiled. "Well, as long as the *government* is happy," he said dryly, spreading his hands in mock sincerity. He paused for a moment in thought. "What about Fleming Executive Protection?"

"Don't worry. We'll make sure your calendar is cleared for the next month and you remain in good standing with them." An amused look crossed Connelly's face. "And rest assured, we'll do it in such a way that won't hurt your career, or your ah . . . reputation." He smiled slightly at this and then added, "Do we have an agreement?"

Desh nodded. "We do."

"Good. I'm sorry to have to pull you back in for one last mission, David, but I know you're the right man for the job."

Desh rose from the chair and prepared to leave. "I hope you're right, Colonel. As always, I'll try not to let you down." He eyed Connelly suspiciously as something he had said earlier finally registered. "You said the wire transfer of the two hundred-K is ready to go?"

"I just need to give the word and it's done."

"So how is it exactly," said Desh, his eyes narrowing, "that you happen to have the wire transfer information for my account, without me having given it to you?"

Connelly raised his eyebrows. "I don't suppose you'd believe it was a lucky guess?" he said with an innocent shrug.

Desh allowed a bemused smile to flash across his face. He opened his briefcase, placed the accordion file inside, and stood.

Connelly also rose from his chair. He reached out and gave Desh a warm handshake. "Good luck, David," he said earnestly. "And be careful."

"I won't be eating any pork products anytime soon, if that's what you mean," said Desh wryly, trying to hide his anxiety.

With that, David Desh picked up his briefcase and walked purposefully out the door.

4

David Desh exited the grounds of Fort Bragg and drove to a nearby shopping center. He parked the Suburban at the outer edge of the sprawling lot, becoming a lone island of privacy cut off from the dense mainland of all other parked vehicles. He pulled out the dossier on Kira Miller and began a careful review. The five-hour drive back to D.C. ahead of him would be the perfect time to digest what he was now reading and plot out his initial strategy.

After a little more than an hour he returned the dossier to his briefcase and began his trek home. Her file hadn't given him much to go on, nor had he expected it to. If the girl's background would have led to an obvious approach, others would have found it by now.

Kira Miller had been able to hide her true nature quite well. From a very young age she had been extremely talented, ambitious, and competitive. When she set her mind to something she had accomplished it. This didn't always win her a lot of friends growing up, and being jumped ahead in school several years did nothing to help her social life.

Even as an adult she tended to make few friends, always keeping her eye on the ball; be it setting the record for youngest ever molecular neurobiology Ph.D. at Stanford or power-climbing up the corporate ladder. In college she had dated some, but she never managed to sustain a relationship for more than eight or nine months. Desh knew that most men would find her brilliance intimidating.

The file elaborated quite extensively on everything that Connelly had told him, laying out her communications with terror groups, how these communications had been found, the airtight evidence gathered against her for the murders of Lusetti and her brother, and the Ebola gene therapy plot.

After the murders, the police investigation had revealed she had spent an inordinate amount of time in NeuroCure's animal labs late at night, but had managed to hide this activity. The employee badge she'd been issued to unlock the door after hours was designed to record the holder's identity and time of entry in the main computer, but she had ingeniously altered the software to prevent this from happening.

Investigators had also found that Kira had ordered far more rodents from suppliers than the company had needed for experiments. Since she was responsible for inventory, this hadn't been caught earlier.

It was clear she had been performing secret animal experiments almost every night. In retrospect, this made sense—chilling sense. She must have brought the Jihadists some evidence that she could execute on the strategy she was proposing to get them to pay her the substantial sums of money she was known to have in banks around the world. An animal proof of concept, as it were.

Connelly and USASOC had vast resources at their disposal, both human and otherwise, and yet they hadn't come close to finding this girl. Only someone extremely careful and extremely clever could possibly elude a government-sponsored manhunt for this long. And that was really the rub on this one. The prey was far smarter than the hunter. Desh didn't feel any macho need to downplay his own intelligence, which was considerable, but it was undeniable that hers was in another league. So how to catch someone smarter than yourself?

It was all in your attitude. You didn't plot a strategy designed to catch her making a mistake. This is what the others probably focused on. Instead, you counted on her *not* making a mistake. You counted on her doing everything exactly right. This was the answer.

As much as he had come to hate the endless violence with which he had long been associated, puzzling out the location of a dangerous adversary intent on eluding capture was a task he found completely absorbing. It was the ultimate challenge. His task was to locate a single human being among the more than six billion inhabitants of the planet, one who could be hiding almost anywhere on the incomprehensibly large surface of the Earth. So how to narrow this down?

He shot by an eighteen-wheeler as if it were standing still, completely lost in thought. His foot was heavy on the gas pedal by nature, and when he didn't actively control himself, his default speed was usually twenty miles per hour over the posted limit. Despite conscious efforts to contain this impulse, he was beginning to feel he was beyond hope and desperately in need of a twelve-step speedaholics program.

Where are you Kira Miller? he said to himself as he changed lanes once again, blowing past two cars and returning to the left lane where he rapidly began pulling away from everyone behind him.

Was she living in a cave somewhere? Maybe. But not likely. He would start by assuming she was still in the States, hiding in plain sight. She was attempting a breathtakingly complex feat of genetic engineering. The report he had read was clear that, at minimum, she would require specialized equipment, cloned genes, ultra-fast DNA sequencers, biological reagents, and genetically identical experimental animals. A terrorist camp in Iran or Afghanistan, or even the best equipped labs in these countries, for that matter, wouldn't be able to readily fulfill her evolving needs in this regard.

Desh decided that regardless of where she was hiding, he would begin by focusing on her computer. No matter how much she may have given up of her past life to elude pursuit, he couldn't believe she'd swear off the Internet, especially given her need to tap into an ocean of biotechnology literature as her research progressed. But there were ways to use computers and the Internet without leaving a trail, and she had already shown an alarming degree of facility with computers when she had modified NeuroCure's security software. Finding a single laptop among untold millions, and then having it happen to be in the lap of Kira Miller when it was found, was like finding a needle in a haystack the size of Texas.

Desh frowned as he realized this analogy fell short. The reality was that the particular needle he was after was not only lost in an enormous haystack, but was also mobile, and would be sure to dive even deeper into the haystack if it sensed someone coming.

5

Desh was thirty minutes from his apartment when his cell phone vibrated inside his shirt pocket. He lifted it out and stole a quick glance at the screen. *Wade Fleming* appeared on the display.

He flipped open the phone. "Hi Wade."

"Hi David," came the reply. His boss wasted no time on small talk. "Do you happen to know a girl named Patricia Swanson?"

Desh's brow furrowed as he searched his memory. "I don't think so," he said. He shrugged. "Of course it's always possible that I met her but just forgot."

"Then you haven't met her. Believe me, you'd remember," he said with absolute conviction "She's a total knockout. I mean like centerfold material," he added for emphasis.

"Okay," replied Desh. "I'll take your word for it. So what about her?"

"She visited the office about an hour ago. Asked for you by name."

"Did she claim she knows me?"

"No. She says she's vacationing at a few choice resort locations around the country for the next month, thinks she might have a stalker, and wants protection. Said she saw your picture and bio on our website and wants you assigned to her. I told her you had a busy month lined up, and offered up Dean Padgett." A note of disapproval entered Fleming's voice. "She wouldn't have it. She wanted *you*, and she was prepared to pay extra to make sure she got you." He paused. "Frankly, David, I think you might be the one who has a stalker, not her. She's probably a bored, spoiled rich girl out for a thrill. What greater thrill than seducing your bodyguard? Must watch too many movies. Bottom line is that I got the feeling she sees you as more of a hired boy-toy than a bodyguard." He paused. "I was tempted to tell her you were gay and offer to take the job myself," he said wryly.

Desh shook his head and a small smile crept across his face. Jim Connelly had promised to clear his calendar, and he must have had quite a laugh when he had hatched this scheme. He sure hadn't wasted any time setting it in motion.

"So when do I start?"

"Tomorrow morning, if you take the job."

"*If* I take the job."

"I told her I needed your okay."

"*Really*? That's a first."

"Look, David, as hot as she is, I'm not running an escort service here. I want to make sure you know what you're getting into. I've *seen* her, and it's hard to imagine how any man could resist her for long if that's her game plan." He paused. "On the other hand, she *is* paying top dollar, and this could be legitimate. It may be that your Delta Force credentials are what impressed her and not your friendly smile. But given my doubts, I won't insist you take this."

"Thanks, Wade. But if I have to risk the attention of a beautiful woman," he said with mock bravado, "that's just what I'll have to do. For the agency's sake, of course."

"Of course," repeated Fleming wryly. "Your loyalty to the agency is legendary, David. I'll e-mail you the assignment details and where to find her so you can get started." There was a long pause on the line. "And I want you to know, while the rest of us are dodging bullets and laser-guided missiles protecting hairy fat guys, we'll be thinking of you lying on the beach with a centerfold model—dodging those dangerous UV rays."

"Don't mention it, Wade. That's just the kind of team player I am."

"Well, I don't want to have to worry about you, David," said Fleming sardonically, "so be sure to use a good sunblock. SPF 30 at least."

"Good tip," said Desh in amusement.

"You know what's really annoying about this one?"

"That she didn't ask for you?"

There was a chuckle at the other end of the line. "Aside from that," said Fleming good-naturedly. "What's really annoying is that you'll probably be bringing in more money to the agency than anyone else this month. Maybe I *should* open up an escort service." Fleming paused. "Take care, David," he said signing off, but couldn't help adding, "you lucky bastard," before hanging up the phone.

6

Desh rapped on the stained wooden door, just below its peephole and above the cheap brass "14D" affixed to it. He had removed his laptop that morning from its docking station in his apartment and it was carefully tucked under his left arm. He was wearing Dockers, a blue polo shirt, and a tan windbreaker that concealed his H&K .45 semiautomatic. A much smaller SIG-Sauer 9-millimeter was shoved in his pants at the small of his back, and identical, sheathed combat knives were strapped to each of his lower legs.

Kira Miller was working with terrorist groups who would stop at nothing to protect her. Groups who celebrated death rather than life, and who would welcome the chance to remove Desh's head with a hacksaw—while he was still using it—if it would further their cause. The closer he got to her, the more dangerous it would be for him. Perhaps these precautions were premature, but why take chances?

Desh heard movement from inside the apartment.

"David Desh?" called a voice questioningly from behind the particleboard door, loudly enough for Desh to hear.

"That's right," confirmed Desh.

"Adam Campbell's friend?"

"In the flesh."

Desh's friend Adam, an ex-soldier who was now a private investigator, had set up this meeting for him the night before, right after he had returned home from his meeting with Connelly.

"Do you have my retainer?"

In answer, Desh removed 60 hundred-dollar bills from an envelope and fanned them out in front of the peephole.

There was a rustle behind the door as a chain was unhooked and a loud click as a dead-bolt lock was turned, followed by the door creaking open.

Desh entered the small, cluttered apartment. It bore the heavy musk of prolonged human habitation that Desh knew could be helped by an open window and the inflow of crisp, autumn air. Four high-end computers straddled a heavy glass-topped desk, all connected to each other through a spaghetti of makeshift wiring. On top of the desk sat a wireless keyboard and three high-definition, plasma monitors. Hanging on the wall above was a framed placard that read:

HACKER-CRATIC OATH
I swear to use my awesome powers for good, not evil.

Other than this and a large black-and-white poster of Albert Einstein sticking out his tongue, the entire living area consisted of the desk, a single couch, a plasma television, and a small kitchen.

Desh appraised the man in front of him. His name was Matt Griffin, and he was a bear of a man. He was at least 6-foot-5 and three hundred pounds, with a bushy brown beard and long, wavy hair—almost a cross between a man and a Wookie. Despite his enormous size he had a harmless air about him that made him completely non-threatening. While his bulk and appearance could quickly lead one to the conclusion he was a dim caveman, his words were spoken with the intellectual affect of an ivy-league professor. Desh handed him the money and waited patiently as he counted to sixty.

Griffin smiled affably. "Okay, Mr. Desh, I'm at your service for a period of one week. What can I do for you?"

Fleming Executive Protection had its share of computer experts, but Desh couldn't use them for this assignment, and he was supposed to be in playboy fantasyland anyway. Matt Griffin was said to be the best in the business. He usually worked for corporate clients doing fairly mundane tasks, but from time to time he helped private investigators if their cause was right, fully prepared to engage in illegal hacking, a victimless crime, if it could result in finding a missing person or stopping a violent criminal. Desh's friend Adam had worked with Griffin several times and had been effusive in his praise for the man, who apparently took his hacker-cratic oath quite seriously, and would only work with someone if he had assurances their intentions were honorable. Adam had vouched for Desh and told Griffin he could trust him implicitly.

Desh set his laptop on the only unoccupied space on the corner of Griffin's desk. The giant eyed it with interest but said nothing. Desh handed him a typed page with Kira Miller's name and last known home and work addresses, e-mail addresses, and telephone numbers.

Griffin scanned the information quickly. "NeuroCure," he said with interest, lowering himself into a black-leather swivel chair in front of his computer monitors while Desh remained standing. "Aren't they developing a treatment for Alzheimer's?"

"Very good," said Desh approvingly. "You're certainly up to speed on your biotech."

Griffin shook his head. "I'm afraid I know next to nothing about biotech," he admitted. "My aunt suffers from the disease so I tend to keep abreast of possible cures."

Tend to keep abreast. The dichotomy between Griffin's Viking appearance and soft-spoken, lofty speech patterns was amusing to him. "I'm sorry about your aunt," offered Desh.

Griffin nodded solemnly. "Why don't you fill me in on what you're after as completely as you can. Nothing you say will leave this room."

"Good. Absolute confidentiality in this case could not be more vital. For your health as well as mine." Desh locked his eyes on Griffin's in an unblinking, intimidating stare, and held it for several long seconds. "You're known to be a man of integrity," he continued, "but betraying my trust would be a very, very bad idea . . ."

"Save your threats," said the giant firmly. "Veiled or otherwise. You have nothing to worry about. I take my responsibilities in this regard very seriously. As I've told you, your information is safe with me."

Desh knew he had little choice but to trust the oversized hacker. He stared at him a while longer, and then finally began to fill him in on Kira Miller's tenure at NeuroCure, and the events that had transpired a year earlier. Griffin scribbled notes on a large pad of paper. Desh didn't mention anything having to do with terrorists or Swiss banks, ending his account when the trail of the elusive Kira Miller had ended at the Cincinnati airport.

Griffin whistled when Desh was finished. "Fascinating," he said. "And very troubling."

Desh noted approvingly that Griffin didn't attempt to explore why Desh had taken it upon himself to look for a psychopath who was wanted by the authorities for the brutal murder of several innocents.

"So here's where I'd like to start," said Desh, "I'd like to know which scientific journals this Kira Miller subscribed to as of a year ago. I'm not interested in any that were sent to her work. I want to know the journals she got at home."

"Do you have a list of probables?"

"I'm afraid not. And, unfortunately, I went online and discovered there are hundreds of scientific journals in her areas of interest."

The giant frowned. "Then this could take a long time. If you tell me the name of a journal I can tell you if she was a subscriber. But there's no way to start with her address and work backwards to the journals." He raised his eyebrows. "Not unless you're prepared to engage in a little social engineering."

Desh was familiar with this euphemism used by hackers. "You mean get information from humans rather than the computer."

"Exactly. Man cannot hack using computers alone. The best hackers are also the most proficient at milking information from humans—the system's weakest links."

Desh eyed Griffin with interest. "Okay," he said. "I'm game."

"Great," said Griffin, beaming happily. He swiveled his chair to face the monitors and his fingers flew over the keyboard, calling up one web page after another as Desh looked over his shoulder. The quartet of pricey computers, linked together, operated at blazing speeds, and Griffin's Internet connection was the best that money could buy, and included custom enhancements. The end result of this was that web pages crammed with data and pictures and graphics each flashed up on the oversized monitor, complete, faster than the eye could follow.

Griffin scrolled through nested menus and clicked on specific options before Desh could even begin to read them. Moments later he was several layers deep in the internal computer files of the D.C. police.

"I'm surprised you can breach a police system so easily," muttered Desh.

Griffin shook his head. "You can't. Their firewalls and security systems are state-of-the-art," he explained. "But I found a way in last year and created a backdoor entrance so I could return anytime I wanted. And I can use the D.C system to query the San Diego Police Department's computers for their file on the Larry Lusetti murder investigation." Griffin continued pulling up pages on the computer as he spoke, and moments later he had the file he was after. He skimmed through it rapidly, pausing to scribble a few names, a telephone number, and a date on his note pad.

Griffin took a deep breath. "I believe I'm ready," he said. He picked up the phone and dialed the number he had written down. A woman named Jill answered, but within a minute he had Roger Tripp on the phone, the postal carrier who had long covered the mail route that included Kira Miller's condo.

"Hello, Mr. Tripp," said Griffin. "Do you have a minute?"

"Well . . . I was just about to head out on my route," he said. "What is this about? Jill said you were a detective."

"That's right, sir. Detective Bob Garcia." Griffin consulted his notepad. "I work with Detective Marty Fershtman. You may remember that Detective Fershtman interviewed you about a Kira Miller on September 28th of last year in regard to a homicide investigation we were conducting."

"I remember," said Tripp warily.

"Great. This won't take but a minute. We've continued our investigation, and we had one additional question we were hoping you could help us with."

"I'll try," said postal worker Tripp.

"Great. Do you happen to remember the titles of any periodicals that you delivered to Dr. Miller? Scientific oriented periodicals," he clarified. "Do you know the type I mean?"

"I think so," said Tripp, showing absolutely no curiosity as to why the police had interest in this information. "They kind of stood out, if you know what I mean. Not exactly light bedtime reading. Let me see." He paused for several long moments to visualize these journals in his head. "*Human Brain Mapping*. That one comes to my memory the clearest. And then, um . . . the *Journal of Cognitive Neuroscience.* Either that or something really close. And then, ah, . . . the *Journal of Applied Gerontology*. I wouldn't bet my life these are the exact titles, but I'm pretty sure."

Griffin scribbled these names on the pad beside his other notes. He winked at Desh before thanking Tripp for his help and ending the call.

"Remarkable," said Desh, his voice filled with respect. He had wanted to begin his search for Kira Miller by identifying the scientific journals he knew would be indispensible to her, but he had been far from certain this would be possible. But Griffin had done so almost *instantly*, and without even breaking a sweat.

"Quite effective, wouldn't you say? If you have the computer skills to get information that establishes instant credibility, like dropping the name of the officer who interviewed Tripp, the world is your oyster. Once you've laid out your bone fides, people will tell you just about anything."

"So it appears," noted Desh with amusement. "Thanks for the demonstration."

"You're quite welcome," said Griffin with a wide grin. "So now what?"

"Can you hack into each journal's database of subscribers?"

"I'll try not to be insulted that you phrased that as a question," said Griffin. "That's like asking *Mozart* if he can play *chopsticks.* This is why you're paying me the big bucks," he added, and then immediately began racing through icons and menus at an Olympic pace.

"Once you're in, ah . . . Amadeus," said Desh, "I'd like to focus in on people who bought online subscriptions to all three journals, or even two of the three, about nine months to a year ago. Chances are, this will be Kira Miller."

"This might take a while," warned Griffin. He got up and walked the few paces to his tiny kitchen, effortlessly lifting one of two large wicker chairs from around the small dinette and dropping it beside his own chair. Desh sat down appreciatively and continued to watch Griffin as he juggled multiple screens and programs with seemingly superhuman agility.

After about an hour he was finally able to hack into the journals' systems, but his subsequent analysis of subscriber databases was fruitless. Over the past year, in fact, not a single person had begun subscribing to more than one of the three journals, either online or by snail-mail.

"She must have decided she could live without them while she was in hiding," suggested Griffin.

Desh pursed his lips in concentration. His best chance to find her was to count on her *not* making mistakes. "All right, Matt," said Desh, "let's try a thought experiment. Let's imagine she has your level of skill with computers," he began.

Griffin looked amused at this thought. "*My* level of skill? My imagination may be prodigious, but that's a lot to ask of it," he said with a twinkle in his eye.

Prodigious. Desh was amused once again at the giant's choice of words. "I wouldn't want to strain your imagination, Matt," he said, rolling his eyes. "So let's make this easy for you. Suppose *you* were on the lam. And you knew that other computer experts were plugged in and trying like crazy to find you. Would you anticipate they'd try to track you through your online journal subscriptions like we just did?"

"Absolutely," came the immediate reply.

"So what would you do if you were still determined to get journals you needed?"

Griffin considered. "I'd put up relays," he responded after only a few seconds of thought. "I'd break through firewalls and shanghai any number of Internet-connected computers around the world, using them as relays, routing the incoming journals through a tangled web of these before it reached me. With enough relays, I'd be virtually untraceable."

Desh considered. "And what if you didn't want searchers to even have the satisfaction of knowing you were out there and receiving the journals," he said. "Even if you *were* untraceable. What if you wanted the world to think you really had vanished—that you might be dead even?"

Griffin answered almost immediately. "In that case, I'd just hack into the journals and *steal* the subscriptions. Then there would be no subscriber record in the databases for experts to find. And you wouldn't have to pay for it either," he noted. "In fact, now that I think about it, that's the best reason of all to do it this way."

"To save money?

"No. To save an identity."

Desh's eyes narrowed. "I see," he said as Griffin's meaning registered. "Because the only way to *buy* an online subscription is by using a credit card."

"Exactly," said Griffin. "So if those searching for you uncovered your purchase, even if they couldn't *trace* you, the false identity you used would be blown."

"Okay. Suppose she did steal the subscriptions. Could you track such a theft?"

Griffin gazed at the ceiling as he considered the various facets of the problem. "I think so," he said finally.

"Come on, Matt," chided Desh. "Someone with *your* prodigious talent? Should be a snap for you."

"I'll take that as a challenge," said Griffin.

"Good," said Desh, determination burning in his eyes. "Because that's exactly the way I intended it."

7

Matt Griffin worked on the problem for an hour while Desh looked on patiently. As it neared lunchtime, Desh offered to go for takeout, an offer that Griffin readily accepted. Desh returned thirty-five minutes later carrying a paper sack containing a number of white, garden-variety Chinese takeout boxes and knocked on the door.

Griffin hurriedly undid the locks and opened the door with a broad, cat-that-ate-the-canary grin on his bearded face. "I did it," he announced triumphantly.

"Fantastic!" said Desh, handing him the bag of Chinese food and shutting the door behind him. "What did you find?" he asked eagerly.

"You were right about her. She's good. Very good."

Griffin sat down at his desk chair and set the bag of food on the floor beside him. "If she really does have a background in biology rather than computers, I think she's earned rookie of the year honors."

Desh lifted the large wicker chair with one arm and moved it a few feet back so it was facing Griffin. Desh sat down, his eyes locked intently on the giant as he continued.

"It turns out that all three journals have a number of, ah . . . *discount* subscribers, shall we say, that they don't know about. Somehow, considering the nature of these journals, that surprised me."

"Didn't think readers of such scholarly journals would engage in petty theft?"

Griffin nodded.

"Nothing surprises me anymore," said Desh cynically. "So how did you sort through them to find her?" he pressed, not allowing the discussion to become sidetracked.

"Two of the journals were being siphoned to the same e-mail address as of about ten months ago. No other stolen subscriptions among the three journals had the same signature."

"Good work," said Desh appreciatively. "Now tell me the bad news."

"What makes you think there is any?"

"It *couldn't* be this easy."

Griffin smiled. "You're right, as it turns out. It's a dead end. She's more sophisticated than I had guessed. The e-mailed journals are routed through an impenetrable maze of computers. Even someone better than me—if such a person existed," he added, grinning, "wouldn't be able to trace through all the relays to find her computer."

Desh frowned. "At least we know she's still alive."

"And still keeping up on the latest research," added Griffin.

Desh nodded at the bag of food. "Dig in," he offered.

Griffin went to the kitchen and returned with large plastic forks and the biggest cardboard plates Desh had ever seen, with a cheerful, orange-and-yellow floral pattern printed on each one. He handed a fork and plate to Desh, and dumped two full containers of cashew chicken along with a container of white rice on his plate. Desh slopped half a box of beef broccoli onto his own plate with some rice, and began picking at it, while Griffin shoveled the food into his giant maw as rapidly as he had navigated the Web.

"You've done a nice job, Matt," said Desh. "We've made faster progress than I expected. But this is about where I thought we'd end up."

"So any ideas of where to go from here?"

Desh nodded thoughtfully. "As a matter of fact, yes. We can't trace her through all her relays, but can we use them to *contact* her?"

Griffin raised his eyebrows. "Interesting thought."

"Well?" pressed Desh.

"Sure. It would be easy. Just name your message and I'll send it," he offered helpfully.

Desh held up a hand. "Not just yet," he said. "I'd like to ping her first. Send in some tracking software that she'll detect and defeat."

"To what end?"

"So she knows someone's out there turning over this particular rock looking for her."

"You sure that's a good idea? It gives her a warning. Also, it's in her best interest to have as much information as possible about whoever is pursuing her. If I were her, I'd trace the ping back to us."

"That's what I'm counting on," said Desh with a thin smile. He rose and lifted his black laptop off the corner of Griffin's desk. "I want you to set everything up on my laptop, so when she does trace the ping, she traces it back to me." He paused. "Assuming she doesn't already know my identity and that I'm after her. I wouldn't rule that out," he added warily. "Set up software that will watch for a breach and record everything possible about its source. I also want you to plant a tracer, so if she does invade my computer, it can latch on and follow the breadcrumb trail back to her."

"She'll be expecting that. I'll try to plant a red herring for her to find and then a more subtle tracking program, but I suspect I won't fool her." Griffin shrugged. "Worth a try though," he acknowledged.

Desh didn't expect a tracer to work either. This wasn't his real plan. What he hadn't told Griffin was that he planned to imbed information on his computer for Kira Miller to find, indicating he was closing in on her. Perhaps he could force her hand. If she really thought he was skilled enough at pursuit to be dangerous to her, perhaps she would take the bait and come after *him*. It was the best strategy he had been able to come up with on the long drive from North Carolina. If you can't bring the mountain to Mohamed . . .

Desh handed his laptop to Griffin and watched carefully as the giant worked his magic, downloading software and setting traps on his system.

About ten minutes into the exercise a troubled look came over Griffin's face. He glanced at Desh but said nothing for several more minutes as he worked the mouse and keyboard. Finally, he stopped what he was doing and met Desh's eyes worriedly. "I'm afraid your plan's not going to work," he said grimly.

Desh tilted his head in confusion. "Why not?"

"Because you were right. She does know you're after her."

"How in the world do you know that?"

"Because she's already paid a visit to your computer," explained Griffin evenly. "Last night."

Desh felt his stomach clench. "You're positive?"

"I'm afraid so. I confirmed it twice. She got through your firewall and invaded your computer. And she downloaded everything she needs."

"What do you mean by 'everything'?"

"I mean everything. She has a copy of it all. Your hard drive, your e-mail logs—everything." Griffin looked back at the computer monitor and shook his head in disbelief. "She may just be as good as me, after all," he said with just a hint of admiration creeping into his voice.

8

Matt Griffin performed computer forensics on Desh's laptop for several hours, but in the end was unable to come up with a single lead. Kira Miller had worn the computer equivalent of gloves for this theft, leaving no fingerprints or DNA behind to help give them a direction in which to search for her.

But Griffin did discover she had created a backdoor entrance for herself: one that would make future journeys into his laptop's inner sanctum to retrieve this and other data routine, regardless of any added security.

Connelly's suspicions were certainly warranted. There *was* a leak in USASOC—wide enough to steer a supertanker through. Whether this was due to a mole or otherwise was unclear, but it was the only way to explain how Kira Miller had known about Desh being put on the operation practically before he had known himself. She had been one step ahead of him before he had even *taken* a step, which was very troubling. If Griffin had not been placing sophisticated tracking software on his computer, Desh would never have known it had been compromised.

Kira Miller must have invaded the computers of all of Desh's predecessors, only they had never discovered the intrusion. If they would have, Connelly would have warned him. Given her access to their computers, it was little wonder they had failed to find her. Not hard to avoid being caught when those searching for you were—quite literally—telegraphing their every move.

Desh knew he had almost been caught with his pants down. But he had been lucky. Once discovered, Kira Miller's computer invasion played right into his hands.

He wanted to lead her to his computer and plant false information: now he had the perfect conduit for this, one that was above suspicion. He instructed Griffin to leave the backdoor entrance alone.

Now, while Desh continued his search for her, he would be planning the specifics of his trap. He knew he needed to be patient. She would never believe he had closed in on her in only a day or two, so he would need to wait a while longer. And the more progress he made prior to setting his trap the better. The closer he got to her, the more clues he uncovered, the more convincingly he could craft his misinformation.

Desh returned to his high-rise apartment in the heart of Washington. He had chosen it almost entirely on the basis of its location and premium fitness center. While his daily workouts couldn't compare to his regime while still with Delta, they still managed to keep him in excellent shape.

While upscale, the apartment was a bit cramped. Not that he cared. Being single, he didn't need much room, and he traveled much of the time on protection assignments, anyway. Saving money while he determined what new course his life would take was more important than additional square footage. His apartment was tidy, but he had been too busy and too numb to personalize it in any way. His taste in art was eclectic, from the reality bending, impossible constructions of Escher, to the surrealism of Dali, to the serene, impressionistic work of Monet. Yet his framed reproductions of favorite works by these artists remained entombed in brown paper in his closet, a telling sign that his spirit had been sapped and he had slipped into a steady depression. Even more telling, he loved books beyond all else, and had collected many thousands over the years: but while being surrounded by shelf upon shelf of his favorites in their myriad of colors brought him great pleasure, he had yet to unbox them.

Connelly had read him perfectly. Even before Iran he had been contemplating leaving the military, struggling mightily with the decision. On the one hand, he had found friendship and camaraderie in Delta, and the importance of what he was doing could not be overstated. His work had saved thousands upon thousands of innocents from horrible suffering and death from dirty bombs, nerve toxins, train derailments, and the like, including children who were in some cases the principal targets of planned attacks, unconscionable as this was. Many Westerners were still blissfully unaware that the future of progressive society was anything but assured. Desh had been on the front lines and seen the fanaticism that threatened to turn the world's clock back a thousand years. He was helping to defeat a rigid and destructive ideology. It was a fire that was blazing across the world that, if left unchecked, would surely consume civilization.

But he had also dreamed of settling down one day. Of becoming a father. Of raising a family. And if he remained in Delta, this was impossible. He was always on the move, being called away overseas on missions about which he couldn't discuss with anyone—including a future wife. Being married was the sharing of two lives, and he would be unable to hold up his end of the bargain. And if he did have children, each time he left his family would wonder if this would be the time Daddy wouldn't be coming back—or be coming back inside a body bag, in pieces—leaving his children fatherless. What kind of life would this be for them? The answer: no life at all. He had refused to even consider it.

But now he had no excuse not to pursue a wife or family. He was no longer in the military and soon wouldn't even be involved in something as dangerous as executive protection. He had wallowed in self-pity long enough. Desh made a vow to himself: once he finished this final mission, he would find a way to get beyond what had happened in Iran and get on with his life.

He rummaged through his near empty refrigerator and found just enough leftover food to cobble together a dinner. He then spent several hours re-familiarizing himself with the contents of his laptop and the thousands of e-mails in his log. He needed to know the full extent of the data to which Kira Miller now had access.

Finally, he sat down in a comfortable chair in his living room and began reading the dossier on his quarry yet again. He knew he would probably read it dozens of times before this was over. And each time, as he learned more and more about her, he would bring a slightly different perspective to the material and would glean fresh insights.

Desh's cell phone began vibrating, an unwelcome intrusion. He reached into his pocket, removed it, and examined the screen. It was a text message from Matt Griffin:

key discovery 4u. visit me asap. don't call. computers, walls, phones: all might have ears.

The message drove Desh to a heightened state of awareness within seconds. Griffin had found something important and had reason to believe Kira had breached more than just Desh's computer. Maybe Griffin was being overly cautious, maybe not, but Desh approved. He had liked the friendly hacker from the start, and the man had already demonstrated that his glowing reputation was well deserved.

Now it was time to find out if his computer expert had truly earned his pay.

Desh armed himself as usual, threw on an oxford shirt and windbreaker, and rushed to Griffin's apartment, his mind racing almost as fast as his armored Suburban. The traffic was light, but even so the trip should have taken forty-five minutes. He made it in just over thirty.

Desh felt butterflies in his stomach as he strode briskly through the short, musty corridor of Griffin's building, anxious to learn what the giant had uncovered. He passed several doors until he came to number 14D. He rapped once on the door and waited, staring at the peephole to help Griffin make a quick identification.

He waited for Griffin to disengage the deadbolt and chain as he had done before, but instead the handle began to turn. Years in the field had trained his subconscious to set off alarms when it encountered anything unexpected, no matter how small, even before his conscious mind could reason out why. He instantly became hyper-alert, just as a woman emerged from behind the door with a gun aimed at his chest.

Already moving forward in anticipation of trouble, Desh lashed out with his right arm to knock the gun lose, and at the same time threw his body sideways to offer a smaller target. But even as he lunged, he realized the woman had anticipated this move, and had begun backpedaling rapidly. She fired as she moved backwards, but despite her rapid retreat, she was forced to jerk her arm aside to avoid Desh's vicious blow.

If the gun had contained bullets, Desh would have won the day. Despite her quick action and reflexes, he had interfered with her aim enough that the shot only hit his leg, and even injured in this way he would have been on his attacker in an instant, easily able to overpower her.

But she hadn't fired bullets. She had fired electricity.

With a stun gun, a hit to the leg was just as effective as a hit to the chest. Instead of bullets, two electrode darts had leapt from her gun and stuck like Velcro to Desh's pants, discharging their massive electric payload in an instant. The electricity completely overwhelmed the tiny electrical signals his brain was sending to control his muscles, causing him to convulse and collapse to the floor, disoriented and paralyzed.

From the instant his assailant had emerged from behind the door, he had known she could only be one person: Kira Miller.

A vague realization came across Desh's addled mind that he was now sprawled on the floor, completely and utterly helpless, while one of the most dangerous women in the world stood calmly over him.

PART TWO
Encounter

9

Desh vaguely felt his legs, arms, and torso being repositioned, and his body being dragged a few feet across the floor like a one hundred and eighty pound sack of cement, and then heard the apartment door shut quietly. He could see Kira Miller out of the corner of one eye. She was holding a large black duffel with three zippered compartments. Her hair was now longer than in the photos he had seen and she had dyed it blond. She was wearing bulky clothing that was far too large for her, in such a way as to add ten pounds to her appearance, and wire-rimmed glasses. Even dazed as he was, Desh was impressed with the simplicity but effectiveness of her disguise. Unless you had reason to suspect this woman was Kira Miller, you'd be hard pressed to pick her out of a crowd.

Matt Griffin was a massive speed bump on the carpet a few feet away; unconscious or worse.

Desh's attacker knew his paralysis would only last about five minutes and didn't waste an instant. She moved as if a *Guinness Book* official had a stopwatch on her, removing his windbreaker and watch and frantically conducting a full body search, not leaving a single inch of David Desh unchecked. She immediately found both guns and both knives and relieved him of them expertly, along with his shoulder holster.

With this completed, Kira Miller pulled a pair of stainless steel fabric shears from her duffel and hastily cut through Desh's button-down shirt and white undershirt, tossing both garments aside and producing a large gray sweatshirt from a bag beside her. She pulled the sweatshirt over his head and slipped his arms through as if he were an infant, with remarkable facility but with a decided lack of gentleness. Finally, she produced an assortment of thin white plastic strips from the bag, between two and four feet long.

Desh recognized these thin strips instantly: plastic handcuffs. These plasticuffs, also called zip-strips, could only be removed if someone cut through the hardened, injection molded nylon plastic; a surprisingly difficult task.

She pulled Desh's right arm out from his body as far as it would go, wrapped the bendable plastic stick around his wrist, and ratcheted it tight. She pulled Griffin's heavy, lifeless left arm closer to Desh and used a long plasticuff bracelet to cuff the two men together.

Finished, she quickly backed fifteen feet away; showing tremendous respect for Desh's training and abilities. She was smart and careful. Even the fastest, most accomplished street fighter or martial artist couldn't disarm a vigilant assailant as long as they maintained a respectful distance. In addition, she had tied him to a virtually immovable anchor—the three- hundred-pound dead-weight of Matt Griffin—who, Desh noted with relief, was breathing shallowly, indicating that at least he wasn't tied to a corpse. For the moment, anyway. So far, her tactics had been flawless.

When the effects of the stun gun were beginning to wear off, Kira Miller held up a sheet of paper on which she had used black marker to write a message in large, block letters.

SAY A SINGLE WORD, EVEN BREATHE TOO HARD, AND I'LL PUT A BULLET IN YOUR HEAD.

She put a finger to her lips to underscore the point and pointed his own gun at him meaningfully. She held up a second sheet.

NOD IF YOU UNDERSTAND.

Desh nodded warily. From the look in her eye, he didn't doubt for a second she would carry out her threat.

She pulled out a third sheet, already prepared, an indication that she had planned her attack with military precision.

STRIP. WAIST DOWN. COMPLETELY NAKED. NO WORDS. NO NOISE.

Desh kicked off his shoes and clumsily pulled off his socks, pants and briefs: a difficult task from a supine position and anchored to Griffin that involved flopping about like a fish out of water and contorting like a circus performer.

Desh was focusing too hard on the imminent threat to his life to waste any energy feeling self-conscious or humiliated about his nudity, but it was human nature to feel more vulnerable when naked, and he was no exception.

Kira tossed him a pair of gray sweatpants that matched the sweatshirt he was now wearing and motioned with her head for him to put them on. He was only too happy to comply. All in all, while she didn't seem to like his taste in clothing, he was encouraged that she was taking the time to see that he was re-clothed. If her plan was to execute him in the apartment, this wouldn't have mattered. On the other hand, Desh remembered Jeffrey Dahmer, and he realized it was dangerous to make any assumptions about her actions or motives. She could be dancing to a song that only she could hear.

When he finished re-dressing, she tossed him a pair of soft leather slip-on shoes from her bag, and he managed to get them on his feet. The fit was perfect. And why not? He had bought several pairs of shoes in the past, online, and she now had ready access to the e-mail confirmations of these orders.

She tossed three plasticuff strips to him, one after another, and he gathered them up wordlessly. She held up another sign.

ONE TIGHT AROUND EACH ANKLE. THE OTHER BETWEEN THEM.

It took several minutes, but Desh did as she had ordered. His feet were now cuffed together in a three-plasticuff chain, leaving about eighteen inches of play between them.

Kira motioned for him to roll onto his stomach and put his arms behind his back, which he found a way to do despite having to drag Griffin's arm along for the ride. She held the gun against his head with one hand and slipped a plasticuff lasso around his crossed wrists with the other, yanking it so tight that it bit into his skin.

With Desh's ankles linked and his wrists now firmly secured behind his back, Kira cut him loose from Griffin using his own knife and retreated rapidly to a safe distance the moment she had. Desh noted she was quite agile and light-footed.

Kira motioned for Desh to get up, which he did awkwardly and with considerable difficulty. She opened the door, checked the hallway, and directed him to enter. Only being able to move his feet a slight distance apart, he was forced to shuffle them in a rapid-fire series of tiny steps. Kira followed about eight feet behind, her gun tucked beneath her oversized sweater but not wavering from the target.

It was now after ten o'clock and the hallway remained deserted. A rental car was parked just outside the exit from Griffin's building; a large Ford sedan. As Desh shuffled toward the car, Kira pushed a button on the remote and the trunk popped open. It was completely empty.

Kira motioned for Desh to climb inside.

Frowning miserably, he bent at the waist and slid into the trunk headfirst, having to curl up into a ball to fit inside the tight quarters.

Kira didn't waste a moment. The instant he was fully inside, she pushed the trunk door closed in a single, smooth motion, and Desh was plunged into an all-enveloping, claustrophobic darkness.

10

Kira Miller drove for about ninety minutes. The air in the trunk was stale to begin with and got steadily worse as time wore on. While there were long stretches during which the ride was relatively smooth, probably indicating highway driving, there were also brief interludes during which Desh was bounced around violently, jarring him inside and out and inflicting several minor cuts and bruises. Finally, after what seemed like forever to Desh, the car stopped for good. A minute later the trunk was popped open again.

"Get out," ordered Kira in hushed tones, shielding Desh as well as she could from any possible onlookers. She held a stun gun in one hand and her black duffel in the other, and it was clear she had no intention of helping him.

"Back out. Legs first," she instructed. "Silently. Call attention to yourself and you're dead," she threatened.

Restrained as he was, not to mention crowded into close quarters, it took a Herculean effort to comply, but he was finally able to manage it. They were at a seedy motel that stretched like a single-story serpent around a pothole-filled parking lot, forming three legs of a rectangle. The building was poorly maintained and the grounds were almost completely lacking in external lighting.

Kira had parked directly in front of one of the rooms and she quickly ushered Desh inside. The unmistakable stench of mildew assailed them as they entered along with a stale, smoky odor that could only have been generated by thousands of cigarettes smoked there through time. The door opened into a short corridor, about five feet long, with the bathroom on the immediate right, and then widened into a main room that was surprisingly large. Long, garish drapes were hung across the only window and a cigarette burn adorned the bottom of a faded bedspread. The room was one of a pair of front-to-back, rather than side-to-side, adjoining rooms. At the back wall, two thin wooden doors were both open, creating a narrow passage between the two separate but identical rooms. Kira had obviously rented both, but had left the lights off in the one adjoining.

"Get on the bed," she commanded once they had entered. "With your back against the headboard."

Desh climbed onto the queen-sized bed as instructed, and she looped a plastic restraint around one of the outer wooden posts that were on both sides of the thin headboard, and then through his plasticuffs.

A lamp sitting on a small end table by the bed currently illuminated the entire room. Kira had knotted a thin rope around its cord, with the free end of the rope tied in a noose. She lifted the noose off the floor and walked to the door, looping it around the handle and pulling tight. This caused the lamp cord to become as taut as it could possibly be and still remain plugged into the wall outlet. She must have measured this carefully beforehand. She then quickly and expertly ran a trip wire across the corridor where it met the main room, about a foot off the ground.

This done, Kira removed a pair of state-of-the-art thermal imaging goggles from her bag and strapped them on, leaving them on her head and ready to be slid over her eyes. She pulled out a black jumpsuit, made from an unusual material that appeared to be partially crystalline, stepped into it, and zipped it up, so that her entire body was completely covered all the way up to her chin. She then retreated to a wooden chair twenty feet away and moved it so that it couldn't be seen from the doorway. All of her activities had been well planned and had been performed with military efficiency.

With her preparations completed, Kira tossed her wire-rimmed glasses into the open duffel, sat in the chair, and shifted her gaze to David Desh.

She let out a heavy sigh. "Are you okay?" she asked with what appeared to be sincere concern.

A look of disbelief came over Desh. After all this, this was her first question of him? Why the pretend concern for his welfare? "What am I doing here?" he snapped, now that speech was apparently no longer punishable by death.

She frowned, almost regretfully. "I needed to speak with you. Convince you that I'm not the villain you think I am. That I'm innocent."

Desh was taken aback. "Innocent! Are you kidding? You go from, 'quiet or I'll put a bullet between your eyes' to claiming you're innocent."

Desh hadn't known what to expect—torture, threats?—but protestations of innocence wasn't on the list. But to what end? He was already at her mercy. Was she simply attempting to keep him off balance?

Kira frowned deeply. "Look, I'm truly sorry for what I just put you through. *Really*. Believe me, this wasn't the first impression I would have liked to make. But I'm innocent nonetheless."

Desh snorted. "Just how stupid do you think I am!" he snapped. "You blast me with enough electricity to light up Broadway. You repeatedly threaten my life. You leave Matt Griffin for dead. And now you have me hogtied to a bed at gunpoint." He shook his head. "I must be missing how this adds up to your being an innocent woman," he finished bitterly.

"I can assure you your hacker friend will be fine. I just hit him with a very potent sleep agent. He'll wake up tomorrow more refreshed than he's been in years," she added. "With no memory of what happened. But I had to handle things this way. You're far too dangerous to be given even a little wiggle room. This was my only option."

"How do you figure?"

"Put yourself in my shoes. If you wanted to have a friendly conversation with someone who's been preconditioned to think you're the devil incarnate, and who also happens to have Special Forces training and is constantly being monitored, how would you go about it?"

Desh ignored the question. "What makes you think I'm being monitored?"

"Because the people behind Connelly won't spare any measure to get their hands on me," she said with absolute conviction. "And not for the reasons you think," she added. "Do you really think they just sent you off on your own recognizance? Just like that? I'm far too important to them for that. Rest assured, they've been tracking your every move since you took this assignment."

Desh raised his eyebrows. "People behind Connelly?" he repeated.

"Connelly is just a dupe in this game. Just like you," she said bluntly. "The people pulling his strings are the ones tracking you."

"If they're tracking me, as you say, how is it they didn't intervene in my kidnapping?"

Kira shook her head. "They don't have a *physical* tail on you," she replied smoothly. "You're too well trained for that. Even if they put two or three cars on you, you'd eventually spot the tail and it would blow up in their faces." She paused. "Besides, it's a waste of manpower. They figured if you managed to find me at all it would take you weeks. Remote monitoring was enough."

"I see," he said patronizingly. "I suppose they imbedded a subtle tracking device in my underwear."

An easy smile lit up her face. "I have to admit, that *is* pretty unlikely," she said sheepishly, an amused twinkle in her eye. "But I wouldn't completely put it past them either. I've been erring on the side of caution and it seems to be working for me so far."

Desh felt himself being instantly drawn in by her incandescent eyes and unselfconscious smile. Kira's effortless charm and physical appeal were more powerful and disarming than he had at first realized. Her features could not have been gentler or more feminine. Her movements were lithe and athletic, despite her bulky clothing, and her voice was soft and appealing. Her eyelashes were long and her jaw and cheekbones delicate. Her wide, blue eyes were warm and expressive.

Desh forced himself to blink and break her momentary spell, annoyed with himself for responding to her with anything other than total revulsion. "You took great pains to ensure quiet in Griffin's apartment. So you obviously think he's bugged."

She sighed. "I'm afraid so."

"How would they possibly even know to bug him? I didn't even know he existed until thirty-six hours ago."

"They're monitoring your phone calls. As soon as you arranged an appointment with him they probably set up listening devices in his apartment. Again, I'm not sure they did, but I operated under this assumption."

"So you sent the text that lured me back to Griffin's apartment?"

Kira nodded.

"Well done," he said with a look of disgust, although this look was reserved for himself. *How had he been so sloppy.* But even as he chastised himself, he realized that Kira Miller's boldness had helped force his error. She had been on to him, probably before he had even taken the assignment, and she had acted with stunning speed and decisiveness; using tactics she had never used before to totally blindside him.

Desh expected her to be gloating, but she appeared more apologetic than ever.

"By your own logic," he said, "you carried out a very successful, silent abduction. My clothes, phone, car, and weapons are far away. Nothing left to bug or track." He nodded toward the door of the motel. "So why the trip wire and other precautions? There's erring on the side of caution and there's irrationality," he pointed out.

"Oh, they'll track us here, all right. If we're lucky, we'll be long gone by the time they do. On the other hand, if *they're* lucky, I need to be prepared."

"And what form do you expect their luck to take?"

"Sooner or later—hopefully later—they'll realize that the homing devices they put in your car, or your clothing, or . . . wherever, haven't moved in a while. They'll track them to Griffin's apartment and realize you aren't there. After you visited Griffin, they may have decided to surveil the parking lot of his building periodically via satellite. If they were lucky and managed to capture an image of the car I'm using, this will greatly accelerate their search." Kira paused. "I just hope they don't arrive before I've accomplished my mission," she finished.

"Oh," he said, raising his eyebrows. "And what mission is that?"

She gazed into his eyes for several long seconds and then sighed. "Recruiting you over to my side," she finally said earnestly.

11

Desh sat on the bed, stunned, for several long seconds. A faint siren could be heard off in the distance through the thin motel walls.

Finally, he shook his head. "Then you can save yourself some time," he said, scowling. "Do whatever you need to do, because I'm not going to join you. Under any circumstances."

"Given what you think you know, this is an admirable position to take," she allowed grimly. "But if it's all the same to you, I'll give it a shot. I say again, the report you have on me is a fabrication." She sighed deeply. "But give the puppet masters their due. They've rigged things to make it very difficult for me to plead my case."

Desh raised his eyebrows questioningly.

"They've told you I'm a brilliant psychopath. A master manipulator. The kind of person who can cut off your limbs one day and pass a lie detector test with flying colors the next. Correct?"

Desh said nothing.

"Which makes everything I say suspect. The more reasonable, the more suspect, since you've been preconditioned to believe it's all manipulation," she said in frustration. "Have you ever seen a faith healer on TV?"

Desh nodded, wondering where she was heading.

"There was a guy who gathered video evidence on one of them, showing it was all a scam. The faith healer's accomplices were researching people waiting in line, feeding him information through a hidden ear piece so he would appear to have divine knowledge; that sort of thing." She paused. "When the devout followers of this faith healer were shown the footage, do you know what happened?"

"They stopped being his devout followers."

"Reasonable guess. But no. They were more his followers than ever. They claimed that the evidence was rigged. That it was the work of Satan who was trying to discredit the work of a great man." Kira shook her head. "If you truly believe you're up against the King Of Lies, no amount of evidence can ever change your mind." She sighed and a weary expression crossed her face. "I just hope that's not the case with you."

Desh furrowed his brow in frustration. "*Why* do you hope it's not the case with me?" he demanded. "Why do you care what I think? And even if you could recruit me, what good will I do you? You have entire terrorist organizations to do your bidding."

"Try to at least entertain the possibility that I'm not who you've been told I am," she said in exasperation. "I am *not* affiliated with terrorists."

"Is your net worth a lie as well?"

"No."

"So even if you're telling the truth, you could hire as many bodyguards and mercenaries as you wanted."

"Yes. I could. But I'm worth too much to the people after me. I'd never be able to fully trust these types. I learned that the hard way," she added gravely. She gestured to Desh. "You, on the other hand, are motivated by doing what's *right* rather than by material rewards. You are a man of integrity and compassion, despite the violent profession you chose. And along with that, you have a very unique personality, philosophy, and array of talents."

Desh raised his eyebrows. "That's quite a character sketch you've put together based on a bit of information on a laptop," he noted.

She smiled knowingly. "Read hundreds of personal e-mail messages and you'd be surprised at how quickly you can get a feel for someone. But your laptop wasn't my first stop—it was my last. Everything is accessible by computer now if you know where to look. Everything. Your college records. Extensive military records and evaluations. The kinds of books you purchase online. Everything."

"Psychiatric evaluations?" added Desh accusingly, recalling how his soul had been laid bare during the few sessions he had had with the military Psychiatrist after his team had been butchered in Iran. Of all the records to which she had access, this would be the biggest violation of privacy of them all.

Kira lowered her eyes and then nodded uncomfortably. "I'm sorry," she said softly, appearing once again to be completely sincere. "From the moment you were assigned, I studied everything I could get my hands on to understand you as a person. Including that. I won't lie to you." She lifted her eyes and locked them onto Desh's once again. "I studied the others Connelly sent after me as well," she said. "Just as thoroughly. But they weren't what I was looking for." She leaned toward Desh intently. "You are. I'm sure of it."

The corners of Desh's mouth turned up in a small, ironic smile, and he shook his head in clear disbelief.

"I know, I know," she said in frustration, "Flattery is also a tool of a master manipulator, and you're not buying it. Be that as it may, it happens to be the truth." She paused. "Look . . . David . . . you yourself pointed out I could have easily recruited others with your skill set."

Desh said nothing, but silently bristled at her use of his first name.

"So why would I choose you and go to such pains to abduct you," continued Kira, "putting myself at this kind of risk, instead of just calling a mercenary—or one of my terrorist friends for that matter—on the phone?"

"Because I have special qualities," he said skeptically. "I get it."

Kira frowned. "I knew this wouldn't be easy," she said resignedly. "There's only one way I can ever hope to gain your trust. I know that. So I'll tell you what, when I've said my piece, I'll remove your cuffs and give you my gun. If that doesn't demonstrate my sincerity, nothing will."

Desh didn't respond. She was trying to get him to lower his guard by giving him false hope, to perhaps stave off an escape attempt, but it wouldn't work. He would believe this when he saw it. In the meanwhile, he would continue to assume that if he didn't escape he was a dead man.

Still, he couldn't help but be intrigued by the unexpected course of the discussion. "Okay," he said finally, pretending to believe her. "It's a deal. By all means begin your persuading. Tell me *your* version of the truth." He pulled at his restraints and added bitterly, "Consider me a captive audience."

She winced at this; regret at having to restrain him etched in every line of her face. Her body language seemed totally genuine, and Desh realized she was as brilliant an actor as she was a biologist.

"The information you have on my childhood and schooling is correct," she began softly. "Except my parents really did die in a tragic accident—I had nothing to do with it."

"The report never said you did."

"But you assumed it, didn't you?"

Desh remained silent.

"Of course you did," she said knowingly.

"Are we going to argue about what I assumed, or are you going to make your case?"

Kira sighed. "You're right," she said unhappily. She visibly gathered herself and then resumed. "I excelled in school and later found my calling in gene therapy. I was told by many in the field I had the kind of insight and intuition that comes around once in a generation. Over time, I came to believe it myself. In fact, I became convinced that I could truly change the world. Make a dramatic impact on medicine." She paused. "But the key to making an impact is choosing the right problem to solve. I wanted to tackle the most challenging problem right from the start. At the risk of sounding immodest," she added, "if you come to realize you're Da Vinci, you owe it to the world to paint masterpieces rather than cartoons."

"Let me guess," said Desh. "You're going to tell me the project you chose has nothing to do with bio-weapons."

"Of course not," she insisted, irritated. "I decided to solve the ultimate problem, one whose solution would make the solutions to all other problems, medical or otherwise, child's play." Her blue eyes twinkled, even in the dim light. "Any guesses?" she challenged.

She looked at him expectantly, obviously wanting him to arrive at the answer on his own. She waited patiently while he mulled it over.

"What?" he said uncertainly after almost a minute of silence. "Build a super-advanced computer?"

"Close," she allowed. She waited again for him to connect the dots.

Desh's forehead wrinkled in concentration. The only way to universally make problems easier to solve was to have better tools to solve them. But if enhancing computer capabilities wasn't the answer, what was? His eyes widened as the answer became obvious. She was a molecular neurobiologist after all, not a computer scientist. "Enhancing intelligence," he said finally. "*Human* intelligence."

"Exactly," she said, beaming, as if pleased with a star pupil. "Just imagine if you could have infinite intelligence. Unlimited creativity. Then you could easily solve any problem to which you turned your attention—instantly." She paused. "Now of course there is no such thing as infinite intelligence. But any significant enhancements to intelligence and creativity would truly be the gift that keeps on giving. What better problem for me to solve?"

"Are you suggesting you actually solved it?" he asked skeptically.

"I did," she confirmed wearily, not looking particularly triumphant or even happy about the supposed accomplishment.

"What, like a *Flowers For Algernon* kind of improvement?" he said, knowing that even *she* wouldn't have the audacity to claim she had achieved increases in intelligence as great as those described in this story.

The corners of her mouth turned up in a slight smile. "No. My results were *far* more impressive than that," she said matter-of-factly.

12

Desh was almost prepared to believe she had managed some kind of improvement in her own intelligence, but not this. "Impossible," he insisted. "Even for you."

"Not impossible. I have a deep knowledge of neurobiology and a genius level intuition with respect to gene therapy. Combine this with single-minded devotion and trial and error and it can be done."

"So what are you trying to say, that I'm talking to someone with an IQ of a thousand? More?"

She shook her head. "The effect is transient. I'm just regular me right now."

"Very convenient," said Desh. "Not that I have an IQ test with me anyway," he conceded. He thought for a moment and then shook his head. "I'm not buying it. We've evolved to become the most intelligent creatures on the planet. I'm sure there's a limit. If we haven't reached it yet we have to be awfully close."

"Are you *kidding*," she responded ardently. "You can't even begin to imagine the potential of the human brain. Without any optimization, it's already faster and more powerful than the most advanced supercomputers ever built. But it's theoretical capacity is staggering: thousands and thousands of times greater than a supercomputer."

"The human brain isn't faster than a supercomputer," argued Desh. "Hell, it isn't even as fast as a dollar calculator."

"We're not wired for math," explained Kira, shaking her head. "We evolved, remember? All evolution cares about is survival and reproduction. The brain is optimized to keep us alive in a hostile world and induce its owner to have sex. Period. And when it comes to preoccupation with sex," she noted, amused, "Male brains are *especially* optimized." She continued to look amused as she added, "But don't get me wrong. I'm not trying to criticize men. I'm sure some of our male ancestors didn't think about sex all the time," she said. "But this trait died out. Do you know why?"

Desh remained silent.

"Because the horny guys had all the children," she said, smiling.

In other circumstances Desh might have returned her smile, but he forced himself to remain expressionless and maintained his icy stare. He was a hostage to a psychopath, and he couldn't afford to let her charm him.

"Anyway," she continued with a sigh, clearly disappointed that her brief attempt at levity had had no effect. "My point is that we're not wired for math. How does a square root help us kill a lion or stay alive? It doesn't. What *does* help us is the ability to throw a spear accurately. Or to dodge a spear thrown by a rival clan," she added. "And remember, unlike a computer, the brain is controlling our every movement, breath, heartbeat, and blink of an eye, and even our every emotion. And all the while it's taking in massive amounts of sensory information—nonstop. Your retina alone has over one hundred million cells constantly relaying visual information to your brain; in ultra-high definition I might add. If a computer had to monitor and manage your every bodily function and download, process, and react to this never-ending barrage of information, it would melt."

Desh was fascinated despite himself. Maybe she *was* the devil, he thought grimly. Here he was fighting for his life and inexplicably, against his will, he continued to respond to her both physically *and* intellectually.

"The roundworm *C. elegans* functions quite well with a nervous system containing just three hundred and two neurons," continued Kira. "Do you know how many neurons the *human* brain has?"

"More than three hundred and two," said Desh wryly.

"One hundred billion," said Kira emphatically. "One hundred billion! And on the order of one hundred *trillion* synaptic connections between them. Not to mention two million miles of axons. Electrical signals are constantly zipping along neuronal pathways like pinballs, creating thought and memory. The possible number of neuronal pathways that can be formed by the human brain are basically infinite. And a computer uses base two. A circuit can either be on or off; one or zero. But your brain is far more nuanced. The number of possible circuits your brain can use for calculation, or thought, or invention, puts the possible number available to computers to shame."

"Okay," said Desh, nodding toward her with his head since his hands were still cuffed to the headboard and unavailable for any gesturing. "Whatever else is true or false, you are an expert molecular neurobiologist, so I'll concede the point. The brain has massive potential." He paused and raised his eyebrows. "But how do you tap into this potential?"

"Good question," she said. "If you're me, you start by studying differences between the brain architecture of geniuses and those that are moderately mentally handicapped."

"What does moderately mean?"

"IQ of forty to fifty-five. They're able to learn up to about a second grade level. The dynamic range in human intelligence is remarkable. From the severely mentally handicapped with IQs less than twenty-five to those rarities with IQs above two hundred. Nature has already demonstrated the plasticity of the human brain and human intelligence before I came along," she pointed out. "I also learned everything I could about autistic savants."

"Is that a new name for what they used to call *idiot* savants?"

"Exactly. Like Dustin Hoffman in the movie *Rain Man*?"

Desh nodded. "I'm familiar with the condition."

"Good. Then you know there are autistic savants who can rival your dollar calculator at math, able to multiply large numbers and even compute square roots instantly. Some of them can memorize entire phone books," she added, snapping her fingers, "just like that."

Desh's eyes narrowed in thought. Idiot savants did provide a unique perspective on the potential of the human brain.

"They can perform amazing feats in a specific area, but their emotional intelligence is very low, and their understanding and judgment is poor. Why? Because they're wired differently than you and I," she explained. "My goal was to understand the genetic basis for these differences in their neuronal patterns. To map the differences between autistic savants and normals. To ultimately find a way to cause a temporary rewiring in a normal brain; to achieve autistic-savant-like capabilities, but differently, more comprehensively, and without the notable deficiencies. Not just to optimize the brain for math and memory tricks, but for intelligence and creativity. Tap into the brain's almost limitless raw power."

"Using gene therapy?"

"Correct," said Kira. "The structure of our brain is always changing. Every thought, memory, sensory input, and experience actually remodels the brain—very, very slightly. I learned that the differences between the brains of autistic savants and normals were surprisingly subtle. And almost like crystal formation, once you nucleate a tiny portion of the brain into a more efficient, optimized structure, you get a chain-reaction that re-orders the rest. There are a number of fetal genes instrumental in setting up neuronal patterns during initial brain development that are turned off after birth. Using gene therapy, I could reactivate whichever of these genes I wanted in a given sequence and at a given expression level."

Kira paused for a few seconds to allow Desh to absorb what she was saying and see if he had any questions.

"Go on," he said.

"I started by experimenting on rodents. I used NeuroCure's facility late at night so I could keep the research secret."

"Why secret? The approach makes intuitive sense—even to a dumb grunt like me."

"I've studied you far too carefully to buy the dumb grunt routine, David."

"I ask again," persisted Desh, "why not pursue this avenue openly?"

"I only wish I could have," said Kira. She held up a finger. "First off, fellow scientists would think it was a wild-goose-chase that couldn't possibly succeed." She held up another finger. "Secondly, the FDA lets you risk putting foreign biologics or chemicals in a person's body, but only to help relieve them of a disease or adverse medical condition. Trying to improve someone who has nothing wrong with them is, ah . . . frowned upon."

"Too much like playing God?" guessed Desh.

"That, and it's also considered an unnecessary risk. The FDA would never sanction something like this. And without the agency's approval, it's illegal to test this approach on humans."

"Even on yourself?"

She nodded. "Even on myself. I was risking my entire career and reputation. If someone found out, believe me, I wouldn't be applauded. Especially in this case. Think about it, trying to alter the brain's architecture, the very seat of the human soul. Playing God, as you said. There's an ethical and moral dimension here that is quite complicated."

"But you didn't let that stop you," said Desh accusingly.

She shook her head firmly but there was a note of regret in her expression. "No," she replied with a sigh. "I was convinced I could succeed. I was only risking myself. And the potential rewards were staggering."

"The ends justify the means?"

"What would you do?" she demanded defensively. "Assume for a moment you had reason to believe you could solve key problems facing humanity; invent technologies that could revolutionize society. But you had to skirt some of society's rules. Do you do it?"

Desh refused to be drawn in. "What *I* would do isn't important," he replied. "It's what you *did* that's important."

Kira was unable to fully hide her disappointment, but she picked up her narrative where she had left off. "NeuroCure's lab was ideal for my needs. We were working on Alzheimer's, so it was already set up for the study of intelligence and memory. I used everything I had learned about the brain and autistic savants and developed cocktails of viral vectors with novel gene constructs inserted. Mixtures I thought would achieve my goals. I tested them on lab rats."

"I'd like to think that rat brains and human brains aren't very similar," said Desh.

"It would be fair to say there are . . . slight differences," she said, amused. "But if you're questioning if there are enough similarities to make the results meaningful, the answer is that there are."

"So, were you able to create your Algernon?"

"Yes. Algernon was a mouse and I worked mostly on rats," she pointed out, "but yes. Rat number ninety-four showed dramatic improvements in intelligence. I spent another year perfecting the cocktail."

"And then you tried it on yourself."

She nodded.

"And what—you became a super-genius?"

"No. It almost killed me." She frowned deeply and looked troubled as she remembered. "Apparently, rat brains and human brains aren't exactly alike," she noted wryly. "Who would have guessed?"

"What happened exactly?"

Kira shifted in her chair and a pained expression crossed her face. "There were a multitude of negative effects. I won't describe them all. Complete loss of hearing. Some 'trippy' hallucinogenic and bizarre sensory effects like those caused by LSD. A killer headache." She paused. "But the worst part was that I found the re-wiring had impacted parts of my autonomic nervous system. My heartbeat and breathing were no longer automatic." She shook her head in horror. "Every single second for the three hours the transformation lasted—while dealing with LSD like hallucinations—I had to consciously instruct my heart to beat and my lungs to inhale, just as you would have to instruct your hand to clench, over and over." She shuddered. "It was the longest, most terrifying three hours of my life—by far."

Desh found himself totally absorbed. "And this result didn't scare you off?"

"Almost," she said earnestly. "Almost. But the rat work had shown me that it was an iterative process. The first seventy-eight rats died, so at least the research with them gave me enough direction that I avoided this fate—narrowly. But starting with rat seventy-nine, I was able to gradually refine the rewiring without further casualties, leading to number ninety-four."

"So you thought you could replicate this result with yourself as the lab rat?"

"Exactly. The next few experiments I conducted inside a flotation tank. This way I didn't have sensory input constantly bombarding my brain and tying up neuronal real estate. I could focus on what was happening in the creative centers of my brain." She paused. "It took me another eighteen months to build to the current, stable level of intelligence, fifty to one hundred IQ points at a time. The more I improved my own intelligence the more obvious additional improvements became. At each new level, problems I had struggled with for weeks became solvable in minutes."

Desh thought about her claim. Could she really have shown this magnitude of improvement? Maybe. The existence of autistic savants certainly made this a possibility.

As she had pointed out, it was undeniable that these rare humans could effortlessly calculate square roots or memorize entire phone books. How long would it take him to match these same feats? The answer was easy—never.

Her story was far-fetched, but at the moment it all held together and explained her after-hours experiments at NeuroCure and why a sensory deprivation tank had been found in her condo.

"And your final IQ?"

"In the end, there was no way to measure it. The most challenging problems on a standard IQ test were instantly obvious. Any number generated on this scale would no longer have meaning."

Desh considered. "So how do you administer this viral gene cocktail of yours?"

"Injections in the beginning. But I ultimately made advances and was able to imbed the solution inside hollowed-out gellcaps. This is basically the same as drinking the mix, except the gellcaps deliver precise doses and are more convenient. A gellcap hits the stomach, dissolves almost immediately, and releases the collection of genetically engineered viruses. They travel to the brain instantly and within a relatively short time they've inserted their payload genes into cellular chromosomes, which are rapidly expressed."

Desh paused in thought. "Were you able to eliminate the negative effects?"

Kira sighed heavily. "For the most part," she said.

"What does that mean?"

"I lost my ability to feel emotions. I became purely analytical, achieving thought in its purest form, divorced from any bias or emotional baggage. I did the experiments in my condo," she explained. "I locked myself in and was alone, so I can't be certain there weren't other personality changes that would have been noticeable to people who knew me." She lowered her eyes. "But there was one effect of the rewiring that was particularly troubling to me," she admitted.

Desh looked on expectantly.

"During the short time the effect lasted," said Kira Miller, "my thoughts became more and more," she paused as if searching for a word. She frowned and shook her head worriedly. "I guess the best word for it would have to be, *sociopathic*," she finished disturbingly.

13

Desh's eyes widened. Once again, Kira Miller had surprised him. She had made such an effort to convince him she *wasn't* a sociopath, chipping away at his resolve with worrisome effectiveness, only to make a statement like *this.*

"That's convenient," said Desh. "You're a model citizen. It's this procedure of yours that somehow brings out the psycho in you. Is that it?" he demanded, annoyed that he had let himself be taken in by her for even a moment.

"Look, David, I didn't have to share this with you. But the only way you'll ever trust me is if I tell you the absolute truth about everything. And no, I still didn't do any of what Connelly says I did. These were thoughts only. I didn't act on them," she insisted. "They were simply strong predispositions, and they went away when my brain architecture returned to normal."

"So tell me about this state of sociopathy," said Desh.

Kira frowned. "Just so I'm clear," she said, "sociopathy isn't the exact right word for it either. Neither is 'psychopath' or 'megalomaniac', although they come almost as close. Basically, it's pure selfishness with a complete and utter lack of conscience. Whatever you choose to call it. A ruthless selfishness, so to speak."

"As opposed to what?"

"As opposed to this same condition with a sadistic element attached."

Desh considered. "I see," he said. "So you don't get your jollies by torturing others, but if you had to do so to achieve an end it wouldn't trouble you in the slightest. Is that about right?"

Kira nodded reluctantly.

"That's comforting," said Desh with a look of disgust. He paused in thought. "This something-like-sociopathy of yours seems like an unlikely side effect of your treatment," he said suspiciously.

Kira frowned. "I thought so too before the experiments. Now I realize it's more of a natural outgrowth of enhanced intelligence than a side effect of the re-wiring."

"How so?"

"The concepts are quite complicated. To be honest, when my intelligence is at normal levels, they're beyond me. But I'll do my best to give you the gist of it." She gathered her thoughts and exhaled loudly. "Let me start at the very beginning. When our ancient relatives first arrived on the scene, they weren't the king of the hill. Far from it. They barely managed to stay *on* the hill. Pre-humans were just one of thousands and thousands of species battling for a tiny niche on a planet teeming with life. If you were a betting man, we were a million-to-one underdog to survive, let alone climb to the top of the food chain. No armor. No speed. No physical weapons."

"But then intelligence came along," said Desh.

"That's right. The polar bear could survive just fine without it. But we *desperately* needed it. Intelligence was the only way out for our ancestors, and they achieved it just in time." She paused and eyed Desh meaningfully. "And intelligence in survival terms means cunning, utter ruthlessness, and utter selfishness." She raised her eyebrows. "What you might consider sociopathic behavior in its primal form."

Desh reflected on what he had seen of the underbelly of human behavior during his time with Delta Force. He had seen things that would make a veteran pathologist vomit. Decapitations and other unspeakable tortures—displays of cruelty that defied the imagination. Without question, violence and brutality—and bloodlust—were intrinsic to human nature. Scratch any century throughout recorded history and staggering displays of cruelty came gushing out: the slaughter of helpless innocents on a massive scale, brutal wars, enslavements, tortures, mass rapes and murders, and other atrocities far too numerous to ignore. Hitler was just one example in a seemingly endless parade. Humanity could wrap itself in the cloak of civilization and pretend this side of its nature didn't exist, but the hostility and savagery that drove the most dangerous predator on the planet to the top of the food chain was always seething, just below the surface.

"To survive," continued Kira, "Homo sapiens evolved intelligence, and a ruthlessness and selfishness hardwired into our genes. That's one side of the equation." She paused. "But a cunning and ruthless intelligence alone wasn't enough. Along with intelligence we had to use teamwork to bring down the mastodon. And our brains were so complex they still needed to develop long after birth. Human infants were helpless for far longer than any other animal on Earth. So our selfishness had to be tempered. We had to evolve some sense of teamwork and fair play. We had to sacrifice for our children and put the clan's survival above our own."

Desh was totally drawn into the conversation intellectually now, temporarily forgetting to remain suspicious of Kira's every word and action.

"So those who were *only* selfish," she continued, "died out in the long run. Those who were wired to be totally ruthless, but could also cooperate and work in a pack, survived to have offspring. To this day, a delicate balance of pure selfishness in some respects and pure selflessness in others is hardwired into our genes. For the sake of discussion, let's use extremes. Call this selfishness sociopathy. Call this selflessness altruism."

"So you believe there is such a thing as altruism? That Abraham Lincoln got it wrong?"

Kira Miller titled her head, intrigued, and gazed at Desh approvingly, impressed that he was familiar with the apocryphal story attributed to Abraham Lincoln.

In the story, Lincoln was traveling on a train and discussing human nature with a fellow passenger. The passenger insisted that such a thing as altruism existed, whereas Lincoln maintained with great vigor that all human acts were purely selfish. During the discussion, Lincoln noticed a baby goat lying across the tracks far ahead. He immediately called for the train to stop, got out, and gently lifted the goat off the tracks. The train started up again and the passenger said, "Why Abe, you just proved my point. You just committed a totally selfless act." To which Abe replied, "Quite the contrary. I just proved *my* point. The act was totally *selfish*." The passenger was confused. "How so?" he asked. To which Lincoln replied, "If I would have done nothing to save that poor animal, I would have felt just *awful*."

Kira's eyes sparkled as she considered her response. "Insightful question," she said. "For what it's worth, I actually think Lincoln was right. But for the sake of this discussion, this is more semantics than anything. Altruistic behavior exists and is hardwired into our genes. Whether it is merely another facet of selfishness isn't germane to my point."

Desh raised his eyebrows. "Which is?"

"Which is that this delicate balance between the competing poles of sociopathy and altruism can be shifted in one direction or another very readily. Granted, some people are born with a strong genetic predisposition one way or the other, but most of us are balanced on a razor's edge. An average man who is the recipient of acts of caring and kindness will often perform charitable acts in return. This same man, given a slight push the other way, will pursue his self-interests even at the expense of others—even at the suffering of his own friends and family. In order to ensure that civilization can exist, that the scales are slightly tipped toward altruism, human intelligence had to invent religion."

Desh frowned. "Invent religion?"

"That's right. There have been thousands of different religions through time. And the followers of each of these religions believe that their founders received the divine answer, and that the religious mythology of all other religions is delusional. Almost everyone agrees that all the *other* religions were invented by man, just not the particular one into which they were born."

Desh decided not to argue the point. "Go on," he said.

"Most religions subscribe to the belief that there is something bigger than us out there," continued Kira. "That there is some purpose to human suffering. That there is a form of continued existence after death. All of this helps to bolster the altruistic side of the human equation. Why not be totally selfish?—especially now that we don't really need clans to survive: we can take down the mastodon alone. The answer: because there will be a reward or punishment in the *next* life." She paused and shook her head. "But what if you knew with absolute certainty that when you died, that was it? There was no afterlife of any kind. Why not be totally selfish? With no God, what is the point to anything? There is no right and wrong: there is only doing what will make you happy. You have a short time to be alive—why not maximize the experience? To hell with anyone else."

Desh looked thoughtful. "Because even if you believed there was no afterlife, altruism is still wired in. That was Lincoln's point: altruism provides its own reward. Being good makes people feel good."

"Excellent," she said. "This is true. So a certainty that there is no afterlife doesn't necessarily imply that pure sociopathy reigns. It isn't perfectly straightforward. But it's definitely a step down that path." She paused. "And our society does have laws. So even if you reasoned that nothing really mattered, that good and evil were relative, and were determined to be completely selfish, you would have to perform a risk-reward analysis. Why not steal that luxury car that you love? One reason is that if you get caught, you'll go to jail. There are risks that your selfish act would lead to a worse existence rather than a better one."

Desh's eyes narrowed. "Unless you had absolute power," he noted.

Kira nodded. "Exactly. I won't resort to the overused cliché, but if you didn't believe in the afterlife and could get away with doing anything you wanted, sociopathic behavior would become more and more likely."

"So that's the connection," guessed Desh. "In your enhanced state you feel that you can do whatever you want."

"Exactly. With intelligence this great, you can't help but feel superior and almost invincible. And you really could get away with almost anything. At the same time, you clearly see the stark reality. There is no God. There is no afterlife."

Desh bristled at this pronouncement. "Why would increased intelligence necessarily make you an atheist?" he challenged.

"The change in brain architecture transforms you into a purely intellectual creature. There is no longer room for faith, something you have to have to sustain a belief in God and the afterlife."

"So how does your enhanced intellect grapple with the question of how the universe came to be? It surely must have been created, which implies a creator."

"I can't come close to understanding my thinking on this subject while in the transformed state. What I do know is that when I'm enhanced, I'm *absolutely convinced* that God does not exist." She paused. "You asked me who created the universe. Let me ask you this: who created God?"

Desh frowned. "God is eternal. He didn't need a creator."

"Really?" said Kira. "Then why does the *universe* need one? If *God* can exist without a creator, why can't the universe? No matter how you slice it, at some point you get to something that existed without being created. Which is impossible for even an enhanced mind to fully comprehend. Conjuring up a God to explain creation is just a convenient cheat unless you're prepared to explain how God originated." She paused. "And even if you accepted God for the sake of argument, why would an omniscient, omnipotent being waste his time creating humanity? The more intellect you bring to bear on the question, with faith out of the picture, the more certain you become that God is just a construct of the human mind, nothing more."

Desh shook his head in irritation and disagreement but didn't argue further. "So enhanced intelligence alters the balance of power in the altruism versus sociopathy war."

Kira nodded. "It takes very little reasoning in this state to justify any selfish act I can contemplate. If someone is in my way—killing them makes perfect intellectual sense. What does it matter if they die now or in thirty years? Either way, existence is meaningless. God is dead. Why shouldn't I do what is needed to achieve my potential?" She raised her eyebrows. "Remind you of anything?" she asked pointedly.

Desh had minored in philosophy in college, as Kira was no doubt aware from her study of him. He looked troubled. "Friedrich Nietzsche's will to power," said Desh unhappily. Nietzsche had glorified the concept of a superman. Not the Clark Kent variety, but a man whose sense of good and evil was based solely on what would help him succeed or fail. Good was anything that would help him achieve his potential. Evil was anything that would hamper him. *What is good? All that heightens the feeling of power in man, the will to power, power itself. What is bad? All that is born of weakness.*

Kira frowned. "I'm afraid so," she confirmed. "In the enhanced state, as soon as you contemplate any of the eternal questions, you quickly reinvent this school of philosophy before taking it to a level of sophistication that the world's greatest philosophers couldn't possibly comprehend."

There was a long silence in the room.

"But you said you haven't acted on any of these sociopathic tendencies," said Desh finally. "Is that right?"

"So far, no," she said gravely. "My inherent sense of altruism and fair play has been strong enough—barely—to prevent me from acting on these impulses. But they're quite strong," she admitted. "It's been tempting to let go of my last bit of pesky Neanderthal wiring and release myself from all moral and ethical bonds," she said, a deeply troubled look on her face. "*Very* tempting."

Desh was unsure of just how to respond to this.

"I haven't enhanced myself for some time now," she continued softly.

"Afraid the pull will become too strong for you to resist?" said Desh

She nodded. The corners of her mouth turned up slightly in a humorless smile. "Sometimes I think of myself as Frodo in the *Lord of The Rings.* In my case the ring's power is that of almost inconceivable creativity and intellect. But like Frodo's burden it is easily accessible, right there around my neck at all times, exerting its magnetic pull. The temptation to use it, especially when I'm desperately in need of some insight, is almost irresistible."

Desh considered. He had never really thought about the ring from the Tolkien trilogy as yet another manifestation of the old cliché regarding power, but of course it was. The ring didn't turn its wearer evil; the power inherent in the ring did this. "Power corrupts," he began, unable to stop himself from reciting the cliché Kira had avoided using. "Absolute power corrupts abso—"

Desh never finished his sentence. With a sound like a shotgun blast the door to the room exploded inward, propelled by vicious, simultaneous kicks expertly applied by two men on the other side.

14

Desh's head jerked violently from the startling intrusion, and his arms were nearly yanked from their sockets as he instinctively tried to assume a defensive posture: his startle reflex not caring that his arms were immobilized behind his back. Along with the thunderous sound of the door crashing in, the room was instantly plunged into impenetrable darkness as the rope Kira had attached to the door handle yanked the lamp cord violently from the wall outlet.

The momentum from the intruders' explosive kicks propelled them into the room, guns drawn, and they hit the trip wire instantly, about the same time their brains registered that they were now blind. With two surprised grunts, followed immediately by two loud thuds, they crashed to the floor only seconds after their attack had begun.

They had counted on a precision surprise attack executed so quickly that even if the girl had been holding a gun she wouldn't be able to stop them. They had not counted on their actions killing the room's only light or being greeted by a trip wire.

Kira Miller had also jumped in shock when the door was kicked open, but she recovered quickly. While the attackers lay sprawled on the floor, dazed, wondering what had hit them and why the world had suddenly gone dark, she slid her thermal imaging goggles down over her eyes. The two intruders instantly became visible as glowing, highly resolved three-dimensional silhouettes.

"Don't move!" she barked.

The taller of the two attackers had now fully recovered his wits after the surprise fall. The girl wasn't as clever as they had been led to believe, he thought arrogantly. The room was as dark as a cave, but she had foolishly given them the upper hand by speaking and giving away her location. He ignored her command and soundlessly lifted his arm and pointed his gun in the direction from which her voice had originated.

She shot him in the chest with her stun gun as he prepared to fire.

The tall man convulsed violently and lay still on the ground while Kira quickly retracted the dual electrode harpoons, ready for another shot. The man's partner silently began to change position on the floor so that he could attempt an attack as well, not having learned from his colleague's miscalculation.

"Just because *you* can't see," hissed Kira, "doesn't mean that *I* can't."

The man froze in place. Like his paralyzed partner, he had assumed she couldn't see him or detect his movements, a foolish and potentially fatal assumption. They had been warned that she was very clever and not to underestimate her.

"That's right," she said smugly. "I'm wearing night-vision goggles. So let's try this again. *Don't. Move.*" She emphasized each word as if speaking to a stubborn toddler.

Desh's mind had been racing since the attack began, considering his options. But he realized that even if he could free himself, escape was hopeless. He couldn't see any better than the attackers could.

Kira pulled a Glock from her bag with a silencer already attached, although given that the sound of the door being forced open would already have awakened every last motel resident—several of whom, at least, were now calling the police—the silencer had questionable value.

"I'm now pointing a gun at you," she explained. "How many others are with you and what is their location?" she demanded.

"No others," replied the man, shaking his head. "Just us."

Kira fired. The silenced gun issued a spitting sound as she sent a bullet tearing through the meaty part of the man's thigh. "I'll only ask once more," she growled. "How many others are with you and what is their location?"

"One other," grunted the man as he desperately began trying to staunch the flow of blood from his leg. "He's taken up a sniper position facing your room to prevent any escape. He's equipped with a thermal imager."

Kira said nothing. She adjusted a setting on the stun gun and fired. The intruder convulsed and lay still, unconscious. She reloaded the gun, adjusted the setting once more, and shot the first man again, rendering him unconscious as well. She pulled a ski mask from her bag, made from the same material as her jumpsuit, and stretched it over her goggles. The material snapped back into shape to fit snugly over her face and nose, fitting perfectly around the goggles and leaving not a single section of her face exposed.

"Shit!" she fumed. "We needed more time. They shouldn't have tracked us here for five or six more hours," she said despondently, as much to herself as to Desh. "By then we would have been long gone." She had been in complete control when dealing with the two attackers, but she was distraught now, as if she had just suffered a terrible loss. Desh was still blind but could hear it clearly in her voice.

"I have to get out of here," she said after a few seconds of silence. "Now." Desh noted that any hint of vulnerability had once again disappeared from her voice. "I can't trust you untied, and I don't have time to drag you with me."

Desh's heart raced furiously. So what would she do with him now? Would she decide to put a bullet in his brain before she left? Desh knew she intended to go through the adjoining room and out the other side of the motel. Her planning had been extraordinary. Just as she had expected, the attackers were only watching the door on the front side of the motel, thinking it was her only exit.

"What if he lied?" said Desh in desperation. "What if they have a sniper watching the back as well?"

"He'll miss," she said simply. "I'm covered head to toe by a jumpsuit, goggles and a ski mask, all designed to completely block my heat signature. I'll be invisible to thermal imaging, from snipers or from the air."

Desh shook his head. "That's impossible," he insisted. "The military has been trying for years. There *is* no such technology."

"There is now," replied Kira smoothly.

Desh's eyes widened. Could it be true? If she could be believed, she had dramatically enhanced her own intelligence. Had she turned her amped-up genius to the problem of defeating thermal imaging technology? If this were true, it would go a long way toward explaining how she had managed to remain in the US and elude the manhunt for so long.

As this was flashing through Desh's mind, Kira approached him and quickly sawed at his restraints with a knife until his hands were free, retreating from him rapidly once they were, despite being armed and having the advantage of sight.

"I have to go," she said hurriedly. "I'll leave the knife and gun in the bathroom of the adjoining room. By the time you shuffle over there and remove your ankle cuffs, I'll have gotten the head start I need."

Desh allowed himself to breathe again. Would she really let him go?

"Damn!" she fumed again. "There's much more to tell. We should be leaving together as allies!" Kira gathered herself. "They'll know I took the risk of kidnapping you," she mumbled rapidly, "but it's unclear how they'll interpret this. They may decide to kill you or they may decide just to use you. I don't know." She paused. "I know you're still not sure about me. But even if you think every word I told you was a lie, your survival depends on believing this: don't trust anyone. Be prepared for anything," she warned anxiously.

Kira gathered her bag and rushed into the adjoining room. After a ten second detour into its bathroom, she unlocked the room's outer door. "We'll have to finish our conversation at another time," she called to Desh through the doors between the two rooms.

There was a slight pause. "Be careful, David," she added earnestly. "I hope you're as good as I think you are."

And with that, Kira Miller opened the door and stepped out into the night.

PART THREE
Fountain

15

Desh moved the instant the outer door of the adjoining room was shut. He scooted to the other side of the bed and reached out cautiously, probing for the lamp on the other end table. It was identical to the one whose cord had been ripped from the wall. His hand connected with it and he fumbled for the switch at its base, managing to find it and flip it on. Although the lamp was on the dim side, after several minutes in darkness he was forced to squint until his eyes adjusted.

The door frame at the room's entrance was shattered where the lock had been, and the door itself hung awkwardly from a single hinge; a splintered mess. The two intruders were awkward heaps on the thin carpet, and neither was moving. Desh slid from the bed and pressed two fingers into each of their necks in turn, feeling for their carotid arteries and signs of a pulse. Both were still alive. Satisfied, he shuffled as quickly as he could to the adjoining room, his ankles still bound. Making sure not to turn on any additional lights, he entered the bathroom, unsure of what he might find there.

He waited until the bathroom door was closed and flipped on the light. No use sending out a beacon to any onlookers that would remind them of the possibility of front-to-back adjoining rooms. True to Kira's word there was a Browning semiautomatic, its clip full, and a combat knife lying on the floor. Desh was shocked to also find the keys to the Ford and what must have been a spare pair of night-vision goggles next to the weapons. She knew he would be coming after her, despite her brief head start, so why arm him and provide him with night-vision and a car?

Desh frowned. Because she was confident it wouldn't matter. She knew he couldn't catch her, even still. She wouldn't have planned an impeccable ambush and a way to exit the motel undetected without planning an escape route as well. He had no doubt she had another car ready to go, parked and waiting for her just on the other side of the stretch of woods that abutted the motel.

Desh pocketed the gun and keys and made quick work of his ankle restraints with the knife. It was a relief to have complete freedom of movement again. He strapped the goggles on his head and grabbed a neatly folded towel from a small shelf in the bathroom. He rushed back to the wounded man as he lay unconscious, wrapping the towel tightly around his thigh.

The men had carried identical guns that were now lying on the floor near them. Desh picked one up and examined it, surprised that he didn't recognize the make. As he pulled the clip his eyes widened. *It was a tranquilizer gun.* Designed to shoot darts instead of bullets.

He patted both men down. While neither possessed any personal items or identification, which didn't surprise him, they each carried semiautomatic pistols along with the tranquilizer guns. They had possessed lethal firepower but had been intent on taking their quarry alive. Interesting. But who were they, exactly? And what were they doing here? Kira Miller's explanation that he was being followed by his own people was the most likely, but still didn't make sense. It wasn't as though he couldn't be trusted to report back once he had found her.

What now? He could charge after her, but he was certain he wouldn't catch her. Desh knew he didn't have much time before the police would be arriving. The man she had shot may have been lying about the sniper, but it was just as likely he hadn't been. And Desh didn't have her supposed ability to become invisible to thermal imagers. He wasn't about to be the first heat-emitting humanoid to rush out the front door. Still, he had to regroup, and the last thing he needed was to be in the room when the police came calling. This left only one choice: he had to leave out the back, through the adjoining room, as she had done.

Kira Miller had told him to trust no one, and regardless of what he might think of the veracity of anything else she said, this was sensible advice. He was in far over his head, and until he had a much better sense of what was happening and who the players were, he wasn't prepared to trust his own shadow.

Desh pocketed the shorter man's cell phone and tranquilizer gun and wrapped the other tranquilizer gun and the two pistols in a towel. He moved into the adjoining room, tossed the towel on the bed, and closed both doors, plunging himself yet again into darkness. He felt for the dead-bolt, locked the adjoining door on his side, and then flipped open the cell phone he had taken. The phone's glow provided enough illumination with which to dial and navigate the room. He had memorized Jim Connelly's private home number and dialed it rapidly.

The phone rang three times while Desh waited anxiously.

"Hello," rasped Connelly sleepily.

"Colonel, it's David Desh."

"David?" mumbled Connelly in surprise. "Jesus, David, it's three in the morning," he complained, but then began to awaken more fully as the significance of the call registered on his barely conscious brain. His voice picked up strength as his adrenaline levels spiked. "Are you okay?"

"Yes, but I need to know something," said Desh in hushed tones.

"Are you under duress?" said Connelly carefully, now fully alert.

"No, I'm alone."

"We need to get to a secure line," insisted Connelly. "I know you remember our discussion. I hadn't expected to hear from you," he added pointedly, as if Desh needed reminding that Connelly had given him explicit instructions not to call him and to stay well clear of military channels.

"Yeah, we wouldn't want to tip off our quarry," said Desh sardonically. He paused and then added, "Unfortunately, it's a little late for that."

"She knows you're on the case?"

"You could say that," replied Desh. "In fact, you could say that I was just abducted," he continued. "And it *wasn't* by aliens."

"What?" whispered the colonel in disbelief. "But why? It makes no sense." He paused in thought. "Unless she thought you were getting close."

"She didn't, and I wasn't," continued Desh hurriedly, acutely aware that the police could arrive at any moment. Worse still, the two men in the adjoining room could regain their consciousness, or their sniper friend could lose his patience with his colleagues and come to investigate. "She tried to convince me she was innocent. I have very little time, so I'll tell you about that later. But I need to know something. Two military types crashed the party and ran her off. Were they yours?"

"I didn't know about the party, so I sure as hell didn't send the party crashers," he replied.

"Did you set them up on their own recognizance to tail me?"

"Why would I do that?" said Connelly, genuinely confused. "You aren't the target here, and I have every confidence you'll do your job and then call your contact."

"Then who are they?"

There was a long pause. "I have no idea," came the uneasy reply.

Desh nodded. "I have to go, Colonel. Do me a favor. Investigate this entire Op from top to bottom. Something's not right. Starting with the party crashers. Make sure you have the straight skinny on this deal."

"After what you've just told me," said Connelly, "you don't need to ask."

"Good. I'll be in touch," said Desh, ending the connection.

Desh pocketed the phone and pushed aside just enough of the curtain to be able to peer out of the window. The coast appeared clear, although this guaranteed nothing.

Desh heard heavy footsteps coming from the adjoining room and jerked his head away from the window, his senses hyper-alert.

"Holy Shit!" bellowed a man in the other room, his shocked voice easily carrying through the wall. "Are they alive?"

"I'll check," said another man. "You call for back-up," he added anxiously.

Desh guessed from their reaction to the two unconscious men they were uniformed cops with no military experience, which was somewhat of a relief. Even so, he didn't wait to hear more. He opened the outer door and cautiously stepped outside, crouching low and keeping to the darkness.

16

David Desh entered the woods near the back of the motel, the night vision equipment that Kira had provided now firmly over his eyes, and picked his way through the trees as quickly as he could. The woods at night provided a spectacle few would ever witness, requiring both the interest and expensive IR night vision equipment to maximize the experience. Desh had been lucky enough to be properly equipped on many occasions and see the woods come alive at night as nocturnal birds, amphibians, mammals, and reptiles scurried onto the stage under cover of darkness, unaware that technology could now offer night-blind humans a peek at their previously hidden universe. Warm-blooded bats, normally invisible against the night sky, now showed up clearly as they winged after insect meals, and owls terrorized rodent populations, often swallowing their prey whole.

Tonight, though, Desh didn't have the luxury of letting himself get distracted. His entire focus was on plotting a path that would allow him to traverse the quarter-mile wide strip of trees as quickly as possible. Ten minutes later he emerged from the trees. A road paralleled the woods, but Desh stayed close to the tree line and out of sight of headlights, continuing to put distance between himself and the motel.

After jogging for a few miles he spotted the steeple of a church across the road, with a small parking area in front, and hurriedly approached it. He passed a sign that read *Saint Peters Lutheran Church.* Pushing aside feelings of guilt, he forced the lock on the front door of the brick building and slid inside.

He went straight to the main sanctuary, stepped onto the altar, and deposited the cell phone he had removed from Kira's assailant behind the pulpit, leaving the phone closed but still on. Within minutes he was back just inside the tree line, staying out of sight and watching all access points to the church carefully.

Desh settled in for what he expected to be a long vigil. Periodically, he retreated farther into the woods and did jumping jacks to keep his blood flowing and to generate warmth on the chilly autumn night. He had the odd feeling that if Kira Miller had had an extra coat in her magic bag, she would have left that in the bathroom for him as well.

So what to make of her? Could her story have been true? It was impossible to say. But regardless, Desh had to admire her competence. She planned brilliantly, was quick on her feet, and was decisive.

But was she too decisive? She had shot one of the intruders to get information with a ruthless efficiency. Few people were capable of acting so callously. On the other hand, she could easily have killed them all. A true psychopath wouldn't have hesitated. Unless for some unfathomable reason it continued to be of importance to her to convince Desh she was innocent, so much so that she was able to sublimate her psychotic nature.

Or was she not a psychopath at all? Had she really been a model citizen before she had altered her own brain chemistry? Maybe. But even if she was, it was equally possible that the changes to her nature she claimed to have come about as a result of her experiments had become permanent, despite her assurances to the contrary.

But this still wouldn't explain the deaths of her parents and uncle and teachers, Desh realized. Even if the murder of her brother and her collaboration with terrorists could be explained as a result of self-induced psychopathic behavior, a horrible side effect of the rewiring of her own brain, these earlier murders could not be. Could it be that she honestly was unaware of her own true nature? What if she had suffered from schizophrenia and had developed a split personality at a young age? Maybe it had always been a Dr. Jekyll, Mr. Hyde thing with her, with the changes to her brain chemistry doing nothing more than allowing the Mr. Hyde personality to become more dominant.

Desh shook his head, annoyed with himself. *Why was he trying so hard to identify some part of her that was innocent!* He knew that she was getting to him, but he hadn't realized just how much until now. Along with a powerful intellect that he found stimulating and those soft, expressive eyes, there was a charm and sincerity to her that was undeniably appealing, even though he knew it was nothing but an accomplished acting job. He had to hand it to the ancient Greeks: they knew that a treacherous woman who could still captivate a man was far more dangerous than the most powerful of sea monsters. How many others had been mesmerized by Kira Miller's siren song, he wondered, letting down their guard and crashing against the cliffs. If their paths crossed again, he had better find a way to tie himself to the mast if he wanted to have any chance of surviving the encounter.

He was still lost in thought, forty minutes after he had abandoned the cell phone, when a large, two-door sedan pulled off the road a hundred yards before the church. Two men with night-vision equipment of their own jumped out and without a word began to double-time it to the church, leaving the driver waiting in the car. They had taken the bait already. Impressive. Whoever they were, they were exceedingly well connected. Despite the police presence in the motel, they had been able to pull the required strings to retrieve their men and track the missing cell phone in record time.

Desh pulled out the tranquilizer gun he had borrowed. Despite the fact they had been tailing him, they were still most likely friendlies. He wasn't exactly in a trusting mood, but he wasn't about to consider lethal force, either, until he knew who they were.

Desh sprinted along the tree line in the opposite direction from the church so he could circle back around behind the car. As the two men entered St. Peters, Desh cut quietly across the road and noiselessly lowered himself into a military crawl. He inched forward toward the passenger door, not even allowing himself to breathe. He was betting the driver had not locked the car.

Desh let out a slow, preparatory breath and quietly removed his goggles, leaving them on the ground next to him. Then, in a single fluid motion, he shot up from the ground—catching the door handle on the way up—and yanked the door wide open. *It wasn't locked.* Wasting no time congratulating himself, Desh pointed the gun at the startled driver, who had just begun reaching for his own weapon. "Hands on the dash!" he barked fiercely.

17

The driver studied Desh thoughtfully, and then calmly placed his hands on the dash as instructed. The tip of Desh's tongue protruded just slightly through his lips as it tended to do whenever he was engaged in any physical activity that required his absolute concentration. He slid through the car's open door and into the back seat, his gun never wavering from its target. "Slide over and close the door," commanded Desh in hushed tones.

The man did as he was told.

"Now slide back and get us on the road. Quickly!" demanded Desh. "Head farther away from the Church." Desh had no interest in passing the man's colleagues who he knew would be exiting the church at any moment after they discovered they had been set up.

The driver did as instructed, and the church rapidly receded in the rear-view mirror.

"Very impressive, Mr. Desh," the driver allowed. "But then, I *have* heard good things."

"Who are you?" demanded Desh. "And why were you and your people following me?"

"Call me Smith," said the driver, a short, wiry man in his late thirties, with short brown hair and a two-inch scar under his ear that followed his jaw line. "After a session with Kira Miller you get a little paranoid, don't you? Don't know who to trust or what to believe."

"Smith, huh," said Desh to himself. The man was unmistakably military. And along with the obvious alias, there was a peculiar arrogance about him, as though he considered himself above it all; unencumbered by rules that might apply to lesser men. "Black-Ops, then?" guessed Desh.

A self-satisfied smile flashed across Smith's face. "That's right," he said. "We had a shot at the girl and we took it. Sorry we surprised you. Given what you've just gone through you're reacting the way any smart soldier would. But we're on the same side you and I. Really."

"Why was I under surveillance then, if we're on the same side?"

"I would be happy to explain that and much more, Mr. Desh. I'm the one who authorized putting you on this Op in the first place. I trust that Colonel Connelly gave you a number to call when you found the girl?"

Desh didn't respond.

"I'm going to lend you a cell phone," said Smith. "I have two of them. I'm going to reach in my pocket for the phone but remain facing the road. I'll throw it back to you. If I begin to pull out a gun, shoot me," he added.

Desh knew that at their current speed any hostile exchange would cause them to crash, killing them both. Mutually assured destruction. Smith would realize this as well.

"Okay," said Desh, nodding warily. "But very slowly."

The man reached into his pocket and carefully inched out the phone, lifting it with his hand facing backward so Desh could see. Still facing the road, he flipped the phone over his shoulder. Desh caught it with his left hand while he continued to train the tranquilizer gun on Smith with his right.

"Dial the number that the colonel gave you," instructed Smith.

Desh flipped open the phone and dialed the number he had memorized. As the call went through, a ringtone melody issued from Smith's shirt pocket. He looked at Desh in the rear-view mirror and raised his eyebrows. "Mind if I get that," he said smugly.

Smith reached into his shirt pocket and flipped open the phone. "Hello, Mr. Desh," he said, his voice arriving in stereo from both the front seat and through the phone in Desh's hand. "I think it's time we had a little talk."

18

Desh still wasn't sure who to trust, but Smith had established his authenticity, even if Connelly hadn't been aware of his activities. Even so, Desh had an uneasy feeling in his gut that wouldn't seem to go away.

"Okay then," said Desh. "Let's talk." He continued to point the gun at the black-ops agent.

"I'll tell you what, Mr. Desh. How about I pull off to the side of the road and we have a disarming ceremony first."

Desh remained silent.

"What do you say?" pressed Smith. "You can keep your gun on me while I toss all of my weapons into a bag in my trunk—including the gun strapped to my ankle. You can frisk me to be sure." He paused. "In return, you can hang on to your weapon. Just don't point it at me."

Desh gazed at the scarred man thoughtfully, but said nothing.

"And while we have a little discussion and get to know each other," pressed Smith, "I'll even drive you home. As long as you sit in the front seat. Be easier to talk that way, and I refuse to be your chauffeur."

Desh thought through all the angles and finally agreed. Five minutes later two guns and a combat knife were tucked in a bag and locked safely away in the trunk, and Desh was satisfied that Smith was now unarmed. After allowing the wiry man to contact his men to give them a quick situation report, Desh settled into the passenger seat, safely restrained in a seat belt, but angling his body so he was facing Smith rather than the road and was out of the man's easy reach.

"All right," said Desh, as Smith accelerated back onto the road, his left hand on the steering wheel and his right arm resting on the storage console between them. "Why don't you tell me what's going on."

"I'm afraid that isn't how this needs to work," said Smith evenly. "I *will* tell you everything. Make no mistake about that. I do understand how confused this woman can make someone and that we surveilled you without your knowledge. So I'm willing to cut you some slack. But we're going to do this my way," he insisted. "First you answer my questions. Then I'll answer yours. Despite heading a black-ops agency that doesn't formally exist and using an alias, I am still your superior officer. I'm sure Connelly told you that."

Desh raised his eyebrows. "Superior officer?" he said, unimpressed. "Come off it, Smith. You've been calling me *Mr.* Desh. You know I'm a civilian. Connelly did tell me to follow your instructions, but *Mr.* Desh can tell you to go to hell anytime he wants."

Smith sighed. "All right, *Mr.* Desh. Let's try this another way, then. If you want to know what's going on, you'll have to answer my questions first. Period. Otherwise, I'll leave you completely in the dark." He glanced sideways at Desh. "Well?"

Desh glared at him for several long seconds but finally nodded irritably.

"Good," said Smith. "So tell me how Kira Miller got the drop on you."

Desh told him about receiving the fake message from Griffin and what had happened at the hacker's apartment. Smith interrupted occasionally for clarification but said very little otherwise. When Desh described how Kira had stripped him and had him dress in sweats, Smith glanced at his gray outfit, considerably worse for wear since Kira had pulled it from her duffel, and an amused smile came over his face.

Smith listened intently as Desh described the precautions Kira had taken at the motel. Smith was well aware that they had worked to great effect on his men. Desh ended his narrative at the point at which Kira had exited through the adjoining motel room, leaving out any mention of her claims of having invented material that could hide her heat signature.

"Damn she's slippery," commented Smith when Desh was finished. "It's uncanny how she manages to stay at large. And then, to risk kidnapping the elite soldier coming after her practically in the middle of the nation's capital—and get away with it. She has balls the size of Texas," he said, partly in frustration and partly in admiration.

Smith paused in thought as they shot along the dark highway, nearly abandoned at this early hour except for the occasional trucker hauling cargo through the night. The car's ride was smooth and its well-tuned engine issued only the softest of roars to interrupt what would have otherwise been a cocoon of silence. Desh's entire universe had been reduced to the luxury interior of an expensive sedan, the twenty-foot swath made by its headlights as they cut through the enveloping darkness, and a stranger using an alias whose motives were currently just as hidden as the stretch of road beyond the headlights.

"Okay," began Smith, having finally plotted his interrogation. "You said she talked with you for an hour or so. What did she talk about?"

"She claimed she was innocent," said Desh. "She wanted to convince me."

"Did she say why this was important to her?"

"No," said Desh. He considered telling the black-ops officer that she had told him her goal was to recruit him to her side, but immediately decided against it.

"Did she explain away all the bizarre deaths and disappearances that occurred around her when she was growing up? Or the death of her boss? Or the murder of her brother?"

"She insisted she didn't kill her parents. The other incidents didn't come up at all. Neither did any mention of Ebola or bio-weapons. She mentioned terrorists only in the context of denying that she had any connection to them."

"I see. Then on what grounds did she claim to be innocent if she made no effort to refute the airtight evidence against her?"

Desh shrugged. "I don't know. Your men interrupted before she got that far."

"Let me understand. She wanted to prove her innocence. Yet after an hour of discussion she had not addressed even a single thing she was accused of?"

"That's right," responded Desh.

Smith took both eyes off the ruler-straight road and studied Desh for several seconds. Finally, apparently unable to find any signs of deceit, he returned his attention to the road. "So what *did* she talk about in that time?"

Desh sighed. "About experiments she conducted to increase her own intelligence. The theory behind it, the results of the experiments; that sort of thing."

Smith raised his eyebrows. "Did she say she was successful?"

Desh nodded. "She claims to be able to enhance her intelligence to immeasurable levels."

"I see," said Smith, noncommittally. "And did she tell you how she applied this newfound brilliance of hers?" he asked.

"Not a word," said Desh.

"Did she *offer* you anything?" asked Smith.

"Like what? Money?"

Smith studied him carefully once again, as if this would enable him to precisely judge the sincerity of Desh's response. "Like anything. Money. Power. Enhanced intelligence of your own." He raised his eyebrows. "Other considerations that might be appealing."

Desh furrowed his brow in confusion. "Other considerations? You can't mean sex," he said in disbelief.

Smith shook his head irritably. "Of course not," he replied.

Desh shrugged. "Then I'm afraid you've lost me. But regardless of what you're trying to hint at, she didn't offer me a single thing. Period. Not a thin dime. Not that I could be bought in any case," he added pointedly.

Smith paused for a long time in thought. "Did you believe her story?" he asked finally, taking a new tack.

"What, about her ability to elevate her IQ, or that she was innocent?"

"Both," said Smith.

"With respect to enhanced intellect—I don't know," said Desh, shrugging. His eyes narrowed in thought. "She's an extraordinary scientist, that's beyond dispute. And she weaved a very convincing scientific rationale around the concept. Autistic savants do exist and do demonstrate what one hundred billion neurons can do when wired slightly differently than normal. As farfetched as it is, she made optimizing her own brain seem possible, even *reasonable,* for someone with her talents." He paused. "Is she innocent? That one is easier. Of course not. Other than claiming she was innocent, she didn't provide a shred of evidence, as we've discussed."

The corners of Smith's mouth turned up in a knowing smile. "But she still got to you a little, didn't she? Even without providing any evidence, you half wanted to believe her, didn't you?"

"What I might have *wanted* to believe and what I actually *do* believe are two different things," snapped Desh defensively.

"I've never met her," said Smith. "But she's brilliant and I'm told she has a way about her. She can suck you in, dazzle you with logic that seems irrefutable, and do it in a way that's absolutely sincere. Not to mention that she has a wholesome, doe-eyed beauty that some men find hard to resist. You must have felt her pull."

Desh frowned. "A little," he admitted. "But I know what she is and my guard was up. She may have intended to provide evidence of her innocence. Maybe she would eventually have even tried to bribe me, but we'll never know. Your men crashed the party and all she talked about was her ability to make herself smarter." He paused and added sharply, "You can believe anything you want. *That's* what happened. That's *all* that happened."

Smith was silent for several long moments as they continued hurtling down the dark highway. Traffic was still sparse but had begun picking up, ever so slightly, with the gradual approach of dawn. "I believe you," he said at last. "I conducted a number of interrogations in a past life and I think you're telling the truth. On the important things at any rate," he added.

"Good," said Desh. "So are you ready to take your turn in this little information exchange of ours?"

Smith considered. "All right," he replied. "First of all, we believe Kira Miller really has found a way to turn herself into the ultimate savant. And our experts seem to agree that, properly organized, there's almost no level of intelligence the one hundred billion neurons you spoke of can't reach."

"Do you have actual evidence of this optimization?"

"Yes. Most of it circumstantial, but enough that we're convinced. What you say she told you fits right in with what we know. It's interesting that she told you she gave herself this immeasurable IQ," continued Smith, "but she didn't say a word about how she applied this intelligence." He eyed Desh meaningfully. "If you had supreme intellect, what problem would you tackle?"

Desh shook his head tiredly. "Look . . . Smith . . . usually I'm up for riddles and guessing games. Really. But I haven't slept in almost twenty-four hours and it's been a tough day, so why don't you just tell me."

"Immortality," said Smith simply.

19

Desh sat in stunned silence, replaying the word in his head to be sure he had heard correctly. A flying insect slammed into the windshield like a tiny missile and became an instant smear. "Immortality," he repeated finally, shaking his head dubiously. "Impossible."

"Yeah, so is amping up your own IQ," shot back Smith. "And no, she hasn't achieved it. Yet. But it's only a matter of time. She has managed to *double* the span of human life, though. Not immortality, but certainly good enough to win the high school science fair," he added wryly.

"You're sure about this?"

Smith nodded. "You can never be positive until the first person treated lives to be a hundred and sixty, but I understand the animal and early human evidence is pretty strong."

"How does she do it?"

"Hell if I know. It takes an injection, repeated once a year. I have no idea what it does. All I know is that it slows aging to a crawl, so that a man of seventy will have all the physical characteristics and abilities of a man of thirty-five."

"Remarkable," said Desh in wonder.

"We believe she sees immortality as a three stage process. She's already completed the first stage. The second stage would be to design microscopic nanorobots that would be injected into the bloodstream, patrolling and repairing the body and replicating themselves as necessary. A vast army of tiny MDs. This could theoretically extend the lifespan five hundred years or more." He paused. "The third stage, her ultimate goal, would be set up an artificial matrix into which she can transfer her intellect. She could repeat this process any number of times. That would be closer to true immortality."

"What do you mean by an artificial matrix to transfer her intellect? Are you saying she plans to transfer her consciousness someday into an artificial body? Turn herself into some kind of cyborg?"

"I don't know. Maybe. Maybe she'll just clone herself every fifty years and transfer her consciousness into a younger version of herself. And what we think she's trying to do may never be possible. Even for her. But that's beside the point. The key for our discussion now is that she has already managed to do the impossible: doubling human life expectancy."

Incredible, thought Desh, as he allowed himself to truly consider the earth shattering implications of this discovery. More than incredible—surreal. But as he thought about it, it all made perfectly logical sense. If he assumed Kira Miller really could optimize her mind and become autistic-savant-like in every area of thought, she wouldn't focus these transcendent abilities on solving pedestrian problems. No, she would go after the ultimate prize: conquering death. The ultimate Holy Grail of the species. And she was a genius in gene therapy even before any enhancements.

Now the journals Kira had been receiving at home made perfect sense. *Human Brain Mapping. The Journal of Cognitive Neuroscience.* Both would be quite useful in her efforts to rewire her own brain. But she had also subscribed to a journal having to do with gerontology, the branch of science that dealt with the aging process. Desh had found this odd at the time, but hadn't thought any more of it. But now the pieces of the puzzle seemed to be fitting together quite nicely.

Desh pulled himself from his reverie. "But if she was able to accomplish something like this," he said, "why didn't she announce it? She'd be recognized as the greatest scientist in history. She'd be an instant billionaire as well."

"You don't really *get* her yet, do you?" said Smith in frustration. "She doesn't get off on extending life or bringing joy to the world. She gets off on the opposite. Think Adolph Hitler, not Florence Nightingale." He paused. "Kira Miller has discovered the ultimate leverage. She can amass wealth and power beyond imagining. Every person on the planet wants to delay their aging. And she's the only game in town. If she takes her treatment public, anyone who pays for it can have extended life. But if she keeps it and only doles it out to a select few, she can acquire a level of power that goes far beyond mere money."

Desh nodded grimly. People had gone to extraordinary lengths throughout history in the pursuit of money alone, but that would pale to the lengths to which they would go for the fountain of youth.

"By using her treatment as currency, we're convinced she has a number of powerful people in her pocket already," said Smith. "Including a mole in USASOC." He shook his head in frustration. "Although it isn't as if anyone she's treating is announcing themselves. She controls supply, so if they do anything to cross her, she cuts them off. Bye-bye fountain of youth."

"Has anyone come forward?"

"Only one. And not willingly. A billionaire industrialist who helped finance her early on."

Desh pursed his lips in thought. "What about intelligence enhancement? Is she leveraging this in the same way?"

"Doesn't have to. Extending life gives her all the power she needs. As far as we know she's keeping enhanced IQ all to herself. Right now she's the goose that lays the golden eggs. The *only* such goose in existence. She can leverage the fruits of her enhanced genius, but why give up her golden-egg laying monopoly?"

"Makes sense," allowed Desh.

"Besides," added Smith, "she'd have far fewer takers for this therapy. People tend to get nervous about a treatment that screws with their brain chemistry. You can't make dramatic changes to the brain without risking irreversible changes in personality." He shook his head in disgust. "Others might not be as eager as she is to transform themselves into something not quite human."

Desh knew that if Kira was to be believed, she was far from eager to undertake any further transformations. In fact, she claimed to be horrified by what her treatment was doing to her and determined to never transform herself again. Whether this was true or not remained to be seen.

They drove on for several minutes as Desh tried to get his mind around the immense implications of what he had been told. Finally, he broke the silence. "Now I understand why you had the colonel make sure I didn't go after her once I found her. And why your men were using tranquilizer darts. You can't risk harming the only being in existence who knows the location of the fountain of youth."

"That's right."

"And if I did catch her, you were worried that she'd hypnotize me with her charm or bribe me. That's what you were getting at when you asked if she had offered me anything. You wanted to know if she tried to buy me off with promises of extended life."

"Yes. She would have had to convince you it really worked, have you talk to some of her other, ah . . . clients, that sort of thing, but I did wonder if she had at least raised the prospect."

"She didn't say a single word about it."

"I believe you. Perhaps she would have if we hadn't intervened." He paused and then sighed heavily. "But you see what we're up against. How can you trust anyone when she can offer them the keys to the fountain of youth?"

"Which is why you didn't share the entire truth with Colonel Connelly," said Desh knowingly. "And why you kept me under surveillance."

"Exactly. I don't trust *anyone* where Kira Miller is concerned. If you ignored Connelly's instructions and captured her, she could offer you the ultimate bribe to gain her freedom. At that point there is no guarantee that you would follow through and call us in. We didn't want to leave that to your discretion."

That could well have been her plan, Desh realized. She had told him her goal was to recruit him to her side, perhaps their discussion was prelude to her revealing what she considered the ultimate recruiting tool.

"I can't be bought," said Desh firmly. "Even with extended life."

Smith nodded. "Again, I believe you. Your military records show that you are a man of impeccable integrity, Mr. Desh. But even so, any man who says he wouldn't be at least a tiny bit tempted to drink from the fountain is a liar."

"Including you?"

"Including me," acknowledged Smith.

Desh pursed his lips in thought. Smith had referred to his military records and said they spoke to his integrity. But Kira had claimed to have made a thorough study of him, including these records. If this was true, she would have known how highly he valued his integrity. In fact, she had said that this trait, among others, was the reason she wanted to recruit him in the first place. But if this were the case, she would have known any attempt at a bribe, regardless of the lure, would have failed. So maybe this hadn't been her plan, after all.

Smith had cleared up some questions but many more remained.

"So what about the terrorist connection and Ebola plot," said Desh. "Is this just a fabrication? Did you invent it to get everyone hunting for her?"

"I wish this were the case," said Smith gravely. He yanked the steering wheel to the left to avoid a grisly mass of fur and blood the headlights had suddenly revealed ahead of them. "But I'm afraid it's very real," he continued a few seconds later, the car steady once again as the unrecognizable road-kill receded behind them. "And with her abilities you can be sure the attack will succeed."

Desh looked confused. "But why would she work with terrorists?" he asked. "It doesn't make any sense. What can she gain from a bio-weapons attack? She has all the money and power she could want."

"You would think," agreed Smith. "But apparently not. We don't know what her angle is on the Ebola plot. But rest assured, whatever it is, it moves her agenda forward. She's a far better chess player than we are. Just because we can't understand one of her moves doesn't mean it's random." He shrugged. "Maybe she plans on blackmailing the government to call off the attack in the eleventh hour. Maybe she wants to get in bed with powerful people on both sides of the war on terror for her own ends. We don't know. All we know is that the threat is very real and she's behind it. Stopping this attack is still the primary purpose of the Op, regardless of any other reason we have for wanting her."

Desh shook his head irritably. "That's bullshit and you know it!" he snapped. "Getting the secret of extended life is the primary purpose of the Op." Before Smith could respond he added, "Suppose I had her in my sights, and I knew for certain that killing her would end the bioterror threat. Would you have me pull the trigger?"

"It's not as easy as that," replied Smith. "We need to know what she knows about the Ebola plot. Taking her alive could well be the only way to stop it."

"You're ducking the question. I asked a hypothetical. Would you support killing her if you knew, *with certainty*, that this would end the threat? Suppose, even, it was the *only* way to end the threat." He stared intently at the wiry driver. "Well?"

Smith hesitated. "It still isn't that simple. If you killed her, you might stop the murder of several million people, but at the expense of extended life for all of humankind now and in future generations. Where do you draw the line? Would you save two million people from dying an average of thirty years sooner than otherwise, even if you knew it was at the cost of preventing more than six *billion* people, in this generation alone, from living longer? Say an average of *seventy years* longer?"

"I see," said Desh in disgust. "So it's just a tradeoff. An easily solved mathematical calculation."

"Not necessarily. But there are important considerations that need to be made. Who's to say that humanity will ever have this chance again?"

"So if two million people have to be sacrificed for the greater good, so be it?"

"Look, the point is we're talking about a hypothetical here. It's unlikely that killing her will stop the bioterror threat. In fact, it's more likely that killing her before she can be interrogated will *end* any chance we'll ever have of stopping it. So no tradeoff needs to be made. Capturing her alive is critical to stopping the Ebola threat *and* to getting the secret of life extension."

"Maybe," said Desh dubiously. "But I doubt it. She's the only one capable of perfecting the virus they're planning to use. Unless it's ready to go, everything I know tells me that killing her will end the threat. But regardless of whether you believe that or not, just do me the favor of not pretending this is mostly about bioterror."

Smith frowned. "Even if I conceded your point, how does this change anything? Kira Miller is still out there somewhere, and we have to find her." He paused and then added pointedly, "And you could be the key. She took a huge risk capturing you. The question is . . . why?"

"I don't have any idea."

"Another move that doesn't make any sense," said Smith in frustration. "If all she wanted was muscle, she could have as much as she needed at any time. You're not wealthy or highly-placed. As good as you are, with her brilliance and resources and unknown benefactors, you had very little chance of finding her. Given everything we know, you don't merit even becoming a pawn in her chess game, let alone a piece of higher value. But the risk she took was uncharacteristic, so we must be missing something."

"I'm just as mystified as you are."

"I doubt we'll ever figure it out," said Smith. "Her enhanced mind can work on a plane that we can't come close to reaching. The question is," he added pointedly, "are you still important to her for some reason?"

"Why do I suddenly feel like a worm right before the fisherman sticks it on a hook?"

"Look, Mr. Desh, you represent an unprecedented opportunity to finally get a handle on this woman. We have to seize this chance. Will you help us?"

Desh considered. There was still something about Smith that he didn't quite trust. His gut told him there was far more to this story. But regardless of Smith's ultimate motivations, there was no question Kira Miller had to be stopped. And Desh knew that, alone, he was overmatched. And even if he refused to help further, this wouldn't stop Kira from coming after him again if she was intent on doing so.

Desh frowned deeply and then nodded. "Okay . . . Smith. I'll help you." He waited until Smith turned from the road to glance at him and then locked onto his eyes with a laser-like intensity. "But this time we're going to do it my way."

20

The darkness was beginning to gradually give way to the coming dawn, and tiny flecks of water appeared on the windshield as the early morning drizzle that had been forecast arrived on schedule. In another month this same precipitation would result in snow flurries. Smith set the wipers to a ten second delay between strokes and waited for Desh to spell out his terms, the silence of the twilight drive broken only by the intermittent squeaking of the wiper blades.

"Pull off here," instructed Desh, pointing.

Smith raised his eyebrows. "A shortcut to your apartment?" he asked.

"No. It makes more sense for you to drop me at Griffin's apartment. I need to retrieve my clothes and watch," he explained. "Not to mention my SUV."

Smith said nothing but exited the highway as instructed, decelerating rapidly to a stop at the end of the long off-ramp. He glanced at the gas gauge and proposed they stop for fuel. Less than a minute later they pulled into a nearby gas station. While Smith began to fill the tank the gnawing in Desh's stomach reminded him just how hungry and thirsty he had become. He also realized that he didn't have his wallet with him and was forced to borrow ten dollars from the black-ops officer, feeling slightly foolish.

Desh entered the store's mini-mart and pulled a thirty-two-ounce bottle of water from the cooler and an orange juice for Smith, and then tore two bananas from a fresh bunch near the register, both for himself, and walked to the counter. The entire time he watched Smith attentively through the transparent storefront to make sure he didn't open the trunk and try to regain access to his weapons. He and Desh appeared to be on the same side, but that didn't mean Desh was prepared to trust him. Whatever was going on, and whoever could be believed, the stakes were very, very high, and he was determined to err on the side of paranoia.

A number of nagging questions still gnawed at him. If Kira Miller really did have some of the wealthiest and most powerful people in the world in her pocket as Smith suggested, then why hadn't she had them use their influence to call off the manhunt? And how was it that she wasn't better protected? The beneficiaries of her therapy would have an enormous vested interest in her welfare and survival. If she died, so did their longevity. Even if she had refused bodyguards, they would have activated armies of guardian angels, staying in the shadows but ensuring that the Smiths of the world didn't get nearly as close to her as they had at the motel.

There was far more going on than Desh understood. He was convinced he was fumbling in the dark, feeling the elephant's trunk and being persuaded it was a snake. He needed to go back to basic principles. If he believed Kira Miller really had been able to optimize her intelligence, it wasn't much of a stretch to believe she had also successfully developed a longevity therapy. And if this were the case, then all bets were truly off. Smith portrayed himself as being on the side of the angels, and maybe this had largely been true in the past. But what about now, in this situation? What would Smith do if he really did have Kira in his grasp? And what about the people above him? Could Desh trust this group to do the right thing once they had her? Would they simply pry the secret from her and give it to the world? It would take but a single weak link for her to bribe herself to freedom or for someone to take her place. She was the key to unlimited power, and if only a single corrupt person was in the loop, he could obtain her secrets for himself, kill her, and disappear; potentially becoming even a bigger monster than she had been.

Desh believed that dangerous character traits such as megalomania, sadism, and sociopathy tended to be enriched in populations of people who had risen to positions of power and influence. This enrichment was even more pronounced at the top of organizations such as the CIA and the military, to which people with these pathologies tended to gravitate preferentially. This was especially true of Black Operations divisions, which existed in the shadows and had little accountability. Not that there weren't plenty of good men high up in the chain of command of these organizations with a passion for serving their country and doing what they thought was right. But all it took was one bad apple at or near the top, and Desh was convinced that with a lure this seductive the odds that one existed were almost a hundred percent. So even if Smith was a saint, turning Kira over to him and his agency could be a disaster.

As Desh walked slowly back to the car, completely oblivious to the drizzle hitting his face, he was hit by a stark realization. If he really believed his own logic, there was only one way he could be absolutely certain the longevity therapy would be unveiled for the benefit all the people of the world: if he did so himself. It was a troubling thought. He had no wish to take matters into his own hands, but unless he could find a flaw in his logic it was a prospect he could not ignore.

A few minutes later they were back on the road. Smith took a sip of orange juice and turned to his passenger. "All right," he said. "We're refueled and I'll have you at Griffin's in less than an hour. So what do you want?" he asked bluntly.

Desh slowly chewed and swallowed a large piece of banana, organizing his thoughts. "First of all," he began. "I'm in charge. You and your men take orders from me." He scanned Smith's face with keen interest, watching for his reaction.

"Go on," said Smith noncommittally, sliding back the center console to reveal two cup holders and shoving his plastic orange juice container into the one nearest him.

"Secondly, kill the listening and homing devices immediately. The only thing these devices and your surveillance will accomplish is guarantee Kira Miller never tries to contact me again."

"They didn't stop her the first time," noted Smith.

Desh shook his head. "I know how she thinks," he said firmly. "The reports all say she's brilliant. And she is. But I know she's also something far more dangerous: she's savvy. And she doesn't make mistakes. She knows you'll try to use me to get to her and she'll be more careful than ever."

"We can track you in a way she can't detect."

"*Really*?" said Desh skeptically. "I wouldn't count on that if I were you. You're underestimating her. Trust me, she'd smell you if you were in the next galaxy. I don't think she'll come within a thousand miles of me now, knowing that I'm bait. But if she does and then catches your scent, she'll bolt and we'll never have another chance." He stared at Smith with an unwavering intensity. "I want your guarantee on this."

Smith paused in thought and then sighed resignedly. "Okay," he said finally, clearly not happy about it.

"Good. I'll continue my efforts to find her as I was tasked to do, since I don't think she'll come to me again. And Smith," he added, "I *will* call you in when I find her as per the original plan." He paused. "Just so you know, I also intend to continue working with Griffin. He's very good at what he does and my gut tells me he's a good man. It goes without saying that the no surveillance rule goes for Griffin and anyone else I'm working with as well," he added pointedly.

"Can he do an effective job for you without having a glimmer of what's really going on?"

"I think so, yes," said Desh. He popped the last piece of his first banana in his mouth, swallowed, and then chased it with a long drink of water.

"So now let's turn to point number three," said Desh. "I have to have full authority to capture her myself. I have the tranquilizer gun I borrowed from your colleague, and I can add other non-lethal weaponry to my arsenal. If I'm wrong and she does come after me again, I won't pass up the chance to take her down."

Smith frowned and looked unconvinced.

"Trust me," added Desh. "Your fountain keeper is in good hands. I'll only act if I think I have to. Otherwise, I'll call you in. And I won't use lethal force."

"It's not like I have a choice," muttered Smith. "If you're in a position to capture her and I'm not there, you're going to do whatever the hell you want, regardless of what I agree to."

"I *will* take her alive. And I can't be bought. You'll just have to trust me."

Smith drained the last of the orange juice as he considered. "Okay," he said, shoving the empty juice container into the cup holder. "I'll agree to your conditions." He eyed Desh intently. "But I have one of my own. My men told me they discovered you had used the cell phone you had, ah . . . borrowed, to contact Jim Connelly. From now on, *I'm* your only contact. You agree not to contact Connelly again no matter what happens. We know there's a mole at USASOC. Calling the colonel plays right into Kira Miller's hands."

"Will you tell him it was you and your men who crashed the party tonight and fill him in on the longevity angle?"

Smith's expression turned to one of disbelief, as if Desh had lost his mind. "She's *doubled* the span of human life," he said emphatically. "There's no greater secret in the world. It's on a need to know basis. And Connelly still doesn't need to know." He frowned and shook his head. "If we don't keep this under wraps we could have dozens and dozens of factions all warring with each other trying to get their hands on her. You think this Op is a clusterfuck now—" He raised his eyebrows and let the thought hang. "I'll tell him it was me at the motel, but that's where I'll stop."

Desh considered. "Agreed," he said. "We have an understanding."

Desh directed Smith to turn right. "I'll expect you to send me an e-mail message with the locations of all bugs and homing devices you've planted anywhere near me or anyone I'm working with."

Smith nodded.

"Oh, and check the list twice, will you," added Desh pointedly. "I wouldn't want you to accidentally forget any."

21

David Desh stood in the parking lot of Griffin's apartment and waited for Smith to drive out of sight. Satisfied, he returned to where he had parked his Suburban and removed a sleek leather case from the passenger seat, which contained state-of-the-art bug detection equipment and an inch-thick sheaf of hundred-dollar bills, compressed tightly by a money clip. Connelly had provided a ridiculously large advance and Desh had withdrawn far more than just Griffin's retainer from the bank the previous morning. Case in hand, he quickly made his way back to Apartment 14 D. He had walked down this same hallway, and into an ambush, only the night before; yet it seemed like ages ago.

Griffin's apartment was unlocked and the giant was sprawled out on the floor right where he had been left, although he was now breathing more deeply and Desh guessed he could be awakened at any time. He carefully cut the plasticuff bracelet from around Griffin's wrist and tossed it into the kitchen trash along with the link Kira had removed the night before.

He removed the bug-detection equipment from the leather case and began a careful sweep of the apartment. Proficiency at detecting and removing listening devices was critical in the executive protection business. Fleming had the most advanced equipment made, which was out of the price range of all but the wealthiest private citizens. Desh found two wireless bugs and placed them in a soundproof container he pulled from the case. Smith had assured Desh he would kill all bugs immediately. Desh didn't believe him for an instant.

Desh changed into his own pants, pulled his cell phone from the pocket where it had spent the night, checked it for messages, and rearmed himself. He retrieved his windbreaker and zipped it over the gray sweatshirt to hide his shoulder holster. His shirt and undershirt had been cut from his body the night before and were ruined. He gathered them up, along with the sweatpants, and piled them nearby for later disposal.

This completed, Desh gently shook Griffin until he began to stir.

Griffin opened his eyes and appeared to be in a fog, struggling to make sense of the man standing before him. Finally, a name and a context must have swum into place to match the face. "David Desh?" he mumbled drunkenly in disbelief.

"Yeah. It's me. Time to wake up."

"Why am I on the floor?" he asked, confused.

"How do you feel?"

Griffin's brain hadn't quite finished rebooting and his responses were slow. "Great," he said at last, almost in surprise. "Never felt better."

Desh nodded. Kira Miller had assured him this would be the case and in this, at least, she hadn't lied.

While Griffin roused himself and finally got up, Desh made a pot of coffee. Several minutes later Griffin joined Desh at his kitchen table, sipping the coffee gratefully.

"You had a visitor last night," began Desh. "Do you remember anything about it?"

Griffin searched his mind but finally shook his head in frustration. "Not a thing."

"It was Kira Miller."

"*Kira Miller!*" repeated Griffin in alarm.

"Don't worry. She just knocked you out and left. She used a benign drug. You'll be fine. And she won't trouble you again, I guarantee it."

"What did she want?"

"Me."

Griffin looked at Desh as if seeing him for the first time. "You really look like hell, you know that?"

Desh smiled weakly. Given that he was sleep deprived, unshaven, uncombed, and had spent part of the night inside the trunk of a car, he didn't doubt it. "Thanks. I feel like hell too."

"What happened to you? And what are you doing here now?" Griffin scratched his head. "For that matter, if she was after *you,* why knock *me* out?"

"I'd love to answer all of your questions, Matt, but I really can't." He held out his hands helplessly.

"Look, David, this secrecy crap has to go. My apartment was broken into and I was knocked out. I'm up to my *ass* in this. I need to know what's going on."

Desh sighed. "You make a good point," he said. "Maybe at some point I'll tell you everything, but not right now. There's too much going on and I don't know who to trust. It's better for both of us if you don't know any more than you do already."

"Then find yourself another hacker," snapped Griffin.

"I don't blame you for being angry," said Desh sympathetically. "A known psychopath and murderer has attacked you, and you want to know what you've gotten yourself into. But I'm asking you to trust me. Eventually, I'll tell you everything." He paused. "And I'll throw in a fifty percent bonus as hazard pay for what you've already gone through."

"You can't spend money when you're dead," noted Griffin, unimpressed.

"I'll see to your safety," Desh assured him. "This was a one time thing. It won't happen again."

Griffin eyed him skeptically but finally nodded. "Okay—for now at least," he added cautiously.

"Good. Now that that's settled," said Desh, changing the subject rapidly so Griffin wouldn't have time to reconsider, "I want you to find everything there is to know about Kira Miller. If it's accessible by computer, I want it. School records, guidance counselor notes, scholarly articles, books she buys online—hell for that matter *anything* she buys online, from perfume to paperclips. I told you about the two teachers from Middlebrook, her high school alma mater. One was murdered and the other went missing about sixteen years or so ago. Find anything you can about this. Newspaper articles, police reports; everything. I want to build as complete a profile of her as is humanly possible."

Griffin studied him carefully. "All right," he said reluctantly. "As long as we're still trying to find a mass murderer, I'm willing to take some personal risk. But this had better not veer off into questionable territory," he warned. He pointed to the plaque on his desk. "Remember, I use my skills for good only."

"And that's what I like about you, Matt," said Desh smoothly. He sighed. "While you're working on this assignment, do you mind if I crash on your couch? I'm exhausted. The prospect of driving home right now without any sleep is looking pretty bleak."

"*Mi sofa es su sofa,*" responded Griffin, his amiable self once again.

"Thanks," said Desh gratefully. He laid down on the couch and closed his eyes.

Desh re-opened his eyes with a start to find the massive figure of Matt Griffin standing over him, shaking him roughly with an anxious but irate expression. Desh glanced at his watch. He had been sleeping for almost two hours. Incredible. He had closed his eyes just an instant before. He was still tired, but this period of concentrated sleep would be enough to allow him to operate at a high level for the rest of the day, if necessary.

"What?" mumbled Desh worriedly as the rage on Griffin's face began to register.

Griffin thrust a scrap of paper in front of his eyes. ARE WE BEING BUGGED?

"No," said Desh aloud, shaking his head "We were, but I cleared them. Why? What's going on?"

Griffin handed him a piece of paper. "You got an e-mail from Kira Miller," he snapped.

Desh bolted upright, now fully awake.

"Read it and tell me what the hell is going on!" barked Griffin angrily.

Desh's heart pounded furiously as he turned to the message.

From: xc86vzi
To: Matt Griffin
Re: Urgent! For David Desh

Matt Griffin:

David probably removed any bugs from your apartment, but remain silent about this message and assume you're being bugged until he indicates otherwise. Please give this message to David immediately.

David Desh:

I bugged the sweatpants I provided to you as a precautionary measure. Once again, I'm sorry about the invasion of privacy. I modified the bug to make it undetectable by your equipment (Impossible—I know). I just finished listening to the record of your conversations with Connelly and Smith that were forwarded to my computer.

Desh stifled a curse and clenched his teeth in fury. She was always one step ahead of him. She had correctly named the two people he had spoken with during the night, which meant she wasn't bluffing. He was being outsmarted at every turn. He retrieved the sweatpants he had worn the night before, opened the door, and threw them as far down the hallway as he could manage. Griffin watched him angrily, not saying a word.

Desh was *furious* with himself, but forced his focus back to the e-mail message, knowing that self-recrimination would have to wait. He continued reading:

We need to finish our discussion. I have precious little time now to provide details (I was planning to last night) but a batch of the gellcaps I told you about were stolen years ago. There is another enhanced human at large (or "golden goose" to use Smith's terminology). He is the one who is ruthless and has powerful people in his pocket, not me. He is also the one behind the effort to find me. It is critical that he be stopped.

Smith is lying to you: the rival who stole my treatment is behind the Ebola plot, not me.

I know you don't trust me, but trust this: Jim Connelly won't live out the day if you don't act. You need to warn him and then bring him fully up to speed. You called him and raised his suspicions and he's in a powerful position to pry and make life uncomfortable for the true psychopaths here. Like you, he is a man who can't be bought, so they will kill him to prevent him from learning the truth. Don't trust me, but please err on the side of caution. Stakes this high bring out the aberrant personality types we spoke of like moths to a flame.

They will kill you as soon as they come to believe you won't lead them to me. They will clean up behind you as well, which means killing Matt Griffin the first chance they get.

Good luck

Kira Miller

Desh looked up from the message in alarm and immediately was met by Griffin's icy stare. "Can you tell me what the hell I've gotten myself into?" he demanded. "Ebola plot! What the hell does that mean? She says some group out there plans to kill you and me both. You said I'd be safe. It sure doesn't sound that way!" he spat.

"Okay, Matt, no more secrets," said Desh, his voice calm. "You're far more involved than I ever expected you to be, and for that I am truly sorry. You deserve the truth. But I need to think through the implications of this e-mail first. How securely was it sent? Could it have been intercepted?"

"No way. She's as good as it gets and my computer is a fortress."

Desh nodded, not surprised. As usual, she was careful and smart. But was the message simply another of her manipulations? Desh was getting awfully tired of being a pawn in a game for which he didn't know either the rules *or* the players.

He made a snap decision. Whether Kira had her own nemesis or not was something he could consider at a later time. But her logic was sound and his gut told him to take her warning about Connelly very seriously. Jim Connelly was a good man and Desh agreed that he couldn't be bought. But the jury was still out on Smith.

Desh was annoyed with himself that even in his current paranoid mindset he had failed to at least consider the possibility that Connelly's digging would make him a target. If Desh was going to survive this mess he would have to do better.

"Do you have a car?" asked Desh.

"Why does that question make me nervous?" answered Griffin guardedly.

"Connelly could be in someone's crosshairs even as we speak. We need to get him in motion immediately and set up a meeting with him so I can bring him up to speed. We can't risk taking my SUV. I'll tell you everything I know on the way."

"This woman is a psychopathic killer. Why would you even *consider* following her advice?"

"If she's wrong, we'll have wasted time and inconvenienced the colonel. But if she's right, we'll have saved his life." Desh paused. "I assume you have a car, correct?" he persisted.

Griffin looked ill but finally nodded unhappily. "What if I'd prefer to stay here and let you meet with this Connelly by yourself?"

Desh shrugged. "Suit yourself. But in that case I won't be able to tell you what you're up against until I see you again. And you have to ask yourself if you feel safer on your own right now—or with me."

Griffin frowned. "I'll go," he mumbled unhappily.

"Good. Can you jump on the computer and find the midway point by car between here and Fort Bragg, North Carolina?"

Griffin sat at his computer and seconds later a satellite map appeared on the large plasma screen. The image of the East Coast of the United States was almost uniformly green and not a single sign of human habitation, including the largest cities, could be detected. The Atlantic Ocean appeared as a much deeper and more vibrant shade of blue than when viewed from the beach. Griffin overlaid the satellite imagery with a driving map that highlighted the route between the two locations, spotting a promising town almost immediately. His hands flew over the keys.

"Emporia Virginia," he announced. "It's a hundred and seventy-two miles from D.C. and a hundred and fifty-five miles from Bragg."

"Good," said Desh. "Any State Parks? Woods? That sort of thing."

Griffin worked the mouse to display a helicopter's-eye view of Emporia and its vicinity and began to fly this virtual helicopter slowly forward. He called up further information on the town and displayed it on one of the smaller monitors. "There's a hydropower dam in Emporia on the Meherrin River. The river flows northwesterly from the dam."

"Find a two-lane road that parallels the river and woods and follow it northwest," instructed Desh. He had decided to borrow from Kira's playbook. Her choice of motels had been tactically ideal. "Try to locate a quarter-mile to a half-mile chunk of woods flanked by roads on either side. Easily accessible but fairly isolated."

Griffin swooped down to the Meherrin River dam and found a nearby road that fit Desh's requirements. He followed the road as instructed, zooming closer when he found a candidate location and back out again when he needed a more panoramic view. Whatever satellite database he had hacked into allowed him to get clearer pictures and zoom in more closely than he would have been able to do using the satellite imagery available to the general public.

"I think I've got it," said Griffin.

Desh studied the screen. Sure enough, about twenty miles from Emporia another road appeared on the right flank, sandwiching the woods between it and the road Griffin had been following. The roads ran parallel on either side of the woods for several miles.

"Continue to follow your original road, but slower and from a lower altitude," said Desh.

Griffin swooped in closer and did as instructed. Desh pursed his lips in concentration and studied the rapidly changing landscape. "Stop," he barked. "Back up just a little."

Desh pointed to an area of road that abutted a section of the tree line that had a break in it. A car could pull off at this point and circle back around without hindrance to a pocket-shaped clearing, about fifty yards away, that couldn't be seen from the road. He only hoped that enough of the trees had retained their leaves to provide adequate cover. Since the satellite data was somewhat dated, it was impossible from the imagery to know for sure.

"Get the GPS coordinates for this break in the tree line and write them down for me while I make a call," said Desh.

Desh lifted the receiver of Griffin's phone. It was cordless but still a landline, which was what he needed. Cell phone traffic was far too easy to intercept. He had checked the phone carefully for listening devices previously and it was clean. He dialed Connelly's scrambled line at his office at USASOC, praying he would be in.

It was picked up on the fist ring. "David?"

"That's right."

"I'm glad you called. And on my secure line at that," added Connelly approvingly. "I've begun looking into this Kira Miller case more carefully and I'm hitting roadblocks that shouldn't be there for someone with my clearance. I think you're right. There's a lot more going on here than meets the eye."

"Colonel, I've learned more since we last spoke. Not enough to complete the picture, but enough to suspect you may have just kicked a hornet's nest. I think you could be in danger. I recommend you leave your office immediately. Write this down," he said. Desh gestured to Griffin who handed him the newly scribed GPS coordinates. Desh read them carefully to Connelly. "The coordinates I just gave you are to a short break in the tree line that parallels the road you'll be on. Otherwise the tree line is unbroken for many miles. If you go off road there you'll find a pocket in the woods, hidden from the road. Meet me there in as close to three hours from now as you can manage. First check your clothing and car for bugs and assume you're being followed."

"Roger that," said Connelly, trusting Desh enough to follow his instructions without asking any questions.

"I'll be with a friend: about six-five, three hundred pounds, bushy beard. I'll explain everything when I see you." Desh paused. "Before we sign off," he added, "has Smith contacted you yet today to explain what last night was all about?"

"Smith?"

"It's an obvious alias. I'm talking about the person you asked me to call in when I found Kira Miller. Black-Ops officer; short, wiry. Scar under his ear."

"I have no idea what you're talking about, David," said Connelly in alarm. "Black-Ops? I was told that number is to the private cell phone of my boss at MacDill: Brigadier General Evan Gordon."

22

The army, navy, air force, and marines each had their own Special Operations Command, but all four reported in to the US Special Operations Command, or USSOCOM, at MacDill Air Force Base in Florida, headed by a four-star general. It made sense that this case warranted attention higher up the chain of command and that the contact information had been for Connelly's boss.

Desh felt his skin crawl. The news that Smith wasn't who he claimed to be significantly increased the chance that Kira had been right and Connelly *was* in imminent danger. This called into question the veracity of everything that Smith had told him. Desh knew he needed to consider the full implications of this new information and discuss this further with Connelly, but that would have to wait for another time. He ended the conversation quickly so the colonel could begin taking steps to protect himself.

"Ready to go?" asked Griffin when Desh was off the phone.

"Not yet. I need to think," said Desh. He lowered his head for almost a full minute as Griffin waited anxiously.

Desh finally lifted his head and looked at Griffin thoughtfully. "It's possible that we're no longer under surveillance or we're being surveilled by friendlies," he said. "But we can't be certain of this, so we need to freeze anyone watching. We need to make sure they don't have any reason to point their satellites at the exits of this building while we're leaving."

"What are you talking about? Whoever is after us can't just access satellites and get real-time imagery of whatever they want on a whim."

Desh raised his eyebrows.

Griffin swallowed hard. "Come on, David," he said nervously. "Are you saying these people are so high up in Big Brother they can authorize real-time satellite surveillance of us?"

"I have reason to believe so, yes."

"Holy Christ!" barked Griffin. "We're totally and completely screwed."

"Don't count us out just yet," said Desh. "I have an idea. If we can convince them we'll be staying here for a while they'll have no reason to point a satellite at your apartment complex."

"How do you know they aren't watching the exits the old fashioned way?"

"I'll reconnoiter the area before we leave, but I don't think they are. They've told me they're calling off the dogs to get my cooperation. They know I'll be checking carefully to see if they've gone back on their word."

Griffin didn't look convinced. "So what's your plan?"

Desh told him. He would remove the bugs from the container in which he had placed them and assume they were still active. Then they would put on a little play for their audience. "For a hacker with your social engineering skills this should be a snap," said Desh encouragingly. "Don't overact, don't speak woodenly as if you're reciting lines, and don't speak directly into the bug. They'll pick up your voice from wherever you are. Just be yourself. If this seems staged it'll blow up in our faces."

Griffin frowned. "Thanks for not putting any pressure on me," he said dryly. He paused for a few seconds to get things straight in his head, took a deep breath, and then gestured for Desh to proceed.

Desh carefully removed the bugs, putting a finger to his lips unnecessarily, and then nodded at Griffin to begin.

Griffin's face was a mask of concentration. "David?" he said in disbelief. "David Desh? Wake up."

"Wha—" mumbled Desh.

"Wake up and tell me what the hell's going on here?" demanded Griffin accusingly. "Why did I just wake up in the middle of my floor? What the hell are you doing here sleeping on my couch?" He delivered the lines convincingly, throwing himself smoothly into the role as Desh had hoped he would.

"Sorry," said Desh, doing a good job of sounding groggy. "I stopped over a few hours ago and couldn't get you awake. I fell asleep myself while I waited for you to sleep it off. I was exhausted." He paused. "Still am for that matter."

Desh went on to repeat the conversation they had had earlier when he had filled Griffin in on the night before. He then repeated the specifics of the assignment he wanted Griffin to work on, an extensive foray into Kira Miller's past. "Look, Matt, I'm really sorry about this, but I still need to regenerate. Do you mind if I continue to sleep on your couch while you work?"

"Go ahead," said Griffin.

"Thanks. Can you wake me in exactly two hours and give me a progress report?"

"Will do," responded Griffin.

Desh gave the thumbs up signal to Griffin and then put his finger to his lips. He carefully returned the bugs to the soundproof container.

"Nicely done, Matt," he said appreciatively.

With any luck anyone keeping tabs on them would relax for a while and decide that any satellite use for the next few hours would be a waste of resources.

Desh continued to visualize different scenarios that might arise and considered making a stop at his apartment for bulletproof vests, but quickly ruled this out. It would be risky and take too much time. Besides, the vests could only stop handgun fire and not rifle-fire. If the military were involved in this, even a small rogue element, they would assume he was wearing a vest and choose their weaponry accordingly. In this case the vests would be a disadvantage rather than an advantage. He enjoyed the *Star Wars* movies as much as the next guy, but had always seen Storm Troopers as the height of stupidity: their head-to-toe white body armor did nothing but slow them down and make their movements awkward while failing to protect them one iota from even the weakest blaster.

Desh removed the thick wad of hundreds from the case he had brought and held them out in front of his face to show Griffin. "An ample supply of cash can prove just as useful in certain emergency situations as a weapon can," he said, and then shoved the bills into his front pants pocket.

Griffin raised his eyebrows. "And here all these years I was under the impression that carrying a huge amount of cash actually put you in *greater* danger, not less. Who knew?"

Desh grinned. "Do you have a cell phone on you?" he asked.

Griffin nodded.

"Leave it. I'm sure you know they can be used as homing beacons."

Griffin pulled his phone from his pocket and set it on his desk. "Okay," he said, nodding toward Desh. "What about *your* phone?"

"It's a special design issued by my firm. It can't be tracked. You can't protect people effectively if their enemies can track you."

Desh slipped out the door and scouted the area for ten minutes, until he was satisfied the coast was clear. Even so, they took separate exits from the building, keeping their heads down and walking as unobtrusively as possible.

Griffin retrieved his car, a blue Chrysler minivan, and met Desh two blocks from the apartment complex. Griffin slid over into the passenger seat. Desh jumped in, quickly adjusted the seat and mirrors, and drove off. The minivan hadn't had a bath in some time and it was cluttered with empty water bottles, Starbucks containers, and even an empty pizza box.

Desh turned to Griffin and raised his eyebrows. "A minivan?" he said with a smile. "Interesting choice for a single guy like you, Matt. I hear these are real chick magnets."

"You Special Forces sissies may need flashy sports cars to attract the fairer sex, but not us hackers," responded Griffin with mock bravado. "Women find us irresistible. We get swarmed like rock stars."

Desh laughed. "I see. So the minivan is actually a tactic to fend them off?"

"Exactly," replied Griffin with a grin.

"Good choice, then."

Griffin laughed. "Actually," he said, "I use it to haul around scores of old computers, sometimes rebuilding and reselling them and sometimes cannibalizing parts." He smiled slyly. "And as for women, I do very well for myself. And I really *don't* need a fancy car. I meet and attract them all the old fashioned way."

Desh gazed at Griffin quizzically.

"Online, of course," he said in amusement.

Desh's smile remained for several seconds. When it was finally gone, a grave expression replaced it. "All right, Matt," he said. "It's time to tell you what I know, incomplete as it is."

Griffin's face reflected both eagerness and anxiety, in equal measure.

Throughout the long drive to Emporia, Desh told Griffin everything he knew and the current state of his analysis, forcing himself to obey the speed limit as he did so; battling his nature so they wouldn't risk getting pulled over. The day remained overcast, with intermittent rain, although it appeared they were driving away from the rain rather than toward it.

When Desh had finished, Griffin was dumbfounded. "This is truly astonishing stuff here, David. If any of this is true the implications are staggering," he said.

Desh pursed his lips and nodded in agreement. "I know I've managed to put you in the middle of all this, but if it makes you feel any better, you and I could be standing at the crossroads of human history. The decisions we make now could well play a role in stopping a bioterror threat and bringing the fountain of youth to the world."

"Thanks David," said Griffin, a pained expression on his face. "Now I feel a lot more relaxed."

"I was shooting for inspiration."

"And you succeeded. I'm inspired and freaked out at the same time."

Desh smiled. "Why don't you tell me what you learned about Kira while I was asleep," he said.

Griffin was five minutes into his report when Desh's cell phone went off. He pulled it from his pocket and eyed the screen warily. It was Connelly. And given the call was unsecured, it had to be urgent. Connelly's cell, like Desh's, was untraceable, but it paid to keep the communication short and to the point.

"Yes," snapped Desh as he answered the call.

"I'm tracking non-stop toward our rendezvous point, with an ETA as planned," said Connelly. "Managed to flush out some company. I think I lost them but can't be sure."

"Understood," said Desh. He paused in thought for a moment and then added, "Stick with the original plan. I'll monitor your perimeter after you arrive."

"Copy that," said Connelly, ending the connection.

Griffin eyed Desh questioningly as he put his phone away.

"The colonel detected a car following him," explained Desh. "But he thinks he lost them."

"*Thinks* he lost them?" said Griffin nervously.

"We have to assume he hasn't."

"But I heard you say, 'stick with the original plan.' Why would you do that if you still think he might have been followed?"

"Because we need information and this might be our best chance to get some."

"How?"

"By setting up an ambush for any unwanted guests," responded Desh gravely.

Griffin shook his head vigorously. "No way!" he croaked, his lofty vocabulary invariably coming down to earth when he was scared or angry. "That's *not* what I signed on for. You may thrive on all this macho military bullshit, but I'm not interested in any of it."

Desh let out a heavy sigh and frowned deeply. "Me either, Matt," he mumbled wearily. "Me either."

23

Desh glanced impatiently at his watch once again and frowned. He was hidden from view behind a large tree trunk at the outer edge of the clearing, which was roughly the size of a basketball court, waiting for Connelly's arrival. He and Griffin had picked up a cab in Emporia. After instructing the driver to drop them off a quarter-mile from the meeting point they had finished their journey on foot. Desh had the tranquilizer gun in one pocket of his windbreaker and two spare clips for his .45 in the other.

Griffin was waiting twenty yards farther into the woods. Few of the trees were totally bare, while many of them held full complements of leaves that hadn't even begun to change color. Given the significant number of evergreens added to the mix, the woods provided adequate cover as Desh had hoped, with a thin cushion of colorful, newly fallen leaves on the ground.

Desh came to full alert. A car was approaching.

He relaxed slightly as it came into view and he recognized the colonel behind the wheel. Connelly carefully chose his route over the hardened ground, which hadn't experienced any of the rain that had fallen to the north, trying to minimize any evidence of the passage of his car. He killed the engine and cautiously got out, alert for anyone following. He was wearing civilian slacks and a heavy green knit sweater. Judging from his bulk, Desh guessed he was wearing a vest as well.

Connelly surveyed the tree line methodically. When his eyes reached Desh's hiding place, Desh moved his head into Connelly's line of sight and nodded meaningfully. The colonel caught his eye and gave him an all but imperceptible nod of acknowledgment in return. Satisfied that Desh was in place as expected, Connelly scooped up an arm-full of fallen leaves and returned to where his car had exited the road, placing the leaves strategically so they would hide any visible tracks but would still look random.

He then carefully returned to the clearing and stood by his car as if waiting for someone.

Desh knew it was possible that Connelly had lost whoever was tailing him, but if these followers could authorize satellite time this would be little consolation. It was also possible that whoever had been following the colonel had no intention of taking any hostile action, but Desh had no choice but to assume otherwise.

Desh quietly made his way to the oversized hacker. "It's showtime," he whispered so softly that Griffin wasn't sure if he had heard it or had simply read Desh's lips. "Don't move. Don't even have noisy thoughts," he continued in hushed tones, his lips almost touching Griffin's right ear. "A single snap of a twig can give away your position."

Griffin glared at him angrily for putting him in harm's way but nodded his understanding.

Desh picked his way through the woods noiselessly, with cat-like grace and light-footedness. The tip of his tongue protruded just slightly from his mouth as he concentrated carefully on avoiding pine cones and twigs, and more plentiful still, fallen leaves that had become dried out and would crunch noisily at the slightest touch.

Desh was convinced that whoever was following Connelly would have enough respect for the colonel not to try a frontal assault. Given Connelly's location in the clearing they were sure to take a textbook approach through the surrounding woods to surprise him on multiple flanks. Desh was on Connelly's southern flank and calculated the angle he would take, coming from the road, if he were attacking Connelly. He chose a post that gave him a full view of this expected approach while keeping him hidden.

He waited behind a dense evergreen, ringed by a thin cushion of needles, now brown, that had fallen from the tree. He remained perfectly still as several minutes ticked by.

He caught movement from the corner of his eye.

A man dressed in black commando gear and wearing a bulletproof vest was stealthily approaching along the exact line Desh had visualized, a militarized and silenced version of Desh's H&K .45 automatic, a favorite of Special Forces commandos, gripped in his right hand. Desh's heart began to jackhammer wildly in his chest but he was able to steady it through force of will alone. The soldier scanned his surroundings alertly while he moved silently and athletically through the woods toward Connelly's position.

Desh leveled the tranquilizer gun at the commando and waited for him to get closer. He had no interest in harming a fellow member of the Special Forces who might just be a dupe in this situation. Given the soldier's body armor, a tranquilizer gun would be his most effective weapon in any case.

The man slowly crept closer. Closer. Closer.

Now, thought Desh, emerging from behind the tree and squeezing off a shot before the man could begin to react. The tranquilizer gun was as silent as a bow. The dart scored a direct hit to the soldier's thigh, and he crumpled to the ground as the tranquilizer took immediate effect.

Desh didn't waste another moment. The man's colleagues were sure to be advancing from alternate flanks. Desh was racing toward the clearing when the word "Freeze!" thundered through the woods. He reached the tree line to see Connelly with his hands up and two men, mirror images of the man he had shot, emerging alertly from the woods on Connelly's northern and western flanks, their weapons held expertly in front of them with two hands and pointing unerringly at the colonel's forehead.

Desh fired. The soldier on Connelly's northern flank collapsed to the ground.

Desh wheeled around the instant the shot was off and fired again at the last remaining commando, but the man had caught Desh's motion and instinctively threw himself into a roll. Instead of hitting an appendage, Desh's shot bounced harmlessly off his vest. The soldier came up firing but Desh had already darted back behind a tree.

Bark flew past Desh's face as a bullet embedded itself in the tree he was using for cover. The soldier was about to shoot again when his arm was blasted backwards and his gun clattered to the ground. A stunned expression came over his face as he realized he had been shot. Blood poured from his arm. Connelly rushed forward and kicked his gun away, and then retreated to a safe distance with his own weapon still trained on the wounded man. Connelly had known Desh was on his southern flank and had been primed to act once Desh had made his expected move.

Desh circled the clearing at the tree line, his gun drawn, looking for additional assailants. There were none. He returned to his original flank and motioned Griffin to leave his hiding place and join him in the clearing. They emerged from the woods and quickly joined Connelly. Desh was calm and alert while Griffin was pale and clammy, looking as if he had seen a ghost.

"All clear?" said Connelly.

"It looks that way," replied Desh, "for the moment at least. Let's question this guy and get the hell out of here."

Connelly motioned to Griffin. "Is this your friend?" he asked.

Desh nodded. "He's a computer expert I've been working with who got drawn in. I think we can trust him." He paused. "Matt Griffin—Jim Connelly," he said.

The men shook hands while Desh turned to the wounded soldier and stared at him intently. "Who are you working for?" he barked. "And what were your orders?"

The soldier remained silent.

"You're obviously US military; ex-Special Forces. I'm guessing you're working for a black-ops group, am I right?" Once again there was no response. "Do you have any idea who it is you were attacking?" He gestured toward Connelly. "You're looking at a highly decorated officer in the US Army Special Operations Command."

The soldier's expression suggested that he knew exactly who it was he was attacking but didn't care.

Desh pocketed the tranquilizer gun, drew his .45, and pulled back on the slide to chamber a round. He pointed it at the prisoner's kneecap suggestively. "I'm only going to ask one more time," he growled. "Why are you after him?"

The soldier's face remained stoic but he glanced from his kneecap to Desh's fiery eyes and swallowed hard. "We were told he went off the reservation."

Desh glanced at Connelly and raised his eyebrows. "How so?"

"We weren't given details. We were just told he had gone rogue and was extremely dangerous. That he was working against the interests of the United States and had to be brought in. The orders came from high up the chain of command."

"Brought in or executed?" said Connelly.

"Brought in."

"But you weren't told he *had* to be taken alive, correct?" said Desh.

The soldier didn't respond, but the look on his face spoke volumes.

"Just as I thought," said Desh. "So if you were able to bring him in without a fight to interrogate him, great, but if you had to kill him, no one would lose any sleep over it."

The soldier glared at Connelly. "You sell out your country and you get what you deserve."

Desh shook his head. "You've been lied to. The colonel hasn't sold out his country. Whoever is ultimately giving the orders has, and is afraid the colonel is on the brink of finding out. So I'll ask again, who gave you your ord—"

Desh jerked his head toward the sky in mid sentence as he detected the faint but unmistakable sound of helicopter blades overhead, his heart accelerating wildly. The chopper was already less than two hundred feet away and was closing fast.

Impossible.

Desh darted for the tree line as a muffled shot rang out from above, and an armor-piercing bullet screamed through Connelly's vest and drilled a hole just below his left shoulder, sending his gun flying. Two soldiers in the helicopter tried to follow Desh's sprinting form with their silenced rifles but held their fire as he entered the woods.

A helicopter was far too noisy to have made it so close undetected, thought Desh in alarm. But this one had. Which meant it was one of the few, next generation choppers designed to have a dramatically reduced acoustic and radar signature. Whoever was after them had access to the military's most advanced equipment, which was extremely disconcerting.

The helicopter approached the clearing and four men, clutching automatic rifles and donned in commando gear, rappelled down a green rope that had unfurled like a streamer from the floor of the chopper. As soon as their boots hit the ground, two of them captured Griffin and Connelly, and two raced into the woods after Desh, fanning out. The helicopter gently settled onto the ground next to Connelly's car as they did so. The man who had called himself Smith was at the controls.

Desh sprinted through the woods ahead of his pursuit, stopping abruptly to take up residence behind a particularly thick tree trunk. The two men approached cautiously, keeping to trees for cover, no doubt aware of Desh's credentials. He was outnumbered, but they had the unenviable task of rooting him out, and he had access to any number of fortified positions. One of the men would circle around and they would coordinate an attack from opposite sides of him. That is if he remained stationary, which he had no intention of doing. Experience told him that he had a better than fifty-fifty chance of escape.

Smith killed the helicopter's engine and entered the woods. "Stand down, Mr. Desh," he bellowed into the trees. "It's Smith," he added, in case Desh failed to recognized his voice.

Desh said nothing.

Smith made several crisp hand signals and seconds later the two commandos retreated back toward their commander. "I'm recalling my men," yelled Smith in Desh's general direction. "We have your two friends," he continued. "Cooperate and they get treated like royalty. Help me get the girl and I'll even let them go." He paused. "Don't cooperate and I'll have them executed. Right here, right now," he bellowed. "So how about it, Desh?"

Smith paused and waited for Desh's response, which didn't come. Desh wasn't about to be goaded into giving away his position.

"Look, Desh, my men and I will be waiting in the clearing for you to come to your senses. Your friends' lives are in your hands. You have three minutes!" he finished, his booming voice reverberating off the trees.

While Desh didn't believe Smith would ever let Griffin and Connelly go, he *did* believe he would execute them if Desh didn't play ball. He had already proven this by shooting the colonel. But as long as they were alive, there was a chance Desh could get them out of this mess. He had no other choice but to give himself up, and Smith knew it.

He approached the edge of the tree line. The colonel and the bearded giant were sitting on the ground next to Connelly's car, their hands and feet bound, while Smith's men were spread throughout the clearing. Desh was relieved to find Connelly still looking alert despite his gunshot wound.

Desh planned to announce himself before he broke from the woods in case any of the soldiers were trigger-happy. He opened his mouth to announce his presence but slammed it closed in shock as he heard something that took him completely by surprise.

The voice of Kira Miller coming from the opposite side of the clearing.

24

"Drop your weapons!" commanded Kira as she calmly entered the clearing, not wearing either glasses or makeup to alter her appearance. She was unarmed and protected by nothing more than a black sweatshirt and tan jacket.

An image flashed across Desh's mind of the sweatpants Kira had provided, which he had unceremoniously thrown into the hall. But he was still wearing the gray sweatshirt from the night before. She must have bugged *both* garments. God, she was clever. She told him she had placed a bug in the sweatpants, knowing he would have changed back into his own pants anyway, but she also knew he would keep the sweatshirt on longer, because she had destroyed his shirt. Like a master magician, she had diverted his attention in one direction while she had continued to operate in another. So she was still listening in when he had read the GPS coordinates of this clearing to Connelly. How had he become so inexcusably sloppy?

"I repeat," said Kira firmly. "Drop your weapons. Now!"

The soldier nearest to Kira shook his head in dismay. "Are you out of your mind! What are you threatening us with, girl power?"

"Girl power. Very witty," she said sarcastically.

"Who *are* you?" said another of the soldiers, his eyes widening in wonder.

Smith had been as stunned as Desh by Kira's sudden arrival, but finally snapped out of his trance. "Don't let down your guard," he instructed his team. "This girl is dangerous. Don't let her appearance and lack of weaponry fool you."

The commandos nodded, but found it hard to take her seriously even so. Desh knew from their reactions they had no idea who she was.

"I'll be damned," continued Smith. "Kira Miller in the flesh. It's nice to finally meet you. But I must say I'm surprised you would just walk into our hands like this after proving so elusive for so long."

"Mr. Smith, I presume?"

"That's what I called myself last night, at least. Which means you must have been listening in to my conversation with Desh."

"Maybe," she said. "On the other hand, maybe I was just paying attention when you shouted your name a minute ago loudly enough to wake the dead."

"Also a reasonable possibility," he conceded.

"I need you to order your men to drop their weapons."

"Or what?" said Smith contemptuously. "Have you invented a super weapon you can activate with your mind that can disable us all? I doubt it. If you had something like this you would have used it already."

Kira's eyes burned with a steely resolve. "I don't need a weapon to get what I want. Either you and your men lay down your weapons—" She paused for effect. "Or I commit suicide."

The commando nearest to Kira smirked. "That's the dumbest threat I've ever . . ." he began, but stopped in mid-sentence as he noticed the expression on Smith's face. Smith wasn't laughing.

"I can have you captured and pacified long before you could kill yourself," said Smith.

"Really?" she said smugly. "I have a cap on a tooth with cyanide enclosed. I bite down on it with all of my strength and I die very quickly. And you can't have that, can you? Because if I die, you're next. Your boss would serve your brains as an appetizer at his next dinner party." She paused and motioned to Smith's men with her head. "Tell them, Smith. You obviously didn't expect me here or you would have warned them already. Tell them what happens to them if they accidentally kill me."

"She's right," said Smith hurriedly, realizing they knew nothing of the stakes and couldn't risk that they would decide to take matters into their own hands. "None of you are to take any hostile action against her if there is any chance—*any* chance—that it could result in her death, accidental or otherwise. Am I clear?" he hissed.

"Clear," responded his men in turn, looks of disbelief across the board.

Desh watched her performance in awe. She was the most remarkable woman he had ever known. She had waltzed into an elite group of heavily armed commandoes without even flinching and was attempting to pull off a plan more audacious than any in his memory.

"Good," said Smith. He turned once again to Kira. "As for you, you've watched too many old spy movies. A suicide tooth? You're bluffing. And even if you aren't, you'll never go through with it." He pulled a tranquilizer gun from his pocket and raised his eyebrows. "I can have you unconscious in a few seconds," he said smugly.

"Even *think* of pointing that at me and I crack the tooth. You might think I'm bluffing, but are you willing to bet your life?" Kira cast a furtive, nervous glance at the tree line in Desh's direction and nodded ever so slightly.

Her nod jolted Desh out of the trance he was in like a cattle prod. "Even if the tooth isn't real," he thundered from beyond the clearing, taking the cue she had given him. "I sure as hell am! I have a gun trained on her head and an itchy trigger finger. I'm happy to be the instrument of suicide for this psychopathic bitch!" he spat hatefully.

"Jesus, Desh!" said Smith in alarm, the smug look vanishing from his face as he realized he had neglected to factor Desh into the equation. "Back off! She could be our only hope of stopping the Ebola attack. You kill her and you're sentencing millions of others to death as well."

"I don't believe that and you know it!" growled Desh. "I think killing her *ends* the threat. So I'll tell you what. Have your men drop their weapons and hug the ground or I put a bullet through her head."

There was no response.

Desh fired, missing Kira's head by inches.

"Do it!" he thundered. "Or be prepared to bend over and kiss your ass goodbye when the powers that be discover you allowed her to be killed. I'll at least die a happy man knowing I stopped her."

Desh could tell that Smith's mind was racing, weighing the possibilities.

"You have ten seconds," said Desh forcefully. "Nine. Eight. Seven. Six—"

"Do what he says!" ordered Smith anxiously. "Now!"

His men were incredulous, but did as ordered: they dropped their weapons and fell to the ground.

Smith remained standing.

"You too, Smith," demanded Desh. "On the ground. You and I need to have a nice long chat."

Smith shook his head. "I'm really not feeling all that chatty," he said.

And then, before Desh could react, Smith pointed his tranquilizer gun at his own leg and pulled the trigger.

PART FOUR
Reunion

25

Kira Miller took the lead as they hiked through the woods. Desh was close behind, his .45 trained on her back, while Connelly and Griffin brought up the rear; all four staying alert for possible ambushes. Their destination was Kira's SUV, rented under an assumed name, which was parked at a campground a half-mile distant and which could not be immediately traced. They were in an untouched section of the woods, blazing their own trail, and their progress was slower than Desh would have liked. Kira had used a small GPS device to find the clearing, and she consulted it periodically to be sure they were taking the most direct line to her vehicle possible.

Desh fumed silently. How had he let Smith slip through his fingers? Smith had known they couldn't wait until he regained consciousness to interrogate him, and dragging his unconscious body along as they made their escape would be equally foolhardy. As expected, the man had carried no identification. *Shit,* thought Desh for the third time. He had been so close to finally learning what was going on and who was pulling Smith's strings. It was maddening.

Desh had tranquilized the remaining commandoes to ensure they couldn't sound an alarm. After he had cut Griffin and Connelly free, he had taken the standard, military first-aid kit from the helicopter and had cleaned and dressed the colonel's wound, giving him a potent pain killer as well. Before they had taken off into the woods, Desh also hurriedly dressed the wound of the now-unconscious soldier Connelly had shot.

All in all, Connelly had been lucky, but he had still lost a considerable amount of blood and the risk of infection was significant. He needed to get to a doctor soon.

Kira stopped walking and gestured toward Desh's gun. "Do you really need to point that at me?" she whispered, taking care that her voice wouldn't carry and advertise their presence.

It was a good question, thought Desh. Did he? She had warned him about Smith; warned him that Connelly was in danger. And she had been right. She had also just bailed them out of a big mess.

But what if this had been nothing but a set-up? For all Desh knew she and Smith were working together. Still, to what end? If she wanted Desh dead she could have accomplished this at the motel. If she was allied with Smith to acquire Griffin and Connelly along with him, they were seconds away from this as well. What's more, she had voluntarily put herself under Desh's control.

Desh wasn't about to holster his gun until they were in more secure territory, but he joined Kira at the front of the procession and no longer pointed it in her direction.

"Thanks," she whispered earnestly.

"So you bugged the sweatshirt, too, didn't you?" asked Desh in hushed tones as they began to move again, barely managing to keep any trace of admiration from his voice.

Kira nodded guiltily.

"What are you doing here?"

"I knew they'd follow the colonel to your meeting place and try to kill him. I decided I couldn't let that happen."

Desh studied her carefully but detected no sign of deceit. "Do you really have a suicide tooth?" he whispered.

A broad smile came over her face. "No," she admitted. "It was all I could think of at the time." She raised her eyebrows. "Actually, I figured my bluster wouldn't keep Smith from deciding I was bluffing for very long. I was counting on you to get the hint and jump in—which is exactly what you did."

Desh knew that he should have done so immediately, but he had been too busy admiring her performance. "How did you know I was watching?" he asked.

"I heard Smith threaten your friends and give you three minutes to return and surrender. I knew you wouldn't let them die," she whispered approvingly. "And I knew if you heard my voice you'd stay hidden to see what was going on."

Desh nodded but didn't respond. In addition to being scientifically brilliant, she could think on her feet as well as anyone he had ever known—and this was saying quite a lot.

Before long they entered a large clearing with a sign that read, "Campground 3B". Eight small wood cabins were arranged in a semicircle within the clearing, and cars were parked beside several of them. A gravel road led away from the campground on the opposite side.

Kira had parked the SUV at the edge of the campground, and soon they were all inside, with Kira driving, Desh in the passenger seat, and Connelly and Griffin in the back.

As Kira started the engine, Desh turned to her and said, "I assume you came here from the road that parallels the one we took. Can you get us back there?"

"Absolutely." She pulled onto the gravel road and slowly moved forward. Connelly winced as the SUV vibrated on the unpaved surface and jostled his injury.

"Where to once we hit the main artery?" she asked.

Desh pursed his lips in concentration. "That depends. Any guess as to when they'll link this car to us?"

"Hard to say," she replied. "It depends on when they discover their raid back there failed, and how many cars are on the road. It shouldn't be immediate, though."

Desh's eyes narrowed as he sorted through various possibilities. "There's a large shopping center between Petersburg and Richmond called the Manor Hill Mall—it's all-enclosed, making it inaccessible to satellite surveillance. We could lose ourselves in the crowds and then leave. They may be able to track us *to* there, but they'll have a hell of a time tracking us *from* there."

Kira looked impressed. "I like it," she said.

"Colonel?" said Desh.

"Me too," said Connelly. "I recommend we split up once we're there."

"Agreed," said Desh. He turned to Kira. "If you can get us on I-95 north, the mall is just off a main exit."

She nodded. "Will do."

The wide gravel road soon ended in a skinny paved one that wound its way through the heart of the woods for a half mile before hitting an arrow-straight main artery. Kira pulled onto the main road and accelerated as rapidly as the rental would allow.

Desh turned in his seat to face Connelly. "Colonel, how are you feeling?"

"I'm fine," said Connelly stoically, but blood was still slowly seeping through his bandages and he looked pale.

"Matt?" said Desh. "How about you? Are you okay?"

"Not really," he said. "But it's hard to complain when I'm sitting next to someone with a bullet wound who isn't," he said dryly.

Desh was encouraged that Griffin had recovered his sense of humor. "When we get to the mall, we'll split up into two groups," said Desh. "I'll go with Kira. Matt, can I count on you to look after the colonel?"

"Look after *him*?"

Desh nodded. "Don't let him fool you. He's not doing as well as he's pretending." He reached into his pocket and pulled out his thick stack of hundreds; passing about forty of them to Griffin in the back seat. "A little spending money," he said. "I need you to see to it that he gets to a doctor."

"I'll do my best," said Griffin solemnly.

"Colonel, any good military doctors you trust with your life?" asked Desh.

Connelly considered. "Yes. Don Menken. He's retired but still lives near Bragg. I can trust him to patch me up and not ask any questions."

Kira opened the SUV's center console and pulled out a cell phone. She passed it back to Griffin. "Use this phone to reach us," she instructed. "I have its mate. Hit *Autodial 1* and it will speed-dial my number. The phone is completely secure."

"No cell phone is secure," said Connelly wearily, the vitality of his voice beginning to wane as his blood loss began to catch up with him.

"The signal can be intercepted easily enough, but the phone can't be connected to me. Even if it could, the audio is sent scrambled. These two phones can unscramble each other's signals, but even top cryptographic experts won't be able to decipher the conversation."

Connelly doubted her code was nearly as tight as she thought it was, but he didn't argue the point.

"Let's come up with a game plan we can use when we get to the mall," suggested Desh.

"Agreed," rasped Connelly. "But first give me the shorthand version of why we're joining forces with enemy number one here."

Kira glanced at Desh with interest, as though curious as to what he would say.

Desh sighed. Connelly was the least well informed of any of them. "We both know there's far more going on here than we understand," he began. "Smith's men crashed the party at the motel. And Smith had a cell phone that responded to the number you gave me and told me you were taking orders from him. But we know that was a lie. Kira claims she's innocent and not involved in any terror plots. She warned me that you were in danger from Smith, and she was right." He raised his eyebrows. "And she did risk herself to rescue us," he added pointedly.

"You've seen her file," responded Connelly. "She's a brilliant manipulator and liar. This could all have been staged."

"This is true. And believe me, I haven't lost sight of that. But she claims she can prove her innocence and explain what's going on, and I'm going to give her that chance. I can assure you that I'll bring a healthy dose of skepticism to the table."

Desh looked at his watch and calculated how long it would take them to reach their destination. "We need to be sure we know what we'll be doing at the mall and think it through so we don't make any obvious mistakes," he said. "But that shouldn't take long. With the time remaining I'll try to give you a thirty-thousand-foot view of what I know. Matt can fill in more of the details when he has the chance."

"Fair enough," said Connelly.

"Before I begin, I need to warn you: without the details you're going to find most of this hard to believe."

Matt Griffin smiled slyly and rolled his eyes. "You can say that again," he muttered from the back of the SUV.

26

The Manor Hill Mall was a hive of activity. Between them, Petersburg and Richmond had a population of over a million people, and it wasn't hard to believe that half of them were shopping at Manor Hill. The mall was four stories high, with all four stories under a vaulted atrium ceiling, and encompassed a total square footage of retail space that was hard to comprehend. Connelly had donned Desh's windbreaker to hide his blood soaked bandages. Desh and Kira had dropped Griffin and the colonel at one end of the mall before driving almost half a mile to enter the mall at its opposite end.

As they had planned during the drive, Griffin and Connelly entered a crowded clothing store and made themselves over from head to toe in an ensemble chosen to help them blend in. They then bought scissors and shaving gear and emerged from a restroom ten minutes later without any facial hair. When Griffin had been told this would be necessary he had almost mutinied; but in the end he had agreed that this was a better alternative than being discovered and shot to death—barely. Connelly was also pained to part with his prized mustache, but he took the loss with military stoicism.

After altering their appearance, the two men ordered a cab under an assumed name and took it to a side entrance of a nearby Hilton hotel. They then passed through the lobby to the front of the hotel and convinced another cabbie to take them all the way to Connelly's doctor friend. The cabbie had adamantly refused to drive this far until he was handed a stack of hundred dollar bills, after which he decided that the customer was always king, and he'd be happy to take them where they wanted to go.

Desh and Kira changed outfits as well. Desh was now wearing a pair of pre-faded jeans and a hooded, burgundy-and-gold Washington Redskins sweatshirt with oversized pockets. Kira replaced the tan jacket she had been wearing with a blue one of a different style, and her hair was now tucked up inside a Redskins ball cap. Both wore tennis shoes for comfort and mobility.

Whoever tracked them to the mall would expect their stay to be brief, just long enough so they could lose themselves among the crowd before racing off by cab or stolen car. The last thing anyone would expect them to do would be to loiter at the mall for several hours in plain sight, which is exactly why they planned to do so, leaving on a bus that wasn't scheduled to depart for several hours yet.

Manor Hill had fourteen restaurants and a Food Court. They found an information booth and asked for a restaurant with a romantic ambiance; shorthand for one that was so poorly lighted they couldn't be easily seen while inside. At the same time such lighting would allow *them* to readily see anyone entering the restaurant from the mall.

Twenty minutes later they were in a booth in the back of *Montag's Gourmet Pizza*, a restaurant whose dusk-like level of lighting was unexpected in a pizza place, gourmet or otherwise, but was perfect for their needs.

The waiter noticed their matching Redskins attire from a distance and assumed they were on a date, but as he got a closer look at the grime and dense shadow of stubble on Desh's face, he changed his mind. They must be married, he thought. No one on a date would have such little regard for personal hygiene.

Desh ordered a soda, Kira iced-tea, and they ordered a large pizza to split. Although Desh knew he had far more important things to worry about, sharing a pizza seemed too much like breaking bread with the devil for his taste;

albeit a devil who had probably saved Connelly's life. He remained determined to keep as much emotional distance from the woman across from him as he could manage.

When the waiter left, Desh stealthily drew his gun and hid it on his lap, under his oversized sweatshirt, with his finger on the trigger. He situated himself at an awkward angle in the booth so he could watch both Kira and the entrance to the restaurant as they spoke.

After the waiter returned with their drinks and then left again, Kira got right to the point. "I assume you remember where we were last night before we were, ah . . . interrupted?"

Desh nodded. It was hard to believe their discussion had taken place just the night before. "You can make yourself smarter, but when you do you turn into a psychopath." As he spoke he continued to anxiously watch the entrance, scrutinizing anyone who approached the hostess podium and scanning all human mall traffic in his view.

"Who knew you had such a way with words," said Kira. She smiled warmly. "That may be the most succinct summation in history."

"We can't be sure when we'll be interrupted again," said Desh icily, subconsciously trying to counter her warmth. "Since you're so eager to convince me you're not working with terrorists, let's not waste any time."

"Agreed," said Kira soberly. She quickly gathered her thoughts. "I left off about two-and-a-half years after I joined NeuroCure," she said. "When I had achieved my breakthrough. Do you have any questions about the treatment before I move on?"

Desh thought about this as he watched a group of teenaged girls stroll by the restaurant, wearing clothing that was several years too old for them along with a colorful assortment of flashy costume jewelry. "How long does the transformation last?" he asked.

"Only about an hour. I was afraid to make it last any longer. Not without better understanding the treatment and what it was doing to me."

"Including your newfound admiration for the work of Nietzsche?"

"Yes."

"I'm surprised the effect is so short."

"It seems longer when you're experiencing it. And at this level of intelligence, the number of insights you can have in a single hour is staggering. To make the effect permanent, I would need to make other modifications to the body. Even in an hour your body becomes depleted of the molecular precursors for neurotransmitters and you get a craving for glucose like you wouldn't believe. After a transformation, I wouldn't feel completely normal for days. I decided not to try it more than once a week, at most."

Desh wondered if anything Smith had told him in the car was true. Since Kira had listened in to this entire conversation there was no reason to be coy. "So where did you decide to focus this towering IQ of yours?" he asked. "Smith said you were working on extending human life and eventually conquering mortality itself."

"He was right," she said. "I'll go into that in more detail later, but this was one of three major goals I set for myself."

Desh considered pressing her to talk more about longevity, but decided to be patient and let her continue in her own way. "What were the other two?"

"One was to achieve another jump in intelligence. In my transformed state it was clear that a level substantially higher than what I had achieved was possible." She took a sip of her iced-tea and set it back down. "My last goal was to um—" She paused and looked slightly embarrassed. "Accumulate massive wealth."

"And here I was beginning to think you were Mother Teresa."

Kira nodded. "I had a feeling that would be your reaction," she said. "In my defense, I didn't want the money for luxuries. I just wanted to be sure that money would never be an issue if I needed equipment or supplies for my other projects, wherever my enhanced intelligence would lead me."

"I wouldn't doubt that immortals would need to have a pretty big nest egg," he allowed. He fished a breadstick from a small wicker basket on the table filled with an assortment of rolls. "Becoming wealthy is the one goal I'm fairly certain you achieved. That is, if I can be certain of anything these days," he added in frustration. "But I'm eager to learn just how it is you were able to accomplish this so quickly," he finished accusingly.

"You think I sold my soul to terrorists?"

"Why not? Even if you aren't sociopathic normally, you admit you are in your enhanced state. Why let a little thing like the deaths of millions slow you down?"

"Come on, David," she snapped in annoyance. "Think it through. Even if I acted on my sociopathic tendencies—which I didn't—I would only be a raving sociopath, not *stupid.* I had achieved immeasurable intelligence. Creativity that would put Thomas Edison to shame. An intellect that would make Stephen Hawking look slow. With capabilities like these, do you really think I'm going to spend years working on a bioterror agent to sell to people who would happily kill me for not covering my face?" She shook her head in exasperation. "I could make millions just selling the cryptographic software that I thought up in ten minutes, or any number of other inventions that could be marketed immediately. What do you think the government would pay for a material that completely shields heat signatures?"

Desh frowned. "When you put it that way, working with terrorists does sound pretty stupid."

"*Thank you,*" she said emphatically. She paused as the waiter came over to check on them.

"Not that it matters," she continued as soon as the waiter was out of earshot, "but I made my fortune in the stock market."

Desh raised his eyebrows. "That wouldn't have been my first guess. How?"

"I analyzed the market while at an elevated level of intelligence," she replied. "When you're in the transformed state you have absolute access to your memory. *All* of your memory. The human brain stores every single input it ever receives: everything you think, read, see, touch or experience. In our normal, un-optimized mode, we're unable to access all but the tiniest tip of that iceberg. But in my enhanced state I can make correlations and logical connections between bits of information I didn't even know I had. Treacherously complex patterns become obvious. Market insights quickly present themselves."

"Did you understand your analysis when you returned to normal?"

Kira smiled. "Not even a little," she admitted. "All I know is that I was right about eighty percent of the time, more than enough to make me very rich, very fast. I underwent my treatment four different times with the sole purpose of analyzing the stock market. And I only placed the riskiest of bets. Currency fluctuations, options, futures—that sort of thing. Over a three-month period I increased my wealth a thousand-fold. The stock market is legalized gambling and I had transformed myself into the ultimate Rain Man."

As usual, she made the most fantastic claims seem eminently plausible. "So why the false identities and Swiss bank accounts?"

"I started to get paranoid, so I began taking precautions."

"Is paranoia another side effect of the enhanced intelligence?"

"No," she replied solemnly. "It's a side effect of getting robbed."

Desh's eyes narrowed. "Is this where the arch nemesis you wrote about in your E-mail comes in? Your Moriarty?"

"I like that," said Kira, smiling. "Gives me hope that you aren't still convinced that *I'm* Moriarty. If you had said, 'Your arch nemesis, Sherlock Holmes,' I'd really be depressed right now."

Desh couldn't help but return her smile.

"One of the things that popped out when I was studying you was how wonderfully well read you are," said Kira earnestly.

"Moriarty isn't exactly an obscure reference. The majority of ten-year-olds know who he is."

She smiled and her eyes sparkled playfully. "That doesn't make what I said any less true. Besides, I wouldn't be too sure about that. I'm not convinced the majority of *adults* even know the name of our Speaker of the House."

A slight smile played across Desh's face. "So tell me about the robbery?"

Desh tensed as a fit man in his thirties with a serious look on his face approached the hostess station and began scanning the restaurant carefully, his eyes moving in an arc that would soon include their booth. "Duck!" whispered Desh as he slipped the gun out from under his sweatshirt and braced himself for action. Kira slid down in the booth as if she had dropped a coin on the floor.

Seconds later the man's eyes stopped shifting as his gaze settled on a booth two over from where they were seated. An attractive woman who was seated with two preschool children waved at him happily. He raised his hand in acknowledgment, his face becoming relaxed, and he hurriedly joined his family.

Desh let out the breath he had been holding. "False alarm," he whispered. "Sorry."

Kira returned to a fully upright position. "Don't be," she said, shaking her head. "Better to err on the side of caution. Besides, I'm sure my pulse will return to normal in an hour or so," she added with a grin.

"You were going to tell me about the robbery," prompted Desh.

"Right," said Kira. "I came home from work one night and my place had been broken into. I had a bottle with twenty-three gellcaps and my lab notebook stored in the false bottom of a dresser drawer. Both were missing."

"You had a dresser with a false-bottomed drawer?"

"I thought putting valuables in a safe would be too obvious. I measured the drawer and had someone at a hardware store cut a platform to my exact specifications. I wallpapered it to match the bottoms of the other drawers and stacked some sweaters on top."

Desh raised his eyebrows, impressed. "Did they take anything else?" he asked, chewing absently on the breadstick he had taken and continuing to watch the entrance.

"Nothing. They knew exactly what they were after."

"Any ideas who it was?"

"Not when it happened, no. I was stunned. I had been careful not to leave a trail. I routinely disposed of the rodents I was using and I never let my lab notebook out of my sight. Until then, I wouldn't have believed it possible that anyone could have known what I was doing. On a hunch, the next day I hired someone at an executive protection agency, like yours, to look for listening devices." She frowned deeply. "He found several in both my office and home. That's the day I truly began to get paranoid."

"That would do it," muttered Desh.

"It was a disaster. Whoever he was, having twenty-three doses of my therapy instantly made him the most formidable man on the planet. I began to take elaborate precautions, learned everything I could about bugs and how to find them, and took some pains to spread my fortune across various accounts. The next time I was enhanced it became clear to me I needed to create a number of flawless false identities as well as invent technologies that would help me stay hidden if I was forced to disappear."

"Enhanced intuition also?"

She nodded. "Intuition is just your subconscious putting together subtle clues and coming to a conclusion that your conscious mind hasn't quite reached. Since my rewiring gives me access to all the memories buried in my subconscious, it unleashes the full power of intuition." Kira paused. "As later events were to prove, this intuition was right on target."

Desh said nothing as he finished the breadstick and drained the last of his soda. There was certainly no arguing this point.

"Three days later," continued Kira, "my boss, Tom Morgan, was killed in a car accident."

Desh nodded, almost imperceptibly. Interesting, he thought. Another piece of the puzzle that was now—possibly—explained.

"I was never able to find any evidence, but I suspect Morgan stumbled onto what I was doing and was responsible for having the bugs planted. My guess is he later approached someone powerful to sell what he knew and access to some of the gellcaps. My unknown enemy. Moriarty, as you called him."

Desh frowned. "And Moriarty had Morgan killed so he would have an exclusive on your treatment."

"That's my guess."

Desh opened his mouth to ask another question but closed it again as the waiter approached with their pizza. As he carefully placed it on the table in front of them, Desh reflected on everything Kira had told him. Her chronology of events explained any number of loose ends. And the central premise of his assignment, that she was working with terrorists on a bioterror plot, had become laughably implausible. And she had warned them about Smith and had risked herself to extricate them.

And although he tried to resist, her looks and personality continued to cast a spell on him. As much as he needed to affix his gaze solely on the entrance and stay alert at all times, he found his eyes inexorably returning to hers as they spoke. He needed to keep the Greek myth of the Siren sea nymphs firmly in his mind. Was he really being as objective in considering her arguments as he needed to be? Were there holes that he was failing to consider?

However much she explained away, he kept returning to the same place: the deaths surrounding her childhood were indisputable. Griffin had verified as much when Desh had been asleep on the hacker's couch. And the evidence against her in the killing of Lusetti and her brother was airtight. As appealing as he found her and as artful as her explanations had been, it was still more likely than not that most of what she said was an elaborate fabrication.

27

They both hungrily ate their first piece of pizza in silence, after which Desh announced his plan to use the restroom and scout the mall once again. He spent a few minutes in the restroom scrubbing his face with soap and cold water, feeling reinvigorated as he did so, and then exited the restaurant.

Throngs of brightly colored shoppers of every description paraded through the mall in all directions, creating a random, ever-changing mosaic of humanity. Some race-walked as if on an urgent mission while others strolled leisurely. Some were empty handed while others carried soft-pretzels, ice cream, elaborate purses, or plastic shopping bags filled to the brim with recent purchases. A young girl pointed excitedly to a pair of shoes though a window as her mother looked on with an amused expression on her face. Desh envied them their untroubled innocence.

He pretended to look in a few store windows and wander through the mall for the next five minutes, furtively scanning the crowd as he did so, but detected nothing out of place and no sign of pursuit.

He returned to the booth to find that Kira was almost finished with her last piece of pizza and the waiter had refilled his drink. Kira eyed him warily as he sat down. "Any suspicious activity?"

Desh shook his head. "I think we're probably in the clear," he said. "If they haven't found us by now, they'll have moved on. They'll never believe we'd do something as stupid as making sitting ducks of ourselves—literally—in the middle of a busy restaurant."

"Stupid like a fox," said Kira with a twinkle in her eye.

Desh smiled. He lifted a large slice of pizza and gestured to Kira. "By all means, continue," he said. "You left off when your boss turned up dead."

Kira gathered herself and resumed her narrative. "After the break-in, Morgan's death, and discovering the listening devices, I became more secretive than ever. I routinely swept for listening devices and I performed all animal experiments in my condo rather than at NeuroCure's facilities." She paused. "I worked on both of my primary goals at the same time, but I achieved the leap forward in neuronal optimization first."

"How long after the break-in?" he asked.

"About nine months."

"I assume you tested it to be sure it worked."

"Yes. I engineered a batch with an exceedingly short half-life in case there were complications. I was only in this state of super-optimization for about two seconds, but it was enough."

"Enough for what?"

"Enough to be certain I'd succeeded. Those two seconds felt like five minutes. The first level of optimization is beyond description. The second level is beyond imagination." Her eyes widened in wonder. "It was a transcendent level of thought. Awe-inspiring. So much so that I was afraid to ever try it again."

This time Desh knew only too well what she meant. Once again, she had been afraid of the corrupting influences of untold power.

"The lower dose was having a cumulative effect," continued Kira. "The more I transformed myself the greater my tendency to embrace the idea of ruthlessly selfish behavior. My emotional side became ever more suppressed, and my feelings of superiority continued to increase. It's hard enough retaining the vestiges of altruism when you become convinced there is no afterlife. And when you're powerful enough to do whatever you want. It's even worse when you begin to see normal human intelligence as pathetically insignificant." She looked troubled. "If this was how I began to view humanity when optimized to the first level, how would I view our species if I spent more than two seconds at an even more elevated level?"

Desh continued eating as she spoke but he was quickly losing his appetite. Was there really a plane of intelligence so elevated that normal human intelligence didn't register? He killed insects without much thought. Beings whose intelligence was as far beyond human intelligence as his was beyond an insect couldn't be blamed for indifference to human life, or even active slaughter of any human that stood in their way.

God as ruthless sociopath?

Or was God, despite infinite power and intelligence, the one exception to the "absolute power corrupts absolutely" rule? Even assuming everything in the bible was completely true, the answer to this question was not obvious. Religions that would be appalled at a characterization of God as anything but a loving father readily accepted that He had wiped all life from the planet, save for two members from each species, simply because He was annoyed at humanity's bad behavior.

Desh pulled himself from his brief reverie and considered the woman in front of him, whose large, expressive blue eyes continued to act as black holes, drawing him into their irresistible gravity wells, defying his every effort at resistance. He needed to stay objective. It was time to get at the heart of the matter. "You're very good," said Desh. "I'll give you that. But before you go any further I'd like to back up. I want you to explain the deaths of your parents and uncle. And the murder of one of your teachers and the disappearance of another."

She frowned and shook her head. "My parents and uncle died in accidents. As far as the teachers go, I have no idea what happened to them. But I had nothing to do with it."

"So you acknowledge that one disappeared and the other was killed horribly, by an obvious psychopath?"

"How could I not? It's the truth. I'll never forget it. It was all anyone could talk about for a long time." She leaned in intently. "Are you suggesting you have evidence that I committed these crimes?"

"No. But the circumstantial evidence is pretty conclusive."

"It's only *conclusive* because of your bias. There's no way I can prove I had nothing to do with those deaths. Whether you believe me or not depends on what lens you view them with. If you're looking for trouble, you're going to find it."

"Meaning?"

"Meaning, if you already think I'm a psycho killer and you examine my past through this lens, you're bound to find evidence to support this contention. This is classic data mining. You draw a conclusion and then mine the data retrospectively to find support for it. You invariably do. I'll bet if we looked at your hometown and vicinity over all the years of your childhood we could find a disappearance or two, some murders, a few *accidental* deaths. Most that you wouldn't even be aware of."

"Probably. A few random events can be explained away as coincidences, but there is a limit. Your teachers—maybe a coincidence. But add in both of your parents and your uncle as well—I'm not buying it."

Kira shook her head, pain etched in every line of her face, as if the wounds from these tragedies had never entirely healed. "I don't know what to say. But I'm willing to bet you can find others who lost parents and also a relative in tragic accidents. Bad luck happens, David," she insisted. "One of the ways I got through it all was by reminding myself of this. I was at least lucky enough to have many good years with my parents. There are orphans and kids in war zones who aren't even that lucky," she finished.

Desh frowned. This line of discussion was getting him nowhere. He wondered why he ever thought it would. What had he expected, a confession? And she did have a point. He *did* bring bias into the equation. If he hadn't already been shown evidence she was a psychopath he would have viewed these events quite differently. He'd probably be consoling her for her loss right now.

Desh sighed. "Let's table this one for a while," he suggested. "Why don't you tell me about your fountain of youth."

Kira nodded as the waiter appeared again with their bill. Desh paid him immediately with cash, including the tip, so he wouldn't have reason to disturb them further.

Kira waited for him to leave and then resumed the discussion. "I had achieved my first goal, a further leap in intelligence, but was afraid to use it. About fourteen months after I was robbed I achieved a breakthrough on my second goal. Smith was accurate. I can double the span of human life."

"How?" asked Desh, not wanting to have the conversation bog down but unable to repress his curiosity. "Just give me the Cliffs Notes version."

Kira paused, as if considering how best to frame her response. "As I said before, our brains aren't optimized for thought. Well, not surprisingly, our bodies aren't optimized for longevity either. Again, all natural selection cares about is reproduction." She took a sip of iced-tea and set it back down on the table. "If you have a mutation that enhances your ability to survive to childbearing age, this mutation will preferentially appear in future generations. But longevity genes don't kick in until you've already done all the reproducing you're ever going to do. The guy who dies at forty has just as much chance of having scores of children, and passing on his *poor* longevity genes, as the guy who dies at eighty has of passing on his *good* ones. There's no evolutionary advantage to long life."

Desh's eyes narrowed. "But parents who live longer can increase their *offspring's* chances of survival. So longevity genes should confer an advantage."

"Very good," she said. "This is true. There is evolutionary pressure on our genes to keep us alive long enough to ensure our children can take care of themselves. But after this point there's no advantage to further longevity. In fact, there might even be evolutionary pressure *against* it."

Desh looked confused.

"The elderly can be a burden on the clan when resources are scarce," explained Kira. "Decreasing the chances of survival for future generations."

A look of distaste came over Desh's face. "So those clans whose elders have the decency to drop-dead early on and not drain further resources thrive more than those whose elders live forever?"

"During times of scarcity at least, yes. This is one probable explanation for why most life on Earth, including ours, is programmed to die."

Desh's brow furrowed in confusion. "What does that mean?" he said "I thought aging was the result of errors accumulating in our DNA."

"Partially true. But a large part of aging is due to a form of planned obsolescence. Our immune systems weaken, we stop producing hormones like estrogen, our hair grays or falls out, our skin shrivels, the acuity of our hearing diminishes, and so on. Our bodies are programmed, at the level of our genes, to die."

"You're the scientist, but it's hard for me to believe that's true."

"That's because it happens gradually," she said. "In some species, like pacific salmon and marsupial mice, it happens all at once. One day they have no signs whatsoever of aging and the next—bam—they're dead from old age." She paused. "Other species aren't programmed to die at all, like rockfish and certain social insect queens."

Desh tilted his head. "But they do die, right?"

"They die. They just don't age as we know it. Eventually accidents or predators or starvation kills them."

Desh had further questions but knew that now was not the time. "Go on," he said.

"I studied these species extensively to understand why they didn't age. I also took DNA samples from people who suffer from a rare aging disease called progeria. By the age of twelve progerics look and sound like elderly people."

Desh shook his head sympathetically. "I've heard about that. What a horrible disease."

He paused. "Can I at least assume their DNA was illuminating?"

"Very. It led directly to the breakthrough I needed," she said. "I had been studying everything I could find on the molecular basis of aging for years. But when I added data on the genetic differences between progeria victims and normals my optimized brain was able to put all the pieces together."

"And you're positive your treatment will work? That it really will double the span of human life?"

"Absolutely certain," she said without hesitation. "One hundred percent."

Desh had become stiff from his angled position in the booth as he continued to watch the entrance, and he shifted temporarily into a more comfortable position. "How can you be so sure?" he asked, rubbing the back of his neck with his left hand while continuing to grip the gun with his right.

"There are a number of ways," replied Kira. "But you'd need a much deeper knowledge of molecular biology and medicine to understand most of them. One way is to look at cellular doubling times. Most people don't know this, but most of your cells will only divide about fifty times in culture. This is called the Hayflick limit. As they approach fifty doublings they take longer and longer to divide and show signs of aging."

"What happens after they divide fifty times?" asked Desh.

"They die," she said simply.

Desh pondered this for a few seconds. "What about cancer cells?" he asked.

"Good question. Cancer cells are the exception. They're the immortals among cells. Not only will they go beyond fifty doublings, they'll continue doubling forever. It's this unconstrained growth that eventually makes them deadly to their host."

Desh was fascinated by all of this but he was out of his league and knew he needed to move on. "Let's say I believe your longevity therapy works the way you say it does," he began. "Let's say I even believe you aren't involved in bioterror. But here's the question: if you really did discover the fountain of youth, why have you kept it a secret?"

Kira raised her eyebrows. "Because I didn't want to be responsible for knocking humanity back to the Dark Ages," she said simply.

28

Desh spotted their waiter and motioned him over. They were in a dark, comfortable little corner of the vast mall and his fear of being discovered was waning by the minute. They had time before they had to catch the bus and he was in no hurry to leave.

"Can you start a new check for us?" asked Desh when the waiter arrived.

"Sure, what can I get for you?"

Desh quickly leafed through the menu. "We'll both have hot fudge sundaes."

The man nodded and hurried off.

"Hot fudge sundaes?" said Kira.

"I want an excuse to stay here longer," he explained. He allowed himself to smile. "Besides, when I'm talking to you my brain needs all the glucose it can get."

She looked almost bashful. "Sorry to have to throw so much at you at once. I know it's like drinking from a fire-hose."

Desh grinned at this. "Not at all. Once again you have me intrigued," he said. "So please go on."

"Smith told you *his* theory as to why I've kept longevity a secret," she said. "To acquire great power and wealth." She shook her head in disgust. "Nothing could be further from the truth. I'd love to share the treatment. The problem is, when I was still enhanced, I considered what the world would be like once I did. The conclusions I reached were shocking."

Desh tried to guess where she was heading, but couldn't.

"If everyone lives to be one hundred and fifty," continued Kira, "what happens to the world's population?"

For a moment Desh wondered if it was a trick question. He shrugged. "It would go up," he said.

"It would go up," she repeated. "A lot. At least as many people would be born each year but far fewer would die. And women would be at reproductive age twice as long. The planet is already overcrowded and getting steadily worse. Introduce my therapy and everyone would need to make room for their great, great, great grandparents." She shook her head emphatically. "Doubling the span of human life would be an absolute disaster."

"It's true our society would have to make changes," acknowledged Desh, "but you can't be sure the effects would be catastrophic."

"Overpopulation doesn't just have physical effects, it has psychological effects as well," she said. "A fascinating experiment was done on Norway rats years ago. The experimenters confined a population of them in a quarter-acre enclosure, provided plenty of food, and removed all predators. They expected the rat population to climb to five thousand, but it didn't. It stabilized at one hundred and fifty. When they *forced* the population to exceed a comfortable density, even with unlimited food, they saw a dramatic increase in pathologic rat behavior. Withdrawal, cannibalism, homosexuality, and other uncharacteristic behaviors emerged." Kira raised her eyebrows and eyed Desh knowingly. "You think human stress goes up a notch or two the more crowded it gets?"

Desh frowned. It didn't take a brilliant scientist to answer this question.

"While enhanced, I quickly realized that if I made the therapy public, the population would reach critical levels very quickly. Within a few generations, at most, humanity would either be reduced to small populations living in Dark Age conditions or extinct. I've since run a number of computer simulations."

"And?"

"And the simulations match my intuition exactly. There are a range of possible scenarios, but I'll give you one of the more likely ones. The skyrocketing population results in vast economic collapse as resources are depleted and the number of jobs can't expand as quickly as the need for them. Economies are geared to a retirement age of sixty-five or so, and an average lifespan of around eighty." Kira paused. "You even joked about the need for an immortal to have a large retirement nest egg," she reminded him.

Desh frowned. He had made the joke but had failed to consider its implications.

"We also spoke about longevity as a burden to younger generations," she continued. "It is. Along with economic collapse, population growth causes conditions to get more and more unsanitary. Contagious diseases spread like wildfire. Massive famines become common. Fighting for survival and fueled by increases in aberrant human behavior, countries war on their international neighbors and soon unleash a nuclear Armageddon on the planet."

Desh blanched. It sounded chillingly plausible. "But wouldn't world governments realize the threat and implement strict birth-control policies?"

"Maybe. Doubtfully, but maybe. But is that what you would want? Buying increased survival at the expense of your offspring? This may sound perfectly reasonable to me when I'm enhanced, but the thought of it sickens me when I'm not." Kira paused. "There is little doubt. Springing a seventy or eighty year life extension on the world would lead to the end of civilization." She frowned and looked utterly disheartened.

The depth of despair on her face took Desh by surprise. "Kira?" he said gently, "are you okay?"

She nodded, but the sadness didn't leave her eyes. "Just feeling sorry for myself," she said softly. "My every effort blows up in my face. I can transform myself to a fantastic level of intelligence, but at the cost of becoming ruthless and losing much of my humanity. I find a way to dramatically slow the aging process, only to realize that doing so will destroy civilization."

Desh sat in silence, unable to think of anything to say. He could understand her frustration. She was a modern day Midas, the king who was thrilled to be granted a touch of gold until he realized the devastating consequences: he couldn't prevent his food or beloved daughter from turning into gold as well.

29

They sat in silence as the waiter arrived with their desserts. Kira put a spoonful of vanilla ice-cream and hot fudge into her mouth and swallowed unhappily. Desh found himself wondering if a being of infinite intelligence would still enjoy the taste of fudge.

As Desh began working on his own sundae he decided to change the subject. Kira still had Lusetti and her brother to explain, but he was beginning to think she would. "So what happened after you realized you couldn't reveal your discovery?"

"I decided to throw in the towel. I vowed to stop all experiments on longevity and to never use my brain optimization therapy again." She waited patiently for excess fudge to finish dripping off her long spoon so she could bring it to her mouth. "But it goes without saying the story didn't end there. Someone had been keeping track of me, not with listening devices but the old fashioned way. I didn't know it at the time, but Larry Lusetti, a Private Investigator, had been hired to keep tabs on me. He went through my garbage and spied on me through my windows like a peeping tom. It didn't take long for him to discover I had stopped all experimentation."

Desh considered. "I'm guessing this signaled Moriarty that you had made a breakthrough and didn't *need* to experiment further."

"That's right. A few days later my condo was broken into again. I had long since stopped keeping records in a lab notebook. By then I was keeping my notes on my computer. The file was encoded and also protected by security I had devised while I was enhanced. Even if someone breached my computer, they'd have to decode the file. But a breach wasn't possible. Not by a member of Homo sapiens at any rate." She frowned deeply. "Which goes to show that just because you're smart doesn't mean you can't be incredibly stupid at the same time."

"Moriarty was able to open the file?"

She nodded. "After he broke into my condo, he must have taken one of the gellcaps that Morgan had stolen. He sat at the computer, enhanced, and was easily able to bypass my security."

Kira scowled, clearly annoyed with herself even now. "I was lucky," she continued. "I had been paranoid enough to only keep records of individual animal experiments on the computer, and philosophical musings. The actual step by step and gene by gene instructions for the longevity therapy, and for the second level of intelligence enhancement, were stored on a key-ring flash drive I kept with me at all times. There was no mention in my computer, whatsoever, that I had been working on an even greater level of intelligence enhancement. Moriarty still knows nothing about this. But I did have notes on the longevity therapy. He couldn't get the recipe, but he learned that I had found a way to extend life."

Desh's eyes narrowed. "Smith knew you had slowed the aging process by half. He also said your ultimate plan on the road to immortality was to design nanobots to patrol the bloodstream, and then find a way to transfer consciousness."

"That's right. This general plan was recorded on my computer. It was my initial thinking before I realized what a disaster even the first step would be. Exactly as Smith described."

"Interesting," said Desh. "So do you think he's Moriarty?"

Kira considered. "Maybe, but my intuition tells me no. I think he's just Moriarty's lieutenant."

"Go on," said Desh, pushing his barely touched dessert to the side, having concluded that he couldn't split his focus between Kira Miller and the entrance and eat a dripping sundae at the same time.

"I knew as soon as Moriarty realized I'd discovered the fountain of youth he wouldn't rest until he had it," continued Kira. "Which meant I was in big trouble. I put the flash drive in a stainless steel pill bottle and buried it where I thought no one would ever find it. I memorized its GPS coordinates. And then I enhanced myself. I was panicked, and my thinking was scattershot, so even though I had just promised myself never to do it again, I felt I had no other choice."

Desh nodded sympathetically. Under the circumstances he couldn't blame her.

"Once I had transformed myself," she continued, "it became clear what I needed to do. The instructions for reconstructing my therapies were dozens and dozens of typed pages long. To be absolutely certain that the secret was safe, even if I was under duress, I imprisoned my memories of the formulas and the GPS coordinates to the buried flash drive: even the memory of the general *area* in which it was buried. I partitioned these memories behind an impenetrable mental wall." She sighed. "It wasn't easy."

"I don't doubt it," said Desh.

"Even enhanced, finding and isolating specific memory traces in my own mind was an extraordinarily difficult challenge."

"But you were able to do it?"

"Yes. I structured these memories so I could only access them if I made a powerful, conscious decision that I wanted to. And like a Chinese finger trap, I set it up so the more I fought to get at the memories while under duress, the stronger the barrier would become." She paused. "As it turned out, I didn't do this a moment too soon."

Desh leaned forward intently.

"A few hours later Larry Lusetti broke into my condo and took me hostage," said Kira. "He wanted the secret to extended life and told me he wasn't leaving without it. He used truth drugs on me. They were very effective. I told him about the discovery and why I hadn't shared it with the world. But when he asked about age retardation, I told him I didn't remember the recipe."

"Which was now absolutely true," said Desh.

Kira nodded. She took a final bite of her sundae, her spoon clinking loudly against the sides of the tall parfait glass as she retrieved it, and pushed it aside. "Unfortunately, I was unable to hold anything else back from him. Under the drugs I told him about the flash drive. I told him exactly how I had partitioned the GPS coordinates in my memory so I couldn't retrieve them under duress. He dutifully reported this to Moriarty."

"And did Moriarty believe you?"

"I assume so. If not, I think he would have had Lusetti use torture in addition to truth drugs, which he never did." Kira paused as if bracing herself to continue, dreading the prospect.

Desh could sense something was very wrong. "What happened then?" he prompted gently.

"I woke up the next morning, still a hostage." She looked off into the distance and a tear slowly formed in the corner of one eye. "And Lusetti told me they had my brother, Alan."

Desh's eyes widened as the connections became obvious.

"Lusetti told me his boss was in Alan's home in Cincinnati," she whispered in horror, "and would burn my brother alive unless I gave him the secret."

"Did you?" said Desh softly.

She looked pale as she shook her head no.

Desh realized he had asked a stupid question. If Moriarty already had the fountain of youth, he wouldn't be so desperate to capture her alive.

"I knew that Moriarty was a man without principles *before* his brain was rewired," she explained somberly. "But if he had the secret to extended life, he could become the biggest monster in history. What could stop him? He could enhance his intelligence and could use the promise of extended life to amass power beyond imagining. The kind of power that Smith accused *me* of wanting."

Kira stopped and a single tear shook itself loose and rolled slowly down her cheek.

Moriarty had forced her to make an impossible decision, Desh realized. He could tell this had caused a deep rift to her psyche that would never heal. "You knew the stakes, and you did what you had to do," he said softly. "I admire you for that."

She shook her head as tears now welled up in both of her eyes. "I wasn't a hero," she said miserably. "I was a weakling. I would have done *anything* to save Alan, even at the risk of unleashing another Hitler on the world. I tried to unlock the memory with all of my might. But I couldn't," she whispered. "The barrier I had constructed was too good." Kira lowered her eyes. "It didn't matter, anyway. I knew in my heart that Moriarty would never let Alan go. Once I gave him what he wanted, he would kill Alan and me both—and Lusetti as well. We would be dangerous loose ends."

Desh realized her analysis was dead on. She had truly been in a no win situation. "So what did you do?" he asked.

"I needed to buy time to rescue my brother. So I told Lusetti the truth. I told him I was trying but couldn't reach these memories. The software I had set up in my mind to guard them wasn't fooled. I explained I was under more duress because of the threat to my brother than if I was being physically tortured."

"Did he believe you?"

"I think so," she said, absently wiping a tear away with the back of her hand. "I pleaded with him to make sure Moriarty wouldn't hurt Alan for twenty-four hours while I found a way to unlock my memories. He told me Moriarty agreed to this."

"And then you killed Lusetti."

She nodded. "He untied me for a bathroom break right after the call with his boss. I knew I had the upper hand in any struggle. I knew he couldn't risk killing me before he had the fountain of youth. I was able to hit him with a marble bookend while he was trying to incapacitate me. I didn't want to kill him," she insisted, her voice distraught. "It just happened that way."

Desh's eyes narrowed. "So you rushed to Lusetti's apartment, hoping you could learn who was pulling his strings," he said.

"That's right. I took his laptop and a file I found with my name on it and went straight to the airport. I took the first flight to Cincinnati, using one of the false identities I already had in place. I studied the file and laptop on the plane, but neither contained Moriarty's identity."

Kira gathered herself. "I'm sure you've guessed the rest by now," she said. "The plane landed and I raced to my brother's house. I was determined to do whatever it took to save his life."

"But you were too late," said Desh solemnly.

A tortured expression came over Kira's face and eyes. "I was too late," she repeated softly, shuddering. She picked up a napkin and wiped away several tears that had begun to roll their way slowly down her face. "I had a special relationship with my brother Alan. He was five years older and always looked out for me. When other kids taunted me because I was different, or because I had skipped a few grades, he defended me. And then when my parents died—"

Her voice broke. She paused and fought to get her emotions under control. "Alan was in college then," she said finally, her voice regaining strength. "At Ohio State. He took a year off to stay with me to make sure I would be okay. I pleaded with him not to put his own life on hold for me, but he wouldn't hear of it. He didn't go back to finish his degree until I left for college myself."

Desh nodded sympathetically and waited for her to continue, but her expression indicated she was emotionally spent and couldn't bear to talk about her brother any further.

"So once you realized you were too late to save him," said Desh solemnly, "you knew you had to vanish from the grid."

She nodded.

"I am truly sorry," he said softly.

Silence hung over them like a rain cloud for several long seconds.

"You killed Lusetti," said Desh finally. "But this was clearly in self defense. If what you say is true then you really *haven't* committed any crimes."

She sighed. "If you don't count illegal human experimentation and misappropriation of corporate resources."

"I don't," said Desh without hesitation.

Kira tried to force a smile but couldn't quite manage it. "Moriarty has been hunting me ever since. He was probably already wealthy and powerful when he got into the game, not to mention ruthless. But it wouldn't take twenty-three hours of superhuman intelligence to create immense wealth and power. I started with very little and created a fortune in no time. Think about what he's been able to do in the last several years."

Desh did and it wasn't a pretty picture. "Any ideas who he might be?"

"None," she said, beginning to recover her emotional equilibrium. "Whoever it is will be very subtle about his wealth and power. You won't find him on the cover of business magazines. The truly powerful don't advertise, they just pull strings from off stage."

Desh thought about this and decided she was almost certainly correct.

"Whoever he is, he didn't waste any time framing me for the murders of Lusetti and my brother. But that wasn't enough to suit him. He decided to pin the Ebola plot on me as well so he could galvanize the entire US military against me. I don't know if he has any other plans with terrorists, but the evidence you've seen is due to his involvement, not mine."

"What does he gain by working with terrorists?" asked Desh.

"I don't know. But there has to be more to it than we're seeing. Because I'm convinced he won't be able to perfect a genetically engineered cold virus capable of delivering Ebola genes."

"Why not?"

"Too complex a project."

"Even with enhanced intelligence?"

"Yes. When my mind is transformed, I have thousands and thousands of hours of the study of molecular biology in my memory for my intellect to draw upon. He almost certainly doesn't. Without this, no matter how great his intelligence, he doesn't have the knowledge base to succeed."

Desh frowned. The more he learned, the more confused he became. He decided to move on. "So why does he want you now? He already knows he can't force the secret of longevity from you."

"I don't know," she said with a shrug. "But he's taking great pains to capture me alive, even knowing I'm his biggest threat and won't rest until I've stopped him. It's obvious he hasn't given up on the fountain of youth."

They sat in silence for several seconds. Finally, Desh glanced at his watch and sighed. "We'd better go," he said. "We have a bus to catch."

Desh paid for the sundaes and they cautiously returned to the main mall. He scanned their surroundings for several minutes but didn't detect anything out of place.

Desh gave Kira a questioning look as they made their way across the mall. "So why me, Kira?" he asked simply.

She sighed. "I already told you. You're a good man. And when the chips are down, you'll do the right thing. You're an expert at finding people. You have Special Forces training. You're smart and well read. I've been trying to find Moriarty and stop him, but I've gotten nowhere."

Kira reached out and placed her hand in front of Desh, signaling him to stop walking. When he did she looked deeply into his eyes and he sensed she was deciding if she wanted to say more. Finally she lowered her eyes. "And I was lonely," she said softly. "I've been on the run for a very long time. Not trusting anyone. Suspicious of everything." She paused. "But I can't stop Moriarty alone. As I studied your history, I realized I needed the help of someone like you; someone I could trust."

So she had risked kidnapping him, even though he couldn't have been more biased against her, to convince him to become her ally. Just as she had told him at the motel. And she had taken an even greater risk by putting herself under his control at the clearing. He still had a few nagging suspicions but he would put them to rest—for now.

Kira gazed into his eyes hopefully. "Will you help me, David?" she asked.

Desh held her stare for several seconds and then nodded, almost imperceptibly. "Yes," he said finally. "I will."

Kira let out the breath she had been holding. "Thank you," she whispered earnestly. "And I really am sorry for bringing you into all of this. It was selfish of me."

"No it wasn't," said Desh firmly. The corners of his mouth turned up into a slight smile. "And you didn't bring me into anything. I was hired by Colonel Jim Connelly to find and stop a psychopathic killer who was off the grid, and that's still what I'm doing."

Kira's features hardened. "I'm going to stop this bastard if it's the last thing I do," she vowed through clenched teeth, her face now a mask of hatred. "I swear on my brother's soul that I'll get him. A tragic accident took my parents from me, but Moriarty murdered the only other person I really ever loved; my only remaining family."

A deadly gleam came to her eye. "And someday—soon—he's going to pay for that."

30

They exited the bus in downtown Richmond and took a cab to a used car lot. There they paid cash for an aging pick-up truck.

Griffin had called while they were on the bus and he and Connelly were doing well, despite the fact, as Griffin had put it, that being forced to shave his beard had surely "scarred and traumatized him for life." They had arrived at the house of Connelly's retired doctor friend without incident and Connelly was getting treatment.

Desh took the driver's seat of the used pick-up when the transaction was completed. "Where to?" he asked.

"Get back on 95 north," replied Kira. "Let's go to my place."

"You have a place? After all this time on the run?"

Her eyes danced playfully. "It's a motor home. I live in a trailer park."

"You're kidding."

"Why do you say that?" she said impishly.

Desh shrugged. "I don't know. You're a brilliant scientist whose discoveries could change the world. You just don't picture someone like that in an RV." He smiled broadly. "Albert Einstein living in a trailer park just seems wrong to me."

She laughed. "That's why it's so perfect. A trailer park is the last place the old me would ever think of living and the last place anyone would think to look. And this way, I can change locations every month or so and still have a sense of home."

It was a sound strategy, Desh realized, once you stopped to think about it. "I'm embarrassed to say that I've never been to a trailer park."

"You're in for a treat then," she said. "I have three RVs as a matter of fact. One on the East Coast, one on the West Coast, and one in the heartland. The last two are just safety valves. I paid for a year at the trailer park in advance so they'll be there for me if I need them."

"I can hardly wait to see it," said Desh, stopping at a red light. "So tell me about your search for Moriarty."

"I will. But not now. I've been doing all of the talking. It's your turn."

"In my defense, I was too busy doing the mistrusting and glaring for that."

"Given what you were told, I can't blame you," she said. "But tell me about *you.* It's been a long time since I've gotten to know anyone. How did you end up in the military?" She paused. "Or did you feel like you really didn't have a choice?"

For just a moment Desh had forgotten that she had made a study of him, but her question reminded him immediately. His father had been a general, a fact that she well knew as evidenced by her question. She certainly hadn't wasted any time on small talk, although with everything they had been through, he realized, small talk at this point would be a little ridiculous.

"I had a choice," he answered. "Definitely. Dad wasn't like that. He loved being in the military but he wanted me and my brother to do what made us happy. In the end, I joined up, not because he pressured me, but because he set such a good example. He was compassionate and friendly and had a great sense of humor." Desh paused. "Most people picture military lifers as rigid, inflexible, authoritarian bureaucrats—and many of them are—but not my father."

"What did your mother think of it all?"

"She had a similar philosophy. She wanted us to be happy. She admired my dad, but she made sure we knew the sacrifices we would be making if we joined up. Funny," he added, "my brother joined up also. Went to Annapolis. I sometimes wonder if either of my folks had put pressure on us if we would have done something else, just to rebel."

Desh hadn't spoken of his father for a long time and his eyes reflected a deep loss.

"I'm sorry about your father," said Kira softly.

He nodded. "If anyone knows about loss, it's you," he said. "Did any of my records say how it happened?"

"No. Just that he died in action."

"Which is a misrepresentation," said Desh dourly. "He was in Pakistan at a weeklong meeting with regional military leaders. He died buying fruit at a market near his hotel. Just another terrorist bombing. Ironic: he had seen a lot of action in his career, but he died off-duty and out of uniform." His lip curled up in disgust. "They probably wouldn't have bombed the place if they knew he was a general. They actually *prefer* killing civilians," he said bitterly. "Generates more terror that way."

Kira sighed supportively. After a few seconds of silence she said, "How's your brother doing?"

"He's doing well. I didn't get to visit with him very often before I left the service. But since I became a civilian I've been seeing more of him."

"Do you regret leaving the military?"

"Honestly, no. I feel a little selfish and maybe a little cowardly; but no. I was ready to leave even before the disaster in Iran. When you're in the Delta Force you don't form strong attachments to anyone outside your team—you can't. Not really. And I didn't want to go through life that way. I wanted to be a husband and father someday."

They drove on in silence for several minutes. "You mentioned Iran," began Kira hesitantly. "What happened there exactly?"

"You must have read the after action report."

"I skimmed through it," she acknowledged. "But it was lengthy and I didn't read it carefully. Besides," she continued, "If we're going to be allies, David, the more insight we have into each other, the better. I'd be interested in hearing these events in your own words."

Desh shrugged. "There's nothing to tell," he lied. He had planned to stop there when it occurred to him that Kira had bared her soul at the restaurant. Maybe it *was* his turn. He sighed heavily. "Okay, I'll give you an abbreviated version."

Desh paused and gathered himself. "Intel had finally located the leader of a terror group, Khalid Abdul-Malik. He was responsible for a series of bombings of churches and synagogues around the world, all timed during religious services to maximize casualties. He was headquartered just outside of Sanandaj, on Iran's western border. We were sent in to capture him if possible, kill him if not. Our insertion was flawless."

Desh tilted his head, remembering. "Satellites had picked up Abdul-Malik and some of his key lieutenants on the move, headed toward the nearby town of Mahabad, and we planned an ambush." He shook his head, a tormented expression on his face. "But we were ambushed instead," he said sullenly. He fell silent for several long seconds and then added, "They had been expecting us."

"You were set up?"

"No question about it. I have no idea how." Desh turned away from Kira and kept his gaze focused steadily on the road ahead, bracing himself to continue. "We were all taken prisoners, me and the three other members of my team. Since I was team commander, the terrorists decided to punish me by torturing my men to death in front of me—men who I loved as brothers." He looked as if he might vomit. "My head was tied in position and my eyes were pried open. I couldn't turn my head and I couldn't look away." He shuddered. "There are tortures beyond the imaginings of the most gifted horror writer," he whispered.

There was a long silence as Kira waited for him to continue.

"I won't describe what happened next," he said finally. "I wouldn't do that to anybody. Suffice it to say they were tortured and then butchered." Hatred welled up in his eyes. "And these sick bastards enjoyed every minute of it, too."

"How did you escape?" asked Kira softly.

"They had finished with my men," said Desh, his voice now dead and emotionless. "I was next. There were three guards with me at the time. While one of them was peeing out back, one of them slipped on a pool of blood and fell. A man has only six quarts of blood in his body. Six quarts doesn't seem like a lot until you're covered in it, and you see the rest spilled on the ground. Eighteen quarts is hard to imagine."

Kira shuddered from the mental picture he had painted.

"I was tied to a chair," continued Desh. "But after the guard fell I gave him a face-full of chair-leg. I dove on the other guard, chair and all, to prevent him from using his gun, but he managed to stab me several times with his knife before I was able to head-butt him into unconsciousness. I escaped and eventually made it across the border to Iraq."

"I do remember this part," said Kira. "I read the soldiers who found you in Iraq couldn't believe you had made it so far in the condition you were in. They were astonished by your stamina and force of will."

Desh grimaced. "I should have died with my men," he whispered. "In the Special Forces, we take the code of leaving no man behind very seriously." His eyes moistened and he shook his head sadly. "The truth is that my men had been so badly butchered there wasn't enough left of their bodies to bring back, even if I could have."

31

Desh accelerated onto the Interstate 95 onramp and merged with highway traffic.

"I don't know what to say," said Kira helplessly.

"There's nothing *to* say. Seems that we've both had our share of bad luck and battle scars. When the stakes are high, the penalties can be high," he said.

They drove on for several minutes until Kira finally broke the silence, deciding a change in subject was in order. "Look, David," she said hesitantly, "at the risk of sounding like a drug pusher, I'd like you to take one of my gellcaps."

Desh eyed her with interest. "Why?" he said simply.

"I appreciate you agreeing to become my ally, but we both know you still don't trust me a hundred percent. How can you? There's been so much going on and so many complexities to this story that only a fool would fail to harbor at least a little doubt. And you're anything but a fool. In the recesses of your mind, you still can't help but wonder if I'm just a great actress and this is all some kind of diabolical plan of mine."

"You're right," he said. "I won't deny it. But the doubt has shrunk from a hundred percent to about five percent, if that makes you feel any better."

"It does. But taking a gellcap will eliminate any remaining reservations. Sure, you might believe intellectually that I've succeeded in radically transforming the human brain, but for you to really trust that all of this is real, you have to experience it for yourself. I could tell you more about what it's like, but until you've experienced it yourself no description I could offer could do it justice. Once you've been enhanced you'll know that everything I've told you is true. Down to the last detail."

Desh pursed his lips. "I don't know, Kira," he said reluctantly. "I'm not sure I like the idea of altering the architecture of my brain."

"After everything I told you, I don't blame you. But I promise the effect will only last about an hour. After that, you'll be the exact same David Desh as always."

"Yeah? How can you be so sure?"

She opened her mouth to answer, but then closed it again. "I guess I can't be. Not absolutely. I know that you won't *feel* any different. And the people I interacted with afterwards never noticed any changes in me—at least none I'm aware of."

"What about the sociopathy?"

"As I mentioned, that effect builds. The first time you're enhanced it's like you're Alice in Wonderland, too awestruck to have many ruthless thoughts. Repeated exposure further numbs the emotions and increases your feelings of omnipotence."

"And then—what?—you graduate from Alice to Frodo to Darth?" he said wryly.

She frowned. "I use too many silly literary metaphors, don't I?"

Desh couldn't help but smile. "Not at all," he said reassuringly. "And I'm the one who came up with Moriarty. So maybe we're two peas in a pod."

Kira caught his eye and sighed deeply. "It would really mean a lot to me, David. You have to experience it to truly understand it."

Desh returned her gaze briefly and then shifted his eyes back to the road as he considered her request. "Okay," he said finally, still with some reluctance. "I'll do it."

"Thanks David," she said in relief. "This *will* erase any lingering doubts. I promise. And it will also surpass your wildest expectations." Her right hand went to her neck and located a silver chain that had been hidden by her clothing. She lifted, pulling the chain up until a silver locket emerged from under her sweatshirt. The locket was heart-shaped and about the circumference of a quarter. She repositioned the necklace so it and the locket were now on the outside of her jacket.

"I just happen to have a dose on hand," she announced.

"There's a gellcap inside that locket?" he said in disbelief.

"Absolutely."

"I don't know, Kira," said Desh, rolling his eyes. "Wearing the One Ring of Power around your neck in pill form? Maybe you *are* taking this Frodo thing a bit far."

Kira grinned. "Okay," she said, amused. "I admit I'm a bit of a geek." She became serious once more. "The truth is that it's a symbolic gesture that strengthens my resolve to never enhance myself again. I want to stop Moriarty, not *become* him. Having a dose around my neck reminds me of the danger of giving in to the lure of power."

"You played a lot of Dungeons And Dragons as a kid, didn't you?" said Desh wryly.

A playful smile lit up her face. "All right," she said. "I can't deny that it's corny. But it really has helped. And, just for the record, I've never played Dungeons And Dragons in my life." She paused and motioned toward the locket. "Are you ready?"

Desh frowned. "Right now?"

"Why not?"

"I'll do it, but let's hold off. I'd rather not be in a car when I take it, and I'd love to have a good night's sleep as well. How about if I try it in the morning?"

Kira nodded. "Whenever you feel up to it. I guess I'm just anxious to develop that deeper level of trust. Besides," she added, "I've never been able to compare notes with anyone."

As they drove they continued a lively conversation. Now that they were allies, Desh found he had an easy rapport with her. About seventy-five minutes into the drive, Kira called a stop for what she called a biological break.

Desh exited the highway and drove into a small gas station with only two pumps and without the ubiquitous mini-store. He pulled up to the pump closest to a small brick structure that contained bathrooms. He exited the pick-up and began to top off the tank while Kira got the restroom key from the attendant.

Kira had just returned the key and was crossing Desh's path as he hung up the nozzle, on her way back to the passenger seat, when Desh's heart leaped to his throat.

Chopper blades. *Again.*

Before Desh could move or call out a warning, Kira collapsed to the ground in front of him, a small dart protruding from her neck.

Desh had already evaluated their current location and knew there was nowhere to run or hide. The chopper was coming closer and he only had an instant to act.

He threw himself to the ground next to Kira to buy himself an additional few seconds while his mind churned furiously. He realized in desperation he had only one option. Reaching out, he clutched the chain around Kira's neck and yanked as hard as he could. The chain snapped and the locket slid to the pavement. Desh tossed the chain as far away from them as he could and snatched the free locket, hurriedly shoving it into his mouth. He used his tongue to push the small, silver heart into the back of his mouth; shoving its point into his cheek to lodge it snugly between his teeth and gums, like a chaw of tobacco, hoping it was too small to cause a visible bulge.

His tongue was still pressed against the locket when he felt a sharp sting in his own neck and he drifted off into a dreamless oblivion.

PART FIVE
Captured

32

David Desh awoke and absently shook his head to clear it, his eyes still closed, vaguely becoming aware of something uncomfortable stabbing into his cheek.

Suddenly, it all came rushing back. The helicopter. Kira falling. So they hadn't used lethal force on him, after all. Either that or he was in heaven, which was unlikely since pain wasn't supposed to be part of that realm, and the ache in his mouth was very real. On the other hand, perhaps he had ended up in that other place . . .

Desh opened his eyes, but only a crack. He wanted to appear unconscious for as long as he could. He and Kira were sitting on the floor, together, their backs against a concrete wall in a gray, dimly lit basement. The room's only light was supplied by an uncovered bulb that hung down from the unfinished ceiling with a pull string hanging down beside it. Heavy steel rungs had been bolted into the wall at even intervals, and his wrists were bound together behind his back and through one of the rungs with plasticuffs. Kira was bound in a similar fashion to a rung five feet to his left. In one corner there was a sump hole, about two feet in diameter, with a pump inside and about ten inches of standing water at its bottom. Three steel poles rose to meet the ceiling in strategic locations to lend structural support to the house.

The basement was empty save a large wooden worktable in the middle of the floor, about eight feet away from the prisoners, with an assortment of tools hanging from a pegboard above it. An unfinished wood staircase at the opposite wall led to the first floor, eventually rising to a door that was out of sight.

They appeared to be alone. It was possible no one had been watching when Desh had first stirred, but he knew it was more likely that someone had picked up his return to consciousness on a video monitor and was approaching even now.

Desh instinctively sized up his position and considered options for escape, but came up empty. As he continued to explore every facet of his surroundings and commit them to memory, he noticed with alarm that a small section of Kira Miller's skull, just over her right ear, had been shaved bald and was now covered by a white bandage.

He pushed at the heart-shaped locket with his tongue and repositioned it in the front of his mouth. As he did so, Kira began to stir. If his movements hadn't been noticed, hers certainly would be. He had no time to spare. He tried to work open the locket's tiny clasp with his tongue and by manipulating it with his teeth, but was unsuccessful. Finally he positioned the locket's seam carefully between his incisors, hoping to force it open like a particularly stubborn pistachio. After a few tries he managed to pry the two halves apart, but only a millimeter. This would have to do. He was afraid of applying too much pressure and having the locket squirt out of his mouth and out of reach. His molars would be safer, but might seal it again for good rather than open it further.

He swallowed the locket whole—its point stabbing the inside of his throat on the way down—knowing his stomach acid would enter the miniscule rift he had opened and begin dissolving the gell that imprisoned Kira's gene therapy cocktail. But how long would this take, given the gellcap was barely exposed? It was impossible to say.

Kira's eyes came open with a start. She shook her head to clear it, wincing in pain as she did so, and turned to Desh with a puzzled expression on her face. But a moment later she must have remembered being at the gas station and hearing a helicopter just before she had lost consciousness.

"Shit," she said dejectedly. "They got us with tranquilizer darts, didn't they?"

Desh nodded.

"I'm not usually hypersensitive to pain," said Kira, "but it feels more like they shot an arrow into my head."

"The dart hit your neck. That's not what you're feeling." Desh frowned worriedly. "A small portion of your head above your right ear has been shaved. There's a bandage there now."

The color drained from Kira's cheeks. "That would explain the intense pain, all right."

"Any idea what they might have done to you?" asked Desh.

"None whatsoever," she replied uneasily.

"Are you going to be okay?"

Kira paused for a moment and then nodded. "It hurts like hell, but not so much that it's debilitating," she replied stoically. "I'll get by." Her eyes darted around the basement. "Where are we?"

"I don't know," said Desh. He was about to continue when the door opened and two men walked down the stairs. As the first man came into view, both prisoners recognized him immediately. The wiry black-ops agent who had called himself Smith.

The same could not be said for the man who followed him. He was in his late forties, of average height but slightly overweight. He was wearing gray suit pants, a blue-striped oxford dress shirt, and black wingtips. He had a small mouth and thin lips, and blond-brown hair that was parted down the middle. There was something about the man that was unsettling, as if the sight of him had set off subconscious alarms that he was a dangerous predator, despite his unassuming appearance.

"Kira Miller," the man said smugly. "At long last."

He put his back to the workbench and hoisted himself to a seated position on the table facing the prisoners, his legs hanging down casually. Smith remained standing, ten feet away from the workbench and facing in the same direction.

"Who are you?" demanded Kira.

"You don't really think I'm going to answer that," he said in amusement. "Call me Sam, and let's leave it at that. And to anticipate your next question, we're in what is called a safe house. There are four heavily armed men upstairs whose job it is to follow any order I give."

Desh had no doubt from their respective postures that this was Smith's boss, which meant he was also probably the man they had been calling Moriarty. And he had access to a safe house and considerable legitimate authority. Not surprising.

"So you must be government," guessed Desh. "Sam as in *Uncle* Sam? Is that supposed to be cute or just psychotic?"

The man moved in a blur, much faster than his appearance would have suggested. He pushed off the table, took the few steps to where Desh was immobilized on the floor, and kicked him savagely in the gut, leading with the point of his black wingtip. Desh tightened his stomach just in time and tried to turn away, but his stomach took the full brunt of the kick, and he reeled from the blow. Pain signals bombarded his nervous system.

Sam, calm again, returned to his perch on the table. "I don't like your tone, Mr. Desh," he said, as if reprimanding a grade-schooler. "You *will* address me with the proper respect. My business is with Dr. Miller here. The only reason you aren't dead yet is because I'm trying to figure out how you factor into this. But I would watch how you speak to me. I'm not *that* curious."

Desh didn't respond as the man who called himself Sam turned once again to Kira. "How's the head?" he taunted.

"What did you do to me?" she demanded.

"Oh, we'll come to that, never fear. But first we have some other business. I don't suppose you'd want to make this easy and just give me the secret to the fountain of youth? The GPS coordinates for that buried flash drive of yours would work just as well."

She said nothing but glared at him icily.

Sam held out his palms innocently. "I didn't think so. Worth a try, though," he said, shrugging. "I thought this might be a bit of a challenge. After all," he added, the corners of his mouth turning up into a cruel smile, "you *were* willing to let me barbecue your brother."

Kira's eyes blazed like twin suns. "You son of a bitch!" she screamed hatefully, pulling against her restraints.

He raised his eyebrows and smiled. "Son of a bitch?" he repeated, amused. "I would normally take offense, but you are technically correct. Mom *was* a bitch. How did you know?" he added wryly.

"I *will* kill you," she growled. "If it's the last thing I ever do."

Sam was unimpressed. "You're hardly in a position to be making threats, my dear." He shook his head in mock regret. "But I see now that killing your brother probably ruined any chance for us to have a romantic relationship."

Desh could tell that Kira was seething inside, but was fighting to stay calm so she wouldn't give this Sam the added satisfaction of getting a rise out of her. The man was purposely pushing her buttons to cloud her thinking, and Desh knew he had to do something to intervene. "So you're the one who broke into her condo," he said, risking the point of Sam's shoe to deflect the conversation from its current course. "And stole her treatment."

Desh braced himself for an attack, but none came. "That's right."

"But you aren't enhanced now," noted Kira, having already regained her equilibrium. "Why not?"

"You of all people know that running your brain at warp speed takes a lot out of it. Can't do it every day." He paused. "But if your real question is, did I run out of pills? the answer is no. I didn't. What's more, I have a molecular biologist working for me who's almost managed to duplicate your work. Another month and I'll have a lifetime supply."

"And will he be signing his own death warrant when he succeeds?" said Kira.

"Why ask questions to which you already know the answer?" Sam shrugged. "Everybody dies sometime." He tilted his head and grinned. "Except for maybe me and you, my dear."

"So who is the molecular biologist working with you?" she asked.

"Oh, I doubt you know him. He was in the bio-defense division at USAMRIID. I discovered he was conspiring with terrorists for money." He rolled his eyes. "He also had a taste for young boys that was quite troubling. So I, ah . . . pressed him into service."

"You mean you blackmailed him," said Kira.

Sam ignored her. "I do have to hand it to you," he continued, shaking his head in admiration. "Even with your lab notebook, even with the instruction manual right in front of him, it's taken him years to duplicate your work."

"Why not just enhance his intelligence?" asked Kira.

"I have. Several times. If not for this, he'd still be trying to figure out how to replicate what you did. But I didn't want to give him too many pills. First, I don't have that many left. Second, that kind of intelligence makes someone extremely difficult to control. You and I both know that. You can't imagine the precautions I had to take each time I souped him up."

Desh searched his own mind for any signs of a change but detected none. Part of him still didn't believe her therapy would really work, but if it did, he had no idea what to expect when it began to kick in.

"How many people other than Desh know about the longevity therapy?" asked Kira.

"Good question," said Sam, smiling. "The wheels are always turning with you, aren't they. Always gathering intel. The answer is, only me. I clean up after myself very carefully. True, the entire US military has been after you, but I'm the only one who *really* knows what's going on."

"Other than me, of course," corrected Smith.

With a burst of motion, Sam pulled a silenced pistol from a holster and put a bullet into Smith's head at point blank range. The impact threw Smith off his feet and he landed roughly on his back, dead before he hit the ground.

Blood mixed with tiny bits of brain matter leaked from Smith's head and began to puddle on the concrete floor next to him.

33

Kira shrank back in horror as blood continued to pour from Smith's head.

Sam returned his gun to its holster. "Now where was I," he said casually, as if nothing had happened

Desh didn't need to consult a textbook to know that this man was a true psychopath.

"Oh, I remember," continued Sam. "I was telling you that I'm the *only one* who really knows what's going on."

Sam nodded at Smith's glassy-eyed corpse on the floor and then his gaze settled back on Kira Miller. "Although, admittedly, there used to be two of us. But now that I have you, Dr. Miller, I won't be needing him anymore," he explained, and then frowning, added, "and to be frank about it, he wasn't all that useful. I had you dead to rights at that motel and he fucked it up."

Desh's last reservations about the veracity of Kira's story had now vanished. Everything she had told him was true. This was the man Connelly had been looking for.

"How will you explain Smith's murder to your men upstairs?" asked Desh.

Sam grinned. "No need for explanations among friends. The men upstairs were handpicked and are all completely loyal to me. I pay them extremely well, but I've always believed in wielding a stick to go along with the carrot. None of them are big believers in the Ten Commandments and have unfortunately committed some major, ah . . . indiscretions . . . in their lives. I have enough dirt on each of them to put them away forever. And if I die, this dirt becomes public automatically." A self-satisfied look settled over his features. "These men would do *anything* for me.

And since they have absolutely no idea what's going on, unlike our dead friend here, they don't have to worry about, ah . . . early termination, so to speak."

Desh knew that Kira had been badly shaken by the ruthlessness of Smith's execution, but she appeared to have composed herself once again. "What's the game here, *Sam*?" she said, spitting out his name hatefully. "You know you can't get the secret of longevity out of me through torture or with drugs. And you'd better believe I'm not going to tell a psychopath like you anything of my own free will. So what am I doing here?"

"We've already established you won't tell me the coordinates." He raised his eyebrows and an amused expression came over his face. "Not even to save your brother's life. But there are sacrifices that are far greater even than this. I've been working ever since that moron Lusetti lost you—paying with his worthless life—to find the proper leverage to get you to, ah . . . voluntarily . . . tell me what I want. And I found it. So here is the question: will you tell me what I want to know to save the future of humanity?"

Kira remained silent, not taking the bait.

"After Lusetti used truth drugs on you, he told me he had learned why you felt it was so important to keep your discovery secret. Overpopulation. Fear of societal upheaval. Well, you're in luck. I can help you out. What if there were no longer any births in the world?" Sam smiled cruelly, quite pleased with himself. "That would solve this problem, wouldn't it? Give you no excuse for not sharing."

"What are you talking about?"

Sam raised his eyebrows. "Sterilization of every woman on the planet," he said simply.

Desh heard Sam but didn't react in any way. His mind had begun to feel strange. It had been painful at first, like a sharp headache, but now the feeling was electric, like the pins-and-needles feeling of a limb falling asleep, only in his head, a place in which he knew there were no sensory receptors of any kind.

Kira looked at Sam as though he were mad. This wild, over-the-top threat could have easily come out of the mouth of a villain on a Saturday morning cartoon. But sadistic and deranged though Sam was, he was clearly formidable, and she sensed that this threat was not entirely an idle one.

"You're out of your mind," she said.

"Am I? My enhanced molecular biologist doesn't think so. He thinks mass sterilization is child's play. Well, child's play for a child trained in molecular biology with an immeasurable IQ," he said in amusement. "A woman is born with all the egg cells she'll ever have. Take them out and it's game over."

"How?"

"I'm not the expert, but I'm told that it's pretty simple if you really make the effort. Lots of ways to target just egg cells. Hell, there are venereal diseases that lead to infertility all by themselves. All you need are determination and an artificially boosted IQ."

As Kira thought about it, she realized he was right. Even a mediocre molecular biologist, his mind transformed by her treatment, could manage something relatively simple like this. And the entire female population wouldn't have to be infected at once. If an engineered virus was set loose, designed just to attack female eggs and nothing else, the attacks would go unnoticed for some time. Each woman infected would have her ability to reproduce destroyed without coming down with as much as a sniffle. And once all human egg cells were destroyed, that was it. Even cloning required an intact egg cell to work, albeit one with its own genetic material removed to get an exact carbon copy of the donor.

"I can see in your eyes that you're beginning to fully grasp the implications of what I'm saying," said Sam, gloating. "The only real challenge is a logistical one: making sure the hyper-contagious virus is spread to every corner of the world. But there are any number of ways to accomplish this." He began ticking them off with his fingers. "Genetically engineered E. coli, designed to be able to out-compete and replace the E. coli found in every human gut—harmless other than having a gamete destroyer on board. Poisoned water supplies. Contaminated cigarette filters."

Kira looked puzzled by this last entry.

"Don't be fooled by the anti-smoking lobby, my dear," said Sam. "Cigarette use is thriving in every corner of the world. Over *five trillion* are smoked each year. Do you think it would be difficult for someone with immeasurable intelligence to figure out a simple way to contaminate a majority of the world's cigarette production lines with a hyper-contagious agent? With all the world's smokers playing the role of Typhoid Mary, it would spread to every human on the planet in no time." He grinned. "I guess second-hand smoke isn't the biggest danger you can face from smokers, after all."

Kira shook her head in disgust but said nothing.

Desh's mind leaped! A massive acceleration of his thoughts occurred in an instant. Like one hundred billion dominoes falling into place at once; like a chain reaction leading to a massive explosion, his neurons had reordered themselves into a more efficient architecture. Thoughts arrived at a furious pace.

Square root of 754, Desh thought to himself, and seemingly before the thought was even finished he saw the answer: 27.459. Time seemed to slow down. His thoughts had been traveling through molasses previously, but now they were jet-propelled.

As Sam delivered a sentence the pauses between each of his words were agonizingly long. Spit . . . It . . . Out! thought Desh impatiently. He studied Sam and realized his body language communicated almost as much as his words—in some cases more. His every movement, breath, eye blink, and facial expression telegraphed what he was thinking.

Sam opened his mouth to speak and a thought flashed into Desh's mind: just to be sure, I'm going to use several strategies. *This is what Sam was about to say, or something very close.* "

Anyway, to ensure maximum exposure, I plan to use multiple strategies," said Sam, right on cue. "But I don't think we'll really need the others. When we unleash the engineered cold virus on the world, that alone will almost certainly do the trick."

"We?" said Kira.

"Me and my terrorist friends, of course. It helps to have a vast organization with cells in every country that follow orders without question. That way we have thousands of epicenters for our little infection."

Desh turned toward Kira Miller handcuffed beside him. In a flash of intuition he knew: he was in love with her! He had been for a while now.

But how did he know this?

A memory of all of his recent vital signs flashed into his mind. Heart rate, levels of brain chemicals, pupil dilation. His body and brain had been responding to her so powerfully his condition was laughingly obvious. The un-enhanced version of David Desh had been clueless, and in fact would have called the idea beyond ridiculous if someone had had the audacity to suggest it, not believing love was even possible in such a short amount of time. But he had been hit by Cupid and hit hard.

Enhanced Desh was not in love, of course. Far from it. He had lost his ability to feel love the instant his mind had transformed, just as Kira had suggested. Now he was able to gaze into Kira's limpid blue eyes and feel nothing. He could study her with clinical detachment. Love was a lizard brain instinct. A survival mechanism bred into the species that was totally separate from reason. Women were extremely vulnerable during pregnancy, and children were helpless for many years. If humans didn't have a mechanism for cementing a pair bond, nothing would remain but selfishness and promiscuity. Certain animal species were wired in the same way.

How did he know that?

And there was more, he realized in amazement. He knew that research on prairie voles, animals known for establishing long-lasting monogamous bonds with their partners, had shown that the male brain became devoted to its partner only after mating, coinciding with a massive release of the neurotransmitter dopamine. Experiments had later shown that the dopamine restructured a part of the vole's brain called the nucleus accumbens, a region that was also found in the human brain.

Desh traced these memory threads to their source. A magazine article. The memories surrounding it were so vivid, it was as if he was there once again. He was a freshman in college, flying home to visit his family. There was a faint smell of microwaved airplane Chicken Marsala in the air. He was sitting next to a older woman who was flying for the first time. He saw her face just as clearly as if he was staring at her now. He had brought a book, but hadn't been able to get into it. He reached for the airplane magazine, the one that was tucked into every seat pocket. He flipped through it. Page twenty-eight had a torn corner. Three words had been filled in on the crossword puzzle by the previous passenger before they had given up.

And beginning on page nineteen, there was an article on the chemistry of love. He could see every word: read and digest them far faster and more efficiently than he could a page of text he was reading for the first time. Prairie vole males only fell in love after sex. Interesting. The pathetic lizard brained Homo sapien he had been before his recent transformation had become smitten with Kira Miller prior to even a single kiss.

Desh would have bet his life he knew nothing about the mating habits of prairie voles. But he would have been wrong. What else was buried in the near-infinity of his memory, ready for instant access?

"Not even terrorists would help you destroy the future of all mankind," said Kira. "Their wives would be affected as well."

"Good point. That's why I didn't tell them," he said smugly.

Kira frowned. She should have seen this coming. "They think they'll be unleashing an Ebola attack against the West, don't they?"

Sam smiled broadly. "I think the bit about the affliction being triggered by pork is what really won them over. It has a nice, 'The finger of Allah striking down the infidels' ring to it. They really loved the PowerPoint presentation," he said sardonically. "Naturally, I had my representative demonstrate the real thing on some of their prisoners, triggered by bacon, and when they saw how horrific a disease it really is, they loved the idea even more."

"You faked the demonstration, didn't you?"

He nodded. "Right you are. Perfecting something like that in the proper time frame would take *your* skills, combined with heightened intellect. My representative saw to it that the prisoners were infected with the genuine Ebola virus before they got the fake, supposedly genetically engineered, cold virus and were forced to eat bacon. Since the real Ebola is highly infectious through contact with blood, he made sure no one got too close while the prisoners were, ah . . . expiring. When the audience left, to make sure the infection was contained, he torched the bodies." Sam smiled cruelly. "Reminds me of your brother," he added coldly.

34

Desh had fought terrorism for many years and had a wealth of knowledge imbedded in his mind. He focused on anti-terror strategy for thirty seconds and had insight after insight. Patterns of sleeper cell organization flashed into his head that US forces had completely missed. There was a better way to find them. It was so obvious. There was a better way to deploy Special Forces teams. There was a better way to arm them.

He was a kid in a candy shop. Wherever he turned his intellect, provided he had a solid knowledge base in the area, and sometimes even if he didn't, breakthrough ideas presented themselves. Desh was able to monitor and analyze the conversation between Sam and Kira with just a small fraction of his attention, and on multiple levels at once. While calm on the outside, Sam was enjoying himself so much he was almost giddy, especially when he was able to taunt Kira about the murder of her brother. And while her pretend stoicism might have fooled other men, Sam knew with certainty, just the way a dog could smell fear, that his barbs were boring into quivering, exposed nerves just as surely as if he were wielding a dentist's drill.

As Desh continued exploring his newfound faculties, he realized with a start that his autonomic nervous system was now under his complete control. It would work as usual, unsupervised, until he decided to assume command.

His resting heart rate was about fifty beats per minute. He lowered it to forty. Then thirty-five. Then back to fifty. He adjusted his body temperature down to ninety-seven and then quickly brought it back to normal. He ordered his circulation to abandon his extremities and concentrate at his core, something the body did naturally in extreme cold to conserve body temperature. His circulation dutifully complied, the blood altering its usual path. He ordered it back to normal and blood immediately rushed back into his extremities. He accomplished all of these feats without any idea how he was doing so.

Desh pondered existence for several minutes. He could use a far more extended analysis, even enhanced, but it was immediately clear that Kira had been right. There was no God or afterlife. He had been a fool. Without emotional baggage, and able to draw on his memory of everything he had ever read or heard, this was crystal clear. Like love, religion was a useful delusion—an opiate of the masses sort of thing. He still harbored some slight interest and affection for Homo sapiens, but could see how this interest could quickly wane. The power of thought he now possessed was intoxicating. How had Kira managed to resist it for so long? To ignore the will to power that was the obligation of every living being? And Kira had achieved a higher level of optimization even than this. Incredible!

Desh had been so quiet that Sam had almost forgotten he was there. His eyes remained locked onto those of Kira Miller. "I hatched the sterilization plan using only *one* of your pills," he boasted, "right after you escaped Lusetti. I began to frame you for the E. coli plot immediately, and I added evidence that it was real—because I was making it real—as I went along. At least real as far as the terrorists were concerned."

"I hate to break it to you," spat Kira condescendingly, "but this plan of yours won't get you what you want. Were you not paying attention the last time you tried to get the secret to longevity? I was *desperate* to save my brother's life, remember. But I couldn't unlock the memory of the flash drive's location. It wasn't that I didn't *want to.* I *couldn't.* Is this ringing a bell? The enhanced me set things up to make sure nothing, or no one, could ever force the secret from me. Not by threatening *me,* my brother, or the entire universe for that matter. Shoot me full of truth drugs again and I'll tell you the same thing: bigger threats and greater duress just make the information *more* impossible to access."

Sam glared at her. "No, my dear," he said evenly. "I haven't forgotten. My strategy takes this into account as well. But I've always believed that you could find a way inside your little memory prison if you were, uh . . . properly motivated." He paused. "Well, I'm giving you plenty of motivation."

Kira shook her head. "I set up a failsafe that I can't fool. *Can't!* If I've been coerced in any way to seek out the information, the failsafe kicks in and locks me out. Even if I enhance myself I can't undo it. I locked the metaphorical gate and fused the keyhole."

"Then this will be your chance to put that to the test, won't it?" said Sam, undaunted. "You *will* tell me the secret," he said, sneering. "Make no mistake. I believe you'll be able to break through your self-imposed memory barrier to prevent me from going forward with my sterilization plan. But if I'm wrong, you'll ultimately tell me anyway—of your own free will."

"If you believe that, you're even more insane than I thought," snapped Kira defiantly.

"Guess again," said Sam icily. "I'll keep you a hostage until you've confirmed that the entire species is sterile, however long this takes. And on that day, you'll know that the survival of humanity will depend on you. Despite your hatred of me, you'll do everything in your power to make mankind's last generation immortal." He held out his hands. "No duress at that point. No threats. You'll honestly *want* to share your secret, of your own accord. At that point your request for the information from your memory will sail right past any failsafe mechanisms in your mind."

A horrified expression came over Kira's face as she realized what he said was probably true.

Sam smiled. "And you won't have to worry about overpopulation. I'll have removed your objections to sharing your secret, and I'll make sure you aren't under any duress." He paused. "But no need to thank me, my dear."

Kira lunged at him, her eyes burning with hatred, and she was yanked back, hard, by the cuffs, which almost pulled her arms from their sockets, and cut into the skin on the back of her hands painfully.

"Look, I'm on your side," said Sam, extending the palms of his hands innocently. "I don't *want* to do this. Really. It's a lot more hassle than it's worth. I'd rather just give all the terrorists vials of aerosolized water to spray about in population centers rather than active virus. All you have to do is give me the secret and agree to work on immortality. Find a way to unlock your own brain before the deadline." He shrugged. "And if not, I'll just wait for you to give it to me by choice."

Kira felt nauseous. "All this just for a few more years of life?"

Sam grinned and shook his head. "A hell of a lot more than a few. We both know that. With the proper use of your gell pills and an extra seventy years, I have every confidence I can push you, nanotechnologists, and others to eventually make your blueprint for immortality a reality. Your treatment will buy me enough time to be certain I'll be alive when immortality is perfected."

Silence hung in the air for several long seconds as Kira glared at him hatefully. "I need information on the viral construct used," she said finally, "and the method for attacking egg cells. I won't even make an attempt to unlock my memory unless I'm convinced this isn't a bluff." She frowned. "Not that my attempts will do any good anyway," she added grimly.

"Trying to buy time already, I see," he said approvingly. "But it's a fair request. I'll give you the information you require. With respect to timing, everything has been ready for a while now, awaiting your capture. But there are some details I have to start in motion now that I have you, so this will give you about three days. After that, if you haven't told me what I want to know, I will begin distribution of the vials. Once they've gone out, not even *I* can recall them, and the terrorist cells around the world can't be reached to abort the mission. At that point it will be out of my hands," he added.

Kira's eyes darted around the room, desperately seeking a way out.

"I can practically see the wheels turning in that brilliant mind of yours, my dear. Think you can trick me somehow? Think you can escape and then stop me? Well, I've gained a very healthy respect for your abilities. As impossible as this would be, I'm not sure I'd put it entirely past you." Sam paused. "Which brings us to our little outpatient surgery on your skull," he said, smirking.

35

Desh turned his attention to the last forty-eight hours of his life. He had been drinking from a fire-hose but now was his chance to sort everything out. Kira's analysis was right, as far as it went, but she had been too shortsighted. Doubling the span of human life in one fell swoop would *lead to disaster. But there was a better answer than just burying the discovery and walking away. And it didn't involve sacrificing the next generation. It simply meant expanding human territorial boundaries to absorb population increases: it meant conquering space.*

If humanity could readily expand into infinity, Kira's therapy could be disclosed to the fanfare it deserved, with no concerns for its effect on the species. Not the pathetic attempts at space travel that were currently being made, focused on incremental improvements, but attempts at revolutionary leaps in technology, with inexpensive interstellar travel as the goal. Leapfrogging the next several generations of space technology in a single bound. Antimatter. Wormholes. Alcubierre's warp drive. Tachyonic drives.

This would require the optimization of top physicists, perhaps with Kira's even more potent potion. This is why she had failed to consider it. She was too used to working and thinking alone, too certain until she had decided to trust Desh that this was critical to her survival. And too certain that her enhancement therapy was too corrupting to be unleashed.

But it didn't have to be that way. With enhanced intellect, there should be a foolproof way to assess someone's inherent trustworthiness and integrity. Yes, the treatment led to a ruthless megalomania, but the ethics and morals of those treated would return to baseline levels when their brains returned to normal.

It would require teamwork among truly good people, but it could be done. Safeguards could be taken to ensure that whoever was enhanced remained under control and working toward joint purposes. Even Sam had managed to enhance someone who was already a psychopath and contain him for the hour. It would simply require a team of Dr. Jekylls to restrain the one chosen to unleash their super-intelligent Mr. Hyde.

He pondered the identity of Smith and Sam and their possible connections to Morgan, Kira's boss at NeuroCure, and also how Morgan had managed to learn of her work in the first place. He called up his every memory since he had first stepped into Connelly's office and let his mind search for patterns and connections. His mind raised a few interesting possibilities to his consciousness for consideration. Very interesting possibilities, in fact.

After a few more minutes of concentrated thought on the subject, the probability that he was on the right track continued to grow, although there were so many unknowns he was far from certain of this. Still, he needed to assume his working hypothesis was true and plan accordingly.

And in the meanwhile, he would attempt to do something about another discovery he had made, one that he had already incorporated into his analysis. To do so would require redirecting untold trillions of his own antibodies and lymphocytes. He wondered if his newfound ability to control his autonomic nervous system applied to his immune system as well. There was only one way to find out.

Sam smiled at Kira and tapped his head, just over his ear, with his index finger, taunting her. "While you were unconscious," he said, "I took the liberty of having a tiny, tamperproof capsule implanted in your skull. With an explosive charge inside. Not much of a charge, I'll admit, but enough to turn the inside of your skull to liquid."

Kira's eyes widened in alarm. The persistent, piercing pain from the minor surgery, obviously performed without anesthetic, served to make Sam's words all the more chilling.

"I've set it to blow at 10 p.m. Eastern Standard Time. And it will, too, unless I transmit the proper encrypted signal from my cell phone before then. If I do, it resets for ten o'clock the next morning. And so on. It resets in twelve-hour increments. You see where this is going?"

Kira glared at him but said nothing.

"Your chances of escape are exceedingly small. But I'm a careful man, and you have an impressive history. So I've implanted this explosive device to be on the safe side. Just in case you do manage to pull off a miracle and escape, or think you see an opening to kill me while you or Desh are still hostages." He paused. "So until you've given me your secret, if I happen to end up dead somehow, you'll have until the clock strikes ten, either a.m. or p.m., whichever is closer, to say your prayers. With me dead, the sterilization plan goes forward automatically. And even if you managed to escape and kill me right after I've reset the timer, you would only have twelve hours to stop my plans. Even with your skills, even taking multiple doses of your treatment, you'd never be able to do it in that short of a time."

"You're bluffing," said Kira. "Implanting an explosive device in my skull would be risking my death, leaving you no way to get the secret of longevity you so desperately want."

Sam shook his head. "No risk at all. I have every intention of resetting it every twelve hours religiously—as long as I'm in good health. The only way you die is if I'm already dead, and at that point the fountain of youth won't do me a lot of good."

"No risk at all?" said Kira scornfully. "You're more insane than I thought. What if the receiver fails? And what if your signal can't make it down to this basement and through my skull? How many bars of reception do you think I get inside my head, anyway?" Her lip curled up in disgust. "Take it out."

Sam's eyes blazed, betraying a rage at having been spoken to in this manner, but only for a moment. His eyes quickly returned to normal and he smiled serenely. "Not to worry. The device has two receivers for redundancy. And while the explosive is a few centimeters deep in your skull, the receivers are affixed just a few millimeters below the surface of your skin. And they're next generation. Won't be available to the public for another year. Nothing but the best for you, my dear. You could be in a coal mine in West Virginia with your head in a freezer and my call would make it through."

Kira glared at him but said nothing.

Sam pushed himself off his perch on the table to a standing position on the concrete floor. "So let's review your options," he said. "Option one: you tell me the secret, and no one's reproductive abilities have to be destroyed. I remove the explosive device from your skull and you live a life of luxury—heavily supervised luxury, but luxury nonetheless—while you continue to work on immortality."

Sam smiled insincerely. "Option two: you don't tell me, our generation will be the end of the line for humanity, and you'll end up telling me your secret and working on immortality eventually anyway."

Kira's eyes continued to burn with a seething hatred. "As I've said," she hissed in barely contained, clipped tones. "I need to verify that you can do what you say before I make any decisions."

Sam nodded. "I'll make sure you get all the evidence you need."

36

Desh realized it was time to turn his attention toward escape. Even though his watch had been removed and he had been unconscious for an extended period since he had last looked at it, his mind had somehow kept perfect track of time. It was nearing ten o'clock. Sam's discussion had come to a somewhat logical conclusion, and he would need to leave and reset the booby trap in Kira's head. He had no doubt planned to end the conversation just prior to having to reset his device for dramatic effect.

When Sam left, would he leave them alone, handcuffed, or would he have them actively guarded? Desh raced through probabilities and options, considering and discarding dozens of strategies. His mind seized on one he thought had a good chance of succeeding. But he would need to interact with the species Homo sapiens dullard, which meant he had to create an avatar personality of the old Desh so he could operate on their delayed level and not arouse suspicion.

Sam's watch began emitting a series of high-pitched beeps, and he smiled in satisfaction. He pushed a button on his watch and the beeping stopped. "I'm afraid I have to go now, my dear," he said to Kira. "I have a helicopter waiting for me. And it's already 9:40. You were unconscious for quite some time. So before I leave, I need to reset the device in your skull. If I don't—" He spread his hands helplessly. "Well, let's just say that neither of us wants that."

He barked an order and seconds later three plain-clothed men had joined him in the basement, each holding a tranquilizer gun. Under any other circumstances they would have been armed with automatic rifles, but Sam was taking no chances that something would go awry and result in Kira's death.

Sam gestured at Smith's corpse lying in a pool of blood ten feet away. "I'll call in a clean-up crew when I'm in the air," he informed the newcomers. He didn't offer any other explanation for the body and the men didn't ask for one.

Sam pointed to the tallest of the three men. "Jim here will be in charge when I'm gone," he announced to his prisoners. "He'll take good care of you." He paused. "Mr. Desh, I'll be back to interrogate you tomorrow morning. As much as I would enjoy slicing off digits and beating you to within an inch of your life, I'm afraid that truth drugs have become just too damn good to justify this sort of thing. Oh well," he said in disappointment. "I'm sure the session will prove interesting, nonetheless."

Sam turned to Kira. "As for you, my dear, you'll have all the information you'll need to confirm the activity of our sterility virus very soon."

Sam paused in thought, and a look of mild amusement came over his face. "Jim, if the girl needs to relieve herself," he continued, "I want one of you in the bathroom with her and one of you outside the door. And don't turn away while she's going either. As for Desh here, if he needs to go—" He shrugged. "Let him pee in his pants."

With that Sam turned and walked to the wood staircase. When he reached it, he turned and faced Kira. "One last thing. Listen for three high-pitched beeps in a few minutes. This will tell you that your twelve-hour clock has been reset." He smiled. "I thought it was considerate of me to provide an audible confirmation for you. I'm trying to minimize your stress until you've come to your senses."

"Yeah, you're a real prince," said Kira bitterly. She paused. "Look, we're handcuffed to a concrete wall. Do you really think you need three guards?"

Sam looked amused. "Just the fact that you asked the question tells me that I do." With that he took a careful look at his watch and rushed up the stairs.

The three guards fanned out in the basement at equal distance from the prisoners.

Kira turned toward Desh with an alarmed look in her eye. There was no getting out of this situation. Moriarty, or Sam, or whoever he was, had won. He had an explosive charge planted in her head and a knife at the throat of the entire species. The situation was hopeless.

Desh winked. The gesture had been completed so quickly she had almost missed it, but it was unmistakable. She wrinkled her forehead in confusion. What did he know that she didn't?

It was time. Desh instructed sweat to exit the pores in his face, and in less than a minute moisture started to bead on his forehead and cheeks. At the same time, at his command, the color drained from his face and lips. He moaned softly.

Hearing the prisoner moan, the guard nearest Desh studied him more closely. "Jesus," he said to his companions. "This guy is sweating like a pig. He looks like death."

"I need a doctor," gasped Desh, the avatar personality he had set up ensuring he said the words in character and with mind-numbing slowness.

Kira struggled to make sense of what was happening. She would have been sure he had come down with the mother of all fevers if it had not been for its sudden onset and the wink he had given her. So this must have been planned. But the sweat sliding down his face was real. They were in a basement and the air was currently cool and dry. No one could cause themselves to sweat. This couldn't be faked. Unless . . .

She glanced down at her chest and stifled a gasp. *The locket was gone.*

Her eyes widened.

The guard named Jim, stationed between his two colleagues, peered at Desh uncomfortably. "What's wrong with you?" he demanded.

"Don't know," uttered Desh feebly. "Gonna vomit," he whispered. "Bathroom. Please."

"It's a trick," said the guard closest to Desh. "It has to be."

"Brilliant conclusion," said Kira mockingly, rolling her eyes. "Can't you tell when someone's feverish? How the hell could it be a trick?" She shook her head in disgust. "Look at him! You can't fake that."

Desh moved his head forward and swallowed hard several times, as if fighting a gag reflex.

"In another few minutes he'll be covered in vomit!" pressed Kira. "Are you prepared to live with that smell all night? You think your psychotic boss will be happy about this when he returns?"

Jim frowned miserably. "Ken," he said, nodding at the guard closest to Desh, "cut him loose. And get him to a toilet."

Ken hesitated.

"Hurry!" barked Jim.

Desh moaned as Ken approached, pulling a combat knife from his belt. The other two guards raised their guns and trained them steadily on Desh, as Ken reached behind him and cut through the tough plastic of his restraint, which fell to the ground, and returned the knife to his belt.

Desh grunted in pain as he rose unsteadily to his feet, hunched over and clutching at his stomach. He glanced at the other two guards. Ken began escorting him to the stairs. When Desh was halfway there, he bent over and made a loud, throaty, heaving sound, as though a week's worth of stomach contents were erupting from his throat.

The guards all glanced away, just for a moment, in disgust.

Desh moved. He snatched Ken's knife with a speed and precision that could never be equaled by a normal man and flicked it toward the guard farthest from him with a smooth, practiced motion. The knife buried itself deep in the guard's chest. The instant Desh released the knife he spun Ken to his right and into the path of the tranquilizer dart that Jim had sent racing toward him. Desh threw his human shield forward and into Jim in front of him, who shoved the dead weight of his tranquilized colleague violently to the concrete floor. As he did so, Desh was on him immediately, landing a vicious kick to his arm and sending his gun flying. The guard attempted a knifehand strike to Desh's throat in combination with a palmhand blow to his nose, but Desh blocked both attempts easily. He had read the guard's body language so precisely he knew the man's intentions before he had begun to move.

Desh now read Jim's defensive posture, and spotting an opening, wheeled around and landed a roundhouse kick on the guard's chest, exploding him back against the staircase. Even as the kick was landing Desh calculated the exact distance to the staircase and the exact speed and force he would need to exert to achieve his goal. As the man's head cracked against the staircase, he crumpled to the ground, unconscious, and Desh knew his calculations had been perfect.

Desh snatched Jim's tranquilizer gun from the floor, stepped over Ken's body, and crouched low under the open staircase. As he had expected, the guard who had remained upstairs bolted through the door to the basement and down several stairs holding an automatic rifle out in front of him. So much for non-lethal force, thought Desh.

The man expertly covered the staircase and entire basement with his gun. He took in the sight of Kira, still bound, and four bodies sprawled on the floor, but could detect no other movement, which he immediately realized suggested his adversary was hidden under the staircase.

His realization came far too late.

Desh casually sent a dart at point blank range through the opening between two stairs and into the guard's leg. He collapsed and slid down four stairs before finally coming to a stop.

Desh was expert in several forms of hand-to-hand combat, and long practice had made his movements precise and cobra-strike quick. And this was *before* his mind was enhanced. With his thoughts so vastly accelerated, the guards' quickest movements had appeared almost deliberate to him. He had been outnumbered four to one and he knew it hadn't been a fair fight—for the four guards.

Desh rushed over to Kira. As he was cutting her free three loud, piercing tones emanated from her skull, startling her but having no effect on him.

Perfect, he thought. His timing had been exact. He ordered the sweat to cease pouring from his face and his blood to flow normally, and the color quickly returned to his face. He considered if Kira could assimilate his speech if he sped it up to more closely match his thoughts, but ruled it out: as intelligent as she was, he would need to continue to relegate a portion of his mind to creating a simulacrum of his old self.

"Are you sure you want to go?" he asked. "You'll need to be sure Sam resets his device by ten o'clock tomorrow morning."

Kira nodded defiantly. "Let's get the hell out of here," she said.

Desh took her hand and led her through the obstacle course of scattered bodies and up the stairs. Sam had said there were four guards, but Desh wasn't about to trust this number. He cautiously peered around the door, counting on his enhanced reaction time to get him safely through any ambushes. There were none.

They found themselves in the kitchen. "Wait here," said Desh.

Before Kira could respond, he rushed off and canvassed the entire house, confirming they were alone, and returned to her a few minutes later. "I want to check the men downstairs for identification. I doubt I'll find any but it's worth thirty seconds."

Desh bounded off and down the stairs, closing the door quietly behind him. He pulled the knife from where he had implanted it in the guard's chest and checked for the man's pulse. He was dead. Desh knelt beside the unconscious men, two in the basement and one on the staircase, and slit each of their throats in turn, careful not to get any blood on himself.

He isolated the memory of these murders and created a temporary dead zone in his mind so they would be hidden when he returned to his vastly inferior normal state, ensuring he would not be improperly burdened by them. He knew that the emotional, un-enhanced version of himself would never sanction the murders of helpless men.

This other Desh was an idiot!

The enhanced version had just ensured that when Sam returned, he would get zero information as to how they had escaped. They needed to keep Sam as off-balanced as possible. The more confused he was, the more intimidated by their magical escape artistry, the better chance they would have.

The stakes were simply too high for squeamishness.

37

Desh rejoined Kira on the first floor. "Did they have any ID?" she asked.

Desh shook his head. "None."

"Doesn't surprise me," she said. "Good news, though. I found our personal items and cell phones in a kitchen drawer."

She held out his watch and cell phone and he took them gratefully. "Good work," he said as he slid his watch back around his wrist.

The fraction of Desh's mind he had used to set up a simulacrum of his slow self waited patiently for the second-and-a-half he expected to pass before Kira's next utterance. The rest of his mind continued to race at fantastic speed, following several trains of thought simultaneously. One train of thought involved their escape. He had learned how to hot-wire a car as part of his general "surviving with what was at hand" training, and he isolated these memories and amplified them in case he turned back into a pumpkin before locating a suitable car.

"Let's get out of here," suggested Kira. "We have to stop this sick bastard," she added with determination. "And we don't have much time."

Desh computed a number of probabilities almost simultaneously. The probability that homing devices had been planted on them or their retrieved personal items. The probability there was detection equipment at hand. The odds that they would find this equipment if it was here, and the amount of time this could be expected to require. The increased risk they were taking with every second they remained where they were. He input all of these figures into a complex equation that he solved the instant it had been formulated:

one course of action was optimal—but just slightly. He transmitted the result to his puppet personality.

Desh held up a hand. "Not just yet. Sam thought escape was impossible, so my gut tells me he didn't plant homing devices on us. Odds are he put the device in your head just to be on the safe side and for intimidation purposes. But we need to be sure. We're in a safe house, so there must be bug detection equipment here somewhere. Let's find it."

They separated and ransacked the house at breakneck speed, tearing through closets and dumping the contents of drawers onto nearby floors. Only four minutes later, Desh found a case in a bedroom closet containing instruments for detecting both homing and listening devices.

He hurriedly scanned both Kira and himself, along with their phones and other personal items. Everything was clean. He checked carefully around Kira's bandage for any signals but detected none.

They cautiously exited the house, wishing they had night vision equipment as they made their way through the darkness, punctuated by the lights from other houses in the neighborhood. Several streets over Desh found an old car that was susceptible to being hot-wired and quickly did so, performing the procedure by the dim light of his open cell phone. He was just pulling away from the curb when—like a hundred billion rubber bands snapping back into their original shape—his hyper-intelligence vanished.

Desh gasped out loud as if he had been hit in the stomach.

Kira glanced at him and nodded knowingly. "Welcome back to the world of the feeble-minded."

He wore an expression of complete disconsolation. "I feel like I've just been blinded," he whispered

She nodded. "Ten minutes from now it will all seem like a dream and you won't miss it so much."

Desh searched his memory. Had he retained *anything*? He was relieved to find that several of the ideas he had had while enhanced were still with him, although the underlying logic he had used to arrive at these concepts was either gone or far beyond his ability to comprehend. Desh forced himself to stop pining for lost brilliance. Time was short.

He gasped again.

He had remembered yet another surprising conclusion reached by his super intelligent alter ego: *he was in love with Kira Miller.*

"What is it?" asked Kira anxiously.

Desh turned to her. He looked into her dazzling blue eyes, and now that his alter ego had shined a spotlight on his emotions he realized it was true: he *was* in love. Or infatuated at any rate. His entire being basked in her presence. She was like a drug to which he had become hopelessly addicted without his knowledge or consent. The rewards of breathless intellect were great, but the primitive lizard brain manufactured rewards of its own. "Nothing," whispered Desh. "Sorry."

Kira looked puzzled but let the subject drop.

Desh knew he could continue to gaze at her beautiful face forever. She truly was an extraordinary woman. But now was not the time to give into these irrational impulses. Now was the time to focus on one thing only: survival.

Desh tore his eyes away from her and focused on the road. "How's your head?" he asked worriedly.

"It's getting better," she said unconvincingly.

Desh suspected she was lying but decided to leave the subject alone. "It won't be long before Sam discovers what happened at the safe house and points a satellite this way," he said. "So in the immediate term, we have to get as far away from this spot as possible." As if to emphasize his point he stepped hard on the accelerator.

"And the not so immediate term?"

"We need to elevate our game. It's time for more desperate measures. And for that we need Connelly."

In response, Kira pulled out her cell phone, the partner to the one she had given Connelly, and flipped it open.

"You're certain the signal can't be unscrambled?" said Desh.

"Absolutely positive," she confirmed. She hit a speed dial button and handed the phone to Desh.

The colonel answered on the first ring and they exchanged greetings.

"What the hell happened to you two?" asked Connelly worriedly.

Desh frowned. "Sorry about the radio silence. We ran into trouble but we're clear now—as far as we know. Assume this is a private channel. What's your status?"

"We're still with my doctor friend at his house," reported Connelly immediately. "I've been patched up and filled with blood and pain-killers. I've gotten plenty of sleep and am recovering nicely. And Matt has brought me up to speed on events."

"Understood," said Desh. "I now have a much clearer picture of what we're dealing with than I had when we separated. I'll brief you further as soon as I can. Bottom line is that I'm now absolutely convinced Kira is innocent and an ally. But a lot of really bad shit is about to happen if we don't move quickly."

"How bad?"

"Bad enough to make me wish for the original Ebola plot you told me about." He didn't wait for the colonel's reply. "The soldiers in the clearing were told you'd gone rogue. Was it just these men who were misinformed, or is it more widespread?"

"It probably wasn't initially, but it sure is now. They've poisoned the entire well. The military is convinced I'm a traitor and will do whatever is necessary to bring me down."

"Understood," said Desh. "You trusted this doctor with your life. Anyone at Bragg you would trust with your life who can fly a chopper; and has access?"

Connelly considered. "Yes."

Desh sighed. "Let me put this another way. Anyone at Bragg who would trust you with *their* life. Someone who will believe you've been framed and will risk their career and life to stick by you." Moriarty would have made sure the misinformation he had put out to frame Connelly had been devastating and airtight. It would take quite a man to put the trust of a friend over damning information put forth by the highest levels of legitimate military authority.

There was a long pause. "I'm as sure as I can be," replied Connelly. "But I guess we're going to find out," he added evenly.

"Make sure to throw all the weaponry and any other military equipment you can find into the chopper before you leave," said Desh. "We don't know exactly what we'll need, so the more the merrier." He paused. "Not to put any added pressure on you," continued Desh soberly, "but getting this chopper is mission critical. I'll brief you fully when I see you, but trust me: the stakes *couldn't* be any higher."

"Understood," said Connelly grimly.

"Good luck, Colonel," said Desh. "Call me when you're in the air and we can choose a rendezvous point."

"Roger that," said Connelly somberly as the connection ended.

38

Desh found a main road and stayed on it for ten minutes until he located an all-night convenience store. A dented four-door Chrysler, filled with teenaged boys whose radio was blasting hip-hop at eardrum-crushing decibel levels, pulled out just as they arrived, leaving the lot empty.

They entered the deserted store. Kira hastily opened a bottle of the most potent pain pills she could find and quickly downed twice the recommended dosage. Desh bought a dozen glazed cake-donuts, each having the density of a neutron star. He finished eating two of the donuts before he had paid for them, wolfing them down as if his life were at stake. He desperately needed to replace the glucose his amped-up brain had devoured, and the speed with which a donut unleashed its glucose into the blood stream—its glycemic index—was legendary.

Desh continued cramming donuts into his mouth like a participant in a hot-dog eating contest as he drove, washing them down with the two quarts of Gatorade he had also purchased at the store. They had learned from the attendant that they were fifty miles east of Lancaster, Pennsylvania, and they headed off in the direction of this city.

Given that Desh had now experienced her gene therapy, Kira was eager to compare notes with him. Before long the conversation turned to Desh's theorics on how her brain optimization could be safely used for the good of civilization, as well as conquering space so extended life could be introduced without threatening disaster.

Now Desh understood precisely what Kira had been afraid of and why she had sworn off her therapy. He had only undergone the treatment a single time, during which his boundless but ruthless intellect had already begun to crowd out much of his innate compassion, and his feelings of kinship with the rest of humanity and concern for human welfare had dramatically diminished.

But this could be managed—and harnessed. The hyper-intelligence only lasted for about an hour, but thankfully, so did the antisocial effects. When the brain's structure returned to normal, so did a subject's true nature. Emotions and compassion and altruism returned as if they had never left.

He explained his vision to Kira. An individual couldn't be trusted with the power of her therapy, but a *team* could—*if* it was properly chosen. Even Frodo hadn't gone it alone.

Desh trusted Connelly with his life and his every instinct told him that Griffin was a good man as well. If Connelly could vouch for the pilot he was even now recruiting, Desh was prepared to trust him also, at least for now. Like it or not, the five of them would already be in the game and would form the core team. But after this, newcomers they wanted to recruit with important expertise would be carefully screened. The first level could be done in the same way Kira had screened Desh, by studying their computer-accessible histories. Once this level was passed the newcomers would be screened further; still without their knowledge. Desh was certain that if he was optimized again, his enormous intellect and enhanced understanding of the nuances of human physiology and body language would enable him to invent a foolproof detector, not just of lies but of intentions; of innate virtue. Those that passed these screens would be added to the team.

Only one subject would ever be enhanced at a time, and this would occur under security conditions that would turn the gold in Fort Knox green with envy. And Desh knew that the people who passed their screens would welcome these precautions, and even *insist* upon them, wanting to be sure their super-intelligent alter egos couldn't escape to do things *they* would regret upon returning to dim-witted normalcy.

The ever growing team, probably organized into a private company, would be sworn to secrecy and would be motivated by a desire to improve the human condition rather than by greed or power—the testing would *ensure* this was the case. And improve the human condition they would. Enhanced economists could derive revolutionary theories to lift third world economies. Physicists could develop clean energy that could be produced at a fraction of the current cost: cold fusion perhaps.

And the team would be ever mindful of the lessons of Midas. They would analyze their breakthrough inventions with great care to be certain their introduction didn't have unintended consequences that might prove disastrous, as had been the case with Kira's age-retardation treatment.

The team would advance civilization, and all the proceeds from their inventions would be poured back into turning additional ideas, conceived by optimized minds, into reality. They would continue to selectively recruit additional top talent: expanding the team's base of expertise and relentlessly extending the frontiers of human knowledge. All the while they would channel massive resources into revolutionary propulsion systems to bring unlimited habitable planets within human reach, and the gift of a greatly extended lifespan to the entire species.

Meanwhile, Kira could work with a team of biologists and psychologists to find a way to enhance someone's intelligence while maintaining their core humanity. To scale up, not just their intellect, but their capacity for selflessness as well. He couldn't believe that hyper-intelligence and compassion could not coexist. If anyone could find a way to accomplish this, she could.

Kira was at first skeptical, but as Desh fleshed out his vision and answered many of her concerns, she became intrigued. It was a utopian dream. But as long as the Mr. Hydes they created were contained by multiply redundant security measures, and foolproof screening technology could be perfected, they could turn this dream into reality. Desh was finally able to persuade her that he was right: that she had thrown in the towel too quickly.

Desh knew that the vision he had had while enhanced was truly breathtaking in scope and ambition, but this didn't change the current stark reality. They were wanted and on the run. Kira had an explosive device in her skull with little time remaining. If they were unable to defeat Moriarty, his utopian vision would be forever unrealized.

They had been driving for close to an hour when Kira's phone rang. Desh took a deep breath and answered. It was the colonel, as expected, and the news was good. He was in the air. His friend, a Major Ross Metzger, had come through.

The colonel handed the phone to Metzger and he and Desh exchanged greetings. Desh offered his heartfelt thanks and gave him their location near Lancaster. Metzger consulted his onboard computer and after a few minutes suggested a rendezvous point. If they caught route 283 northwest toward Elizabethtown, they would find a high school just outside the city limits. The helicopter would land on the fifty yard-line of the school's football field.

Desh spotted the school forty minutes later. He parked in the lot, and they walked the short distance to the field. They had been unable to find a flashlight in the stolen car so their vision was severely limited on this dark night. They stationed themselves under the bleachers and awaited their ride. Even by helicopter, it would take Metzger a while to cover the distance from Bragg, probably another hour or so.

This wasn't the first time he had been under the bleachers with a beautiful girl, Desh reflected, but never as an adult, and never a girl like this. He desperately wanted to hold her. He suppressed this ridiculous impulse, disgusted with himself. Civilization was coming to a fork in the tracks, with one track leading toward heaven and the other toward hell, and his actions could determine who controlled the switching station. What an epitaph that would make: the future of humanity destroyed because the man in a position to stop the threat was in the thrall of infatuation and couldn't keep his head in the game.

After what seemed like an eternity they heard the sound of a chopper cutting through the night sky, and minutes later an elongated helicopter appeared above the field, its body dimensions roughly those of a dragonfly. It hovered noisily over the fifty-yard line and lowered itself to the ground. Desh and Kira jumped through a wide opening in the middle of the aircraft and were greeted heartily by Griffin and Connelly as the helicopter lifted off once again. Despite the presence of eight steel troop seats facing the front of the craft and two side-facing gunner seats, all the passengers remained standing, holding on to straps to help maintain their balance.

Connelly was wearing a sling on his left arm to prevent movement, but looked surprisingly good. Griffin looked somewhat ridiculous without his facial hair—a clean-cut Wookie—but Desh pretended not to notice any difference in the man.

"Jesus, Colonel," shouted Desh appreciatively over the din of the helicopter. "You got us a *Blackhawk*?"

"Only because Bragg was all out of Harriers," replied Connelly wryly.

39

Jim Connelly handed them both a sophisticated set of padded black headphones, with a speaker arm they could position under their mouths. They slipped them over their heads while Connelly repositioned the set he had been using, which he had removed while greeting them.

Metzger was in the pilot's seat in the front of the chopper. He looked back over his right shoulder. "Where to?" he said into his own headset. He was about the same age as the colonel, with black hair and bushy eyebrows.

"Hagerstown, Maryland," said Kira in a normal tone of voice. Even so, the entire group could easily hear her through the headphones, which did a remarkable job of insulating their ears from the unrelenting din of the chopper. "It's about seventy miles northwest of D.C."

Metzger nodded and the Blackhawk swooped off on a southwesterly heading. He dialed up a map on his computer and within minutes settled on a flight plan. When he had the aircraft under control he reached back and shook hands with Desh and then Kira in turn.

"We appreciate the ride, major," said Desh. "Do you think you got away cleanly?"

"I think so," he answered. "I altered some computerized flight logs to disguise the theft. Hopefully this will buy us a day." He shrugged. "I also disabled the transponder so they can't locate us immediately when they do discover the unauthorized use."

"Well done," said Desh.

Metzger nodded to acknowledge the compliment. "We should be there in about thirty minutes," he announced. "Where do we land?"

The four passengers eyed each other for inspiration, but no one offered any immediate thoughts. A Blackhawk wouldn't be easy to hide.

"We need abandoned areas that don't get any traffic," said Metzger. "Think."

Kira pursed her lips in concentration. She had been living in a trailer park just outside of Hagerstown for months. She should be able to come up with *something*. "There's a community pool near the town's northern border," she said. "After summer it's drained and the facility is chained up. It has a very large deep-end we could land in."

Metzger shook his head. "Won't be deep enough. This bird's almost seventeen feet high."

Damn, thought Kira in frustration. She turned back to sorting through additional possibilities. They had been picked up in a football field. While this was a nice wide-open space, it couldn't conceal the chopper. She smiled. Perhaps she just had the wrong sport. "There's a minor league baseball team in Haggerstown," she said. "The Suns. They play in Municipal stadium. Seats over four thousand. Enclosed by bleachers and a home-run fence."

"How tall are the bleachers?" asked Metzger.

She had never been to a game but had driven by the stadium on many occasions. "At the entrance, behind home plate, taller than seventeen feet."

"Is it locked up in the off-season?"

"Can't imagine it's not," replied Kira.

"How close to residential areas?"

"Not," she replied. "Fairly industrial. No bars or stores in the area open at night."

"Sounds like we have a winner," said Metzger. "Let's give it a go."

With this decided, Desh motioned to Connelly to join him in the back of the chopper. The two men knelt beside two large, green canvas bags that Connelly had loaded aboard that contained a wide assortment of weapons and other equipment. Desh unzipped the first bag and inspected the contents approvingly: four combat knives, plasticuffs, metal handcuffs, rope, tape, six flashlights, a first aid kit, a wire cutter, a bolt cutter, and six pairs of night vision goggles. Desh also found several assault vests sporting multiple pockets for weapons, spare clips and grenades.

The second bag contained a wide variety of electronic and communication equipment, four H&K .45s, four MP-5 machine pistols, and a dozen stun grenades. These grenades were also known as flashbangs. Like this name implied, they would create such an intensely bright flash and earsplitting bang that they would blind and deafen an enemy for about ten seconds. Several pairs of eye protectors and electronic earplugs were present as well to minimize the effects of the stun grenades on those who were using them. Finally, Desh located several empty rucksacks that could be filled for specific missions as needed.

Connelly had done well. He had loaded the chopper for bear as Desh had requested.

As Desh continued inspecting the equipment he removed his headphones and motioned for the colonel to do the same. He leaned in close to Connelly's ear. "This Metzger really came through for you," he shouted. "But it's inner circle time. I'm going to lay out information so sensitive I don't trust *myself* with it." He looked at Connelly meaningfully.

"He's solid," bellowed Connelly, but even so Desh could barely hear him. "He was on my team back in the day. We've been on dozens of missions together, including some that went bad. Real bad. Clusterfucks. He's as good as it gets."

"Integrity?" asked Desh.

Connelly nodded. "We took out a Columbian drug lord once. Just the two of us. The guy had a silk drawstring bag in his safe filled with diamonds the size of marbles." He raised his eyebrows. "Ninety-nine guys out of a hundred would have at least raised the philosophical question: who would know if some went missing? But Metzger pulled the bag from the safe, looked inside, and tossed it to me. Never mentioned it again." Connelly locked his eyes firmly on Desh. "He's one of us, David. He prides himself on doing what's right."

Desh nodded. "Thanks Colonel. Good enough for me. I assumed as much, but I had to ask." He slid his headset back over his ears and Connelly did the same. The two men carried the heavy canvas bags to the front end of the helicopter.

When they were within twenty miles of Hagerstown, Desh passed out night vision goggles and Metzger killed the helicopter's lights. They were now invisible from the ground. Piloting a helicopter blind using night-vision equipment wasn't for the faint of heart, but Metzger had considerable experience doing so. Five minutes later they were over Hagerstown and Kira directed Metzger to the stadium. He circled it quickly and landed as close to the bleachers as he could, well behind home plate.

As expected, the gate entrance had a heavy chain around it and was padlocked. Desh pulled a pair of bolt-cutters from one of the canvas bags, and they were soon on their way.

They came upon some parked cars about three blocks from the stadium, and Desh expertly broke into one and hotwired it. They returned the night vision equipment to one of the canvas bags, threw both bags in the trunk, and climbed into the car. Kira drove, Connelly took the passenger seat to protect his injury, and Griffin, Desh and Metzger crammed themselves into the back.

Kira pulled away from the curb. "Next stop, my place," she announced. "We'll be there in fifteen minutes."

PART SIX
Moriarty

40

They parked at the outskirts of Kira's trailer park and made their way silently to her class A motor home. It was nearing three in the morning, and the other residents of the park were sound asleep and didn't stir at their arrival. Kira had taken care to select a park at which there was ample spacing between RVs.

Kira's RV was forty feet long and eight wide. The drapes were already closed and she kept the lighting low. Despite the limited space, Kira had decorated the dwelling tastefully with several well-placed knickknacks and plants that gave it a homey and unmistakably feminine feel. The RV was packed with cherry cabinetry and had a self-contained bathroom, kitchen, dining area, living room, and bedroom. Desh had never been inside an RV of any kind and marveled at how much could be fit inside, and how cleverly. The kitchen had an oven, a three-burner stove, and a microwave, along with a large stainless steel refrigerator-freezer. There were two tan leather couches along either wall, facing each other, with about four feet of space between them. A high-end computer rested underneath the small kitchen table with a full-sized keyboard and three monitors on its surface. Desh couldn't imagine wanting or needing more than a single monitor, but after the last few days he was beginning to think this was a minority opinion.

Kira gestured for Connelly to take one of the two couches and for Griffin and Metzger to take the other. The driver and passenger seats were cushioned, soft-leather captain's chairs, capable of being swiveled around one hundred and eighty degrees to become additional living room furniture; a configuration Kira used whenever the vehicle was parked.

She sat in one and motioned for Desh to take the other. The only hint that the group was gathered inside a mammoth vehicle rather than a tiny house was the presence of a large steering wheel protruding into the living room.

"We need to brief you and we need to do it quickly," began Desh as soon as he was seated. "There's a lot to tell, so let's get right to it."

For over an hour, Desh and Kira reviewed everything they knew: intelligence enhancement, Kira's longevity therapy, her self-imposed memory blockade, the murder of her brother, the Ebola frame, and finally, their recent interaction with the ruthless man they had called Moriarty. They did their best to impart the information succinctly, but understood the importance of being thorough. The team had to know the entire truth; no matter how much valuable time was consumed in the process. Desh observed the major carefully throughout the briefing, finding him to be intelligent, inquisitive, and a positive addition to the team.

It was Desh's passionate description of the awesome power of an enhanced intellect that persuaded the three men to believe the rest, as utterly fantastic as it all was. If the level of intelligence that could be attained was truly as phenomenal as Desh described, they readily agreed that age retardation could be achieved after a number of sessions in this altered state, and that a hyper-infective virus targeting egg cells could be perfected as well.

Thirty minutes into their briefing, Kira had brewed up a pot of coffee and provided a cup to each member of the team, who were unanimous in expressing their gratitude for the caffeine.

Finally, at just after four in the morning, the briefing was complete.

Metzger leaned forward on the couch, so he could see around the now clean-shaven giant seated beside him, and glanced worriedly at the bandage-covered bald spot on the side of Kira's skull. "I hate to bring this up," he said, "but the explosive is set to go off in only six hours."

Kira nodded, but remained silent.

"Is something like this really possible?" asked Griffin, directing his question to Connelly who was across from him in the compact living room.

The colonel sighed. "I'm afraid so," he said. "C-4 is the explosive everyone knows about, but the military has developed plastic explosives even more potent than this. Shape the charge correctly and it wouldn't take much. Easy to booby-trap a device so it can't be removed."

"Jesus," said Griffin in revulsion. "I am *so* sorry, Kira," he added gently. "This Sam is truly a monster."

Kira attempted a half-hearted smile. "I appreciate the concern, Matt, but I'll be okay. Remember, he didn't implant the device to kill me. He did so as an insurance policy: to make sure I don't kill *him.* If he dies, I die. In the meanwhile, he'll continue to reset it. He needs me alive to get his hands on the fountain of youth. He'll expect me to try to stop him for a few days, get nowhere, and then let myself be recaptured: giving him my secret rather than letting him carry out his plan."

Griffin nodded, but the frown didn't leave his face.

Metzger pursed his lips in concentration. "Kira," he said, "you told him you couldn't give him the secret to your longevity therapy, or the location of the flash drive, even if you desperately wanted to. Is that true, or partially a bluff?"

"Unfortunately, it's absolutely true," replied Kira with a troubled look on her face. "He knows firsthand that with the extraordinary capabilities enhancement gives you, manipulating memory in this way is possible. Despite this, he thinks with proper motivation I'll find a way. But he's wrong about that."

"That's unfortunate," said the major. "It means that negotiating a stop to the threat isn't even an option." He frowned. "What if his plan succeeds? Is he right? Would you then publically disclose your longevity treatment?"

Kira sighed. "I would," she replied. "The bastard is right. At that point there would be no reason not to. Humanity's only hope would be to achieve true immortality, or figure out how to coax the production of new egg cells. Enhanced molecular biologists might eventually discover a way to do this, but I wouldn't count on it."

Metzger frowned deeply. "If we want to have any chance of stopping this threat," he said, "I'd suggest that our first order of business is learning who this Sam really is."

"Agreed," said Desh.

"Do we have anything to go on?" asked Griffin.

Desh raised his eyebrows. "Actually, yes," he said confidently. "I think we do."

41

All eyes were instantly upon David Desh, including Kira's. He hadn't yet shared his theory even with her.

"First, it's almost certain Sam is in the government," began Desh. "We know he has considerable legitimate authority. Not to mention access to next generation military helicopters and to safe houses. Second, he kept boasting of the men he had in his pocket, be they molecular biologists or military muscle. He apparently has dirt on a large and diverse cast of characters." Desh leaned forward intently. "So how would someone be able to get that much dirt on that many people?" He turned his gaze to Connelly and raised his eyebrows. "Remind you of anybody, Colonel?"

Connelly thought for a moment and his eyes widened as he realized where Desh was headed. "J. Edgar Hoover," he whispered.

"J. Edgar Hoover," repeated Desh, nodding. "Head of the FBI for forty-nine years under eight different presidents. Rumored to have used the power of the FBI to wiretap and spy on citizens of personal interest to him. Kept secret files on his enemies containing compromising or embarrassing information. Nobody could be sure what he had on them. Rumor has it that several presidents called him in, intent on firing him, but he left unscathed each time."

"Many believe he was the most powerful man in the history of the US, including presidents," pointed out Connelly.

"Exactly," said Desh excitedly. "I think Sam is taking a page out of Hoover's playbook, trying for the same results. And my guess is he's well on his way. He claims to be blackmailing numerous men. He has also demonstrated considerable power to move men and equipment like so many chess pieces, not to mention arranging to have the colonel provide me with Smith's telephone number as my contact. Since Hoover's time, Congress has added more stringent safeguards against domestic surveillance, of course—" He raised his eyebrows doubtfully.

"But this wouldn't hinder him in the least," said Kira, completing Desh's sentence. "Enhanced, he can circumvent any safeguards. And the word ruthless is completely inadequate to describe him. Here's a man who was a psychopath *before* he was enhanced. A man who bragged about burning my brother alive."

Desh nodded gravely.

"So you think Sam's with the FBI?" asked Metzger.

Desh shook his head. "No. The FBI isn't the best agency to carry out this strategy any longer. A modern day Hoover would choose differently."

Griffin's eyes widened. "The NSA," he whispered.

"Exactly."

"We better hope you're wrong," said Griffin anxiously, "because if you're not, then this just became even a bigger nightmare. The NSA makes Big Brother look like the ACLU. They're the largest intelligence gathering organization in the world, which also makes them the most *powerful* agency in the world. They're in charge of cryptology for the US, which puts them in charge of signal's intelligence: radio, microwave, fiber-optic, cell phones, satellites—everything."

"You certainly know your NSA, Matt," said Desh, standing and pouring himself another cup of coffee. "They've been involved in this from the beginning," he continued. "In some capacity." He shifted his eyes to Kira. "Someone had to order satellites to track you, Kira. But that didn't necessarily mean our Moriarty—or Sam if you will—worked there. Given everyone was convinced you were behind the Ebola threat, the NSA would have been called in regardless."

"But if he did work there, that would explain a lot," said Metzger. "The NSA sends daily intelligence reports to numerous agencies—and even to the White House on occasion. If this Sam was operating from within the NSA he could readily spread false intelligence. He could spread misinformation about Kira that would be accepted as fact. And he put together a tight frame of the colonel in record time. I've known Jim Connelly forever, and I know that nothing could ever get him to betray his country. Yet the evidence they put together against him almost had *me* convinced."

"The more you think about it," said Desh, "the more sense it makes. The NSA would be the ideal place for Sam to reinvent Hoover's strategy, using capabilities that Hoover could only dream of. The combination of being able to doctor intelligence reports and eavesdrop on whoever he wanted to at the highest levels of government—and blackmail them—would make him the ultimate puppet master."

"He'd be high up in the organization," said Kira. "But not the Director. Not enough anonymity that way."

Metzger pursed his lips. "It feels right," he said, his bushy eyebrows almost touching as he wrinkled his forehead in thought. "But how much does this help us? Even if we knew this were true, could we find him?"

"David and I know what he looks like now," said Kira.

"Yeah, but they don't just advertise employees of the NSA in an online directory with pictures and addresses," said Connelly.

"How many employees do they have?" asked Kira.

Griffin smiled. "It's classified," he said. "So is their budget. Their headquarters is at Fort Meade, Maryland, just outside D.C. I read online that someone counted eighteen thousand parking spaces there. The *Post* published an article a few years back estimating the total number at all their facilities around the world at close to forty thousand. Their security is legendary," he added grimly.

"How do you happen to know so much about them, Matt?" asked Connelly curiously.

"Are you kidding," replied Griffin, grinning. "The NSA is to conspiracy theorists and hackers what Area 51 is to UFO freaks. Massive, powerful, shadowy. Not to mention that they have a supercomputer center with the largest accumulation of computer power ever housed on Earth."

Desh smiled mischievously. "Ever hack into it?"

"Absolutely not!" said Griffin, looking shocked. "It's the third rail of the hacking world. First, they have the best security on the planet. Impenetrable as far as I know. Second, if you did make it in, they would find out, and they'd come after you—with a vengeance."

Desh looked amused. "If it makes you feel any better, they're already coming after you with a vengeance," he pointed out. "Surely simple employee records and photographs don't warrant the NSA's maximum protection."

"Maybe not," allowed Griffin. "But even their minimum protection is pretty unbeatable."

"You're the only chance we have," said Kira gently. "Can you do it?"

Griffin sighed. "Maybe, given three or four days, I could get employee records. Maybe. But we don't have time for that." He shook his head helplessly. "Kira is as good a hacker as I am, so together we might be able to do it faster." He frowned. "But still not fast enough to stop this Sam character from unleashing his engineered virus."

Kira shook her head. "I'm only as good as you when my intelligence has been enhanced. Otherwise, you're orders of magnitude more accomplished than I am."

"What about enhancing Matt, then?" suggested the colonel. "If this mental transformation is all it's cracked up to be, with his vast base of knowledge, he should be able to beat even the NSA." Connelly pulled a pain-relief capsule from his pocket, placed it on his tongue, and washed it down with some now lukewarm coffee.

Desh sighed. "I have no doubt that he could." He eyed Kira warily. "But I don't know if we want to take that chance right now."

"You're *that* worried about the side effects of this pill?" said Connelly.

"I've compared notes with Kira," replied Desh, "and the sociopathy effect hit me harder and faster than it hit her."

Metzger stroked his chin once again. He turned to Kira. "Do you think it hit David harder because there was testosterone added to the mix?" he asked.

Kira considered. "An interesting hypothesis," she said. "But I don't know."

"It's possible Matt won't display any antisocial tendencies the first time," said Desh. "Kira tells me her therapy didn't affect her that way to any major degree until she had been transformed a number of times." He frowned. "But we can't rule out the possibility the effect will hit him even harder than it did me. That would be dangerous for everyone."

"How hard did it really hit you?" asked Metzger. "It didn't sound to me as though you had turned into a total monster."

"Not a total one, no," said Desh. "But reflecting now on some of the thoughts I had in this state scares me. I still had some loyalty to Kira and humanity—which is why I helped her escape. But the effect on me was to the right of Kira. What if the effect on Matt is to the right of me?" There was no mistaking the worried look on his face. "Eventually, all of you need to experience the effect, but under far more secure and controlled conditions."

Kira sighed. "You know that I agree with you, David," she said. "But there's too much at stake not to risk this. And it would only be his first time." She paused and then smiled sheepishly. "While we're having this discussion, we should probably ask Matt if he's even willing to do this," she added.

All eyes turned toward Griffin.

"Well?" said Kira.

Griffin nodded. Then, smiling, he turned to Desh and winked. "I guess this is my chance to become even *more* prodigious," he said wryly.

The smile vanished from Griffin's face as he realized that Desh's dour expression hadn't changed. "I understand your concerns, David," he said. "If it will make you feel any better, you can tie my legs together."

"Oh, I plan on doing far more than that," said Desh.

"Okay," said Griffin, slightly taken aback. "That's fine. But even if I turned into the devil, what do you think an overweight, out of shape computer expert could do against three highly trained members of the US military?"

A troubled look came over Desh's face. "Far more than you might imagine," he said worriedly.

42

Kira Miller retreated to her bedroom at the back of the RV. She turned to Desh before she entered and said, "The gellcaps are in a secure spot. I'll need about five minutes with a screwdriver to get at them."

Desh nodded as she disappeared behind the curtain that separated the bedroom from the rest of the vehicle. "Let's get you ready, Matt," he said. He gestured for the hacker to take a seat at the kitchen table in front of Kira's keyboard and monitors.

Once he was seated, Desh and Metzger wasted no time roping him securely to the chair. They bound his ankles with both metal and plastic handcuffs and taped his calves to the chair's two front legs with a stronger version of duct tape.

They had just finished when Kira emerged with a small stainless steel canister and handed it to Desh. He removed a single pill and gave it to Griffin while Kira took a small glass from a cabinet and filled it with tap water. Griffin took the water from Kira and downed the pill without ceremony.

"When will this take effect?" he asked.

"In about five minutes," replied Kira.

Desh pulled an MP-5 from the canvas bag and handed it to Metzger. "Take a position in Kira's bedroom as far from Matt as you can get," he said, "and cover him."

Metzger did as instructed, opening the curtain to have a clear view of the entire vehicle, while Desh stacked both canvas bags on the floor in front of the passenger seat and pulled an MP-5 for himself. "Colonel, you're with me."

Desh turned the passenger seat around so it faced the road again and knelt on it, extending his head above the high seatback with the machine pistol protruding over it. He insisted that Connelly sit normally in the comfortable driver's seat, unarmed. The colonel argued that he could carry his own weight and help cover Griffin, but Desh wouldn't hear of it, reminding him that a rifle shot had recently torn a hole through his shoulder, mere inches away from his heart. "Save your strength, Colonel," Desh told him. "I have a feeling you're going to need it."

Reluctantly, Connelly took the seat as requested.

"Kira, I want you in the bedroom, safely behind the major," said Desh.

Kira opened her mouth to argue but thought better of it. She had been in charge, and alone, for far too long. The reason she had wanted to team up with Desh in the first place was to get help. With a slight smile she realized she should let herself enjoy not making all the decisions for a change. She walked to the back of the RV and for once played the role of the damsel, taking a position behind and to the left of the war-hardened major.

"Major," Desh called out.

Metzger caught his eye from thirty feet away.

"If he shows any suspicious behavior whatsoever, shoot him in the leg immediately. No hesitation. Don't forget that he'll be much faster than we are, mentally and physically."

Metzger nodded.

The group took consolation from the fact that in addition to being bound, Griffin was slow and untrained, so that even if the transformation tripled his speed they should be able to handle him. Should be. No one was in a hurry to test this theory.

Griffin began navigating the web so he would be poised at the entrance to the NSA's system when the mental transformation took effect. He didn't have to wait long. "Holy crap!" he yelled the instant it did. He continued speaking after this but at a rate too fast for the rest of the group to decipher.

Griffin turned back to the keyboard and his fingers flew over it like those of a possessed concert pianist, filling all three monitors with an ever-changing parade of menus, data, and web pages. He had worked too fast for most people to have any hope of following before he was enhanced, but now his speed was off the charts. He continued working at a dizzying pace for twenty minutes while Desh and Metzger kept their weapons carefully trained on him.

"Matt, how is it looking?" said Desh finally. "Can you do it?"

Griffin snapped an unintelligible response.

"We can't understand you," said Desh.

"Can't-operate-at-your-pathetic-speed-so-leave-me-the-hell-alone," blurted out Griffin harshly, having slowed just enough that Desh could separate the words.

"Divert a portion of your mind to act as a slow version of yourself," instructed Desh. "Less frustrating speaking with normals that way."

"Done," said Griffin.

"How are you feeling?" asked Desh cautiously.

"Idiot question!" snapped Griffin immediately. "What you're really asking is: have I turned into the devil? If not, I would tell you no. If so, I would lie and *still* tell you no. Moron!" he finished disdainfully.

It may have been a stupid question, Kira thought, but Griffin's response had been illuminating nonetheless. "You realize—"

"That I was as pathetic and slow as you are a few minutes ago. Yes, I know." The blistering pace of Griffin's keyboard and mouse manipulations didn't slow as he spoke nor did conversation seem to affect his ability to digest entire screens of information at a glance.

Desh caught Kira's eye worriedly, and she knew exactly what he was thinking. Griffin was also handling the transformation less well than had Kira. Less well, perhaps, even than Desh. So perhaps it *was* a testosterone effect after all.

The group let Griffin continue working in silence for the next fifteen minutes, not wanting to provoke the demon within. Kira finally decided it was time for a status report. "How is it coming, Matt?" she called from the other end of the vehicle.

Griffin's hands hadn't once stopped moving over the keyboard since he had begun. "Child's play," he said smugly. "I'll be in NSA's personnel database in about ten minutes." He paused. "Meanwhile," he announced with a superior air, "I've broken into the Federal Reserve and diverted five hundred million dollars into your numbered Swiss bank account."

Kira drew back, stunned.

"Relax," snapped Griffin, correctly having predicted her reaction despite her being well out of his sight. "It's a victimless crime. Just numbers in a computer. I didn't steal anyone's money, just created five hundred million more. And yes, even though it's a numbered and oh-so-secret Swiss account, I'm sure I put the funds in the correct one."

"Why, Matt?" said Kira, concerned. "What prompted you to do that?"

"Sadly, I'm forced to live most of my life as a moron," Griffin shot back. "I'll soon return to my pathetic former self who will be joining this sanctimonious team of yours. The better capitalized we are, especially in the beginning before invention money pours in, the faster we can achieve our ultimate goals."

The four other members of the group exchanged meaningful glances and raised eyebrows. Griffin had become ultra-arrogant, certainly, but in his own way he knew that the future of his lesser self was tied to the team, which was at least somewhat comforting.

"You have to reverse this transaction, Matt," said Kira softly. "It's not right."

"Don't preach to me!" barked Griffin. "Spare me your brainless and misguided moralizing. A sum this great will help our cause, and you know it."

"But—"

"This discussion is over!" thundered Griffin.

Kira sighed deeply and decided not to push it further. The truth was that he was right. It was a victimless crime and would help them accomplish a greater good. She was certainly no stranger to these hard choices. She had broken the law to develop her treatment. She had killed Lusetti and she had injured several others to avoid capture. That night alone she had been involved in the theft of two cars and a misappropriation of a military helicopter.

But this was while she was her normal self. Those experiencing the mind altering effects of her treatment wielded too much power, and had too little conscience, to be allowed even the smallest step onto this slippery slope. The team would need to make sure that in the future those they enhanced had no ability to directly affect the outside world while still in the thrall of the transformation.

"I'm in," announced Griffin. "Quickly, describe Sam."

"Well," began Desh, "His height is about—"

"Too slow," barked Griffin. "I'll find him without you." There was the briefest of pauses and then, "This is him, correct?"

A headshot security photo of a man filled an entire screen. For the first time since Griffin had become transformed he left something on a monitor for more than a few seconds.

Desh's eyes widened. "But—"

"How?" Griffin interrupted, anticipating Desh's question once again. "Without hearing your description?" As he spoke, his fingers once again sped over the keyboard and Sam's picture disappeared to be replaced by a screen of what looked like computer code. Once Griffin had learned from Desh's reaction he had found the right person he continued to pursue other projects he had been working on in parallel. "I can access the log-in patterns of any employee. I know Sam's locations over the past few days and the timing of some of his activities. From your story I know his approximate age and I can guess the precise level and position in the organization that would allow him to achieve all that he has. I narrowed it to five men. His name is S. Frank Putnam. The S stands for Samuel. He's among the top twenty people in the NSA."

Kira was speechless. *He had done it.* At long last, she knew the identity of the man who had killed her brother and turned her life into a nightmare. "Do you have—"

"Yes, of course," snapped Griffin. "His address and more."

"What are you doing now?" asked Desh, his weapon still trained on the hacker. Finally, Griffin's slower-witted avatar had allowed someone to get out an entire question without being interrupted.

"Clearing Kira's and the colonel's good names," he replied.

Given that Griffin appeared to have almost free rein of the cyber domain, Kira was encouraged that he continued to work toward helping the team. "But won't—"

"That be a tip-off to S. Frank Putnam," finished Griffin. "No. The records will remain as they are for twenty-four hours. Kira and Connelly will continue to be wanted fugitives."

"And in twenty-four hours?" called out Kira from her post in the bedroom with extreme interest.

"The record will show that the accusations and evidence against Kira Miller were false, but that she was shot and killed before this was discovered. You'll be off the grid for good, Kira. I'll set up a new identity for you later. When I'm finished, you'll be able to ride naked on a horse through Fort Bragg without attracting military attention."

"I'd take money on that bet," mused Desh, who then quickly winced as if he couldn't believe he had said this out loud.

A smile came to Kira's face, knowing this was meant as a compliment, but she didn't respond. "And the colonel?" she asked Griffin.

"New evidence will emerge that he is completely innocent, with prior information to the contrary an attempt by an unnamed NSA employee with a personal vendetta to frame him."

"And what will—"

"Enough!" thundered Griffin. "I've been more than patient."

He continued his work with the computer unabated; as if unaware he had just made an outburst. Eight minutes later he gasped and looked as if his best friend had just died.

Desh caught Kira's eye and nodded knowingly. "Welcome back, Matt," he said.

"This well and truly sucks," complained the giant.

"Give yourself a few minutes," said Desh. "It won't annoy you so much."

"Do you think you could untie me?" asked Griffin.

Desh shook his head. "I'm afraid not. Not for ten minutes. I need to be sure this isn't a ruse."

Griffin didn't look happy about this but didn't argue. Having been transformed, he now was one of the few people who would know firsthand why Desh had been so cautious.

"Do you remember what happened?" asked Connelly.

"Good question," said Griffin, tilting his head for several long seconds. "I remember what I accomplished," he said finally. "I only have the vaguest idea how." He held out his hands in wonder. "I was like a hotrodding God," he said in awe. "What I was able to do in an hour, I couldn't do normally if I was given a thousand years."

Griffin continued to take inventory of the past hour and a guilty expression came over his face. "I was a bit of an asshole, wasn't I?"

"I wouldn't say that at all," said Desh. "You were a *total* asshole." He grinned. "But don't worry about it. Your work was phenomenal."

Griffin turned to Kira and shook his head in wonder. "That's quite a treatment you've got there," he said admiringly. Still facing her, he let out a heavy sigh and the smile retreated from his face. "Got anything to eat?" he asked eagerly.

43

Matt Griffin quickly proceeded to devour four bagels and then started in on a large bag of corn chips Kira had given him. Desh released the giant from his bonds while crumbs rained onto his head at a steady pace.

Once Griffin had been restored to full freedom, the entire group gathered around him as best they could in the tight space. "My superhuman alter ego may not win any Miss Congeniality awards," he said, "but he sure was a God of the cyber domain. Allow me to demonstrate." Griffin hit a few keys and a satellite photo came up on one of the monitors. It showed a central residence and two small, red barns, contained within the expansive grounds. The house was nestled among several mature trees. About thirty yards from the house a number of tiny horses could be identified milling about inside a fenced-in area about the size of a football field.

"This is the Sam Putnam residence," explained Griffin.

"He lives on a farm?" said Kira in surprise.

"A small one," said Griffin. "And he doesn't actually farm anything. But he does have eight horses and two barns."

"A perfect layout for him," noted Desh. "It lets him be isolated from near neighbors without seeming to be a recluse. He's just a rugged outdoorsman. And while the farm must have been expensive, it isn't showy enough to make anyone wonder how he could afford it."

"And the isolation leaves open numerous options for security," added Metzger.

"Where is it?" asked Kira.

Griffin worked the mouse and zoomed out, showing the scene from a far higher altitude. Putnam's farm disappeared. As if by magic, a map with borders and place names was overlaid onto the satellite image. Griffin pointed at the center of the screen. "Putnam lives here," he said. "In Severn Maryland."

The town was directly between Washington to the southwest and Baltimore to the northeast. It was at most fifteen minutes away from NSA headquarters at Fort Meade.

While the group studied the map, Griffin pulled up a page of information about the town and left it on the adjacent monitor. Severn had been a small rural town for most of its existence, but in the past several decades it had seen explosive growth given its proximity to D.C. and Baltimore and the growth of the government, including the NSA. While much of the town was originally zoned as rural farmland, the vast majority of land had now be rezoned for residential purposes. Putnam owned one of the few remaining properties that could be designated as a farm.

Griffin changed the view of Putnam's property, zooming in to give the view from about a hundred feet overhead. "He has enough video cameras blanketing the property that there are virtually no blind spots. They all feed into two separate banks of monitors, one bank inside his bedroom and the other," he said, pointing to the barn that was the farthest from the residence, "inside here."

Griffin moved the view a few hundred yards from the residence and zoomed in until a relatively unassuming fence came into view. "This is a chain-link fence, ten feet high, completely encircling the periphery of the property," he announced. "It looks innocent enough—almost inviting. No razor wire, no electricity. But don't be fooled. It has vibration sensors. Try to climb over it or cut through it and your exact location is revealed."

Griffin showed a closer view of the main dwelling. "There's a microwave perimeter exactly twenty feet out from the house. Break the beam and once again Putnam will know about it." He raised his eyebrows. "Presupposing you could get over the first fence without any alarms going off, and he didn't see you on the monitors."

"How do you know all this?" asked Metzger.

"He has a very advanced system," explained Griffin. "He has a computer devoted just to home security, and this is tied into the Internet. That way, anyone with the proper codes can check all of the video feeds and security monitors from any computer."

"And you hacked into this computer?" said Kira.

"Yes. And reprogrammed it while I was inside," said Griffin proudly. "For the next twenty-four hours the system will ignore certain inputs. Cut through the fence and break the microwave barrier and the system won't notice. The video monitors are set to show the same benign view of the estate on a continual basis."

Desh scratched his head. "It doesn't make sense to have a security system online that's vulnerable to what you just did," he said.

"I agree," said Griffin. "But it *isn't* vulnerable. A top-drawer hacker could hack into the system and identify what security safeguards are in place. But anyone skilled at storming this kind of heavily protected castle could do that in other ways. But reprogramming it the way I did simply isn't possible with normal human faculties. Trust me on this one."

"Did you get anything useful from his personal computer?" asked Kira eagerly. "Anything that might give us a lead to the sterilization plot?"

Griffin frowned. "No. He didn't have any computers online during the time I was altered. I suspect he only allows an online connection to be active when he's using it, and then physically disrupts the connection when he isn't."

This was a bad break, thought Desh. But all things considered, Griffin had accomplished more than Desh could ever have hoped for.

"Let's get back to Putnam's security," said Desh. "Are you telling us that we can just waltz in there undetected for the next twenty-four hours?"

"Almost," said Griffin. He worked the mouse and different views of Putnam's property came into view, one of which showed a tiny human figure. He zoomed in closer and a man came into focus wearing jeans, a t-shirt and a cowboy hat. He was putting out hay for the horses. He wasn't wearing a jacket, which meant the footage Griffin had tapped into was probably several months out of date.

"Security information from the monitors and alarms is fed to two men," said Griffin as he zoomed in tight on the man's waist, revealing an automatic weapon and walkie-talkie. "He's one of them."

"Interesting," said Metzger. "This guy's cowboyed up so most people will take him as a farmhand."

"He doubles as a farmhand from the look of it," commented Connelly.

"You said two men," said Desh. "Where is the other one?"

"The security computer logs indicate that one of the men is almost always in the barn, manning the monitors."

"Won't the guard in the barn realize something is wrong when his colleague fails to show up on the monitors?" asked Desh.

Griffin grinned broadly. "When Kira makes you smart, she makes you *prodigiously* smart," he said happily. "I took this into account. I only altered the outer cameras, focusing on the chain-link fence and the grounds beyond the outer barn. He'll be able to see his friend, all right," he said happily. "But not anyone sneaking up on him from the outer perimeter."

Desh nodded approvingly. "Anything else we should know?" he asked.

Griffin considered. "I don't think so," he replied. "An alarm would normally go off if the house was breached in any way, but my modifications won't allow this to happen."

He eyed Desh. "Unfortunately, I can't program these two guys to ignore you," he said.

Desh didn't appear concerned about this in the least. "You've done great, Matt," he said warmly. "With no alarms or video of our approach, they shouldn't be much trouble."

"So what's the plan?" asked the major.

All eyes turned to Desh. Even though he was no longer in the military—and even if he was, both Connelly and Metzger would have outranked him—everyone knew this was his show.

"I don't think confronting Putnam right now buys us much," began Desh. "Capture, followed by torture, might be an option at some point, but I wouldn't suggest it as a first move." He paused. "Comments? Disagreements?"

There was silence for several long moments, but no one objected.

"When do you think capturing Putnam *would* be the right move?" asked Connelly.

"When we've tried all other avenues," said Desh. "As a last resort. And just after he's reset Kira's implant." He paused. "Putnam's probably been conditioned to withstand truth drugs. But given twelve hours we might be able to persuade him, in ways he wouldn't find pleasant, to stop his viral attack and give us the code to disarm the device in Kira's head."

"But then again, we might not," noted Metzger.

"Right," said Desh. "That's why we should try other approaches first."

"I assume we start with his house," said Metzger.

Desh nodded. "It'd be a shame not to after super-Matt here went to all the trouble to make it easy for us. I propose we wait for Putnam to leave for work and then break in. That will probably give us a good eight hours to search his house, and for Matt to have quality time with his computer. The goals will be twofold: one, learn anything we can about Putnam's connection to terrorists and how to stop his plan from succeeding. Two, try to find out anything we can about the device in Kira's skull and how to disarm it."

Desh surveyed the group, looking each member of the team firmly in the eye. Each nodded in turn.

"Sounds like a plan," said Kira supportively.

Desh looked at his watch. He was exhausted, as they all were, but they wouldn't have the luxury of rest for a long time yet. A stanza from a favorite Robert Frost poem drifted across his consciousness:

The woods are lovely, dark and deep,
But I have promises to keep,
And miles to go before I sleep,
And miles to go before I sleep.

Desh sighed and turned toward Griffin. Time to figure out just how many additional miles were in *their* immediate futures. "Matt, can you pull up directions to Severn and get a distance."

Griffin's fingers flew over the keyboard and fifteen seconds later a map was on the monitor with the driving path outlined by a bold line. "Seventy-five miles," he announced.

Desh locked his eyes onto Kira. "Kira, we need to get moving. Can you disconnect us from the trailer park cable and gas lines, and do whatever else needs to be done for us to hit the road."

Kira nodded. "We'll be ready to roll in five minutes," she said.

44

It was already a quarter to eight before Kira's forty-foot behemoth pulled off onto an old dirt road a few hundred yards from the outer perimeter of Putnam's property. Desh and Metzger jumped out of the vehicle immediately and fanned out in opposite directions, each carrying a pair of green binoculars, rubberized for shock resistance. During the trip each had donned assault vests and were armed to the teeth. The entire team now wore walkie-talkie earpieces with wires that disappeared beneath their shirts. Kira, who had taught herself how to handle a weapon, was armed with a familiar Glock 9-millimeter pistol while Griffin, given his complete lack of experience, remained unarmed.

Desh and Metzger had only been in place for a few minutes when a large black Cadillac pulled onto the road nearest to Putnam's spread. The car's windows weren't tinted, probably once again to prevent any raised eyebrows in the neighborhood, but Desh knew a heavily armored car when he saw one and this one was armored to the gills—more tank than car.

Desh carefully turned a dial on the binoculars and focused in on the driver. *Bingo.* It was Sam. Samuel Frank Putnam in the flesh. They had been lucky. If they had arrived even five minutes later they would have missed his departure.

Within minutes the car was out of sight, heading in the opposite direction from where they were stationed, toward Fort Meade. Desh signaled to Metzger and they both returned to Kira's motor home.

"Showtime," announced Desh to the group. He handed Metzger and Griffin a gellcap from the stainless steel bottle Kira had given him. "Put these in your pockets," he instructed. "Use them only in an absolute emergency." He held the pill bottle out to Kira. "Kira?" he said.

She shook her head. "No thanks," she said with a sigh. "Just kicked the habit."

Desh and Metzger strapped rucksacks on their backs that had been stuffed full of gear during the drive to Putnam's farm.

The colonel had gotten another hour of concentrated sleep while they drove, but was now fully awake. Desh had insisted that he stay behind to man the RV and to guard their flank.

Desh turned to the major, who was waiting for him. "Go with Matt and Kira and take up a concealed position just outside the chain-link fence," he instructed. "I'll be with you in a minute."

Metzger looked puzzled but didn't question Desh's order. He took a last glance at Desh and Connelly and exited the vehicle with the two civilians in tow. They arrived at the outer perimeter of the property and waited behind a group of trees for Desh to join them. Five minutes later he arrived.

"What was that all about?" Kira whispered to Desh.

"I needed to be sure the colonel was all right," he whispered back, "and to bury the pill canister away from the RV. Just in case."

Desh pulled a pair of wire cutters from one of many pockets in his vest. After a few minutes of snipping links he carefully removed a three-foot square section of the fence, hoping that the transformed Matt Griffin was as good as he thought and the vibration alarm really had been rendered impotent.

They each scurried through the hole in the fence and advanced, crouching low to the ground until they came to another grouping of trees, which the entire team knelt behind. Desh removed his rucksack and propped it behind one of the trees, along with his submachine gun. Metzger held his MP-5 at the ready to protect Kira and Griffin while Desh peered around a tree with binoculars.

He scanned the area for several minutes. Finally, turning back to the others he mouthed, "Back in five minutes," and then, pulling a tranquilizer gun from his vest, he stole away without a sound. The team had agreed they would only use lethal force on Putnam's security people as a last resort. While this was being decided, Desh had an odd feeling that he was forgetting something important about the events at the safe house, but try as he might he couldn't put his finger on what this might be.

Desh had waited until the roving security guard had moved well out of sight of his planned approach to the outer barn. The guard was still dressed as a farmhand, although his clothing was considerably warmer than it had been in the satellite photos. He and his colleague were probably quite competent, but they were overmatched by someone with Desh's training and field experience, and lulled into a false sense of security by their faith in the perimeter alarms.

Desh crept to the side of the outermost barn and peered inside. The second guard was seated with his back to him, at a large bank of twelve monitors, twenty yards away. Desh glided forward noiselessly with his gun extended, rapidly closing the distance between them. He was able to get to within five feet of the man before he began to spin around, startled. Desh shot him in the thigh and he slumped in his chair, unconscious.

Desh studied the monitors to confirm the other security guard hadn't moved from his position near the large horse pen, and plotted his approach. He exited the barn and circled around the property so he could come up behind the second guard. Once he had a bead on the man, he stalked him for several minutes, gradually working his way closer. He silently covered the last few feet and fired. This time the guard hadn't had any warning at all and melted to the ground as the tranquilizer took immediate effect.

Desh pulled out his binoculars and surveyed the area. Everything looked to be in order. He double-timed it to where Metzger could see him and signaled for the rest of the group to join him. Minutes later they were at the back of the house. Desh chose a suitable window and shattered it with the back of his submachine gun, using the weapon to quickly clear away the jagged glass remaining around the perimeter of the sill. All four intruders climbed through the window one at a time until they were all safely inside the residence.

45

Putnam's house was large, about five thousand square feet. The front door opened into a living room on the left and a glass enclosed study on the right. The kitchen was spacious, with large stainless steel appliances, blue granite countertops, and a large cooking island in its center. The interior of the house was in direct contrast to its simple, rustic exterior, and managed to clash atrociously even with itself. While all of the furniture was a minimalist, ultra-modern steel, glass, and silver, the rest of the interior was reminiscent of a European palace, with crystal chandeliers and baroque oil paintings displayed in elaborate, carved wooden frames.

It was 8:30 and they still hadn't heard the three telltale tones that would tell them that Putnam had reset the device that threatened Kira Miller, providing a twelve-hour stay of execution. No one had brought it up, but it was weighing on all of their minds.

Griffin sat at the computer in Putnam's study and called up several screens. The rest of the team stood behind him, eagerly looking over his shoulder. "This might take a while," he said after a few minutes. "I have to break through security and then try to find a needle in a haystack. That's presupposing Putnam left any evidence on this computer in the first place." He sighed. "And I'll be trying this the old fashioned way. As much as I'd like to become a hotrodding God of a hacker again, I'm not sure I'm up to it yet. It takes a lot out of you."

"No question about it," said Desh.

"If I haven't made solid progress by one or two this afternoon," said Griffin earnestly, "I'll take another gellcap and go to town."

Desh nodded but wasn't certain he liked the idea. The antisocial effect was cumulative and Griffin hadn't handled his altered state well the first time.

Griffin bent to work on the keyboard while the three armed members of the team conducted a systematic search of Putnam's home, looking for any clues or information that might prove useful. After forty minutes of searching, Desh activated the small microphone dangling from a cord running down his neck and checked in with Connelly in the RV. The colonel reported that all was well, and that he had not observed any suspicious activity in the vicinity.

Desh was searching through an upstairs room when Metzger's voice came through his earpiece. "David, meet me in the basement. Something I want to show you."

"Roger that," he said.

Desh moved briskly and arrived at the basement just ahead of Kira, who Metzger had also summoned. The room was nicely finished, including the ceiling and walls, and was carpeted. Metzger was standing next to a door in the far corner of the basement. He motioned for Desh and Kira to join him as he opened the door and stepped through.

They entered a small, unfinished section of the basement with its original concrete floor and walls. There was a sump hole in one corner and a water heater in another.

A large, square piece of plywood was standing up against the wall, about eight feet on a side. Metzger went to an edge and pushed. The plywood slid fairly readily across the smooth floor.

Desh's eyes widened as a square opening in the concrete wall was revealed, hidden behind the plywood. It was about six feet on a side and formed the entrance to a tunnel leading away from the house.

Metzger pulled a small flashlight from his vest and pointed it down the passageway. The tunnel continued for about thirty yards and then curved out of sight.

"Interesting," said Desh. "Were you searching specifically for an escape hatch?" he asked the major.

Metzger nodded. "Blackmail too many powerful men and you create a few enemies. Even if Putnam convinced them the dirt he had collected would be released automatically if he was killed, he would still want to have a means to escape a frontal assault—just in case."

"Not all that well hidden," noted Kira.

"Doesn't need to be on this side," said Metzger. "Putnam would count on his security monitors giving him a head start. I'm sure the tunnel exit is well concealed. Once Putnam emerges, he can probably collapse the tunnel behind him to prevent anyone from following."

"Let's get out of here," said Desh. "Even though Putnam is convinced of the strength of his signal and receiver, I want Kira aboveground," he said protectively. "Why take any chances we don't have to? We can search this tunnel later." He paused. "Nice work, Major."

Desh caught Kira glancing nervously at her watch as they climbed the stairs. "I'm guessing you would have told me if you had heard three high-pitched beeps recently," he said softly.

Kira sighed. "He'll reset it," she said, although with less confidence than before.

When the three of them emerged from the basement, Griffin saw them through the glass wall of the study and motioned them over.

"I haven't found anything linking Putnam to terror or the sterilization virus," he said when they had joined him, "but I did find files on a number of powerful people in politics and the military."

"Compromising ones?" guessed Kira.

"Very," he replied. "Hoover would be proud. Putnam has a number of taped phone calls implicating the callers for taking bribes, cheating on spouses, engaging in criminal activity—the works." He paused and shook his head. "He also has a lot of these." A video of a chubby, balding older man having sex with a buxom young beauty appeared on the screen. None of them recognized the man. "According to the file," explained Griffin, "Baldy is the CEO of a major corporation. Putnam has videos of a number of powerful men engaged in either homosexual activity or having sex with women who aren't their wives. But I'll spare you any more samples," he said.

"Thank you," said Desh in sincere appreciation.

"Not exactly the kind of thing you'd want to be shown to your wife or children," noted Metzger unnecessarily.

"Or your constituency," added Desh.

A digital clock appeared at the bottom of Putnam's computer monitor. It read 9:45. Desh eyed Kira worriedly. She was trying to keep a stiff upper lip but he could read the tension in her face.

There was a knock at the front door.

Desh grabbed Kira's arm and rushed from the room, taking up a position on the wall flanking the front door. Metzger hurried Griffin with him into position on the other side. Both men trained their weapons at the door.

There was another knock and then the rattle of keys. Finally, the door swung slowly open.

"Hello in there," yelled S. Frank Putnam from the entrance. "I'm alone and unarmed. I'm coming in," he announced.

Putnam calmly entered and closed the door behind him. Once the door had closed, Desh rushed to the window and peered out. He raised his binoculars and scanned the vicinity, but didn't see any evidence of anyone else approaching.

"Congratulations on escaping from the safe house and discovering my identity," said Putnam sincerely. "One of these days you'll have to tell me how you did it," he added.

"What are you doing here?" growled Kira disdainfully.

"Making sure you don't violate my property any further, my dear. My men will be arriving here in about ten minutes," he said, "but I thought I'd say hello and give you a chance to surrender first."

"Why?" asked Desh suspiciously.

"I don't want to risk any injury to Dr. Miller, of course."

"Other than your implanted bomb that's set to go off in twelve minutes, you mean," said Desh.

"Twelve minutes is plenty of time for me to reset it; which I fully intend to do. I just wanted to tell you personally that you'll soon be greatly outnumbered, and urge you to surrender when my men arrive."

Desh spoke into the microphone of his walkie-talkie. "Colonel, possible incoming hostiles converging on our position. Do you have a visual?"

There was no answer.

"Colonel, come in." He paused and lifted the tiny microphone to his mouth. "Come in," he said anxiously. "Say again, possible incoming hostiles."

"What's the matter, Desh?" taunted Putnam. "No answer?"

"What did you do!" demanded Kira in alarm.

"You think my men wouldn't spot a fucking RV?" said Putnam contemptuously. "That thing's a monstrosity."

"What did you do!" persisted Kira.

"As it turns out, absolutely nothing, my dear. Your friend the colonel did it to himself."

"Did what to himself?" snapped Desh.

"When my people boarded the RV, your colonel friend was hiding in the bedroom. Thought he'd be cute and wear electronic earplugs and goggles and toss out a stun grenade. He figured he would recover his sight and hearing before we did." Putnam shook his head in amusement. "He didn't count on the vibration knocking him off his feet. His head slammed into the corner of an end table. Killed him instantly." He paused, milking the moment. "It wasn't pretty."

The four intruders traded horrified glances. Even Kira and Griffin, who hadn't known the colonel very well, looked ill at the loss of such a good man.

Putnam made a show of looking at his watch. "You have five minutes to come out with your hands raised," he said. "After that my men will come in after you." The corners of his mouth turned up in a cruel smile. "But I really have to go now, my dear. If I'm late resetting that little device in your head, I might end up with brain splatter on my drapes." He raised his eyebrows. "Can't have that, can we?"

Kira raised her gun and pointed it at Putnam. "Don't take another step!" she growled.

"Or what?" he said scornfully. "You're going to *shoot* me?" He shook his head and laughed. "You're going to give yourself five minutes to live? You're going to kill the only chance you have to keep the lid on Pandora's box? *I don't think so.*"

A bullet exploded from Kira's gun and tore through Putnam's chest, slamming him back against the door. "Think again," she whispered, her face a mask of rage. She walked toward him and emptied the entire magazine into his body.

"Kira, what are you doing!" screamed Desh.

"He had to die," she spat hatefully.

Kira Miller turned away from the body and gathered herself. "David, take Putnam's escape tunnel and get out of here. Using my treatment the three of you can stop Putnam's plot. I *know* you can. But with the leverage he had over me, I was hurting our chances. Beat this bastard and then carry out your vision. You're a good man. I have confidence in you."

Desh said nothing, but reached out to hold her. She melted into his arms and several tears escaped from her eyes and ran down her cheeks.

"David," she whispered, still in his arms, "I'm going to give you the GPS coordinates to my flash drive. If for some reason you aren't able to stop the virus, I'm counting on you to give the secret of longevity to the world."

Kira Miller wiped away her tears with the back of her hand and focused with all of her heart on unlocking her memory. Not because some external force was demanding it, but because she *wanted* to give it freely. To this man. A man she had come to trust and admire. Her instincts in choosing David Desh had been perfect. Had things been otherwise, who knew where their relationship might have led.

She gasped. Like a dam bursting, her memory came flooding back into her mind.

Kira cupped her hands around Desh's ear and whispered the coordinates. She repeated the coordinates several times until Desh was able to whisper them back to her. Even if he forgot them, she knew, his enhanced mind would remember them with perfect clarity, along with the exact feel of her breath in his ear and her exact pronunciation of every number.

Now she knew that her life extension discovery would live on, even if she didn't. And Desh would only reveal it if Putnam's plan couldn't be stopped. She was certain of it.

Kira pushed Desh away as several more tears began to slide down her face. "You need to keep your distance," she said.

It was 9:59 and the second hand on Desh's watch was sweeping around the dial at a sickening pace. "Kira, you're the most extraordinary woman I have ever known," said Desh with absolute sincerity.

She forced a brave smile for the benefit of Desh and the two other members of the team. "Thanks. I just hope I was wrong about that afterlife thing," she said.

And with that, Kira Miller closed her eyes and awaited oblivion.

46

Kira's three companions closed their eyes with her. Precious seconds continued ticking.

An explosion rocked the room.

It was intense beyond reason. The flash from the explosion was as bright as a supernova and blinded everyone in the room, even through closed eyelids.

Desh realized he couldn't hear and then instantly realized something else: the explosion had been from a stun grenade, not from the device in Kira's head.

He swung around to defend himself but it was too late. Two men grabbed him roughly, one of them pressing a gun to his face. The other pulled his arms behind his back and tightened an all too familiar plasticuff restraint around his wrists. He knew not to resist. Deaf and blind with a gun in your cheek was not an ideal tactical position in which to be. He was pushed roughly into the wall and was frisked expertly, his weapons quickly removed.

Desh's eyesight and hearing gradually returned. The room began to come into focus once again.

Kira Miller was standing next to him. Alive. And it was after ten o'clock.

Desh and Kira had been forced next to each other, flanked by two armed commandoes who had each worn electronic earplugs and goggles during the raid. Griffin and Metzger had been herded together about ten yards away, flanked by their own heavily armed guards. Putnam's bloody, bullet riddled body lay between the two groups.

The commandoes must have arrived through Putnam's tunnel in the basement, Desh realized, lobbing in a few flashbangs to easily overpower the inhabitants of the living room.

A handsome, clean-cut civilian of average size and weight, wearing casual slacks and a sport coat walked briskly and arrogantly into the living room. His blue eyes were eerily calm, but there was also both a shrewdness and a menace to them; like those of a poisonous snake just before a strike.

Kira Miller gasped. She reached out to steady herself, having momentarily become dizzy.

"*Alan?*" she croaked in dismay, barely able to get the name out.

"Hello, Kira," he said cheerfully. "Happy to see your big brother alive?"

Kira was too stunned to reply. She stood facing him with her mouth open.

"Or just happy that the device Putnam put in your skull was a bluff?"

Kira's mind awakened from its paralysis. She didn't understand. *Anything.* Her brother was alive! And Putnam's bomb had been a bluff! Her emotions were at such a fever pitch she was afraid she would explode after all.

"Search their pockets carefully," Alan Miller instructed the men. "If any of them have small pills on them, it's important thcy bc found."

The men conducted a full body search and quickly found the gellcaps Desh and Metzger were carrying in their pockets. The soldiers handed them to a delighted Alan Miller. He pocketed the gellcaps and turned to his sister. "Thanks, Kira. I can use all of these I can get."

"What's going on Alan?" pleaded Kira, recovering some of her equilibrium.

Her brother grinned. "Isn't it remarkable. As brilliant as you are and you have no fucking clue." He sighed. "I suppose I can spoon feed it to you. But not here. Let's adjourn to more comfortable surroundings—at least for me," he said, quite pleased with himself.

As he finished speaking, the all-too-familiar sound of helicopters filled the living room. "Right on schedule," noted Alan. He gestured to the front door. "After you," he said.

Two commandoes raised automatic weapons and motioned them toward the door.

"What about them?" said Kira, gesturing to Griffin and Metzger.

Alan frowned. "They won't be coming with," he shouted over the incoming helicopters. "We'll see. If I think I can use them as leverage with you, perhaps I'll let them live out the day."

Alan Miller exited the house with his sister and Desh in tow as three helicopters landed on Putnam's property. The two outer choppers were of military design, but the one in the middle was civilian. It was white with red accents and was roughly the same size as a Blackhawk. The word *Sikorsky* was printed tastefully on its shell. This model was very exclusive, the type used by CEOs and heads of state, and could seat up to ten passengers in decadent luxury.

Alan nodded at the commandoes. "Secure them," he ordered.

The soldiers opened the door to the chopper and pushed the two captives inside. The passenger compartment was truly spectacular: more opulent than the most luxurious limousine. There was enough headroom to walk through the cabin comfortably, a fully stocked bar, lacquered wood cabinetry, mirrors and inlaid video screens. The seats were all cushioned captain's chairs covered by the finest leather, with burled walnut finishes, separated from each other by spacious armrests with compartments for wine glasses and phones.

Desh moved. He head butted one of the commandoes to the floor of the cabin and threw his shoulder into the other, slamming him against the cockpit door. The man on the floor recovered with remarkable rapidity and rammed his rifle into the back of Desh's leg. Desh fell to his knees. By this time the other soldier had recovered and landed a fierce blow to Desh's face. He then clutched a fistful of Desh's hair and threw him back into a captain's chair at the back of the Sikorsky. "Don't try that again, asshole," growled the solider. "Next time I won't be so gentle."

The soldiers proceeded to bind the two prisoners securely to the chairs. As an added precaution one of the men strung razor wire across the aisle just below their chins. If they moved forward the wire would slice into their necks.

When his men reported that all was secure, Alan Miller entered the helicopter and nodded for the commandoes to leave. He opened the door to the cockpit. "Make sure we aren't being followed," he directed the pilot. "Let me know if you see anything suspicious."

Alan closed the cockpit door and walked a few paces to the bar. He added several ice cubes to a cocktail glass and then calmly, deliberately, filled it with equal parts Scotch and club soda as though he didn't have a care in the world. Finally he sat across from his sister and Desh and took a sip of his drink, closing his eyes to savor it.

"Now, that's more like it," he said. "No reason not to be civilized," he added smugly.

He reached out and rapped on the cabin door twice, and moments later the helicopter lifted off.

"Finally," said Alan Miller, "we can have a private conversation. The pilots can't hear anything being said in this compartment."

The all-enclosed cabin was carefully designed to keep the din of the helicopter blades from encroaching, and Kira realized they would be able to converse without shouting. Executives demanded a quiet ride and had the money to ensure they got it.

Kira was wounded to the depths of her soul. The pain in her eyes was profound. "It was you all along," she said numbly to her brother.

He nodded. "For someone so brilliant, you don't catch on very fast," he commented.

"My teachers," she said weakly. "Mom and Dad. Uncle Kevin. It was you?"

Alan grinned. "Who else?" he said proudly. "But don't beat yourself up. I was the model big brother around you. A perfect angel. Otherwise, I'm sure you'd have at least considered a possibility so obvious it could have bit you in the ass."

Kira trembled and for a moment thought she might vomit. "Did anyone suspect?" she croaked.

"Of course," he said. "How could they not? But I was clever. I did most of my killing away from home. And I knew enough to cultivate a saintly image around *you.* You had the potential to be my Achilles' heel. I couldn't kill you, that would arouse too much suspicion after the other deaths. Yet if I let you glimpse my true nature, I was sure you would put two and two together and turn me in." He paused. "Look at the Unabomber. Brought down by his own brother." He shook his head in mock disgust. "Whatever happened to sibling loyalty?"

A tear ran down Kira Miller's face. She had thought that nothing could hurt her more than she had already been hurt. But she was wrong. This was the older brother she had adored. But he had been a psychopath all the while. His had been the ultimate betrayal, and he had made a fool of her. *How could she have been so blind?*

"What's wrong, Kira?" he said, sneering. "Thought you were a better judge of human nature?" His lip curled up in contempt. "You were so easy to fool. So needy."

"You're a monster," she whispered, now loathing the creature in front of her and loathing herself even more for having cared for him so deeply.

Alan laughed. "Someone had to balance out your nauseating self-righteousness," he replied. "But you know how it is. Us psychopaths don't really see anything wrong with our behavior. And if it makes you feel any better, Mom and Dad's life insurance policy was a great leg up for a struggling college student."

She glared at him hatefully. "So you murdered Mom and Dad and then pretended to come to my rescue. So I would adore you even more."

Alan smiled serenely.

"And then you framed me in a way that would lead people to believe that *I* was a psychopath and responsible for these murders. Murders that *you* had committed."

"Nice touch, don't you think?"

"The worst part of it all," she said in disgust, "is that you made me care about you. I loved you!" She turned her eyes away. "And you made me think I had caused your death," she added in outrage.

"Well, now you know better," he replied smoothly. "So cheer up."

47

Thin shades made of cherry-wood, which could be raised or lowered with the touch of a button, were completely covering the chopper's large windows, giving the prisoners no indication as to their heading. The helicopter's ride was so smooth and the noise so unobtrusive it was easy to forget they were flying.

"So how do you fit into all of this?" asked Desh.

"Fascinating story," said Alan, amused. "I was visiting my dear little sister in her condo in La Jolla while she was working for NeuroCure. Naturally, she insisted I stay at her place. She always did. After all, she truly adored me."

Kira's eyes blazed in fury at this but she remained silent.

"She had to go into work a few times," continued Alan. "So, as is my nature, I thought I would explore her place. See what I could find. Didn't take me long to find her false bottomed drawer with her lab notebook and gellcaps inside." He paused. "So I tried one," he said simply. "It didn't take a super-genius, which I soon became, to grasp the possibilities."

Desh frowned. "So you decided to stage a break-in and steal them all."

"Not right away," replied Alan with an air of superiority. "I waited until a few months after my visit so my sister would never suspect I was responsible. And I didn't just take the gellcaps. I took a sample of Kira's hair as well, in case I ever needed it to frame her." He looked quite pleased with himself. "I like to plan ahead."

Desh shook his head in disgust. He had used a strand of the hair he had taken to frame her for his own murder.

"Then I waited a few days and killed Kira's boss to throw her a head fake," said Alan. "When you're under the influence of her treatment, things become crystal clear. I was certain that if I killed Morgan, she would jump to the conclusion that *he* had stolen the pills and was double-crossed by a powerful partner."

Desh knew this was the exact conclusion Kira *had* reached. "And then you hired Lusetti to watch her."

"I thought it best to leave her alone to make other ah . . . mind-blowing . . . discoveries, and then swoop in and steal these as well. Meanwhile, I was using her pills judiciously to set up my empire."

"Where does Putnam fit in?" asked Desh.

"As I'm sure you're aware, with intelligence this great fortunes can be amassed in any number of ways," he replied, swirling his drink around absently. "But if power is your drug, pulling strings at the most powerful intelligence gathering organization in the history of mankind has certain advantages."

"But why Putnam? Did you know him?"

Alan shook his head. "While using Kira's therapy, I broke into the personal computers of a number of mid-level NSA operatives. Putnam was one of them. We were like-minded and he was particularly savage. I was able to dig up enough dirt on him to guarantee him the death sentence several times over. So I recruited him and masterminded his climb up the ladder. We made a great team."

"Did you give him any gellcaps?" asked Kira.

"Of course not," he snapped disdainfully. "Do I look like an idiot. Putnam was far too ruthless and ambitious to be trusted. If he ever became transformed, I was certain he would find a way to turn the tables on me." He paused. "The only person I ever allowed to become transformed, other than myself, was a molecular biologist Putnam was blackmailing. And this was done under extraordinarily secure conditions, and only to ensure I would have an unlimited supply of your treatment."

"So when Putnam was boasting about his activities, he was really describing what you had done," said Desh.

"That's right," he replied. "We rehearsed everything he said to you. I even instructed him to kill the man you know as Smith in front of you. Putnam had no idea why I wanted him to pretend to be me." Alan sneered. "But he knew better than to question me," he added icily.

Alan Miller walked a few steps to the bar and began pouring himself another drink. He turned to Desh once again. "I recruited Putnam and began building wealth and power all the while my sister was working on extended life. I always knew what she was up to. I made it a point to know, despite the precautions she thought she was taking after my break-in." He added ice to his glass and returned to his seat. "When Lusetti reported she was closing up shop, I suspected she had made a breakthrough."

"So you flew to San Diego to find out," said Desh.

"When I learned the secret wasn't in her computer and would have to be coerced from her, I figured I could kill two birds with one stone. With emphasis on *kill*," he added sardonically. "I had been considering faking my own death, anyway, and starting over with a new identity that was off the grid."

"And you knew your sister worshipped you. So you decided to pretend to be a hostage and use the threat of your own death as leverage."

Alan nodded. "It was a brilliant plan, if I do say so myself." He paused for a moment and his features hardened. "But I didn't count on the memory trap she had made," he growled through clenched teeth. "That fucked *everything* up." He swirled his drink and stared at it in his hand, as if mesmerized, until he was icy calm once again.

"So given the memory blockade, why even bother with Kira?" asked Desh. "Why not just optimize your molecular biologist until he repeated her work, saving yourself the headache?"

"Because compared to my freak of a sister, he's a moron. It took him years to duplicate her brain optimization therapy—and he had the instructions. Even enhanced, I doubt there are even three or four scientists in the world who could duplicate her longevity work." He shook his head. "No, she was the only game in town. But as if her memory trick wasn't annoying enough, she managed to kill that dumb bastard Lusetti and vanish from the grid. I'm man enough to admit that this *really* pissed me off," he said with apparent calm, but his tone couldn't fully disguise an unmistakable undercurrent of barely contained rage at this memory, even now. "But only for a short while," he added. "I regrouped. I took another of her smart pills, and I came up with my grand plan the very next day."

"Putnam told us," said Kira in disgust. "Mass sterilization of women just so you can extend your twisted existence for a few years."

Alan laughed. "Mass sterilization?" he repeated in amusement. "Don't believe everything you're told."

"I don't understand," said Kira.

"That's because you're so sanctimonious you refuse to give yourself the very gift you created. If you would have taken one of your own pills, you would have seen through this ruse in an instant." He shook his head in disappointment. "You really are a lot less intelligent than I remembered." He spread his hands innocently. "Why would I possibly want to sterilize anybody?"

She looked confused. "First, to motivate me to unlock my memories."

Alan shook his head. "When I enhanced myself after I had faked my death, I pondered the likely properties of your memory prison. I realized right away that no threat, no matter how great, would enable you to crack it." He gestured toward her encouragingly. "By all means, guess again."

"Because if you succeeded—if ours really did become mankind's last generation—I would be forced to give you my secret for the survival of the species. Or to Putnam, at any rate."

"Give it to *Putnam*?" he hissed, as if outraged. "Give it to *me*? Kira, you would never give your secret to *either one of us*. You can only unlock your memory if you truly want to. And you would never *want to* for me or Putnam. You would bide your time, knowing we wouldn't kill you, until you could escape. That way you'd make sure we didn't hoard the secret and use it for our own ends. Make sure the entire world was a beneficiary." He scowled. "You and I both know that's what you'd do."

Kira nodded. "You're right," she acknowledged reluctantly.

"Of course I am. And if I kept you hostage and tried to *force* it out of you, I'd be back where I started. Catch 22. So the only way I could get it is if I let you go and you gave it to the entire world." He paused. "And while this would, indeed, ensure I lived longer along with the rest of the masses, I would lose the use of the most powerful lever in history." He smiled cruelly. "You see, I'm a little selfish. I want the secret all to myself. To use as I see fit."

"I still don't see it," said Kira. "The Ebola cold-virus was a bluff. The explosive in my head was a bluff. The sterilization plot was a bluff. Why? How do they all fit together? And what did all of these machinations buy you?"

Her brother smiled broadly. "As it turns out, Kira . . . everything."

48

Alan Miller took a sip of his drink, a delighted gleam in his eye, obviously reveling in finally being able to share his warped maneuverings with a rapt audience. He was savoring the telling of a story that would twist the knife in his prisoners over and over again. "As I said, I knew with certainty that you couldn't be coerced. So I had to ask my unfathomably brilliant transformed self this question: under what conditions would my little sister give up her secret? Once I answered this, all I had to do was establish these conditions." He rolled his eyes. "A lot easier said than done, I must admit."

"So what were the conditions?" asked Kira, but a sick feeling had grown in the pit of her stomach. She realized she had just given Desh the location of the flash drive. She knew exactly what combination of conditions this had taken. But for Alan to suggest he had orchestrated things from the start to bring about these conditions was *preposterous.* Besides, she had whispered the coordinates directly in Desh' ear, and no listening device was sensitive enough to catch *that.*

"First," began Alan, "you had to respect someone enough to trust them with your secret. If you were forever a loner and didn't have anyone to trust, no combination of circumstances would do."

He turned to Desh. "That's where you come in. You were handpicked for this role."

"What are you talking about?" snapped Desh in confusion.

"Who do you think set you up in Iran?" he said smugly, a Cheshire grin on his face.

"Impossible!" barked Desh. "You're saying you expected me to team up with your sister even then?"

Alan Miller nodded. "I wanted to ensure she had someone to confide in. Believe me, Desh, I know my sister's taste in men. I've met the guys she's dated and she's told me, in nauseating detail, the kind of man she's looking for. I studied the records of scores of Special Forces operatives before stumbling onto a ringer like you. You're her exact type physically. Brilliant in your own right. Personable. You studied philosophy for Christ's sake. You like poetry. Incredibly well read. Sickeningly righteous." He grinned. "You're catnip to her. The transformed me was convinced that if you two were thrown together under desperate circumstances, there's no way she doesn't fall in love with you."

Alan gazed at his sister knowingly. "Go ahead, Kira. I know I chose well. Tell him. You're in love with him already."

Kira lowered her eyes but said nothing.

A startled look flashed over Desh's face, and he appeared totally dumbstruck. His eyes darted to the side as if desperately trying to read Kira's expression.

Alan laughed. "I'll be damned!" he said, studying Desh. "You're in love with *her,* also. I can see it in your face." He laughed again. "I should be a fucking matchmaker."

Kira gazed at Desh and her eyes widened. She had been feeling like an idiot, desperately trying to hide her feelings from him, convinced that true love was something that happened over years rather than days. But she sensed her brother, evil as he was, had guessed correctly. Desh had fallen for her as well.

Alan shifted his attention back to his sister. "I had hoped this would happen. When both parties can subconsciously pick up on each other's signals of infatuation, the effect is accelerated. My in-depth study of Desh suggested he liked girl-next-door types who were his match intellectually, but frankly, Kira, I was convinced your irritating personality would turn him off." He raised his eyebrows. "Despite not having a firsthand knowledge of Desh's taste in women, my brilliant, transformed self calculated there was a good chance he would fall for you too." He shook his head in wonder. "Ironic that a being of pure intellect could so accurately predict a largely irrational, involuntary response."

"You should feel very proud of yourself," spat Desh bitterly.

Alan looked back and forth between his two prisoners and smiled in delight. "What's the matter, you two? You look angry and confused. Feeling manipulated? Feeling like experimental animals? Does the fact that *I* orchestrated your feelings for each other to serve *my* purposes taint them?"

At this, Desh's expression became thoughtful, and he shook his head ever so slightly, as though the moment Alan had voiced what he had been feeling, he had realized these feelings were misguided. "No taint Alan. My feelings for Kira are my own. If you were responsible for allowing me to meet such a remarkable woman, than I thank you, regardless of your motives." Desh paused. "And if you predicted we would fall for each other," he continued, "so what? Someone might be able to predict my loathing of you, but that doesn't make it any less real."

Alan Miller laughed. "Your loathing of me is about to take a sharp turn for the worse," he said icily. "Allow me to continue. Once I knew you were the right man, I made sure you encountered tragedy, so you would be a wounded soul and would break all ties with other women. To make you more appealing to my sister. After all, what could possibly be more appealing than a tortured, unattached hero?"

"You really did set us up in Iran, didn't you?" whispered Desh in horror.

"Putnam arranged for that particular—what do you grunts like to call it—oh yeah . . . clusterfuck. He didn't have any idea why. Those stupid-assed terrorists were well paid to make sure you escaped alive, but they almost blew it. I needed you injured, but not as injured as you were."

"You're saying they *let* me escape?"

"That's right."

"Why did you need me injured? So I'd cut an even more sympathetic figure for Kira?"

Alan smiled. "I'll answer that a little later. I don't want to get too far ahead of myself. And I really do want to share with you how brilliantly you were both manipulated. After all, you're the only two people in the world who will ever have a chance to appreciate my mastery." He paused. "Shall I continue?"

Desh nodded while Kira glared at her brother hatefully.

"The optimized me figured there was a fifty-fifty chance Desh would leave the service. Either way, it didn't really matter to my plan."

"If your plan was to get me to team up with Kira, why did you wait so long?"

"She wasn't ready yet. I wanted her harried. Chasing her; almost catching her; isolating her. Making her feel persecuted and alone. Crushing her spirit. I needed her primed for the arrival of her white knight. When I judged she was at the end of her rope, I pulled the strings to have you come in."

Kira knew this is exactly what had happened. She had recruited David because she was lonely and fatigued. Alan's execution had been flawless.

"Are you saying you could have captured her earlier?" said Desh.

Alan shrugged. "Possibly," he said. "If I had made more balls-out attempts. I tried to capture her in the early days, but failed. My enhanced self had calculated that if I captured her, tortured her a bit, and then let her find a way to escape, this would accelerate her readiness to seek out an ally like you, and I could move up my time table." An annoyed look came over his face. "But she was a lot better than I thought she'd be. And when I got close she would take bold risks with her own life to elude capture, which I couldn't have. So I changed gears and made harassment my primary objective."

"How did you get me assigned?" asked Desh.

Alan grinned. "With the powerful people Putnam and I have in our pockets, it was laughably easy. I had an influential politician with plenty of skeletons in his closet arrange for it all with Connelly's bosses. And I had long since made sure the identities of all of the agents sent after her were recorded in a database I knew she could breach."

"Because you knew she would study them," said Desh. "You *needed* her to study them."

He nodded. "She studied others that were sent after her without effect, but I knew if she was properly primed and studied your photo and history, she would try to recruit you."

Kira Miller felt bile rise in her throat. This thing pretending to be her brother was distilled evil. What twist of fate had led to her parents giving birth to two mutant children: a daughter with unequaled genius for molecular biology and a son born entirely without a conscience.

"She took the bait just as I knew she would," boasted Alan. "I had planned on having the two of you captured by my black-ops dupe, Smith, and held together as prisoners for a few days to allow love to blossom. But you kept eluding him." Alan shrugged. "Served my purposes anyway. In fact, your escapes from the motel and woods probably cemented your relationship." A content, self-satisfied expression came over his face. "Then all that was left to do was have Putnam capture you both and pretend to be me, initiating a perfect storm of circumstances that would cause Kira to tell her lover-boy her secret."

The helicopter banked, reminding the prisoners they were tearing through the air at great speed to an unknown destination, something easy to forget given the near perfect stillness of the opulent, enclosed cabin. "How did you know you would be able to find us when you needed to?" asked Desh.

"This is where the need for you to get seriously injured in Iran comes in. We ordered a military surgeon to add a few implants in addition to fixing you up. The orders came from the highest military channels. He was told this was being done because you were a known traitor." Alan smirked. "He was even told you had set up your own men."

Desh lunged forward in fury, his neck catching enough of the wire in front of him to draw blood, if only shallowly. "You sick bastard!" he screamed, his rage finally spilling out.

Alan Miller continued calmly as if Desh's outburst had never happened. "The surgeon implanted a tiny, remote homing device on your elbow, just under the skin. The device was designed to lie completely dormant until pinged by a coded signal, upon which point it would activate. You could scan for bugs all you wanted when it was dormant and it wouldn't register. While the bomb in Kira's head was a bluff, the advanced receivers Putnam told you about are very real. As Kira well knows, when you've taken one of her pills, improving electronics becomes child's play."

"So you could have captured us at any time David was with me?" said Kira in shock.

"That's right. But after you avoided capture, I didn't want to reacquire you too quickly. You two had to have some time to bond." He paused and watched blood slowly roll down Desh's neck with fascination. "When you escaped from the safe house, I was forced yet again to alter my plans. I had planned on the two of you remaining prisoners for several days there and then arranging for your escape, with Putnam being killed in the process." He shrugged. "No matter. I was able to make some adjustments and everything still worked out as planned."

"You still don't have the coordinates," said Kira defiantly.

"Don't I?" said her brother, smirking. "The homing device wasn't the only thing the surgeon in Iraq implanted when he was operating on Desh. He also gave him cochlear implants—one for each ear. It's a standard procedure for people deaf or very hard of hearing. Only the implants *he* received were silicon-chip based recording units. They record digitally and can be downloaded to a computer for playback." He sipped his drink and smiled. "They have a finite battery life and only record from ten to eighteen hours, depending on the amount of input, so I had these set to be activated by my signal as well."

"And you activated them within the past ten hours, I presume," said Desh.

"Right you are," said Alan happily. "Using the homing device I had implanted, I easily tracked you to Putnam's house. After all my painstaking planning, at long last I had created the perfect storm." He gazed at his sister smugly. "A man you trusted and were falling in love with. A credible threat to species survival. And you convinced that you had but minutes to live."

Much of the fire had left Kira Miller as the realization hit her with full force that this monster had won. And she had dutifully played her role as the perfect little pawn. She glanced at her bonds and the razor wire at her throat. Escape was impossible. And even if she could escape, what would she do? Would she kill her own brother?

She clenched her fists. This *wasn't* her brother, she told herself forcefully. This was a twisted imposter. Believing this was the only way her psyche could survive a betrayal this vast. Her brother had died in a fire in their childhood home. The monster in front of her was a complete stranger.

"The finishing touch to my masterpiece," continued Alan, "was for you to think your arch-enemy was dead."

"Why?" said Desh.

"If Kira suspected a powerful enemy with access to her treatment was still at large, she would have been far less comfortable disclosing the GPS coordinates." He raised his eyebrows. "Putnam had no idea what my real plan was. Certainly not that his extermination was a key ingredient.

With the arch-enemy who had killed your brother dead, you were free to whisper your secret right into Desh's cochlea."

Alan paused to let his prisoners ponder just how utterly they had been manipulated; just how complete his victory.

"What if Kira hadn't killed Putnam?"

"I suspected she would. I made sure he boasted about killing me just to rub salt in her wound. And my sister is so fucking predictable. So fucking noble. I can't tell you how disappointed I am that we sprang from the same womb."

"Believe me," said Kira Miller, scowling, "your disappointment *pales* in comparison to mine."

"But to answer your question, Desh," said Alan, as if his sister had not spoken, "I was the one who sent Putnam into his house to talk with you in the first place. I had a sniper targeting him while the rest of my men came up through his tunnel. If Kira had failed to shoot him, my sniper would have done so the moment he opened the door." He paused. "You wouldn't know who had killed him or why, but that wouldn't matter. With the only man capable of resetting the supposed explosive charge in Kira's skull dead, she would once again tell you her secret, believing she had but minutes to live and having no guarantee that the sterilization plot could be stopped."

Desh nodded miserably. "It appears you thought of everything," he said, looking defeated for the first time.

"You're damn straight," said Alan smugly.

49

The helicopter had landed almost five minutes before but Alan Miller was clearly enjoying himself too much to put a temporary halt to the proceedings, and the pilots knew better than to interrupt their boss. Finally, Alan decided a change in venue was in order.

Six soldiers, once again dressed in commando gear, had surrounded the helicopter and were waiting patiently for Alan Miller to open the helicopter door. "Bring them inside," he barked. He then nodded toward Desh at the back of the chopper. "And make sure this one is completely immobilized on the gurney. He's ex-Special Forces."

Gurney? Desh didn't like the sound of that. The blood had stopped dripping from his neck, but he was battered and bruised from the melee on the helicopter. It was getting difficult to remember when he had last showered or a time when he wasn't bound. Perhaps in years past a captor would have felt secure simply holding a gun on him without feeling the need to immobilize him as well, but this was no longer the case. The almost superhuman portrayal of Special Forces soldiers by the media and in fiction had unfortunately ensured that he was rarely underestimated.

Three soldiers entered the chopper and removed all restraints but the plasticuffs binding the prisoners' wrists behind their backs. They were marched off the helicopter. A mansion that would not have been out of place in ancient Greece loomed in front of them. Massive white pillars flanked its entrance, and it was centered on acres and acres of meticulously manicured grounds, complete with ponds, gardens and winding streams. Two large, multi-tiered marble fountains stood at its entrance, with life-sized statues of Greek Gods drinking nectar from massive chalices. No other houses were visible for as far as the eye could see in any direction.

They were ushered through the oversized front door and into a vaulted room with twice as much floor space as Kira's entire RV. The floor was white marble, and a ninety-five-inch plasma television hung on the wall like a massive work of modern art, with ten movie-theater style seats facing it. The mansion's interior contained numerous statues and paintings, all depicting Greek Gods, as if Alan Miller considered himself a modern Zeus and had built himself an Olympus in which to reside.

Desh was shoved roughly on his back onto the wheeled, stainless steel gurney of which Alan had spoken, his hands still cuffed behind him. Two of the mercenaries strapped him down and checked to be sure he couldn't escape. Kira's hands were also cuffed behind her and were now cuffed to the gleaming steel gurney as well.

Alan Miller entered the room briskly and stood beside the gurney, so both prisoners could see him well. "This is my media room," he announced proudly. "What do you think?"

Desh looked up at him icily. "I think I'm going to enjoy watching you die," he said intently.

"Very good," said Alan approvingly. "What bravado. No wonder my sister likes you so much. I'm afraid you're at a bit of a disadvantage, though. While I don't have fancy electronic security systems, I do have twelve war-hardened mercenaries who patrol the grounds. I pay them extremely well." He shook his head, unimpressed. "Forgive me for not feeling threatened."

"So what now?" said Desh.

"A surgeon of my acquaintance is on his way. He'll be here in about ten minutes. He'll remove your implants and then, at long last, I'll take my first step toward immortality."

"A surgeon? Isn't that a little delicate for a butcher like you," said Desh. "Why not just kill me?"

"Fair question," he said. He held his hands out, palms up, and sighed. "Technology these days. It's remarkably reliable on the whole, but you just never know. If for some reason the recorder failed to activate or to capture the GPS coordinates properly, I'm going to need you alive so you can tell me the coordinates yourself."

Desh eyed Alan Miller with contempt. "You'd better hope your recorder worked then, because you'll never get the coordinates from me. With truth drugs or otherwise."

Alan laughed. "Part of me almost hopes it didn't work, just so we can find out."

"And if it did?" said Desh.

"I may keep you alive as leverage. I still need my sister to continue her longevity work. She is still the best biologist of her generation."

There was a long silence during which Alan Miller appeared to be lost in thought. "Now that I've answered all your questions," he said finally. "I have one of my own." He raised his eyebrows. "How did you escape from the safe house?"

Desh smiled. "I'm afraid I can't tell you that," he said.

"Oh, you'll tell me all right. What you—"

Outside, the Sikorsky helicopter erupted into flames.

The explosion rocked the mansion as if an earthquake had struck.

Alan Miller rushed to a window. *All hell was breaking loose.* The military helicopter that had fired a missile into the Sikorsky was now strafing the grounds with its machine guns. At least two of Alan's mercenaries were dead and several others had taken positions in preparation for a firefight, or were racing to take cover. Billowing smoke from the flaming helicopter created a surreal haze over the entire scene, and heavy gunfire could be heard from multiple quarters.

Alan could tell his sister had been as stunned as he was. But he had caught a certain gleam in David Desh's eye as he ran to the window. Desh had not been surprised.

Alan raced over to the gurney and looked down at Desh. "What's going on?" he demanded, speaking loudly to be heard over the raging battle taking place outside, the room's marble floor doing nothing to dampen the noise.

"I don't have any idea," said Desh, raising his voice to a near shout as well.

Alan grabbed Desh's head and slammed it into the gurney. "*I repeat,*" he screamed menacingly, "*what is going on?*"

Desh's face remained stoically impassive, despite the blow to his head, and it was clear he would not be responding.

"Okay, lover boy," he spat at Desh. "Let's see how brave you are when it comes to my sister."

Alan walked rapidly to a desk and returned with a sharply pointed silver letter-opener. Without warning he plunged it savagely into his sister's arm.

Kira issued a startled shriek as blood began to soak her sweatshirt.

Alan wrapped his left forearm tightly around his sister's neck from behind and extended his right arm in front of her, the now bloody letter-opener pointed at her face. "Tell me exactly what's going on," he barked at Desh. "The first time I even suspect you're lying to me, she loses an eye."

Desh looked into Alan's eyes and had no doubt he would do it. He would *enjoy* doing it. "I set you up," said Desh quickly.

"Impossible," said Alan, holding the point of the letter-opener a few inches from his sister's left eye and slowly moving it forward.

"I used one of Kira's pills," said Desh hurriedly, desperate to convince Alan he was telling the truth. "That's how we escaped from Putnam's safe house."

Alan's eyes narrowed. He lowered the letter opener as he considered this new information worriedly. Without saying anything more, he reached into his pocket, pulled out a gellcap, and hurriedly swallowed it.

"You know the awesome ability of an enhanced mind to see patterns and make connections," continued Desh. "And I'm not your sister, whose every memory is of the saintly Alan Miller. Kira was at the epicenter of the deaths of her parents and uncle and teachers—*but so was her brother.* And there was nothing left of your body but ashes. Very convenient. I realized this exact endgame was a likely possibility immediately. The *most* likely possibility. My surprised reactions since you arrived at Putnam's have been nothing but an act."

Kira Miller couldn't hide her shock.

"You're lying," snapped Alan. "I can tell from Kira's reaction."

"She didn't know."

"You suspected all of this and you didn't tell her?" said Alan in disbelief.

"There was a chance I was wrong," replied Desh. "That Putnam was behind everything and the situation was exactly as it had been portrayed. I didn't want to give Kira false hopes that the bomb implant was a fake, or tarnish her memory of you if I was wrong." Desh paused. "There was also one other consideration," he said, trying to stall by divulging information as piecemeal as he thought he could get away with.

"What?" snapped Alan impatiently.

Desh paused for another second before answering. "I wanted her reactions to be real," he said. "The same with Griffin and Metzger. When the explosive device failed to go off, when you arrived, I couldn't count on their acting abilities. I didn't want to tip you off that I was on to you."

Alan shook his head vigorously. "Bullshit!" he snapped. "If you suspected, you wouldn't have let Kira give you the GPS coordinates, and you wouldn't have let me capture you."

"Think again, *psycho,*" said Desh in contempt. "I didn't know how to find you. I needed you to reveal yourself. And I wanted you to brag about your achievements so I could be sure I hadn't missed anything." Desh raised his eyebrows. "Not to mention that I detected your implanted cochlear recorders while I was enhanced and used my immune system to deactivate them." He smiled broadly. "*Who's feeling manipulated now, asshole!*" he spat hatefully.

Gunfire continued to rage unabated on the lush, well-tended acreage surrounding the mansion, now transformed into a killing field, violated by explosions and countless bullets, and fertilized with copious amounts of blood.

Alan glared at Desh. "Make no mistake," he barked. "Whatever is happening outside, my men will handle it. And in just a few minutes I'll be transformed and able to slip out of any noose."

"Don't count on it," said Desh.

"Who *are* they?" demanded Alan. "Even if you suspected me, you couldn't have set me up. You couldn't possibly know where I live. And no one followed us here. I'm sure of it."

"Wrong again, *asshole,*" hissed Desh. "Before we broke into Putnam's house, I had a private conversation with my friend the colonel. I knew you would spot the RV. How could you not? I told him to take one of Kira's pills at the first hint of trouble. I outlined how it would be possible to fake his own death." Desh winked. "I'm sure you know that when you're enhanced you can control your heart rate. Smear blood on your head, pretend to be dead, and don't have a pulse when someone is checking for it. Presto, you're declared dead." Desh raised his eyebrows. "But to give credit where it's due," he continued. "I did get the idea of faking Connelly's death from you, Alan." He smiled mockingly. "Thanks."

The veins in Alan Miller's neck were standing out as his fury mounted. Desh knew his best bet was to keep him here until his team arrived, hoping against hope this would happen soon, before Kira's treatment transformed her brother.

"Even though the colonel is injured," continued Desh, "with his mind enhanced, it must have been easy for him to best your men at Putnam's farm and free Metzger and Griffin. I told him to give a pill to the major and come after me." Desh raised his eyebrows. "You see, I hid a homing device on myself that the colonel could use to track me. And your men were good enough to arrive at Putnam's in military choppers so the major could borrow one. The colonel's mind is now back to normal, no doubt. But just one Ross Metzger, enhanced, along with a military helicopter, is more than a match for your mercenaries."

Instead of responding, Alan Miller appeared to be listening for gunfire. But after a deafening barrage that had seemed to go on forever, everything was now utterly silent. This seemed to totally unnerve him, and he shoved the gurney near the wall, dragging his sister along with it. He pulled out a gun and crouched behind his two prisoners, his back to the wall, using their bodies as shields.

"What's the matter?" taunted Desh. "Not so sure of your mercenary force anymore?"

Before Desh completed his sentence, Connelly and Metzger entered the room. Metzger moved with the elegance of a ballet dancer and took in the scene with superhuman acuity.

Alan peered around his sister. "Take one step closer and I'll kill them both," he threatened.

Metzger looked bored. "Thanks. It will spare me the trouble," he said.

Alan's eyes narrowed and it was clear the wheels were turning in his head. "Look, Major," he said amicably, "we can team up, you and I. Surely in the state you're in now you can see the logic of this. Why hitch yourself to my sister's wagon? I already have more power and money than *God.* Once we begin to leverage the secret of extended life, you and I will be the most powerful people on the planet."

"Ross, *please,*" pleaded Kira Miller. "Kill him! Don't worry about hitting me. He took a gellcap and he'll be enhanced any second. This is your chance!" she insisted emphatically. "Remember what Matt said: the vast majority of your life will be lived as you *were,* unenhanced. And that Ross Metzger couldn't live with himself if he teamed up with this psychopath."

"*Shut the fuck up, you bitch!*" thundered Metzger.

Kira flinched and drew back from the fury of his words.

Metzger pulled the trigger and put a bullet cleanly between Alan Miller's eyes. He slammed back against the wall and then fell forward, face first.

Kira gasped in shock. The shot had missed her by the thickness of a piece of paper.

No one moved. No one even breathed. All eyes were on Ross Metzger.

The major calmly lowered his gun. "Sorry about that, Kira," he said matter-of-factly. "You were in the way of a clean shot. I calculated that if I shouted a curse at you, your head would twist just enough for me to kill him."

Kira stared at him in bewilderment, her eyes blinking rapidly. She glanced at her brother on the floor and then turned her head to take in as much of her surroundings as she could. All was quiet.

Could it be? After all this time, was it now really over? It had happened so fast. Metzger's actions had been so decisive; so final. The immense pressure that had been bearing down on her psyche for so long was so crushing that its sudden removal was surreal; disorienting. She took a deep breath and let the reality seep into the deep recesses of her consciousness: her interminable waking nightmare had truly ended. It had ended with a venomous curse, and a single shot delivered with superhuman accuracy. Several tears escaped from the corners of her eyes and raced down her cheeks.

The major turned to Desh. "David, while I am more ruthless than I was, I'm not like Griffin or you. It isn't testosterone related. I believe I've come through the transformation with more of my soul intact even than Kira did the first time. I have some theories but you wouldn't understand." He paused; or had his simulacrum pause at any rate. "Kira, I'm sorry about your brother."

Kira Miller took a long, hard look at the body lying on the floor and then firmly turned away, as if determined to close the book on this part of her life forever. She turned to Metzger and shook her head resolutely; only her eyes betraying her deep pain. "That's not my brother," she said bitterly, drying her tears with the back of her hand. "My brother died in a fire a year ago."

50

The grounds were still smoking from the carnage that had taken place there, and the outside world was now eerily silent, as if even birds and insects had been cowed into silence by the bloodshed they had witnessed.

"I've got to hand it to you David," said Kira appreciatively. "You're certainly full of surprises."

"Sorry about that," he replied guiltily.

"Don't be. I understand why you made the choices you did, and your plan was flawless." Her gaze shifted to Connelly and Metzger. "Gentlemen, I can't thank you enough."

The colonel smiled warmly. "No need for thanks, Kira. We're a team now, after all."

"Judging from the past twenty-four hours," said Desh, "we're about as formidable a team as you could want."

"Hard to argue with that," said Connelly cheerfully. "But it does help that your alter ego had it all figured out ahead of time," he said to Desh.

As Metzger freed the two prisoners and tore a piece of Alan's shirt to wrap around Kira's arm where the letter-opener had entered, Desh reflected on the enormity of all that had happened.

The colonel was right—for the most part. Desh's enhanced mind *had* solved the puzzle. He had correctly guessed what had happened in Iran and why. He had guessed Alan Miller was behind it all, and that he had chosen Desh because he was someone whose integrity his sister would respond to, and who she would therefore attempt to recruit.

But ironically, even after having realized the nature of his own feelings for Kira, *his enhanced self had completely missed that those feelings were reciprocated.* A warm glow came over him at the thought, along with a smile that refused to leave his face.

Desh wished he could freeze this moment forever. He had never felt this way about a woman before. And never in his life had he felt so relieved. Or triumphant. Or hopeful.

They had done it. Against incredible odds they had prevailed.

They had been charging ahead at a dizzying pace; so busy fighting for their lives and struggling to peel back the onion it had seemed as if this state of affairs would never end: or would end, inevitably, with their deaths. But they had battled their way to victory, and in the process they had earned themselves a future. A future in which Kira's discoveries could be harnessed to better mankind, rather than being used by a psychopath to become the most powerful and dangerous man in history.

Desh could only imagine the elation Kira must be feeling now that her long ordeal was finally over. She had faced these powerful, shadowy forces for an eternity longer than he had, and utterly alone.

Desh pulled himself from his reverie. He was now standing beside the steel gurney to which he had been strapped, and Metzger had just finished wrapping Kira's arm. "Is Matt okay?" he asked.

"He's fine," said Connelly. "I gave him the keys to the RV and told him we'd meet up with him later at a location I gave him. After the fireworks at Putnam's house, when I took out the men who were holding him and the major hostage, he didn't look so hot." Connelly smiled. "Not that we would have brought him on this little raid anyway," he admitted.

"How are *you* doing, Colonel?" asked Kira in concern.

"Great," he said happily. "Your treatment is unbelievable. I was able to direct my body's autonomous functions and greatly accelerate the healing process."

"I hate to spoil the party," said Metzger soberly, "but we need to go. As isolated as this place is, we have to assume we attracted some attention. We need to lay low for a while. As soon as Matt is up to it, we can give him a gellcap and let him clean up behind us."

Desh raised his eyebrows. "Can I assume you have a strategy in mind?"

"Of course," said Metzger. "Step one: Enhanced Matt alters secure military databases to show that Alan Miller was in league with terrorists on an imminent attack. Step two: he plants secret orders, backdated to yesterday, calling on me to take out Miller using any means necessary."

Desh was impressed with the simplicity but effectiveness of the plan. This would instantly legitimize Metzger's appropriation of the helicopter from Bragg and the carnage at the mansion. "That should do it," he said. "You'll probably earn a medal." Having a member of the team capable of subverting the most secure computer systems in the world did have its advantages.

"Kira," said the major, "you and David stay here for a few minutes. The colonel and I will make certain we didn't miss any hostiles and start the chopper."

Connelly looked puzzled. "Shouldn't we all leave right now?"

"They've been through a lot," explained Metzger. "Let's give them a few minutes alone."

The colonel still looked confused, but didn't argue.

Desh knew that Metzger was still in the thrall of Kira's treatment, which meant he was undoubtedly focusing on ridiculously complex problems at the same time his avatar personality was speaking with them. And he must have also read their body language like a neon sign, picking up on their mutual infatuation and Desh's desire to have a few minutes alone with Kira. He would have to remember to thank the major later.

Metzger turned back toward Desh as he and Connelly reached the front door. "You're welcome," he said knowingly, and then, guns drawn, both men cautiously exited the mansion.

The corners of Desh's mouth turned up into a wry smile in response to Metzger's words, but his smile quickly vanished as he made a visual inspection of Kira's arm. "Are you all right?" he asked softly.

She smiled, almost bashfully. "Never better," she said simply.

Desh paused awkwardly. "Kira," he began. "About this whole being in love thing—" He looked at her uncertainly. "I feel a bit silly. I never believed it could happen so suddenly."

She nodded. "Me either."

"We've been through hell together," he continued, "and we've bared our souls to each other. We know more about each other than couples who have been together for months." He sighed. "What we *don't* know is how we'll be together when the pressure is *off*. So I was thinking—even if it might seem a bit ridiculous at this point in our relationship—maybe we should go on an old-fashioned, boring first date. No commandoes or adrenaline allowed."

"A first date, huh," said Kira, considering. "Not a bad idea." She grinned and then added playfully, "But I should warn you, I don't kiss until the *third* date."

Desh laughed. "In that case," he said, "I'm prepared to call our time together at Montag's Gourmet Pizza a date." He raised his eyebrows. "And you did take me to a motel and tie me to the headboard of a bed. Does that count?"

"Nope. I'm afraid not. Normally it would, but given that I brought you there in the trunk of a car, I have to disqualify it."

"Okay, then. What about the nature hike we shared together?"

"We weren't alone."

"Damn," said Desh. "Your definition of a date is awfully picky. You also took me to your place for the night, but since we weren't alone then, either, I suppose you won't count it." Desh shook his head. "If I had known," he added wryly, "I would have ditched the major and the colonel at the baseball stadium when we landed."

Kira laughed and leaned closer to him, well within an inescapable gravity well that was impossible for either of them to resist, even had they wanted to. They kissed hungrily, and only the sure knowledge that they wouldn't remain alone for long in what had become a war zone enabled them to, finally, separate.

Kira sighed dreamily. "I'll tell you what," she whispered with a contented smile. "I'm prepared to count our entire time together as the equivalent of two dates."

"Two?" whispered a euphoric Desh, who felt as though he surely must be floating. "I thought you didn't kiss 'till the third."

"That was just a sample," she said.

"An incredibly effective one," he said contentedly.

"Good. Because after we've showered and gotten some sleep, I'll be ready for that third date. We can go out to dinner. *I'm* buying."

"*Really*," said Desh, amused. "That sounds like too good of a deal to pass up."

"Well, you did bring Matt Griffin to the team. And he did just deposit half a billion dollars in my account. So I suppose I owe you a nice dinner."

"A half billion dollars only gets me dinner?"

Kira flashed an incandescent smile. "That remains to be seen," she said, her eyes dancing.

Desh grinned. There was a long silence as he gazed deeply into her eyes. As he did so, he couldn't help but feel they were truly in love. But he knew this could well be an illusion. It could prove to be nothing more than a passing infatuation, catalyzed by their being thrown together in desperate circumstances and forced to fight for their lives side by side.

If only emotions were as simple as pure reason, he thought. But they weren't. They were primal, and often incomprehensible.

But that's what made emotion the most critical part of being human, Desh realized. If life could be reduced to the purely rational, to a solvable equation, there would be no mystery, no excitement. Life would become utterly predictable; a tedious movie that could never surprise. The truth was that neither he nor Kira, normal or enhanced, could know for sure if their feelings for each other would diminish or grow as time marched on.

Desh knew that Connelly and Metzger were waiting for them. "We'd better go," he said softly, pulling his eyes away from Kira's and nodding toward the oversized front door of the mansion. "Our chariot—and our future—await," he added.

"Gallantly said," noted Kira with a smile. She raised her eyebrows. "Any guesses as to what that future might hold?"

Desh shook his head. "Not a one," he replied. "But I can tell you this," he added happily. "I suddenly can't wait to find out."

EPILOGUE

"The brain is the last and grandest biological frontier, the most complex thing we have yet discovered in our universe. It contains hundreds of billions of cells interlinked through trillions of connections. The brain boggles the mind."

—James D. Watson, Nobel Laureate and co-discoverer of the structure of DNA.

"Anyone who is not shocked by quantum theory has not understood a single word of it."

—Niels Bohr, Nobel Prize winning physicist.

David Desh studied his wife through the thick Plexiglas barrier as anxiety ate at his stomach. Jim Connelly, Matt Griffin, and Ross Metzger stood quietly beside him, each lost in their own thoughts.

The core team had debated taking this step for the better part of a year and had finally reached a decision. They had to know. Even if it cost them everything. They had to know what might await human consciousness at the next level of optimization, a level Kira had experienced for all of two seconds: long enough to understand that she had achieved intelligence as far beyond her first level of optimization as that level was beyond normalcy.

If anything was universally accepted as the hallmark of humanity, it was the insatiable curiosity at the heart of the species. But would this insatiable curiosity cost them everything?

It was impossible to predict.

Kira had extended the effect of this second level of enhancement from two seconds to five minutes in duration. For five minutes she would exist in a realm that approached the theoretical limit of thought that could be achieved by one hundred billion neurons; a level staggering in its power. If the sociopathic tendencies scaled up as well, and they failed to contain her, the consequences would be unpredictable and potentially disastrous—even given the limited duration of the effect.

So they had taken precautions. A steel chair had been bolted to the floor, and Kira was immobilized in it more securely than any human had ever been immobilized in history. She sat in the middle of a thick plexiglass cube that looked like a transparent racquetball court, with enough sleeping gas to tranquilize a herd of elephants poised above her head, ready to be triggered by any of her observers. In case her enhanced mind was able to direct her body's enzymes to metabolize the gas before it could affect her, the chair was rigged with plastic explosives that were also controlled from the outside. She had insisted upon this herself.

In the past year they had recruited dozens of top people from every field, carefully vetted according to Desh's plan, who had made breathtaking discoveries that would soon transform the world. But the original five who were gathered together now still formed the core leadership, and it seemed only fitting that they be the sole witnesses to the greatest experiment of them all.

Inside the plexiglass enclosure, Kira gasped. She clenched her teeth in agony. The transformation had begun.

David Desh watched his wife helplessly as her agony intensified for almost thirty seconds.

Just as suddenly as it had begun, the tortured expression left her face and was replaced by a look of serenity more complete than any Desh had ever witnessed. There was a radiance to her now; an ethereal glow. Desh knew that while her outer demeanor was utterly peaceful, her mind was now churning at an inconceivably furious pace. He shook his head in awe and trepidation. Through what new galaxies of thought was she now traversing?

The five minutes ticked by with agonizing slowness. Kira's vital signs were being monitored, and her breathing and heartbeat had become as steady as an atomic clock; a sure sign she was in the enhanced state. Her eyes had been closed since the transformation had begun, and she hadn't moved a centimeter; nor had she uttered a single word.

Without warning her vital signs lost their perfect rhythm. *She was back.* She had returned from her extraordinary voyage.

Desh blew out the breath he had been holding for some time now, relieved.

The countenances of his three friends all brightened beside him as well.

But there was a hurdle yet to jump, Desh knew. Would she be the same woman with whom he had fallen in love, or would this experience, this new reordering of her neurons, change her in unpredictable ways?

Forty seconds passed and her eyes remained closed. David Desh suddenly found it hard to take a breath. Had something gone wrong?

He checked the digital clock counting down on the monitor next to her still-strong vital signs. They had agreed not to enter her cell until a full ten minutes after the effect appeared to have reversed, just to be sure. Desh's desire to rush in and hold her, and confirm that nothing was amiss, was so all consuming it took every ounce of his will to suppress it.

He stared at the digital clock as the seconds continued to pass; willing them to go faster.

Kira slammed into normalcy like a starship traveling at warp speed crashing into an immovable object. The return to normalcy had been jarring before, but nothing could compare to *this*.

She shook off the shock of it and hastily searched her mind. Had she contemplated evil acts while on this transcendent plane of intelligence? Had she found Nietzsche's will to power even more difficult to resist than before? Had she been even more contemptuous and dismissive of the species Homo sapiens?

Memories flooded back to her. They were but a pale shadow of a shadow of a shadow of her thoughts during the five-minute period—which had seemed to her to last for many hours—and the memories were in clumsy English rather than the precise and expansive symbolic logic her mind had been able to effortlessly manipulate while transformed.

But these wisps of memory were enough. *She knew*. Their greatest hopes had been realized. Their greatest fears put to rest. David had been right. Compassion and pure intellect were *not* mutually exclusive. And as her normal mind brushed over the faint echo of the conclusions she had reached while transformed, feelings of profound joy and contentment surged through her.

The baseline level of human thought was so plagued by emotion and instinct, so limited in power and rationality, that individuals could be readily fooled into believing almost any conjecture. At the first level of enhancement with which she and her team had become familiar, faith did not exist, and any logic that called for the existence of a deity was quickly seen to be fatally flawed. At this level of thought it became clear that existence was without meaning, and selfishness became an imperative.

But now, having achieved a second level of optimization that was truly staggering, she had gained a perspective far different from that she had achieved at the first level. She marveled at the preposterous hubris she and the others had exhibited at this level. Incredible. Now that she had achieved a truly transcendent plane of thought she was sure of only one thing: *she understood absolutely nothing!*

The universe was infinite, and there were most likely an infinite number of universes. To sit on one tiny planet in an ocean of infinite infinities and believe you understood *anything* about the true nature of existence and reality was absurd. The convictions of the arrogant minds of those at the first level of enhancement were just as flawed as any they had replaced.

Was there an afterlife? Maybe. Perhaps there wasn't even a need for one. Perhaps all consciousness was *already* immortal. The widely embraced Many-Worlds interpretation of the bizarre experimental results found in quantum physics suggested that whenever different possibilities for the future existed, *all of them were realized.* The universe was constantly splitting into multiple universes, like branches on a tree, with each branch continuing to branch an infinite number of times.

In the past a bullet fired from a helicopter had been hurtling toward Jim Connelly as he stood in a clearing. In this universe it had missed killing him by a few inches.

But as the bullet was hurtling toward him the universe had branched. There were now an infinite number of universes in which the bullet had killed him, and an infinite number in which it had missed entirely. But within these infinities going forward, until the end of time, there would always be at least one universe in which the colonel's consciousness survived.

The possibility of quantum immortality was accepted by a number of mainstream physicists as they used their normal human faculties to understand the fantastic implications of quantum effects. But there were possibilities her alter ego had glimpsed that human scientists had not even *begun* to suspect. There were at least as many reasons to believe in the existence of immortality or an afterlife as there were not to.

Was there a God? It was impossible to answer this question for sure, but the level of human understanding was so insignificant it was the height of arrogance to rule it out. She had posed the question: if God could exist without need of a creator, why couldn't the universe? But the converse was also true. If the universe could exist without being created, why couldn't God?

But even if God existed, there was no guarantee this being would have all the answers; would fully understand the nature of reality. An omniscient being could be all-knowing and yet have far more to learn. Infinite infinities yet again. Even if God's mind could grasp and contain within it the infinity of numbers between 0 and 1, there were still an infinity of numbers outside of this set.

But if *God* might be unable to fully comprehend the true nature of existence, where did this leave poor humanity? To what end should this lowly species aspire?

Miraculously, Kira's alter ego had come up with an answer to this question: one she found immensely satisfying. *The purpose of consciousness—any consciousness—was to achieve infinite comprehension.* It was as simple as that. If a God existed, humanity must strive to discover this God and help this deity become omniscient, not just in one infinity, but in an infinity of infinities.

This was one possible purpose for her species. But her alter ego, using symbolic logic, had arrived at a possibility she considered much more likely: that humanity's purpose, together with all life across all universes, was not to *discover* God—*it was to become God.*

If a single human egg could possess consciousness at the instant of fertilization, how would it view itself? It couldn't possibly predict or comprehend the multi-trillion-celled being it would ultimately become. The entirety of humanity could well be that single, fertilized cell, unaware that it would grow a trillion-fold more complex and eventually become God, *perhaps had already become God,* in a universe in which all pasts, presents, and futures existed side by side.

Humanity was composed of separate individuals now, but an embryo at early stages was also nothing more than a ball of separate cells. But these separate cells would ultimately become connected in wondrous ways to create something unimaginably greater than themselves.

And seen in this light, altruism and sociopathy were far from straightforward concepts, beyond even the complexities that Abraham Lincoln had revealed. Absolute altruism on one level could be absolute selfishness in disguise on another, and vice-versa. The cells making up the human body were selfless; gladly sacrificing themselves when necessary for the good of the organism. On the microscopic level they were being foolishly altruistic, foolishly suicidal, but on the *macroscopic* level they were being purely selfish—ensuring the survival of the body. And what happened when an individual cell became selfish and exhibited Nietzsche's will to power? It became a cancer. The cell would break free of the restraints on its own division and become immortal—for a while—until its very immortality choked the entire organism to death, killing the selfish cell in the process.

Humanity had no choice but to assume that it would evolve into God, either alone or in combination with all other conscious beings and all other life. The stakes were too high to assume anything else. Life would evolve into God, and then God would create the multiverse and all life, in a circular process extending through all of space-time, with no beginning and no end, which only this ultimate intelligence could comprehend. Some forms of life would play starring roles in this process and some would play lesser roles—which might even call for their extinction. Yet the purpose of all life would be to foster a healthy God; just as the purpose of all human cells was to enhance the health of the entire organism, even at the cost of their own survival, if necessary.

In this case, the questions posed by Nietzsche would be answered in a far different way than this philosopher had answered them. What is good? All that fosters life in its myriad forms, subject to the overriding needs of emerging Godhood. What is bad? All that stands in the way of life and its struggle to become God.

So now their fledgling team would have a clear purpose. And the means to enhance themselves to a previously unimaginable level of thought, without fear of sociopathy. Kira realized that this wouldn't make their problems disappear, it would only expand them and increase their difficulty. A myriad of tough questions and challenges remained, even in the near term. Could this transcendent transformation be made permanent? Should it be? Should mankind take a hand in its own evolution? If so, could the essence of humankind be preserved? *Should* it be preserved? What if some wanted to make the switch and others didn't?

There would be no easy answers. But these were questions for another day.

Right now, it was time to report the phenomenal success of the experiment to the team, and describe the profound new vistas of thought this second level of enhancement had opened.

And she also needed to speak with her husband. To tell him something she knew he was eager to hear.

She was pregnant.

The fertilization had taken place just two days before. It was too soon for her normal self to have known, but her transformed alter ego had realized it immediately.

She could struggle with the nature of existence for all eternity without achieving complete understanding. But she knew this for certain: when their baby came into the world, she and David would be taking their own steps toward immortality. Toward infinity. Their child would take its place in a procession of life that she knew in her soul would end with the creation of God.

Kira prepared to open her eyes for the first time since the transformation had begun and gaze happily into the eyes of the man she loved. It was time to tell him he was going to be a father.

From the Author: Thanks for reading *WIRED*! If you enjoyed this book, I would greatly appreciate it if you could help spread the word. Feel free to Friend me on Facebook at *Douglas E. Richards Author*, which is the best way to stay updated on new releases.

Novels by Douglas E. Richards

Adult
WIRED (Technothriller/Science-fiction)
AMPED (The WIRED Sequel)
THE CURE (Technothriller/Science-fiction)

Middle Grade/YA (Enjoyed by kids and adults alike)
THE PROMETHEUS PROJECT SERIES (Science Fiction Thrillers)

Book 1: *TRAPPED*
Book 2: *CAPTURED*
Book 3: *STRANDED*

THE DEVIL'S SWORD (Mainstream Thriller)
ETHAN PRITCHER, BODY SWITCHER
OUT OF THIS WORLD (Science Fiction/Fantasy)

Made in the USA
Lexington, KY
23 August 2014